MA

The rays of the late sun shone fitfully from a cloud-serried sky, and shadows fled across the sward, across the faces of those who stood before me, swelled up in arrogance, petty men who would summon a king to an accounting. One stood forth among them, a-glitter in rich stuff, and made much of flourishing the scrolls from which he spelled out those demands by which they thought to bind my royal power.

To the end I let him speak his treason for all to hear. Then I gave my answer.

From the dark forest roundabout, my picked archers stepped forth, and in a dread silence bent their bows. And my heart sang as their shafts sang, finding their marks in traitors' breasts. And under my eyes were the false barons slain, every one, and when the deed was done I walked forth from my pavilion and spurned with my foot that scrap of parchment they called their "Charter."

That's not the way it happened? It is where you're going,

Look for all these TOR books by Keith Laumer

KEITH LAUMER
BEYOND THE IMPERIUM

A TOM DOHERTY ASSOCIATES BOOK

BEYOND THE IMPERIUM

Copyright © 1981 by Keith Laumer

The parts of this work have been published separately as follows:

Book I, **The Other Side of Time,** appeared serially (in a substantially different version) in **Amazing Stories,** copyright © 1965 by Ziff-Davis Publishing Company, and is also copyright © 1965 by Keith Laumer. Book II, **Assignment in Nowhere,** is copyright © 1968 by Keith Laumer.

First printing: November 1981
Second printing: February 1986

A TOR Book

Published by Tom Doherty Associates
49 West 24 Street
New York, N.Y. 10010

Cover art by Bob Petillo

ISBN: 0-812-54381-5
CAN. ED.: 0-812-54382-3

Printed in the United States

0 9 8 7 6 5 4 3 2

BOOK I:

ASSIGNMENT IN NOWHERE

CHAPTER ONE

It was one of those tranquil summer evenings when the sunset colors seemed to linger on in the sky even longer than June in Stockholm could explain. I stood by the French windows, looking out at pale rose and tawny gold and electric blue, feeling a sensation near the back of the neck that always before had meant trouble, big trouble, coming my way.

The phone jangled harshly through the room. I beat the track record getting to it, grabbed the old-fashioned Imperium-style, brass-mounted instrument off the hall table, and waited a moment to be sure my voice wouldn't squeak before I said hello.

"Colonel Bayard?" said the voice at the other end. "The Freiherr von Richthofen calling; one moment, please . . ."

Through the open archway to the dining room I could see the dark gleam of Barbro's red hair as she nodded at the bottle of wine Luc was showing her. Candlelight from the elaborate chandelier over her head cast a soft light on snowy linen, gleaming crystal, rare old porcelain, glittering silver. With Luc as our household major domo, every meal was an occasion, but my appetite had vanished. I didn't know why, Richthofen was an old and valued friend, as well as the head of Imperial Intelligence. . . .

"Brion?" Richthofen's faintly accented voice came from the bell-shaped earpiece of the telephone. "I am glad to have found you at home."

"What's up, Manfred?"

"Ah . . ." he sounded mildly embarrassed. "You have been at home all evening?"

9

"We got in about an hour ago. Have you been trying to reach me?"

"Oh, no. But a small matter has arisen . . ." There was a pause. "I wonder, Brion, if you could find the time to drop down to Imperial Intelligence Headquarters?"

"Certainly. When?"

"Now. Tonight. . . .?" the pause again. Something was bothering him—a strange occurrence in itself. "I'm sorry to disturb you at home, Brion, but—"

"I'll be there in half an hour," I said. "Luc will be unhappy, but I guess he'll survive. Can you tell me what it's about?"

"I think not, Brion; the wires may not be secure. Please make my apologies to Barbro—and to Luc too."

Barbro had risen and come around the table. "Brion—what was the call—" She saw my face. "Is there trouble?"

"Don't know. I'll be back as soon as I can. It must be important or Manfred wouldn't have called."

I went along the hall to my bedroom, changed into street clothes, took a trench coat and hat—the nights were cool in Stockholm—and went out into the front hall. Luc was there, holding a small apparatus of spring wire and leather.

"I won't be needing that, Luc," I said. "Just a routine trip down to HQ."

"Better take it, sir." Luc's sour face was holding its usual expression of grim disapproval—an expression I had learned masked an intense loyalty. I grinned at him, took the slug gun and its special quick-draw holster, pulled back my right sleeve and clipped it in place, checked the action. With a flick of the wrist, the tiny slug gun—the shape and color of a flattened, water-eroded stone—slapped into my palm. I tucked it back in place.

"Just to please you, Luc. I'll be back in an hour. Maybe less."

I stepped out into the gleam of the big, square, thick-lensed carriage lights that shed a nostalgic yellow glow over the granite balustrade, went down the wide steps to the waiting car, and slid in behind the thick oak-rimmed wheel. The engine was already idling. I pulled along the gravelled drive, out past the poplars by the open iron gate, into the cobbled city street. Ahead, a car parked at the curb with headlights burning pulled out, took up a position in front of me. In the rearview mirror I saw a second car ease around the corner, fall in behind me. Jeweled highlights glinted from the elaborate star-burst badge of the Imperial Intelligence bolted to the massive grill. It seemed Manfred had sent along an escort to be sure I made it to headquarters.

It was a ten-minute drive through the wide, softly lit streets of the old capital, superficially like the Stockholm of my native continuum. But here in the Zero-zero world of the Imperium, the center of the vast Net of alternate worlds opened up by the M-C drive, the colors were somehow a little brighter, the evening breeze a little softer, the magic of living a little closer.

Following my escort, I crossed the Norrbro Bridge, made a hard right between red granite pillars into a short drive, swung through a set of massive wrought-iron gates with a wave to the cherry-tunicked sentry as he presented arms. I pulled up before the broad doors of polished ironbound oak and the brass plate that said KUNGLIGA SVENSKA SPIONAGE, and the car behind me braked with a squeal and doors slammed open. By the time I had slid from behind the wheel, the four men from the two cars had formed a casual half-circle around me. I recognized one of them—a Net operative who had chauffeured me into a place called Blight-Insular Two, a few years back. He returned my nod with a carefully impersonal look.

"They're waiting for you in General Baron von Rich-thofen's suite, Colonel," he said. I grunted and went up the steps, with the curious feeling that my escort was behaving more like a squad of plainclothesmen making a dangerous pinch, than an honor guard.

Manfred got to his feet when I came into the office. The look he gave me was an odd one—as though he weren't quite sure just how to put whatever it was he was about to say.

"Brion, I must ask for your indulgence," he said. "Please take a chair. Something of a . . . a troublesome nature has arisen." He looked at me with a worried expression. This wasn't the suave, perfectly poised von

Richthofer I was used to seeing daily in the course of my duties as a colonel of the Imperial Intelligence. I sat, noticing the careful placement of the four armed agents in the room, and the foursome who had walked me to the office, standing silently by.

"Go ahead, sir," I said, getting formal just to keep in the spirit of the thing. "I understand this is business. I assume you'll tell me what it's all about, in time."

"I must ask you a number of questions, Brion," Richthofen said unhappily. He sat down, the lines in his face suddenly showing his nearly eighty years, ran a lean hand over smooth iron grey hair, then straightened himself abruptly, leaned back in the chair with the decisive air of a man who has decided something has to be done and it may as well be gotten over with.

"What was your wife's maiden name?" he rapped out.

"Ludane," I answered levelly. Whatever the game was, I'd play along. Manfred had known Barbro longer than I had. Her father had served with Richthofen as an Imperial agent for thirty years.

"When did you meet her?"

"About five years ago—at the Royal Midsummer Ball, the night I arrived here."

"Who else was present that night?"

"You, Hermann Goering, Chief Captain Winter . . ." I named a dozen of the guests at the gay affair that had ended so tragically with an attack by raiders from the nightmare world known as B-I Two. "Winter was killed," I added, "by a hand grenade that was meant for me."

"What was your work—originally?"

"I was a diplomat—a United States diplomat—until your lads kidnapped me and brought me here." The last was just a subtle reminder that whatever it was that required that my oldest friend in this other Stockholm question me as though I were a stranger, my presence here in the world of the Imperium had been all his idea in the first place. He noted the dig a moment before going on to the next question.

"What is your work here in Stockholm Zero-zero?"

"You gave me a nice job in Intelligence as a Net Surveillance officer—"

"What is the Net?"

"The continuum of alternate world lines; the matrix of simultaneous reality—"

"What is the Imperium?" he cut me off. It was one of those rapid-fire interrogations, designed to rattle the subject and make him forget his lines—not the friendliest kind of questioning a man could encounter.

"The overgovernment of the Zero-zero A-line in which the M-C generator was developed."

"What does M-C abbreviate?"

"Maxoni-Cocini—the boys that invented the thing, back in 1893—"

"How is the M-C effect employed?"

"It's the drive used to power the Net shuttles."

"Where are the Net operations carried out?"

"All across the Net—except for the Blight, of course—"

"What is the Blight?"

"Every A-line within thousands of parameters of the Zero-zero line is a hell-world of radiation or—"

"What produced the Blight?"

"The M-C effect, mishandled. You lads here in the Zero-zero line were the only ones who controlled it—"

"What is the Zero-zero line?"

I waved a hand. "This universe we're sitting in right now. The alternate world where the M-C field—"

"Do you have a scar on your right foot?" I smiled—slightly—at the change of pace question.

"Uh-huh. Where Chief Inspector Bale fired a round between my big toe and—"

"Why were you brought here?"

"You needed me to impersonate a dictator—in a place called Blight-Insular Two—"

"Are there other viable A-lines within the Blight?"

I nodded. "Two. One is a war-blasted place with a Common History date of about 1910; the other is my native clime, called B-I Three—"

"You have a bullet scar on your right side?"

"Nope; the left. I also have—"

"What is a Common History date?"

"The date at which two different A-lines' histories diverge—"

"What was your first assignment as a Colonel of Intelligence?"

I answered the question—and a lot of other ones. For the next hour and a half he covered every facet of my private and public life, digging into those odd corners of casual incident that would be known only to me—and to himself. All the while, eight armed men stood by, silent, ready. . . .

My pretense of casual acceptance of the situation was wearing a little thin by the time he sighed, laid both hands on the table—I had the sudden, startled impression that he had just slipped a gun into a drawer out of my line of vision—and looked at me with a more normal expression.

"Brion, in the curious profession of which we are both members one encounters the necessity of performing many unpleasant duties. To call you here like this . . ." he nodded at the waiting gun handlers, who quietly faded away. "Yes, under guard—to question you like a common suspect—has been one of the most unpleasant. Rest assured that it was necessary—and that the question has now been resolved to my complete satisfaction." He rose and extended a hand. I got up, feeling a little suppressed anger trying to bubble up under my collar. I took his hand, shook it once, and dropped it. My reluctance must have showed.

"Later, Brion—perhaps tomorrow—I can explain this farcical affair. For tonight, I ask you to accept my personal apologies for the inconvenience—the embarrassment I have been forced to cause you. It was in the interests of the Imperium."

I made polite but not enthusiastic noises, and left. Whatever it was that was afoot, I knew Richthofen had a reason for what he had done—but that didn't make me like it any better—or reduce my curiosity. But I was damned if I'd ask any questions now.

There was no one in sight as I went along to the elevator, rode down, stepped out into the white marble-paved corridor on the ground floor. Somewhere at the far end of the wide hallway feet were hurrying. A door banged with a curious air of finality. I stood like an animal testing the air before venturing into dangerous new territory. An air of crisis seemed to hang over the silent building.

Then I found myself sniffing in earnest. There was a smell of burning wood and asphalt, a hint of smoke. I turned toward the apparent source, walking rapidly but quietly. I passed the wide foot of the formal staircase that led up to the reception hall one floor above—and halted, swung back, my eyes on a dark smudge against the gleaming white floor tiles. I almost missed the second smudge—a good two yards from the first, and fainter. But the shape of both marks was clear enough: they were footprints. Six feet farther along the corridor there was another faint stain—as though someone had stepped into hot tar, and was tracking it behind him.

The direction of the prints was along the corridor to the left. I looked along the dimly lit way. It all seemed as peaceful as a mortuary after hours—and had that same air of grim business accomplished and more to come.

I went along the hall, paused at the intersection, looking both ways. The odor seemed stronger—a smell like singed paint now. I followed the prints around the corner. Twenty feet along the corridor there was a large burn scar against the floor, with footprints around it—lots of prints. There was also a spatter of blood, and on the wall the bloody print of a hand twice the size of mine. Under a sign that said SERVICE STAIR there was a second hand-print on the edge of a door—a hand-print outlined in blistered, blackened paint. My wrist twitched—a reflex reminder of the slug gun Luc had insisted I bring along.

It was two steps to the door. I reached for the polished brass knob—and jerked my hand back. It was hot to the touch. With my handkerchief wrapped around my hand, I got the door open. Narrow steps went down into shadows and the smell of smouldering wood. I started to reach for the wall switch, then thought better of it, closed the door silently behind me, started down. At the bottom, I waited for a moment, listening, then gingerly poked my head out to look along the dark basement hall—and froze.

Dim shadows danced on the wall opposite—shadows outlined in dull reddish light. I came out, went along to a right-angle turn, risked another look. Fifty feet from me, a glowing figure moved with erratic, jerky speed—a figure that shone in the gloom like a thick-limbed iron statue heated red hot. It darted a few feet, made movements too quick to follow, spun, bobbed across the narrow passage—and disappeared through an open door, like a paper cutout jerked by a string.

My wrist twitched again, and this time the gun was in my hand—a smooth, comforting feeling—nestling against my palm. The odor of smoke was stronger now. I looked down, and in the weak light from behind me made out blackened footprints against the wood plank flooring. The thought occurred to me that I should go back, give an alarm, and then carry on with a few heavily armed guards; but it was just a thought. I was already moving along toward the door, not liking it very well, but on the trail of something that wouldn't wait.

The odor was thick in the air now. The hot cloth smell of a press-'em-while-you-wait shop, mingled with the hot metallic tang of a foundry, and a little autumnal woodsmoke thrown in for balance. I came up smooth and silent to the door, flattened myself against the wall, covered the last few inches like a caterpillar sneaking up on a tender young leaf. I risked a fast look inside. The glow from the phantom intruder threw strange reddish shadows on the walls of an unused storeroom—dusty, dark, scattered with odds and ends of litter that should have been swept up but hadn't.

In the center of the room, the fiery man himself leaned over a sprawled body—a giant figure in a shapeless coverall. The fiery man's hands—strange, glowing hands in clumsy looking gauntlets—plucked at his victim with more-than-human dexterity; then he straightened. I didn't take time to goggle at the spectacle of a three-hundred-degree centigrade murderer. There was a chance that his victim wasn't dead yet—and if I hit him quick enough to capitalize on the tiny advantage of surprise . . .

I forgot all about the slug gun. I went through the door at a run, launched myself at the figure from whom heat radiated like a tangible wall and saw it turn with unbelievable, split-second speed, throw up a hand—five glowing fingers outspread—take one darting step back—

Long, pink sparks crackled from the outflung hand, leaping toward me. Like a diver hanging suspended in

midair, I saw the harsh electric glare, heard the *pop!* as
the miniature lightnings closed with me. . . .

Then a silent explosion turned the world to blinding
white, hurling me into nothingness.

For a long time I lay, clinging to the dim and formless
dream that was my refuge from the hazy memory of
smouldering footprints, a deserted room, and a fantastic
glowing man crouched over his victim. I groaned,
groped for the dream again, found only hard, cold
concrete against my face, a roiling nausea in the pit of
my stomach, and a taste like copper pennies in my
mouth. I found the floor, pushed hard to get my face up
out of the grit, blinked gummed eyes . . .

The room was dark, silent, dusty and vacant as a
robbed grave. I used an old tennis shoe someone had left
in my mouth as a tongue, grated it across dry lips, made
the kind of effort that under other circumstances had
won luckier souls the Congressional Medal, and sat up.
There was a ringing in my head like the echo of the
Liberty Bell just before it cracked.

I maneuvered to hands and knees, and, taking it by
easy stages, got to my feet. I sniffed. The burning odor
was gone. And my quarry hadn't waited around to see
whether I was all right. He—or it—had been gone for
some time—and had taken the corpse with him.

The light in the room was too weak to show me any
detail. I fumbled, got out a massive flint and steel
Imperium-style lighter, made three tries, got a smoky
yellow flame and squinted to find the trail of blackened
prints that would show me which way the fiery man had
gone.

There weren't any.

I went all the way to the door, looking for the scars I
had seen earlier, then came back, cast about among
empty cardboard cartons and stacked floor wax drums.
There were no footprints—not even the old-fashioned
kind—except for mine. The dust was thick, undisturbed.
There were no marks to show where the body had lain,
not a trace of my wild charge across the room. Only the
scrabble marks I had made getting to my feet proved
that I wasn't dreaming my own existence. I had heard of
people who pinched themselves to see if they were

dreaming. It had always seemed a little silly to me—you could dream a pinch as well as any other, more soothing, sensation. But I solemnly took a fold of skin on the back of my hand, squeezed hard. I could hardly feel it.

That didn't seem to prove anything one way or another. I made it to the door like a man walking to the undertaker's to save that last cab fare, and went into the hall. The lights were out. Only a dim, phosphorescent glow seemed to emanate from the walls and floor. The sight of the wood planking gave me no comfort at all. The prints burned here had been dark, distinct, charred. Now the dull varnish gleamed at me, unmarked.

The buzzing in my head had diminished to a faint hum, like that of a trapped fly, as I pushed through the door into the ground floor hallway. The milk glass globe hanging from the high ceiling glared at me with an unhealthy electric blue. A blackish haze seemed to hang in the still air of the silent corridor, lending a funereal tinge to the familiar vista of marble floor and varnished doors. Behind me, the door clicked shut with a shockingly loud, metallic clatter. I took a few breaths of the blackish air, failed to detect any hint of smoke. A glance at the door showed me what I had expected—smooth dark brown paint, unmarked by burning handprints.

I crossed the hall, pushed into an empty office. On the desk, a small clay pot sat on a blotter, filled with hard, baked-looking dirt. One dry leaf lay on the desk beside it. The desk clock said twelve-oh-five. I reached past it, picked up the phone, jiggled the hook. The silence at the other end was like a concrete wall. I jiggled some more, failed to evoke so much as a crackle of line static. I left the room, tried the next office with the same result. The phones were as dead as my hopes of living to a ripe old age outside a padded cell.

My footsteps in the corridor had a loud, clattering quality. I made it to the front entrance, pushed out through the heavy door, stood on the top step looking down at my car, still sitting where I had left it. The two escort vehicles were gone. Beyond the car, I noticed that the guard shack at the gate was dark. The street lamps seemed to be off too, and the usual gay pattern of the lights of the city's towers was missing. But a power failure wouldn't affect the carbide pole lights. . . . My glance went on to the sky; it was black, overcast. Even the stars were in on the black out.

I got into the car, turned the switch and pressed the starter button on the floor. Nothing happened. I muttered an impolite suggestion, tried again. No action. The horn didn't work either, and twisting the light switch produced nothing but a dry *snick!*

I got out of the car, stood undecided for a moment, then started around the building for the garages in the rear. I slowed, halted before I got there. They were dark, the heavy doors closed and barred. I fetched up another sigh, and for the first time noticed the dead, stale smell of the air. I walked back along the drive, passed the guard post, unaccountably deserted, emerged onto the street. It stretched into shadows, silent and dark. Predictably, there were no cabs in sight. A few cars stood at the curb. I started off toward the bridge, noticed a dark shape halfway across it: a car, without lights, parked midway in the span. For some reason, the sight shocked me. A small, uneasy feeling began to supplant the irritated frustration that had been gathering strength somewhere down below my third shirt button. I walked along to the car, peered in through the rolled up windows. There was no one inside. I thought of pushing the car to the side of the street, then considered the state of my constitution at the moment and went on.

There were more abandoned cars in Gustav Adolfstorg, all parked incongruously in midstream. One was a boxy, open touring car. The ignition switch was on, and the light switch too. I went on, checked the next one I came to. The switches were on. It appeared that there had been an epidemic of automotive ignition trouble in the city tonight, as well as a breakdown in the power plants—a coincidence that did nothing to improve my spirits.

I walked on across the square with its heroic equestrian statue, past the dark front of the Opera House, crossed Arsenalsgatan, turned up Tradgarsgatan, walked past shuttered shops, bleak in an eerie light like that of an eclipse. The city was absolutely still.

No breeze stirred the lifeless air, no growl of auto
engines disturbed the silence, no clatter of feet, no
distant chatter of voices. My first faint sense of un-
easiness was rapidly developing into a full-scale cold
sweat.

I cut across the corner of the park, skirting the glass
display cases crowded with provincial handicrafts, and
hurried across a stretch of barren clay.

The wrongness of it penetrated my preoccupation. I
looked back across the expanse of sterile earth,
searching on across the garden—the oddly naked
garden. There were the gravelled paths, the tile lined
pools—their fountaining jets lifeless—the band shell,
the green painted benches, the steel lampposts with
their attached refuse containers and neatly framed tram
schedules. But not one blade of grass, not a tree or
flowering shrub—no sign of the magnificent bed of
prize rhododendron that had occupied a popular
magazine's rotogravure section only a week earlier. I
turned and started on, half-running now, the unease
turning to an undefined dread that caught at my throat
and surged in my stomach like foul water in a
foundering galley's bilge.

I pushed through the iron gates of my house, wheezing
like a blown boiler from the run. I stared at the blank
black windows, feeling the impalacable air of abandon-
ment, desolation—of utter vacantness. I went on up the
drive, taking in the bare stretch of dirt that had been
verdant only hours before. Where the poplars had stood,
curious foot-wide pits showed black against the grey
soil. Only a scatter of dead leaves was left to remind me
that once trees had stood here. The crunch of my feet on
the gravel was loud. I stepped off onto the former lawn,
felt my feet sink into the dry, crumbling earth. At the
steps, I looked back. Only my trail of footmarks showed
that life had ever existed here—those, and a scatter of
dead insects under the carriage lamps. The door opened.
I pushed inside, stood savoring the funereal hush, my
heart thudding painfully, high in my chest.

"Barbro!" I called. My voice was a dry croak—a croak
of cold fear. I ran along the unlighted hall, went up the
stairs four at a time, slammed through the sitting room

door, on through into the bedroom. I found only silence, an aching stillness in which the sounds of my passage seemed to echo with a shocked reproach. I stumbled out of the room, yelling for Luc, not really expecting an answer now, yelling to break the awful, ominous stillness, the fear of what I might find in the dark, dead rooms.

I searched room by room, went back and tried the closets, shouting, slamming doors wide, not fighting the panic that was welling up inside me, but giving it vent in violent action.

There was nothing. Every room was in perfect order, every piece of furniture in its accustomed place, every drape discreetly drawn, every dish and book and garment undisturbed—but on the marble mantelpiece, the brass clock sat silent, its tick stilled. And in the pots where the broad-leafed plants had lent their touch of green, only the dead soil remained. I stood in the center of the dark library, staring out at the grim, metallic glow of the night sky, feeling the silence flow back in like a tangible thing, trying now to regain my control, to accept the truth. Barbro was gone—along with every other living thing in the Imperial capital.

CHAPTER TWO

I didn't notice the sound at first. I was sitting in the empty drawing room, staring out past the edge of heavy brocaded drapes at the empty street, listening to the thud of my empty heart. . . .

Then it penetrated: a steady thumping, faint, far away—but a sound—in the silent city. I jumped up, made it to the door and was out on the steps before the idea of caution occurred to me. The thumping was clearer now: a rhythmic slap, like the feet of marching troops, coming closer—

I saw them then, a flicker of movement through the iron spears of the fence. I faded back inside, watched from the darkness as they swung past, four abreast, big men in drab, shapeless coveralls. I tried to estimate their number. Perhaps two hundred, some laden with heavy packs, some with rifle-like weapons, one or two being helped by their comrades. They'd seen action somewhere tonight.

The last of them passed, and I ran softly down the drive. Keeping to the shelter of the buildings along the avenue, I followed a hundred yards behind them.

The first, stunning blow was past now, leaving me with a curious sense of detachment. The detachment of the sole survivor. The troop ahead swung along Nybroviken, grim, high-shouldered marchers a head taller than my six feet, not singing, not talking—just marching, block after block, past empty cars, empty buildings, empty parks—and a dead cat, lying in the gutter. I paused, stared at the ruffled, pathetic cadaver. They turned left into Uppsalavägen—and I realized

22

then where they were headed—to the Net Terminus Building at Stallmästargården. I was watching from the shelter of a massive oak a hundred yards away as the end of the column turned in at the ornate gate, and disappeared beyond the massive portal that had been smashed from its hinges. One man dropped off, took up a post at the entry.

I crossed the street silently, followed the walk around to the side entrance, wasted a few seconds wishing for the keys in my safe back at the house, then headed for the back of the building. Stumbling through denuded flower beds, I followed the line of the wall, barely visible in the blackish light—a light that seemed, curiously, to shine upward from the ground rather than impinge from the starless sky. A masonry wall barred my way. I jumped, caught the top edge, pulled myself over, dropped into the paved court behind the Terminal. Half a dozen boxy wheeled shuttles were parked here, of the special type used for work in some of the nearer A-lines—worlds with Common History dates only a few centuries in the past, where other Stockholms existed with streets in which a diguised delivery van could move unnoticed.

One of the vehicles was close to the building wall. I climbed up on its hood, reached, tried to lift the wide, metal frame, double-hung window. It didn't budge. I went back down, fumbled in the dark under the shuttle's dash, brought out the standard tool kit, found a hammer, scrambled back up, and as gently as I could, smashed the glass from the frame. It made a hell of a racket. I stood listening, half expecting to hear indignant voices calling questions, but the only sound was my own breathing, and a creak from the shuttle's springs as I shifted my weight.

The room I clambered into was a maintenance shop, lined with long workbenches littered with disassembled shuttle components, its walls hung with tools and equipment. I went out through the door at the far end of the room, along the corridor of the big double doors leading into the garages. Faint sounds came from within. I eased the door open a foot, slipped inside, into the echoing stillness of the wide, high vaulted depot. A double row of Net shuttles reared up in the gloom—heavy, ten-man machines, smaller three-man scouts, a pair of light new-model single-seaters at the far end of the line.

And beyond them—dwarfing them—a row of dark blocky machines of strange design, massive and ugly as garbage scows, illogically dumped here among the elegantly decorated vehicles of the Imperial TNL service. Dark figures moved around the strange machines, forming up into groups beside each heavy transport, responding to gestures and an occasional grunted command. I walked along behind the parked shuttles, eased forward between two from which I had a clear view of the proceedings.

The doors to the first of the five alien machines were open. As I watched, a suited man clambered in, followed by the next in line. The troops—whoever they were—were reembarking. They were clumsy, slope-shouldered heavyweights, covered from head to toe in baggy, dull grey suits with dark glass faceplates. One of the Imperial machines was impeding the smooth flow of the moving column; two of the intruders stepped to it, gripped it by its near side runner, and, with one heave, tipped it up, dumped it over on its side with a heavy slam and a tinkle of breaking glass. I felt myself edging farther back out of sight; the scout weighed a good two tons.

The first shuttle was loaded now. The line of men shuffled along to the next and continued loading. Time was slipping past. In another ten minutes all the suited men would be aboard their machines, gone—back to whatever world-line they had come from. It was clear that these were invaders from the Net—a race of men, unknown to Imperial authorities, who possessed an M-C drive of their own. Men who were my only link with the vanished inhabitants of desolated Stockholm Zero-zero. Waiting here wouldn't help; I had to follow them, learn what I could. . . .

I took a bracing lungful of the stale Terminal air and stepped out of my hiding place, feeling as exposed as a rat between holes as I moved along the wall, putting distance between myself and the strangers. My objective was one of the two-man scouts—a fast, maneuverable machine with adequate armament and the latest in instrumentation. I reached it, got the door open with no more than a rattle of the latch that sent my stomach crowding up under my ribs; but there was no alarm.

Even inside, there was enough of the eerie light to see my way by. I went forward to the control compartment, slid into the operator's seat, and tried the main drive warm-up switch.

Nothing happened. I tried other controls, without response. The M-C drive was as dead as the cars abandoned in the city streets. I got up, went back to the entry and eased it open, stepped silently out. I could hear the invaders working away two hundred feet from me, shielded from view by the ranked shuttles. An idea was taking form—an idea I didn't like very well. The first thing it would require was that I get around to the opposite side of the Terminal. I turned . . .

He was standing ten feet away, just beyond the rear corner of the shuttle. At close range he looked seven feet tall, wide in proportion, with gloved hands the size of briefcases. He took a step toward me, and I backed away. He followed, almost leisurely. Two more steps and I would be clear of the shelter of the machine, exposed to the view of any of the others who might happen to glance my way. I stopped. The stranger kept on coming, one immense, stubby-fingered hand reaching for me.

My wrist twitched, and the slug gun was in my hand. I aimed for a point just below the center of the chest, and fired. At the muffled *slap*! of the gun, the monster-man jacknifed, went down backward with a slam like a horse falling in harness. I jumped past him to the shelter of the next machine, and crouched there, waiting. It seemed impossible that no one had heard the shot or the fall of the victim, but the sounds from the far end of the vast shed went on, uninterrupted. I let out a breath I just realized I had been holding, feeling my heart thumping in my chest like a trapped rabbit's.

With the gun still in my hand, I stepped out, went back to the man I had shot. He lay on his back, spread-eagled like a bearskin rug—and about the same size. Through his shattered faceplate, I saw a broad, coarse, dead-grey face, with porous skin, and a wide, lipless mouth, half-open now to show square, yellow teeth. Small eyes, pale

blue as a winter sky, stared lifelessly under bushy
yellow brows that grew in a continuous bar across the
forehead. A greasy lock of dull blonde hair fell beside
one hollow temple. It was the most appallingly hideous
face I had ever seen. I backed off from it, turned and
started off into the shadows.

The last in line of the alien shuttles was my target. To
get to it, I had to cross an open space of perhaps fifty
feet, concealed by nothing but the dimness of the light. I
stepped out, started across the exposed stretch as
silently as slick leather soles would let me. Every time
one of them turned in my direction, I froze until he
turned away. I had almost reached shelter when one of
the officers tallying men turned to stare toward the
other end of the huge shed. Someone had missed the one
I had shot. The officer called—a sudden hoarse cry like a
bellow of mortal agony. The others paid no attention.
The officer snapped an order, started off to investigate.
I had perhaps half a minute before he found his
missing crewman. I slipped into the shadow of the
supply shuttle, worked my way quickly to the last in
line, slid around the end. The coast was clear. I made it
to the entry in three quick steps, swung myself up, and
stepped inside the enemy machine.
There was a sickish animal odor here, a subtle alien-
ness of proportion. I took in the control panels, the
operator's chair, the view-screens, and the chart table in
a swift glance. All were recognizable—but in size and
shape and detail they differed in a hundred ways from
the familiar Imperial patterns, or from any normal
scheme of convenience. I hitched myself into the high,
wide, hard seat, stared at squares and circles of plastic
glowing in clashing shades of brown and violet. Curious
symbols embossed on metal strips labelled some of the
baroquely curved levers which projected from the dull
ochre panel. A pair of prominent foot pedals, set awkwardly wide apart, showed signs of heavy wear.
I stared at the array, feeling the sweat begin to pop out
on my forehead. I had only a few seconds to decide—and
if my guess were wrong—
A simple knife switch set in the center of the panel
drew my attention. There were scratches on the panel

around it, and worn spots on the mud-colored plastic
grip. It was as good a guess as any. I reached out
tentatively—

Outside, a horrific shriek ripped through the silence. I
jerked, smashing my knee against a sharp corner of the
panel. The pain brought a warm flood of instinctive
anger and decision. I ground my teeth together, reached
again, slammed the lever down.

At once, the lights dimmed. I heard the entry close
with an echoing impact. Heavy vibration started up,
rattling ill-fitting panel members. Indicator lights began
to wink; curious lines danced on a pair of glowing
pinkish screens. I felt a ghostly blow against the side of
the hull. One of the boys wanted in, but he was a trifle
too late. The screens had cleared to show me a view of
black desolation under a starless sky—the familiar
devastation of the Blight. The M-C field was operating;
the stolen shuttle was carrying me out across the Net of
alternate worlds—and at terrific speed, to judge from
the quicksilver flow of the scene outside as I flashed
across the parallel realities of the A-lines. I had made
my escape. The next order of business was to determine
how to control the strange machine.

Half an hour's study of the panel sufficed to give me a
general idea of the meanings of the major instruments. I
was ready now to attempt to maneuver the stolen
shuttle. I gripped the control lever, tugged at it—it
didn't move. I tried again, succeeded only in bending the
metal arm. I stood, braced my feet, put my shoulders
into it. With a sharp clang, the lever broke off short. I
sank back in the chair, tossed the broken handle to the
floor. Evidently, the controls were locked. The owners
of the strange shuttle had taken precautions against any
disgruntled potential deserter who might have an
impulse to ride the machine to some idyllic world line of
his own choice. Once launched, its course was pre-
determined, guided by automatic instruments—and I
was powerless to stop it.

CHAPTER THREE

Two hours passed while the shuttle rushed on into the unexplored and uncharted depths of the Net. I sat watching the fantastic flow of scenes beyond the view screens—the weird phenomenon that Chief Captain Winter of the TNL Service had called A-entropy. At the speed at which I was travelling—far greater than anything ever managed by Imperial technicians—living creatures would not be detectable; a man would flash across the screen and be gone in a fraction of a microsecond. But the fixed features of the scene—the streets, the buildings, the stone and metal and wood—loomed around me. And as I watched, they changed. . . .

The half-familiar structures seemed to flow, to shrink or expand gradually, sprouting outré new elements. I saw doorways widen, or dwindle and disappear; red granite blocks rippled and flowed, changed by degrees to grey polished slabs. The nearly legible lettering on a nearby shop window writhed, reformed itself, the Roman capitals distorting into forms like Cyrillic letters, then changed again, and again, to become lines of meaningless symbols. I saw sheds and shacks appear and swell, crowding among the older structures, burgeoning mightily into blank, forbidding piles that soared up out of sight. Balconies budded as window ledges grew into great cantilevered terraces, then merged, shutting out the sky—and then they, in turn, drew back, and new facades stood revealed: grim, blackish ribbed columns, rearing up a thousand feet into the unchanging sky, linked by narrow bridges that shifted, twitching like nervous fingers, widening, spreading into a vast network that entangled the spires like a spider's

28

web, then broke, faded back, leaving only a dark bar here and there to join the now ponderous squat towers like chains linking captive monsters. All this is a frozen, eternal instant of time, as the stolen shuttle rushed blindly across the lines of alternate probability toward its unknown destination.

I sat entranced, watching the universe evolve around me. Then I found myself nodding, my eyes aching abominably. I suddenly realized that I hadn't eaten my dinner yet—nor slept—in how many hours? I got out of the chair, made a quick search of the compartment, and found a coarse-woven cloak with a rank odor like attar of locker room blended with essence of stable. I was too weary to be choosy, though. I spread the cloth on the floor in the tiny space between the operator's seat and the power compartment, curled up on it, and let the overwhelming weariness sweep over me. . . .

. . . and awakened with a start. The steady drone of the drive had changed in tone, dropped to a deep thrumming. My watch said I'd been on the way a little less than three and a half hours—but brief as the trip had been, the ugly but fantastically efficient shuttle had raced across the Net into regions where the Imperial scouts had never penetrated. I scrambled up, got my eyes open far enough to make out the screens.

It was a scene from a drunk's delirium. Strange, crooked towers rose up from dark, empty canyons where footpaths threaded over heaped refuse among crowded stalls, doorless arches, between high-wheeled carts laden with meaningless shapes of wood and metal and leather. From carved stone lintels, cornices, pilasters, grotesque faces peered, goggled, grimaced like devils in an Aztec tomb. As I gaped, the growl of the drive sank to a mutter, died. The oddly shifting scene froze into the immobility of identity. I had arrived—somewhere.

But the street—if I could use that term for this crowded alley—was deserted, and the same odd, fungoid light I had seen in the empty streets of Stockholm glowed faintly from every surface under the dead, opaque blackness of the sky above.

Then without warning a wave of nausea bent me double, retching. The shuttle seemed to rise under me, twist, spin. Forces seized me, stretched me out as thin as copper wire, threaded me through the red-hot eye of a needle, then slammed me into a compacted lump like a metal-baler cubing a junked car. I heard a whistling noise, and it was me, trying to get enough air into my lungs to let out a yell of agony—

And then the pressure was gone. I was sprawled on my back on the hard floor, but still breathing and in my usual shape, watching lights wink out on the panel. I felt the sharp, reassuring pain of an honest cut on my knee, saw a small dark patch of blood through a tear in the cloth. I got to my feet, and the screen caught my eye. . . .

The two-foot rectangle of the view-plate showed me a crowd packing the narrow street that had been deserted a moment ago. A mob of squat, hulking, long-armed creatures surging and milling in an intricate play of dark and light where vivid shafts of sunlight struck down from high above into deep shadow—

Then behind me metal growled. I whirled, saw the entry hatch jump, swing open. The shuttle trembled, lurched—and a vast, wide shape stepped in through the opening—a fanged monstrosity with a bulging, bald head, a wide, thin-lipped, chinless face, huge, strangely elaborate ears, a massive, hulking body buckled into straps and hung with clanking bangles, incongruous against a shaggy pelt like a blonde gorilla's.

The muscles of my right wrist tensed, ready to slap the slug gun into my hand, but I relaxed, let my arms fall to my sides. I could kill this fellow—and the next one who stepped inside. But there was more at stake here than my own personal well-being. A moment before, I had seen the miracle of a deserted street transformed in the wink of an eye into a teeming marketplace packed with sunlight and movement. If these grotesque, golden-haired apes knew the secret of that enchantment then maybe my own Stockholm could also come back from the dead . . . if I could find the secret.

"All right, big boy," I said aloud. "I'll come along peacefully."

The creature reached, clamped a hand like a power shovel on my shoulder, literally lifted me, and hurled me at the door. I struck the jamb, bounced, fell out into an odor like dead meat and broccoli rotting together. A growl ran through the shaggy mob surrounding me. They jumped back, jabbering. I made it to my feet, slapping at the decayed rubbish clinging to my jacket, and my captor came up from behind, grabbed my arm as though he had decided to tear it off, and sent me spinning ahead. I hooked a foot in a loop of melon rind, went down again. Something hit me across the back of the shoulders like a falling tree. I oofed, tried to get to hands and knees to make my white god speech, and felt a kick that slammed me forward, my face ploughing into spongy, reeking garbage. I came up spitting, in time to take a smashing blow full in the face, and saw bright constellations burst above me, like a Fourth of July display long ago in another world.

I was aware of my feet dragging, and worked them to relieve the gouging of hard fingers under my arms. Then I was stumbling, half dragged between two of the hairy men, who shouldered their way through the press of babbling spectators that gave way reluctantly, their eyes like blue marbles staring at me as though I were a victim of a strange and terrible disease.

It seemed like a long way that they hauled me, while I gradually adjusted my thinking to the reality of my captivity by creatures that awakened racial memories of ogres and giants and things that went bump in the night. But here they were, as real as life and twice as smelly, scratching at hairy hides with fingers like bananas, showing great yellowish fighting fangs in grimaces of amazement and disgust, and looming over me like angry goblins over a small boy. I stumbled along through the hubbub of raucous sound and eye-watering stench toward whatever fate trolls kept in store for mortals who fell among them.

We came out from the narrow way into a wider but not cleaner avenue lined with curious, multitiered stalls, where grey-maned merchants squatted, peering down from their high perches, shouting their wares, tossing down purchases to customers, catching thick, square coins on the fly. There were heaped fruits, odd-shaped clay pots of all sizes capped and sealed with purplish tar, drab-colored mats of woven fiber, flimsy-looking contraptions of hammered sheet metal, harnesses, straps of leather with massive brass buckles, strings of brightly polished brass and copper discs like old English horse brasses.

And in this fantastic bazaar a horde of variegated near-humanity milled. A dozen races and colors of shaggy sub-men, half-men, ape-men: man-like giants with great bushes of bluish hair fringing bright red faces; incredibly tall, slim creatures, with sleek, black fur, curiously short legs and long, flat feet; wide, squat individuals with round shoulders and long, drooping noses. Some wore great loops and strings of the polished brasses, others had only one or two baubles pinned to the leather straps that seemed to constitute their only clothing. And others, the more bedraggled members, with strap-worn shoulders and horny bare feet, had no brass at all. And over all, great blue and green flies hovered, droning, like a living canopy.

I saw the crowd part to let a great, slow-moving beast push through, a thing as big as a small Indian elephant, and with the same ponderous tread; but the trunk was no more than an exaggerated pig's snout, and from below it two great shovel tusks of yellow ivory thrust out from the underslung jaw above a drooping pink lower lip, looped with saliva and froth. Wide strips of inch-thick leather harnessed the beast to a heavy cart stacked with hooped barrels, and a shaggy driver atop the load slapped a vast braided whip across the massive back of the animal. Farther on, two of the short, burly man-things—they would weigh in at five hundred pounds apiece, I estimated—toiled in harness beside a mangy mastodon-like animal whose blunt tusks were capped with six-inch wooden knobs.

We reached the end of the boulevard and after a short delay to kick a few determined spectators back, my bodyguard urged me roughly up a wide, garbage-littered flight of steep, uneven stone steps—on through a gaping, doorless opening where two lowbrowed louts in black straps and enamelled brasses rose from crouching positions to intercept us. I leaned on the wall and worked on getting my arms back into their sockets while the boys staged a surly reunion. Other members emerged from the hot, zoo-smelling gloom of the rabbit warren building; they came over to wrinkle brows and

grimace at me, prodding and poking with fingers like
gun barrels. I backed away, flattened myself against the
wall, remembering, for some unfortunate reason, a
kitten that Gargantua had been very fond of until it
broke. . . .

My guards pushed through, clamped onto my arms
again in a proprietary way, hooted for gangway, and
dragged me into one of the arched openings off the
irregularly-shaped entry hall. I tried to follow the
turnings and twisting and dips and rises of the tunnel-
like passage with some vague idea of finding my way
back later, but I soon lost track. It was almost pitch dark
here. Small, yellowish incandescent bulbs glowed at
fifty-foot intervals, showing me a puddled floor, and
rough-hewn walls with many branching side passages.
After a couple of hundred yards, the hall widened into a
gloomy thirty-foot chamber. One of my keepers, rooted
in a heap of rubbish, produced a wide strap of thick
blackish leather attached to the wall by a length of rope.
He buckled it around my right wrist, gave me a shove,
then went and squatted by the wall. The other cop went
off along a corridor that curved sharply up and out of
sight. I kicked enough of the damp debris aside to make
a place to sit, and settled down for a wait. Sooner or
later someone in authority would be wanting to
interrogate me. For that, communication would have to
be established—and as a Net-travelling race, I assumed
my captors would have some linguistic capability. After
that . . .

I remember stretching out full length on the filthy
floor, having a brief thought that for slimy brick, it was
amazingly comfortable; then a big, hard foot was
kicking at me. I started to sit up, was hauled to my feet
by the rope on my arm, and marched along another
dingy passage. My feet were almost to heavy to lift now,
and my stomach felt like a raw wound. I tried to
calculate how many hours it had been since I had eaten,
but lost count. My brain was working sluggishly, like a
clock dipped in syrup.

The chamber we arrived at—somewhere high in the
squat building, I thought; the walk had been mostly
along upward-slanting corridors—was domed, roughly

circular, with niches set in the irregularly-surfaced walls. There was a terrible odor of dung and rotting hay. The room seemed more like a den in a zoo than an apartment in a human dwelling. I had an impulse to look around for the opening the bear would emerge from.

There were heaps of greyish rags dumped in some of the niches. One of them moved, and I realized that it was a living creature—an incredibly aged, scruffy specimen of my captors' race. The two escorting me urged me closer to the ancient. They had a subdued air now, as though in the presence of rank. In the poor light that filtered in from an arrangement of openings around the walls, I saw a hand like a grey leather-covered claw come up, rake fitfully at the thin, moth-eaten chest hair of the oldster. I made out his eyes then—dull blue, half-veiled by drooping upper lids, nested in the bloodred crescents of sagging lower lids. They stared at me fixedly, unblinking. Below, great tufts of grey hair sprouted from gaping half-inch nostrils. The mouth was puckered, toothless, as wide as a hip pocket. The rest of the face was a mass of doughy wrinkles, framed between long locks of uncombed white hair from which incredible long-lobed ears poked, obscenely pink and naked. The chin hair, caked with foreign matter, hung down across the shrunken chest, against which bony, bald knees pocked up like grey stones. I accidentally breathed, choked at a stench like a rotting whale, and was jerked back into position.

The patriarch made a hoarse, croaking noise. I waited, breathing through my mouth. One of my jailers shook me, barked something at me.

"Sorry, fellows," I croaked. "No kapoosh."

The bearded elder jumped as though he'd been poked with a hot iron. He squalled something, spraying me in the process. He bounced up and down with surprising energy, still screeching, then stopped abruptly and thrust his face close to mine. One of my guards grabbed my neck with a hard hand, anticipating my reaction. I stared into the blue eyes—eyes as human as mine, set in this ghastly caricature of a face—saw the open pores as big as match heads, watched a trickle of saliva find its way from the loose mouth down into the beard. . . .

He leaned back with a snuffle, waved an arm, made a

speech. When he finished, a thin voice piped up from the left. I twisted, saw another mangy bearskin rug shifting position. My owners propelled me in that direction, held me while the second oldster, even uglier than the first, looked me over. While he stared and drooled, my gaze wandered up to a higher niche. In the shadows, I could barely make out the propped bones of a skeleton, the empty eye sockets gazing down, the massive jaws grinning sardonically, a thick leather strap still circling the neck bones. Apparently promotion to the local Supreme Court was a life appointment.

A jerk at my arm brought me back to more immediate matters. The grandpa before me shrilled. I didn't answer. He curled his lips back, exposing toothless yellowish gums and a tongue like a pink sock full of sand, and screamed. That woke up a couple more wise men; there were answering hoots and squawks from several directions.

My keepers dutifully guided me over to the next judge, an obese old fellow with a bloated, sparsely-haired belly over which large black fleas hurried on erratic paths like bloodhounds looking for a lost trail. This one had one tooth left—a hooked, yellow-brown canine over an inch long. He showed it to me, made gobbling noises, then leaned out and took a swipe at me with an arm as long as a dock crane. My alert guardians pulled me back as I ducked; I was grateful; even this senile old reprobate packed enough wallop to smash my jaw and break my neck if he had connected.

At a querulous cry from a niche high up in a dark corner, we steered in that direction. A lank hand with two fingers missing groped, pulled a crooked body up into a sitting position. Half a face looked down at me. There were scars, then a ragged edge, then bare, exposed bone where the right cheek had been. The eye socket was still there, but empty, the lid puckered and sunken. The mouth, with one corner missing, failed to close properly—an effect that produced a vacuous, loose-lipped smile—as appropriate to this horror as a poodle shave on a hyena.

I was staggering now, not reacting as promptly as my leaders would have liked. The one on the left—the more vicious of the two, I had already decided—lifted me up

by one arm, slammed me down, jerked me back to my
feet, then shook me like a dusty blanket. I staggered, got
my feet back under me, jerked free, and hit him hard in
the belly. It was like punching a sandbag; he twisted me
casually back into position. I don't think he even noticed
the blow.

We stood in the center of the room for a while then,
while the council of elders deliberated. One got mad and
spat across the room at the big-bellied one, who replied
with a hurled handful of offal. Apparently that was the
sign for the closing of the session. My helpers backed
off, shoved me out into the corridor, and hustled me off
on another trip through the crooked passages, with
hoots and snarls ringing from the chamber behind us.

This journey ended in still another room, like the
others no more than a wide place in the corridor. There
was a stone bench, some crude-looking shelves big
enough for coffins in one corner, the usual dim bulb,
heaped garbage, and odds and ends of equipment of
obscure function. There was a hole in the center of the
chamber from which a gurgling sound came. Sanitary
facilities, I judged, from the odor. This time I was
strapped by one ankle and allowed to sit on the floor. A
clay pot with some sort of mush in it was thrust at me. I
got a whiff, gagged, pushed it away. I wasn't that
hungry—not yet.

An hour passed. I had the feeling I was waiting for
something. My two proprietors—or two others, I wasn't
sure—sat across the room, hunkered down on their
haunches, dipping up their dinner from their food pots,
not talking. I could hardly smell the place now—my
olfactory nerves were numb. Every so often a newcomer
would shamble in, come over to gape at me, then move
off.

Then a messenger arrived, barked something
peremptory. My escorts got to their feet, licked their
fingers carefully with thick, pink tongues as big as shoe
soles, came over and unstrapped the ankle braclet, and
started me off again. We went down, this time—taking
one branching byway after another, passing through a
wide hall where at least fifty hulking louts sat at long
benches, holding some sort of meeting, past an entry
through which late evening light glowed, then down

again, into a narrow passage that ended in a cul-de-sac.

Lefty—my more violent companion—yanked at my arm, thrust me toward a round, two-foot opening, like an oversized rat-hole, set eighteen inches above the floor. It was just about wide enough for a man to crawl into. I got the idea. For a moment, I hesitated; this looked like the end of the trail. Once inside, there'd be no further opportunities for escape—not that I had had any so far.

A blow on the side of the head slammed me against the wall. I went down, twisted on my back. The one who had hit me was standing over me, reaching for a new grip. I'd had about enough of this fellow. Without pausing to consider the consequences, I bent my knee, smashed a hard, ikedo-type kick to his groin. He doubled over, and my second kick caught him square in the mouth. I got a glimpse of pinkish blood welling—

The other man-ape grabbed me, thrust me at the burrow almost casually. I dived for it, scrambled into a damp chill and an odor as solid as well-aged cheese. A crawl of five feet brought me to a drop-off. I felt around over the edge, found the floor two feet below, swung my legs around and stood, facing the entrance with the slug gun in my hand. If Big Boy came in after me, he'd get a surprise.

But I saw the two of them silhouetted against the light from along the corridor. Lefty was leaning on his friend, making plaintive squeaking noises. Then they went off along the corridor together. Apparently whatever their instructions were, they didn't include taking revenge on the new specimen—not yet.

CHAPTER FOUR

The traditional first move when imprisoned in the dark was to pace off the dimensions of the cell, a gambit which presumably lends a mystic sense of mastery over one's environment. Of course, I wasn't actually imprisoned. I could crawl back out into the corridor—but since I would undoubtedly meet Lefty before I had gone far, the idea lacked appeal. That left me with the pacing off to do.

I started from the opening, took a step which I estimated at three feet, and slammed against a wall. No help there.

Back at my starting point, I took a more cautious step, then another—

There was a sound from the darkness ahead. I stood, one foot poised, not breathing, listening. . . .

"*Vansi pa' me' zen pa'*," a mellow tenor voice said from the darkness. "*Sta' zi?*"

I backed a step. The gun was still in my hand. The other fellow had the advantage; his eyes would be used to the dark, and I was outlined against the faint glow from the tunnel. At the thought, I dropped flat, felt the cold wetness of the rough floor come through my clothes.

"*Bo'jou', ami*," the voice said. "*E' vou Gallice?*"

Whoever he was, he was presumably a fellow prisoner. And the language he had spoken didn't sound much like the grunts and clicks of the ogres outside. Still, I had no impulse to rush over and get acquainted.

"*Kansh' tu dall' Scansk . . .*" The voice came again. And this time I almost got the meaning. The accent was horrible, but it sounded almost like Swedish. . . .

"Maybe Anglic, you," the voice said.

"Maybe," I answered, hearing my voice come out as a croak. "Who're you?"

"Ah, good! I took a blink from you so you come into." The accent was vaguely Hungarian and the words didn't make much sense. "Why catch they you? Where from commer you?"

I edged a few feet to the side to get farther from the light. The floor slanted up slightly. I thought of using my lighter, but that would only make me a better target if this new chum had any unfriendly ideas—and nothing I had encountered so far in giant-land led me to expect otherwise.

"Don't be shy of you," the voice urged. "I am friend."

"I asked you who you are," I said. My hackles were still on edge. I was tired and hungry and bruised, and talking to a strange voice in the dark wasn't what I needed to soothe my nerves just now.

"Sir, I have honor of to make known myself: Field Agent Dzok, at the service."

"Field agent of what?" My voice had a sharp edge.

"Perhaps better for further confidences to await closer acquaintance," the field agent said. "Please, you will talk again, thus allowing me to place the dialect more closely."

"The dialect is English," I said. I eased back another foot, working my way up-slope. I didn't know whether he could see me or not, but it was an old maxim to take the high ground. . . .

"English? Ah, yes. I think we've triggered the correct mnemonic now. Not a very well-known sub-branch of Anglic, but then I fancy my linguistic indoctrination is one of the more complete for an Agent of Class Four. Am I doing better?"

The voice seemed closer, as well as more grammatical. "You're doing fine," I assured it—and rolled quickly away. Too late, I felt an edge under my back, yelled, went over, and slammed against hard stone three feet below the upper level. I felt my head bounce, heard a loud ringing, while bright lights flashed. Then there was a hand groping over my chest, under my head.

"Sorry, old fellow," the voice said up close. "I should

have warned you. Did the same thing myself my first day here. . . ."

I sat up, groped quickly, found the slug gun, tucked it back into my cuff holster.

"I guess I was a little over-cautious," I said. "I hardly expected to run into another human being in this damned place." I worked my jaw, found it still operable, touched a scrape on my elbow.

"I see you've hurt your arm," my cell-mate said. "Let me dab a bit of salve on that. . . ." I heard him moving, heard the snap of some sort of fastener, fumbling noises. I got out my lighter, snapped it. It caught, blazed up blindingly. I held it up—and my jaw dropped.

Agent Dzok crouched a yard from me, his head turned away from the bright light, a small first aid kit in his hands—hands that were tufted with short, silky red-brown hair that ran up under the grimy cuffs of a tattered white uniform. I saw long thick-looking arms, scuffed soft leather boots encasing odd long-heeled feet, a small round head, dark-skinned, long nosed. Dzok turned his face toward me, blinking deepset yellowish eyes set close together above a wide mouth that opened in a smile to show square, yellow teeth.

"The light's a bit bright," he said in his musical voice. "I've been in the dark for so long now. . . ."

I gulped, flicked off the lighter. "Sorry," I mumbled. "Wha—who did you say you were?"

"You look a trifle startled," Dzok said in an amused tone. "I take it you haven't encountered my branch of the Hominids before?"

"I had a strange idea we Homo sapiens were the only branch of the family that made it into the Cenozoic," I said. "Meeting the boys outside was quite a shock. Now you. . . ."

"Ummm. I think our two families diverged at about your late Pliocene. The Hagroon are a somewhat later offshoot, at about the end of the Pleistocene—say half a million years back." He laughed softly. "So you see, they represent a closer relationship to you sapiens than do we of Xonijeel. . . ."

"That's depressing news."

Dzok's rough-skinned hand fumbled at my arm, then gripped it lightly while he dabbed at the abrasion. The cool ointment started to take the throb from the wound.

"How did they happen to pick you up?" Dzok asked. "I take it you were one of a group taken on a raid?"

"As far as I know, I'm the only one." I was still being cautious. Dzok seemed like a friendly enough creature, but he had a little too much hair on him for my taste, in view of what I'd seen of the Hagroon. The latter might be closer relatives of mine than of the agent, but I couldn't help lumping them together in my mind—though Dzok was more monkey-like than ape-like.

"Curious," Dzok said. "The pattern usually calls for catches of at least fifty or so. I've theorized that this represents some sort of minimum group size which is worth the bother of the necessary cultural analysis, language indoctrination, and so on."

"Necessary for what?"

"For making use of the captives," Dzok said. "The Hagroon are slave raiders, of course."

"Why 'of course'?"

"I assumed you knew, being a victim..." Dzok paused. "But then perhaps you're in a different category. You say you were the only captive taken?"

"What about you?" I ignored the question. "How did you get here?"

The agent sighed. "I was a trifle incautious, I fear. I had a rather naïve idea that in this congeries of variant hominid strains I'd pass unnoticed, but I was spotted instantly. They knocked me about a bit, dragged me in before a tribunal of nonagenarians for an interrogation, which I pretended not to understand—"

"You mean you speak their language?" I interrupted.

"Naturally, my dear fellow. An agent of Class Four could hardly be effective without language indoctrination."

I let that pass. "What sort of questions did they ask you?"

"Lot of blooming nonsense, actually. It's extremely difficult for noncosmopolitan races to communicate at a meaningful level; the basic cultural assumptions vary so widely—"

"You and I seem to be doing all right."

"Well, after all, I *am* a Field Agent of the Authority. We're trained in just such communicative ability."

"Maybe you'd better start a little farther back. What authority are you talking about? How'd you get here? Where are you from in the first place? Where did you learn English?"

Dzok had finished with my arm now. He laughed—a good-natured chuckle. Imprisonment in foul conditions seemed not to bother him. "I'll take those questions one at a time. I suggest we move up to my dais now. I've arranged a few scraps of cloth in the one dry corner here. And perhaps you'd like a bit of clean food, after that nauseous pap our friends here issue."

"You've got food?"

"My emergency ration pack. I've been using it sparingly. Not very satisfying, but nourishing enough."

We made our way to a shelf-like flat area high in the right rear corner of the cell, and I stretched out on Dzok's neatly arranged dry rags and accepted a robin's-egg-sized capsule.

"Swallow that down," Dzok said. "A balanced ration for twenty-four hours; arranged concentrically, of course. Takes about nine hours to assimilate. There's water too." He passed me a thick clay cup.

I gulped hard, got the pill down. "Your throat must be bigger than mine," I said. "Now what about my questions?"

"Ah, yes, the Authority; this is the great Web government which exercises jurisdiction over all that region of the Web lying within two million E-units radius of the Home Line. . . ."

I was listening, thinking how this news would sit with the Imperial authorities when I got back—if I got back—if there was anything to go back to. Not one new Net-traveling race but two—each as alien to the other as either was to me. And all three doubtless laying claim to ever-wider territory. . . .

Dzok was still talking, ". . .our work in the Anglic sector has been limited, for obvious reasons—"

"What obvious reasons?"

"Our chaps could hardly pass unnoticed among you," Dzok said drily. "So we've left the sector pretty much to its own devices—"

"But you *have* been there?"

"Routine surveillance only, mostly in null time, of course—"

"You use too many 'of courses', Dzok," I said. "But go on, I'm listening."

"Our maps of the area are sketchy. There's the vast desert area, of C—" he cleared his throat. "A vast desert area known as the Desolation, within which no world lines survive, surrounded by a rather wide spectrum of related lines, all having as their central cultural source the North European technical nucleus—rather a low-grade technology, to be sure, but the first glimmering of enlightenment is coming into being there. . . ."

He went on with his outline of the vast sweep of A-lines that constituted the scope of activities of the Authority. I didn't call attention to his misconceptions regarding the total absence of life in the Blight, or his seeming ignorance of the existence of a line with Net-traveling capabilities. That was information I would keep in reserve.

". . . the scope of the Authority has been steadily extended over the last fifteen hundred years," the agent was saying. "Our unique Web-transit abilities naturally carry with them a certain responsibility. The early tendency toward exploitation has long been overcome, and the Authority now merely exercises a police and peace-keeping function, while obtaining useful raw materials and manufactured products from carefully selected loci on a normal commercial basis."

"Uh-huh." I'd heard the speech before. It was a lot like the pitch Bernadotte and Richthofen and the others had given me when I first arrived at Stockholm Zero-zero.

"My mission here," Dzok went on, "was to discover the forces behind the slave raids which had been creating so much misery and unrest along the periphery of the Authority, and to recommend the optimum method of eliminating the nuisance with the minimum of overt interference. As I've told you, I badly under-estimated our Hagroon. I was arrested within a quarter-hour of my arrival."

"And you learned English on your visits to the, ah, Anglic Sector?"

"I've never visited the sector personally, but the

language libraries naturally have monitored the developing dialects."

"Do your friends know where you are?"

Dzok sighed. "I'm afraid not. I was out to cut a bit of a figure, I realize now—belatedly. I envisioned myself reporting back in to IDMS Headquarters with the solution neatly wrapped and tied with pink ribbon. Instead—well, in time they'll notice my prolonged absence and set to work to find my trail. In the meantime. . ."

"In the meantime, what?"

"I can only hope they take action before my turn comes."

"Your turn for what?"

"Didn't you know, old chap? But of course not; you don't speak their beastly dialect. It's all because of the food shortage, you see. They're cannibals. Captives that fail to prove their usefulness as slaves are slaughtered and eaten."

"About how long," I asked Dzok, "do you suppose we have?"

"I estimate that I've been here for three weeks," the agent said. "There are two poor sods here when I came—a pair of slaves of a low order of intelligence. As well as I could determine, they'd been here for some two weeks. They were taken away a week ago. Some sort of feast for a high official, I gathered. Judging from the look of the menu, they'd have need of those ferocious teeth of theirs. Tough chewing, I'd say."

I was beginning to see through agent Dzok. His breezy air covered a conviction that he'd be in a Hagroon cooking pot himself before many more days had passed.

"In that case, I suppose we'd better start thinking about a way to get out of here," I suggested.

"I hoped you'd see that," Dzok said. "I have a chance of sorts—but it will require two men. How good are you at climbing?"

"As good as I have to be," I said shortly. "What's the plan?"

"There are two guards posted along the corridor. We'll need to entice one of them inside so as to deal with him separately. That shouldn't be too difficult."

"How do we get past the other one?"

"That part's a bit tricky—but not impossible. I have some materials tucked away here—items from my survival kit as well as a number of things I've salvaged since I arrived. There's also a crude map I sketched from memory. We'll have approximately one hundred meters of corridor to negotiate before we reach the side entry I've marked as our escape route. Our only hope lies in not running into a party of Hagroon before we reach it. Your disguise won't stand close examination."

"Disguise?" I had the feeling I had stumbled into somebody else's drunken dream. "Who are we going as? Dracula and the wolf man?" I was light-headed, dizzy. I lay back on my rags and closed my eyes. Dzok's voice seemed to come from a long way off:

"Get a good rest. I'll make my preparations. As soon as you wake, we'll make our try."

I came awake to the sound of voices—snarling, angry voices. I sat up, blinking through deep gloom. Dzok said something in a mild tone, and the voice snapped back—a booming, animal snort. I could smell him now—even in the fetid air of the cell, the reek of the angry Hagroon cut through. I could see him, a big fellow, standing near the entry. I wondered how he'd gotten through; the opening was barely big enough for me. . . .

"Lie still and make no sound, Anglic," Dzok called in the same soothing tone he had been using to the Hagroon. "This one wants me. My time ran out, it seems. . . ." Then he broke into the strange dialect again.

The Hagroon snarled and spat. I saw his arm reach, saw Dzok duck under it, plant a solid blow in the bigger creature's chest. The Hagroon grunted, crouched a little, reached again. I came to my feet, flicked my wrist, felt the solid slap as the slug gun filled my palm. Dzok moved back and the jailor jumped after him, swung a blow that knocked the agent's guard aside and sent him spinning. I took two quick steps to the Hagroon's side, aimed, and fired at point-blank range. The recoil kicked me halfway across the room as the monsterman reeled back, fell to the floor, kicking, his long arms wrapped around himself. He was making horrible, choked sounds, and I felt myself pitying the brute. He was tough. The blast from the slug at that range would have killed an ox, but he was rolling over now, trying to get up. I followed him, picked out his head against the lesser dark of the background, fired again. Fluid spattered my face. The huge body gave one tremendous leap and lay still. I wiped my face with a forearm, snorted the rusty odor of blood from my nostrils, turned back to Dzok. He was sprawled on the floor, holding one arm.

"You fooled me, Anglic," he panted. "Damned good show. . .you had a weapon. . . ."

"What about that plan?" I demanded. "Can we try it now?"

"Damned . . . brute," Dzok got out between his teeth. "Broke my arm. Damned nuisance. Perhaps you'd better try it alone."

"To hell with that. Let's get started. What do I do?"

Dzok made a choked sound that might have been a laugh. "You're tougher than you look, Anglic, and the gun will help. All right. Here's what we have to do . . ."

Twenty minutes later I was sweating inside the most fantastic getup ever used in a jail break. Dzok had draped me in a crude harness made from strips of rags—there had been a heap of them in the den when he arrived—luxurious bedding for the inmates. Attached to the straps were tufts of greasy hair arranged so as to hang down, screening my body. The agent had traded his food ration to his former cell-mates in return for the privilege of trimming hair samples from their shaggy bodies, he explained. The dead Hagroon had supplied more. Using adhesives from his kit, he had assembled the grotesque outfit. It hung down below my knees, without even an attempt at a fit.

"This is fantastic," I told him. "It wouldn't fool a newborn idiot at a hundred yards in a bad light!"

Agent Dzok was busy stuffing a bundle inside what was left of his jacket. "You'll look properly bulky and shaggy. That's the best we can do. You won't have to pass close scrutiny—we hope. Now let's be going."

Dzok went first, moving awkwardly with his broken arm bound to his chest, but not complaining. He paused with his head out in the corridor, then scrabbled through.

"Come on, the coast is clear," he called softly. "Our

warden is taking a stroll."

I followed, emerged into air that was comparatively cool and clean after the stale stink of the den. The light was on along the passage as usual. There was no way to tell the time of day. A hundred feet along, the corridor turned right and up; there were no openings along the section we could see. The guard was presumably loitering farther along.

Dzok moved silently off, slim-hipped, low-waisted, his odd, thin legs slightly bent at the knee, his once natty uniform a thing of tatters and tears through which his seal-sleek pelt showed. Before we reached the turn, we heard the rumble of Hagroon voices. Dzok stopped and I came up beside him. He stood with his head cocked, listening.

"Two of them," he whispered. "Filthy bit of luck. . . ."

I waited feeling the sweat trickle down inside my clown suit of stinking rags and dangling locks of hair. There was a sudden sharp itch between my shoulder blades—not the first since I had been introduced to Hagroon hospitality. I grimaced but didn't try to scratch; the flimsy outfit would have fallen to pieces.

"Oh-oh," Dzok breathed. "One of them is leaving. Changing of the guard."

I nodded. Another minute ticked by like a waiting bomb. Dzok turned, gave me a large wink, then said something in a loud, angry snarl—a passable imitation of the Hagroon speech pattern. He waited a moment, then hissed: "Count to ten, slowly—" and started on along the passage at a quick, shambling pace. Just as he moved out of sight around the corner, he looked back, shouted something in a chattering language. Then he was gone.

I started my count, listening hard. I heard the Hagroon guard snort something, heard Dzok reply. Five. Six. Seven. The Hagroon spoke again, sounding closer. Nine. Ten—

I took a deep breath, tried to assume the sort of hunch-shouldered stance the Hagroon displayed, moved on around the turn in a rolling walk. Twenty feet ahead, beyond the light, Dzok stood, waving his good arm, yelling something now, pointing back toward me. A few yards farther on, the guard, squat, bristly figure like a pile of hay, shot a glance in my direction. Dzok jumped closer to him, still shouting. The Hagroon raised an arm, took a swing that Dzok just managed to avoid. I came on, getting closer to the light bulb now. Dzok dashed, in, ducked, got past the guard. The Hagroon had his back to me, fifteen feet away now, almost within range. I flipped the gun into my hand, made another five feet—

The guard whirled, started an angry shout at me—then suddenly got a good look at what must have been only a dim silhouette in the bad light at his first glance. His reflexes were good. He lunged while the startled look was still settling into place on the wide, mud-colored face. I got the shot off just as he crashed into me, and we went down, his four-hundred-pound body smashing me back like a truck hitting a fruit cart. I managed to twist aside just enough to let the bulk of his weight slam past before I hit the pavement and skidded. I got some breath back into my lungs, hauled my gun hand free for another shot. But it wasn't necessary—the huge body lay sprawled half on me, inert as a frozen mammoth.

Dzok was beside me, helping me to my feet with his good hand.

"All right, so far," he said cheerfully rearranging my hair shirt. "Quite a weapon you have there. You sapiens are marvelous at the sort of thing—a natural result of your physical frailty, no doubt."

"Let's analyze me later," I muttered. My shoulders were hurting like hell where I had raked them across the rough paving. "What next?"

"Nothing else between us and the refuse disposal slot I told you about. It's not far. Come along." He seemed as jauntly as ever, unbothered by the brief, violent encounter.

He led the way down a slanting side branch, then up a steep climb, took another turnoff into a wider passage filled with the smell of burning garbage.

"The kitchens," Dzok hissed. "Just a little farther."

We heard loud voices then—the Hagroons never seemed to talk any other way. Flat against the rough-hewn wall, we waited. Two slope-shouldered bruisers waddled out from the low-arched kitchen entry, and went off in the opposite direction. We went on, following a trail of spilled refuse, ducked under a low doorway and into a bin layered with putrefying food waste. I thought I had graduated from the course in bad smells, but this was a whole new spectrum of stench. We splashed through, looked out a two-yard-wide, foot-high slot crusted with garbage. The view was darkness, and a faint glistening of wet cobbles far below. I twisted, looked up. A ragged line of eaves showed above my head.

"I thought so," I said softly. "The low ceilings meant the roof had to be next. I think these people stacked this pile of stone up here and carved the rooms out afterward."

"Precisely," Dzok said. "Not very efficient, perhaps, but in a society where slave labor is plentiful and architectural talent nonexistent, it serves."

"Which way?" I asked. "Up or down?"

Dzok looked doubtfully at me, eyeing my shoulders and arms like a fight manager looking over a prospective addition to his stable. "Up," he said. "If you think you can manage."

"I guess I'll have to manage," I said. "And what about you, with that arm?"

"Eh? Oh, it may be a bit awkward, but no matter. Shall we go?" And he slipped forward through the opening in the two-foot thick wall, twisting over on his back; then his feet were through and out of sight, and suddenly I was very much alone. Behind me the growl of voices and an occasional clatter seemed louder than it had before. Someone was coming my way. I turned over on my back as Dzok had done, eased into the slot. The garbage provided adequate lubrication.

My head emerged into the chilly night. Above I saw the cold glitter of stars in a pitch-black sky, the dim outlines of nearby buildings, a few faint lights gleaming from openings cut at random in the crude masonry walls. It was a long reach to the projecting cornice just above me. I stretched, trying not to think about the long drop below—found a handhold, scrambled up and over. Dzok came up, as I rolled and sat up.

"There's a bridge to the next tower a few yards down the far side," he whispered. "What kept you?"

"I just paused to admire the view. Here, help me get rid of the ape suit." I shed the costume, caked and slimy with garbage now, while Dzok slapped ineffectually at the samples adhering to my back. He looked worse than I did, if possible. His sleek fur was damp and clotted with sour-smelling liquid.

"When I get home," he said, "I shall have the longest, hottest bath obtainable in the most luxurious sensorium in the city of Zaj."

"I'll join you there," I offered. "If we make it."

"The sooner we start, the sooner the handmaidens will ply their brushes." He moved away across the slight dome of the roof, crouched at the far edge, turned, and slipped from sight. It appeared that there was a lot more monkey in Dzok than I'd managed to retain. I got down awkwardly on all fours, slid over the edge, groped with a foot, found no support.

"Lower yourself to arm's length," Dzok's voice came softly from the darkness below—how far below I couldn't say. I eased over the edge, scraping new abrasions in my hide. Dangling at full length, I still found nothing under my toes.

"Let go and drop," Dzok called quietly. "Just a meter or so."

That was a proposal I would have liked to mull over in the quiet of my study for a few hours, but it wasn't the time to argue. I tried to relax, then let go. There was a dizzy moment of free fall, a projecting stone ripped my cheek as I slammed against a flat ledge and went down, one hand raking stone, and the other stabbing down into nothingness. Dzok caught me, pulled me back. I sat up, made out the dim strip of dark, railess walk arching off into the night. I started to ask if that was what we had to cross, but Dzok was already on the way.

Forty-five minutes later, after a trip that would have been unexceptional to the average human fly, Dzok and I stood in the deep shadow of an alley carpeted in the usual deposit of rubbish.

This place would be an archaeologist's paradise," I muttered. "Everything from yesterday's banana peel to the first fling that ever chipped is right here underfoot."

Dzok was busy opening the bundle he had carried inside his jacket. I helped him arrange the straps and brasses taken from the Hagroon I had killed in the cell.

"We'll exchange roles now," he said softly. "I'm the

captor, if anyone questions us. I may be able to carry it off. I'm not certain just how alien I may appear to the average monster in the street; I saw a few australopithecine types as they brought me in. Now, it's up to you to guide us to where you left the shuttle. About half a mile, you said?"

"Something like that—if it's still there." We started off along the alley which paralleled the main thoroughfare I had traversed under guard eighteen hours earlier. It twisted and turned, narrowing at times to no more than an air space between crooked walls, widening once to form a marketplace where odd, three-tiered stalls slumped, deserted and drab in the postmidnight stillness. After half an hour's stealthy walk, I called a halt.

"The way these alleys wander, I'm not a damned bit sure where we are," I said. "I think we'll have to risk trying the main street, at least long enough for me to get my bearings."

Dzok nodded, and we took a side alley, emerging in the comparatively wide avenue. A lone Hagroon shambled along the opposite side of the street. Wide-spaced lamps on ten-foot poles shed pools of sad, yellow light on a littered walk that ran under windowless facades adorned only by the crooked lines of haphazard masonry courses, as alien as beehives.

I led the way to the right. A trough of brownish stone slopping over with oil-scummed water looked familiar; just beyond this point I had seen the harnessed mastodon. The alley from which the shuttle had operated was not far ahead. The street curved to the left. I pointed to a dark side way debouching from a widening of the street ahead.

"I think that's it. We'd better try another alley and see if we can't sneak up on it from behind. They probably have guards on the shuttle."

"We'll soon know." A narrow opening just ahead seemed to lead back into the heart of the block of masonry. We followed it, emerged in a dead end, from which an arched opening like a sewage tunnel led off into utter darkness.

"Let's try that route," Dzok suggested. "It seems to lead in the right general direction."

"What if it's somebody's bedroom?" I eyed the looming building; the crudely mortared walls gave no hint of interior function. The Hagroon knew only one style of construction: solid-rock Gothic.

"In that case, we'll beat a hasty retreat."

"Somehow the thought of pounding through these dark alleys with a horde of aroused Hagroon at my heels lacks appeal," I said. "But I guess we can give it a try." I moved to the archway, peered inside, then took the plunge. My shoes seemed loud on the rough floor. Behind me I could hear Dzok's breathing. The last glimmer of light faded behind us. I was feeling my way with a hand against the wall now. We went on for what seemed a long time.

"Hssst!" Dzok's hand touched my shoulder. "I think we've taken a wrong turning somewhere, old boy . . ."

"Yeah . . ." I thought it over. "We'd better go back."

For another ten minutes we groped our way back in the dark, as silently as possible. Then Dzok halted. I came up behind him.

"What is it?" I whispered.

"Shhh."

I heard it then: a very faint sound of feet shuffling. Then a glow of light sprang up around a curve ahead, showing a dark doorway across the passage.

"In there," Dzok whispered, and dived for it. I followed, slammed against him. There was a sound of heavy breathing nearby.

"What was that you said about bedrooms?" he murmured in my ear.

The breathing snorted into a resonant snore, followed by gulping sounds. I could hear a heavy body moving, the rustle of disturbed rubbish. Then an eerie silence settled.

Suddenly Dzok moved. I heard something clatter in the far corner of the room. His hand grabbed at me, pulling me along. I stumbled over things, heard his hand rasping on stone, then we were flat against the wall. A big Hagroon body rose up, moved into the light from the open door through which we had entered. Another of the shaggy figures appeared outside; this would be the one we had first heard in the alley. The two exchanged guttural growls. The nearer one turned back into the room—and abruptly the chamber was flooded with wan light. I saw that Dzok and I were in an alcove that partly concealed us from view from the door. The Hagroon squinted against the light, half-turned away—then whirled back as he saw us. Dzok jumped. The gun slapped my hand—but Dzok was past him, diving for another opening. I was behind him, ducking under the Hagroon's belated grab, then pelting along a tunnel toward a faint glow at the far end, Dzok bounding ten yards in the lead. There were yells behind us, a horrible barking roar, the pound of feet. I hadn't wanted a horde of trolls chasing me through the dark—but here I was anyway.

Ahead, Dzok leaped out into the open, skidded to a halt, looked both ways, then pointed, and was gone. I raced out into the open alley, saw Dzok charging straight at a pair of Hagroon in guards' bangles—and beyond him, the dark rectangular bulk of the shuttle. The agent yelled. I recognized the grunts and croaks of the Hagroon language. The two guards hesitated. One pointed at me, started forward, the other spread his arms, barked something at Dzok. The latter, still coming on full tilt, straight-armed the heavier humanoid, dodged aside as the Hagroon staggered back, and made for the shuttle. I brought the slug gun up, fired at extreme range, saw the Hagroon bounce back, slam against the wall, then reach—but I was past him. Dzok's opponent saw me, dithered for a moment, then whirled toward me. I fired—and missed, tried to twist aside, slipped, went down and skidded under the Hagroon's grasp, leaving a sleeve from my coat dangling in his hands. I scrambled, made it to all fours, dived for the open entry to the shuttle. Dzok's hand shot out, hauled me inside, and the door banged behind me as the sentry hit it like a charging rhino.

Dzok whirled to the operator's seat.

"Great Scott!" he yelled. "The control lever's broken off short!" The shuttle was rocking under blows at the entry port. Dzok gripped the edge of the panel with his one good hand; the muscles of his shoulder bunched, and with one heave, he tore it away, exposing tight-packed electronic components.

"Quick, Anglic!" he snapped. "The leads there—cross

them!" I wedged myself in beside him, grabbed two heavy insulated cables, twisted their ends together. Following the agent's barked instructions, I ripped wires loose, made hasty connections from a massive coil—which I recognized as an M-C field energizer—to a boxed unit like a fifty KW transformer. Dzok reached past me, jammed a frayed cable end against a heavy bus bar. With a shower of blue and yellow sparks, copper welded to steel. A deep hum started up; abruptly the shattering blows at the entry ceased. I felt the familiar tension of the M-C field close in around me. I let out a long sigh, slumped back in the chair.

"Close, Anglic," Dzok sighed, "But we're clear now. . . ." I looked over at him, saw his yellowish eyes waver and half-close; then he fell sideways into my lap.

CHAPTER FIVE

Dzok was lying where I had dragged him, in deep grass under a small, leafy tree, his chest rising and falling in the quick, shallow, almost panting, breathing of his kind.

The shuttle rested fifty feet away, up against a rocky escarpment at the top of which a grey, chimp-sized ape perched, scratching thoughtfully and gazing down at us. My clothes were spread on the grass along with what remained of Dzok's whites. I had given them a scrubbing in the sandy-bedded stream that flowed nearby. I had also inventoried my wounds, found nothing worse than cuts, scrapes and bruises.

The agent rolled over on his side, groaned, winced in his sleep as his weight pressed against his bound arm; then his eyes opened.

"Welcome back," I said. "Feel better?"

He groaned again. His pale tongue came out, touched his thin, blackish lips.

"As soon as I'm home again I shall definitely resign my commission," he croaked. He moved to ease the arm, lifted it with his good hand and laid it across his chest.

"This member seems to belong to someone else," he groaned. "Someone who died horribly."

"Maybe I'd better try to set it."

He shook his head. "Where are we, Anglic?"

"The name's Bayard. As to where we are, your guess is better than mine, I hope. I piled the scout along full tilt for about five hours, then took a chance and dropped in here to wait for you to come around. You must have been in worse shape than you told me."

"I was close to the end of my resources," the agent admitted. "I'd been beaten pretty badly on three

55

occasions, and my food pellets were running low. I'd been on short rations for about a week."

"How the devil did you manage to stay on your feet—and climb, and fight, and run—and with a broken arm?"

"Small credit to me, old fellow. Merely a matter of triggering certain emergency metabolic stimulators. Hypnotics, you know." His eyes took in the scene. "Pretty place. No sign of our former hosts?"

"Not yet. It's been about four hours since we arrived."

"I think we're safe from intrusion. From what little we'd learned of them, they have very poor Web instrumentation. They won't trail us." He studied the ragged skyline.

"Did you maneuver the shuttle spatially? We seem to be out in the wilds."

I shook my head. "These cliffs here," I indicated the rising pinnacles of warm, reddish-brown stone that ringed the glade. "I watched them evolve from what were buildings back in the inhabited regions. It gives you the feeling that we men and our works are just a force of nature, like any other catastrophe."

"I've seen the same thing," Dzok agreed. "No matter what path you choose to follow across the alternate world-lines, the changes are progressive, developmental. A puddle becomes a pond, then a lake, then a reservoir, then a swimming pool, then a swamp filled with dead trees and twenty-foot snakes; trees stretch, or shrink, grow new branches, new fruits, slide away through the soil to new positions; but always gradually. There are no discontinuities in the entropic grid—excepting, of course, such man-caused anomalies as the Desolation."

"Do you know where we are?" The grey ape on the cliff top watched me suspiciously.

"Give me a moment to gather my forces," Dzok closed his eyes, took deep breaths. "I'll have to drop back on self-hypnotic mnemonic conditioning. I have no conscious recollection of this region."

I waited. His breathing resumed its normal rapid, shallow pattern. His eyes popped open.

"Right," he said briskly. "Not too bad, at all. We're about six hours' run from Authority Central at Zaj, I'd guess." He sat up, got shakily to his feet. "May as well get moving. I'll have a bit of work to do calibrating the instruments; bit awkward navigating with dead screens." He was looking at me thoughtfully. "Which brings me to wonder, Bayard, ah . . . just how did you manage to control the shuttle?"

I could feel my forehead wrinkling. I couldn't tell yet whether I was going to frown or grin.

"I may as well confide in you, Dzok," I said. "I know a little something about shuttles myself."

He waited, looking alert and interested.

"Your Authority isn't the only power claiming control of the Net. I represent the Paramount Government of the Imperium."

Dzok nodded kindly. "Glad you decided to tell me. Makes things cosier all around. Lends an air of mutual confidence, all that sort of thing."

"You already knew?"

"I must confess I used a simple hypnotic technique on you while you were resting, back in our digs. Dug out some fascinating data. Took the opportunity to plant a number of suggestions, too. Nothing harmful, of course. Just a little dampening of your anxiety syndrome, plus, of course, a command to obey my instructions to the letter."

I looked at him, gazing airily at me. My expression settled into a wide and rather sardonic grin.

"I'm very relieved to hear it. Now I don't feel like such a stinker for working on you while you were out."

For a moment he looked startled, then his complacent expression returned.

"Sorry to disappoint you, old chap, but of course I'm well protected against that sort of thing—" he broke off, looking just a little worried, as though a thought had just struck him.

I nodded. "Me too."

Suddenly he laughed. His cannonball head seemed to split in a grin that showed at least thirty-six teeth. He leaned and slapped his knee with his good hand, doubled over in a paroxysm of hilarity, staggered toward me, still roaring. I took a step back, tensed my wrist.

"You have an infectious laugh, Dzok," I said. "But not infectious enough to let you get me in range of that pile driver arm of yours."

He straightened, grinning rather ruefully now. "Seems to be a bit of an impasse," he conceded.

"I'm sure we can work it out," I said. "Just don't keep trying those beginners' tricks. I've had to learn all about them."

He pursed his wide, thin lips. "I'm wondering why you stopped here. Why didn't you press on, reattain the safety of your own base while I was unconscious?"

"I told you. I don't know where I am. This is unfamiliar territory to me—and there are no maps aboard that tub."

"Ah-hah. And now you expect me to guide you home—and myself into an untenable position?"

"Just rig up the board and calibrate it. I'll do my own steering."

He shook his head. "I'm still considerably stronger than you, old fellow—in spite of my indisposition." He twitched his broken arm. "I fail to see how you can coerce me."

"I still have the gun we sapiens are so clever about making."

"Quite. But shooting me would hardly be to your advantage." He was grinning again. I had the feeling he was enjoying it all. "Better let me run us in to Xonijeel. I'll see to it you're given all possible aid."

"I've had a sample of hairy hospitality," I said. "I'm not yearning for more."

He looked pained. "I hope you don't lump us australopithecines in with the Hagroon, of all people, just on the basis of a little handsome body hair."

"Are you promising me you'll give me a shuttle and turn me loose?"

"Well . . ." he spread his wide, deeply-grooved hands. "After all, I'm hardly in a position . . ."

"Think of the position you'd be in if I left you here."

"I'd have to actively resist any such effort, I'm afraid."

"You'd lose."

"Hmmm. Probably. On the other hand, I'd be much too valuable a prisoner in this Imperium of yours, so it's just as well to die fighting." He tensed as though ready to go into action. I didn't want that.

"I'll make another proposal," I said quickly. "You give

me your word as an officer of the Authority that I'll be given an opportunity to confer with the appropriate high officials at Zaj—and I'll agree to accompany you there first."

He nodded promptly. "I can assure you of that much. And I'll take it upon myself to personally guarantee you'll receive honorable treatment."

"That's a deal." I stepped forward, put out my hand, trying not to look as worried as I felt. Dzok looked blank, then reached out gingerly, took my hand. His palm felt hot and dry and coarse-skinned, like a dog's paw.

"Empty hand; no weapon," he murmured. "Marvelous symbolism." He grinned widely again. "Glad we worked it out. You seem like a decent sort, Bayard, in spite—" The smile faded slightly. "I have a curious feeling you've done me, in some obscure way. . . ."

"I was wondering how I'd talk you into taking me to Zaj," I said, grinning back at him now. "Thanks for making it easy."

"Ummmm. Trouble at home, eh?"

"That's a slight understatement."

He frowned at me. "I'll get to work on the instruments, while you tell me the details."

One hour, two skinned knuckles, and one slight electric shock later, the shuttle was on its way, Dzok in the operator's seat crouched over the jury-rigged panel.

"This curious light you mentioned," he was saying. "You say it seemed to pervade even enclosed spaces, cut off from any normal light source?"

"That's right. A sort of ghostly, bluish glow."

"There are a number of things in your account that I can't explain," Dzok said. "But as for the light effect, it's plain you'd been transposed spontaneously into a null-time level. The Hagroon are fond of operating there. The apparent light is due to certain emanations arising from the oscillation of elementary particles at a vastly reduced level of energy; a portion of this activity elicits a response from the optic nerve. Did you notice that it arose particularly from metal surfaces?"

"Not especially."

Dzok shook his head, frowning. "A fantastic energy input is required to transfer mass across the entropic threshold. Far more than is needed to set up the drift across the A-lines, for example. And you say you found yourself there, without mechanical aid?"

I nodded. "What is this null time?"

"Ah, a very difficult concept." Dzok was busily noting instrument readings, twiddling things, taking more readings. As a shuttle technician, he was way ahead of me. "In normal entropy, of course, we move in a direction which we can conveniently think of as forward; with Web travel, we move perpendicular to this vector—sideways, one might say. Null time...well, consider it as offset at right angles to both: a stunted, lifeless continuum, in which energies flow in strange ways."

"Then it wasn't the city that was altered—it was me. I had been ejected from my normal continuum into this null-time state—"

"Quite correct, old fellow," Dzok blinked at me sympathetically. "I can see you've been laboring under a ghastly strain, thinking otherwise."

"I'm beginning to get the picture," I said. "The Hagroon are studying the Imperium from null time—getting set for an attack, I'd guess offhand. They've got techniques that are way beyond anything the Imperium has. We need help. Do you think the Authority will give it to us?"

"I don't know, Bayard," Dzok said. "But I'll do my best for you."

I had a few hours' restless nap on the floor behind the control seat before Dzok called me. I climbed up to lean over his chair, staring into the screen. We were among spidery towers now; minarets of lofty, fragile beauty, soaring up pink, yellow, pale green, into a bright morning sky.

"Nice," I said. "We're close to your home line now, I take it?"

"Ah, the towers of Zaj," Dzok almost sang. "There's nothing to equal them in all the universes!"

"Let's hope I get a reception to match the pretty buildings."

"Look here, Bayard, there's something I feel I ought to ...ah...tell you," Dzok said hesitantly. "Frankly, there's a certain, well, ill-feeling in the minds of some against the sapiens group. Unreasonable, perhaps—but it's a factor we're going to have to deal with."

"What's this ill-feeling based on?"

"Certain, ah, presumed racial characteristics. You have a reputation for ferocity, ruthless competitiveness, love of violence. . . ."

"I see. We're not nice and mild like the Hagroon, say. And who was it that I saw bounce one of the Hagroon out of the way in order to steal this scout we're riding in?"

"Yes, yes, all of us are prey to a certain degree of combativeness. But perhaps you noticed that even the Hagroon tend to enslave rather than to kill, and though they're cruel, it's the cruelty of indifference, not hate. I saw you kick one of them just as you entered the cell. Did you note that he took no revenge?"

"Anybody will fight back when he's been knocked around enough."

"But only you sapiens have systematically killed off every other form of hominid life in your native continua!" Dzok was getting a little excited now. "You hairless ones—in every line where you exist—you exist alone! Ages ago, in the first confrontation of the bald mutation with normal anthropos—driven, doubtless, by shame at your naked condition—you slaughtered your hairy fellow men! And even today your minds are warped by ancient guilt-and-shame complexes associated with nudity!"

"So you're holding the present generation responsible for what happened—or may have happened—thousands of years ago?"

"In my world sector," Dzok stated, "there are three major races of Man: we australopithecines, to employ your English terms; the Rhodesians—excellent workers, strong and willing, if not overly bright; and the Pekin derivatives—blue-faced chaps, you know. We live together in perfect harmony, each group with its societal niche, each contributing its special talents to the common culture. While you sapiens—why, you even set upon your own kind, distinguishable only by the most trivial details!"

"What about me, Dzok? Do I seem to you to be a

raving maniac? Have I indicated any particular distaste for you, for example?"

"Me?" Dzok looked amazed, then whooped with laughter. "Me!" he choked. "The idea . . ."

"What's so funny?"

"You . . . with your poor bald face—your spindly limbs—your degenerate dentition—having to overcome your natural distaste for *me!*" He was almost falling out of his chair now.

"Well, if I had any natural distaste, I at least had the decency to forget it!" I snapped.

Dzok stopped laughing, dabbed at his eyes with a dangling cuff. He looked at me almost apologetically.

"You did, at that," he conceded. "And you bound up my arm, and washed my poor old uniform for me—"

"And your poor old face too, you homely galoot!"

Dzok was smiling embarrassedly now. "I'm sorry, old boy; I got a bit carried away. All those personal remarks—a lot of rot, actually. Judge a chap on what he does, not what he is, eh? None of us can help our natural tendencies—and perhaps overcoming one's instinct is in the end a nobler achievement than not having the impulse in the first place." He put out his hand uncertainly.

"Empty hand, no weapon, eh?" He smiled. I took the hand.

"You're all right, Bayard," Dzok said. "Without you I'd have been rotting in that bloody cell. I'm on your side, old fellow—all the way!"

He whirled as a buzzer went, slapped switches, threw out the main drive, watched needles creep across dials, flipped the transfer switch. The growl of the field generators faded down the scale. Dzok beamed at me.

"We're here." He held a thumb up. "This may be a great day for both our races."

We stepped out into a wide sweep of colorfully tiled plaza dotted with trees, the bright geometric shapes of flower beds, fountains splashing in the sunlight. There were hundreds of australopithecines in sight, strolling leisurely in pairs, or hurrying briskly along with the air of urgency that was apparently as characteristic of Xonijeelian bureaucrats as of their hairless counterparts at home. Some wore flowing robes like

Arab djellabas; others were dressed in multicolored pantaloon and jacket outfits; and here and there were the trim white uniforms that indicated the IDMS. Our sudden arrival in the midst of the pack caused a mild stir that became a low murmur as they caught sight of me. I saw noses wrinkle in flat, toothy faces, a few hostile stares, heard snickers from here and there. Someone called something to Dzok. He answered, took a firm grip of my arm.

"Sorry, Bayard," he muttered. "Mustn't appear to be running loose, you know." He waved an arm at a light aircraft cruising overhead. I thought it was a heli until I noticed its lack of rotors. It dropped into a landing and a wide transparent hatch opened like a clamshell. A close relative of Dzok's showed a fine set of teeth and waved, then his gaze settled on me and his grin dropped like a wet bar rag. He fluted something at Dzok, who called an answer back, took my arm, urged me along.

"Ignore him, Bayard. A mere peasant."

"That's easy. I don't know what he's saying."

I climbed into the well-sprung seat. Dzok settled in beside me, gave the driver an address.

"This adventure hasn't turned out too badly after all," he said expansively. "Back safe and sound—more or less—with a captive machine and a most unusual, ah, guest."

"I'm glad you didn't say prisoner," I commented, looking down on a gorgeous pattern of parks and plazas and delicate spires as we swooped over them at dashing speed. "Where are we headed?"

"We're going directly to IDMS Headquarters. My report will require quick action, and of course you're in haste as well."

There didn't seem to be much more to say. I rode along, admiring the city below, watching a massive white tower grow in the distance. We aimed directly for it, circled it once as though waiting for landing instructions, then hovered, dropped down to settle lightly on a small pad centered in a roof garden of tall palms, great banks of yellow and blue blossoms, freeform reflecting pools with caged birds and animals completing the jungle setting.

"Now, just let me do the talking, Bayard," Dzok said,

hurrying me toward a stairwell. "I'll present your case to our Council in the most favorable light, and I'm confident there'll be no trouble. You should be on your way home in a matter of hours."

"I hope your Council is a little less race-minded than the yokels down below—" I started, then broke off, staring at a camouflaged cage where a hairless, tailless biped, two-feet tall, with a low forehead, snouted face and sparse beard stared out at me with dull eyes.

"My God!" I said. "That's a man—a midget—"

Dzok turned sharply. "Eh? What?" He gaped, then grinned. "Oh, good Lord, Bayard, it's merely a tonquil! Most amusing little creature, but hardly human—"

The little manikin stirred, made a plaintive noise. I went on then, feeling a mixture of emotions, none of which added to my confidence.

We descended the escalator, went along a wide, cool corridor to a glass door, on into a wide skylighted room with a pool, grass, tables, and a row of lockers at the far side. Dzok went to a wall screen, talked urgently, then turned to me.

"All set," he told me. "Council's in session now, and will review the case."

"That's fast action," I said. "I was afraid I'd have to spend a week filling out forms and then sweat out a spot on the calendar."

"Not here," Dzok said loftily. "It's a matter of pride for local Councils to keep their dockets clear."

"Local Council? I thought we were going to see the big wheels. I need to make my pitch to the top level—"

"This is the top level. They're perfectly capable of evaluating a situation, making a sound decision, and issuing appropriate orders." He glanced at a wall scale which I assumed was a clock.

"We have half an hour. We'll take a few moments to freshen up, change of clothes and all that. I'm afraid we still smell of the Hagroon prison."

There were a few other customers in the room, lanky, sleek Xonijeelians who stroked to the length of the pool or reclined in lounge chairs. They stared curiously as we passed. Dzok spoke to one or two, but didn't linger to chat. At the lockers, he pressed buttons, used an attached tape to measure me, worked a lever. A flat package popped out from a wide slot.

"A clean outfit, Bayard—not exactly what you've been used to, but I think you'll find it comfortable—and frankly, the familiar garments may be a help in overcoming any initial—ah—distaste the Council Members may feel."

"Swell," I muttered. "Too bad I left my ape suit. I could come as a Hagroon."

Dzok tutted and selected clothing for himself, then led me into a shower room where jets of warm, perfumed water came from orifices in the domed ceiling. We stripped and soaped down, Dzok achieving a remarkable lather, then air-dried in the dressing room. My new clothes—a pantaloon and jacket outfit in blue and silver satin with soft leather-like shoes and white silk shirt—fitted me passably. Dzok snickered, watching me comb my hair. I think he considered it hardly worth the effort. He gave the mirror a last glance, settled his new gold-braided white pillbox cap on his round head, fitted the scarlet chin strap under his lower lip, gave the tight-fitting tunic a last tug. "Not often an agent returns from the field with a report he'd justified in classifying Class Two Sub-Emergency," he said in a satisfied tone.

"What's the emergency? Me or the Hagroon slave-runners?"

Dzok laughed—a bit uneasily, perhaps. "Now, now, don't be anxious, Bayard. I'm sure the Councillors will recognize the unusual nature of your case. . . ."

I followed him back into the corridor, thinking that one over.

"Suppose I were a 'usual' case, what then?"

"Well, of course, Authority policy would govern in that instance. But—"

"And what would Authority policy dictate?" I persisted.

"Let's just wait and deal with the situation as it develops, eh?" Dzok hurried ahead, leaving me with an unpleasant feeling that his self-confidence was waning the closer we came to the huge red-gilt doors that blocked the wide corridor ahead.

Two sharp sentries in silver-trimmed white snapped to as we came up. Dzok exchanged a few words with

them. Then one thumbed a control and the portals
swung open. Dzok took a deep breath, waiting for me to
come up. Beyond him I saw a long table behind which
sat a row of faces—mostly australopithecines, but with
representatives of at least three other types of Man, all
with grey or grizzled heads, some in red-ornamented
whites, a few in colorful civvies.

"Stiff upper lip, that's the drill," Dzok muttered. "To
my left and half a pace back. Follow my lead on
protocol...." Then he stepped off toward the waiting
elders. I adjusted a nonviolent, uncompetitive look on
my face and followed. A dozen pairs of yellow eyes
watched me approach; twelve expressions faced me
across the polished table of black wood—and none of
them were warm smiles of welcome. A narrow-faced
grey-beard to the left of center made a smacking noise
with his mobile lips, leaned to mutter something to the
councillor on his left. Dzok halted, executed a half-bow
with a bending of the knees, spoke briefly in his staccato
language, then indicated me.

"I introduce to the Council one Bayard, native to the
Anglic Sector," he said, switching to English. "As you
see, a sapiens—"

"Where did you capture it?" the thin-faced member
rapped out in a high, irritable voice.

"Bayard is not...ah...precisely a captive,
Excellency," Dzok started.

"Are you saying the creature forced its way here?"

"You may ignore that question, Agent," a round-faced
councillor spoke up from the right. "Councillor
Sphogeel is venting his bias in rhetoric. However, your
statement requires clarification."

"You're aware of Authority policy with regard to bald
antropoids, Agent?" another put in.

"The circumstances under which I encountered
Bayard were unusual," Dzok said smoothly. "It was only
with his cooperation and assistance that I escaped
prolonged imprisonment. My report—"

"Imprisonment? An Agent of the Authority?"

"I think we'd better hear the Agent's full report—at
once," the councillor who had interrupted Sphogeel
said, then added a remark in Xonijeelian. Dzok replied
in kind at some length, with considerable waving of his

long arms. I stood silently at his left and a half pace to the rear as instructed, feeling like a second hand bargain up for sale, with no takers.

The councillors fired questions then, which Dzok fielded crisply, sweating all the while. Old Sphogeel's expression failed to sweeten as the hearing went on. Finally the round-faced councillor waved a long-fingered, greyish hand, fixed his gaze on me.

"Now, Bayard, Agent Dzok has told us of the circumstances under which you placed yourself in his custody—"

"I doubt very much that Dzok told you any such thing," I cut him off abruptly. "I'm here by invitation, as a representative of my government."

"Is the Council to be subjected to impertinence?" Sphogeel demanded shrilly. "You speak when ordered to do so, sapiens—and keep a civil tongue in your head!"

"And I'm also sure," I bored on, "that his report included mention of the fact that I'm in need of immediate transportation back to my home line."

"Your needs are hardly of interest to this body," Sphogeel snapped. "We know quite well how to deal with your kind."

"You don't know anything about my kind!" I came back at him. "There's been no previous contact between our respective governments—"

"There is only one government, sapiens!" Sphogeel cut me off. "As for your kind . . ." His long, flexible upper lip was curled back, showing shocking pink gums and lots of teeth, in a sneer like that of an annoyed horse. ". . . we're familiar enough with your record of mayhem—"

"Hold on there, Sphogeel," another member broke in. "I for one would like to hear this fellow's account of his experiences. It appears the activities of the Hagroon may have some significance—"

"I say let the Hagroon do as they like insofar as these fratricidal deviants are concerned!" Sphogeel came back. He seemed to be even more upset than his prejudices warranted. I could see the line he was taking now: he didn't intend even to give me a hearing. It was time for me to get my oar into the water.

"Whether you like it or not, Sphogeel," I cut across

the hubbub, "the Imperium is a first-class, Net-traveling power. Our two cultures were bound to meet sooner or later. I'd like to see our relations get off to a good start."

"Net-traveling?" the fat councillor queried. "You failed to mention that, Agent." He was looking at Dzok.

"I was about to reach that portion of the briefing, Excellency," Dzok said smoothly. "Bayard had made the claim that although he was transported to the Hagroon line in a Hagroon shuttle, his people have a Web drive of their own. And, indeed, he seemed to be somewhat familiar with the controls of the primitive Hagroon machine."

"This places a different complexion on matters," the official said. "Gentlemen, I suggest we take no hasty action which might prejudice future relations with a Web power—"

"We'll have no dealings with the scum!" old Sphogeel shrilled, coming to his feet. "Our present policy of expl—"

"Sit down, Councillor!" the fat member roared, jumping up to face the thin one. "I'm well aware of the policies pertaining to this situation! I suggest we refrain from announcing them to the world!"

"Whatever your policy has been in the past," I interjected into the silence, "it should be reevaluated in the light of new data. The Imperium is a Net power, but there's no need of any conflict of interest—"

"The creature lies!" Sphogeel snarled, staring at me across the table. "We've carried out extensive reconnaissance in the entire Sapient quadrant—including the so-called Anglic Sector—and we've encountered no evidence whatever of native Web-transit capability!"

"The Zero-zero line of the Imperium lies within the region you call the Desolation," I said.

Sphogeel gasped. "You have the audacity to mention that hideous monument to your tribe's lust for destruction? That alone is sufficient grounds for your expulsion from the society of decent Hominoids!"

"How is that possible?" another asked. "Nothing lives within the Desolation. . . ."

"Another of the debased creature's lies," Sphogeel snapped. "I demand that the Council expel this degenerate at once and place a Class Two reprimand in the file of this agent—"

"Nevertheless," I yelled the councillors down, "a number of normal lines exist in the Blight. One of them is the seat of a Net government. As an official of that government, I ask that you listen to what I have to say, and give me the assistance I ask for."

"That seems a modest enough demand," the fat member said. "Sit down, Councillor. As for you, Bayard—go ahead with your story."

Sphogeel glowered, then snapped his fingers. A half-grown youth in unadorned whites stepped forward from an inconspicuous post by the door, listened to the oldster's hissed instructions, then darted away. Sphogeel folded his arms and glowered.

"I submit," he snapped. "Under protest."

Half an hour later I had finished my account. There were questions then—some from reasonable-sounding members like the chubby one whose name was Nikodo, others mere inflammatory remarks of the "Are you still beating your wife" type. I answered them all as clearly as I could.

"We're to understand then," a truculent-looking councillor said, "that you found yourself in a null-time level of your native continuum, having arrived there by means unknown. You then observed persons, presumably Hagroon, boarding transports, preparatory to departure. You killed one of these men, stole one of their crude Web-travelers, only to find yourself trapped. Arriving at the Hagroon world line, you were placed under confinement, from which you escaped by killing a second man. You now present yourself here with the demand that you be given valuable Authority property and released to continue your activities."

"That's not fairly stated, Excellency," Dzok started, but a dirty look cut him off.

"The man is a self-confessed double murderer," Sphogeel snapped. "I think—"

"Let him speak," Nikodo barked.

"The Hagroon are up to something. I'd say an attack on the Imperium from null time would be a likely guess. If you won't give us assistance, then I'm asking that you lend me transportation home in time to give a warning—"

The young messenger slipped back into the room, went to Sphogeel, handed him a strip of paper. He glanced at it, then looked up at me with a fierce glitter in his yellow eyes.

"As I thought! The creature lies!" he rasped. "His entire fantastic story is a fabric of deceit! The Imperium, eh? A Web Power, eh? Ha!" Sphogeel thrust the paper at the next councillor, a sad-looking, pale tan creature with bush muttonchop whiskers and no chin. He blinked at the paper, looked up at me with a startled expression, frowned, passed the paper along. When it reached Nikodo, he read it, shot me a puzzled look reread it.

"I'm afraid I don't understand this, Bayard." His look bored into me now. His dark face was getting blackish-purple around the edges. "What did you hope to gain by attempting to delude this body?"

"Maybe if you'll tell me what you're talking about, I could shed some light on it," I said. Silently, the paper was tossed across to me. I looked at the crow tracks on it.

"Sorry. I can't read Xonijeelian."

"That should have been sufficient evidence in itself," Sphogeel growled. "Claims to be a Web operative, but has no language background . . ."

"Councillor Sphogeel had your statement checked out," Nikodo said coldly. "You stated that this Zero-zero world line lay at approximately our coordinates 875-259 within the area of the Desolation. Our scanners found three normal world lines within the desert—to that extent, your story contained a shred of truth. But as for coordinates 875-259 . . ."

"Yes?" I held my voice steady with an effort.

"No such world exists. The uninterrupted sweep of the destroyed worlds blankets that entire region of the Web."

"You'd better take another look—"

"Look for yourself!" Sphogeel thrust a second paper across the table toward me—a glossy black photogram, far more detailed than the clumsy constructions used by the Imperial Net mapping service. I recognized the familiar oval shape of the Blight at once—and within it the glowing points that represented the worlds known as Blight-Insular Two and Three—and a third A-line within the Blight, unknown to me. But where the Zero-zero line of the Imperium should have been—was nothing.

"I think the Council has wasted sufficient time on this charlatan," someone said. "Take the fellow away."

Dzok was staring at me. "Why?" he said. "Why did you lie, Bayard?"

"The creature's purpose was clear enough," Sphogeel grated. "Ascribing his own base motivations to others, he assumed that to confess himself a citizen of a mere sub-technical race would mean he'd receive scant attention. He therefore attempted to overawe us with talk of a great Web power—a veiled threat of retaliation! Pitiful subterfuge! But nothing other than that would be expected from such a genetic inferior!"

"Your equipment's not working properly," I grated. "Take another scan—"

"Silence, criminal!" Sphogeel was on his feet again. He had no intention of losing the advantage his shock technique had gained him.

"Sphogeel has something he doesn't want known," I yelled. "He faked the shot—"

"That is not possible," Nikodo rapped out. "Wild accusations will gain you nothing, sapiens!"

"All I've asked for is a ride home." I flipped the scan photo across the table. "Take me there, and you'll see soon enough whether I'm lying!"

"Suicidal, he asks that we sacrifice a traveler and crew to play out his folly," someone boomed.

"You talk a lot about my kind's murderous instincts," I barked. "Where are the sapiens types here in this cosy little world of yours? In concentration camps, getting daily lectures on brotherly love?"

"There are no intelligent hairless forms native to Xonijeel," Nikodo snapped.

"Why not?" I rapped back at him. "Don't tell me they died out?"

"Their strain was a weak one," Nikodo said defensively. "Small, naked, ill-equipped to face the rigors of the glacial periods. None survived into the present era—"

"So you killed them off! In my world maybe it worked out the other way around—or maybe it was natural forces in both cases. Either way you slice it, it's ancient history. I suggest we make a new start now—and you can begin by checking out my story—"

"I say we put an end to this farce!" Sphogeel pounded on the table for attention. "I move the Council to a formal vote! At once!"

Nikodo waited until the talk died away. "Councillor Sphogeel has exercised his right of peremptory motion," he said heavily. "The vote will now be taken on the question, in the form to be proposed by the Councillor."

Sphogeel was still standing. "The question takes this form," he said formally. "To grant the demands of this sapiens..." he looked around the table as though gauging the tempers of his fellows.

"He's risking his position on the wording of the Demand Vote," Dzok hissed in my ear. "He'll lose if he goes too far."

"... or, alternatively..." his eyes were on me now "... to order him transported to a sub-technical world line, to live out his natural span in isolation."

Dzok groaned. A sigh went around the table. Nikodo muttered. "If you'd only come to us honestly, sapiens," he started—

"The vote!" Sphogeel snapped. "Take the creature outside, Agent!"

Dzok took my arm, guided me out in the corridor. The heavy panels clicked behind us.

"I don't understand at all," he said. "Telling them all that rubbish about a Web power. You've prejudiced the Council hopelessly against you—and for what?"

"I'll give you a clue, Dzok," I said. "I don't think they needed any help—they already have their opinion of Homo sapiens."

"Nikodo was strongly inclined to be sympathetic," Dzok said. "He's a powerful member. But your senseless lies—"

"Listen to me, Dzok—" I grabbed his arm. "I wasn't lying! Try to get that through your thick skull! I don't care what your instruments showed. The Imperium exists!"

"The scanner doesn't lie, sapiens," Dzok said coldly.

"It would be better for you to admit your mistake and plead for mercy." He pulled his arm free and smoothed the crease in the sleeve.

"Mercy?" I laughed, not very merrily. "From the kindly Councillor Sphogeel? You people make a big thing of your happy family philosophy—but when it gets right down to practical politics, you're as ruthless as the rest of the ape-stock!"

"There's been no talk of killing," Dzok said stiffly. "Relocation will allow you to live out your life in reasonable comfort—"

"It's not my life I'm talking about, Dzok! There are three billion people living in that world you say doesn't exist. A surprise attack by the Hagroon will be a slaughter!"

"Your story makes no sense, Anglic! Your claims have been exposed for the fancies they are! There is no such world line as this Imperium of yours!"

"Your instruments need overhauling. It was there forty-eight hours ago—"

The Council Chamber doors opened. The sentry listened to someone inside, then beckoned Dzok. The agent gave me a worried look, passed inside. The two armed men came to port arms, silently took up positions on either side of me.

"What did they say?" I asked. Nobody answered. Half a minute went by, like an amputee on crutches. Then the door opened again and Dzok came out. Two of the Council Members were behind him.

"An . . . ah . . . decision has been reached, Bayard," he said stiffly. "You'll be escorted to quarters where you'll spend the night. Tomorrow . . ."

Sphogeel shouldered past him. "Hesitant about performing your duty, Agent?" he rasped. "Tell the creature, His plots are in vain! The Council has voted relocation—"

It was what I had expected. I stepped back, slapped my gun into my hand—and Dzok's long arm swept down, caught me across the forearm with a blow like an axe, sent the slug gun bouncing off along the carpeted hall. I whirled, went for the short flit gun the nearest sentry was holding. I got a hand on it too—just as steel hooks clamped on me, hauled me back. A grayish-tan hand with black seal's fur on its back was in front of my face, crushing a tiny ampoule. An acrid odor hit my nostrils. I choked, tried not to breathe it in. . . . My legs went slack as wet rope, folded. I hit the floor without feeling it. I was on my back, and Dzok was leaning over me, saying something.

". . . regret . . . my fault, old boy . . ."

I made the supreme effort, moved my tongue, got out one word—". . . Truth . . ."

Someone pushed Dzok aside. Close-set yellow eyes stared into mine. There were voices:

". . . deep mnemonics . . ."

". . . finish the job . . ."

". . . word of honor as an officer . . ."

". . . devil take him. An Anglic's an Anglic . . ."

Then I was falling, light as an inflated balloon, seeing the scene around me swell, blur, fade into a whirling of lights and darkness that dwindled and was gone.

CHAPTER SIX

I watched the play of sunlight on the set of gauzy curtains at the open window for a long time before I began to think about who owned them. The recollection came hard, like a lesson learned but not used for a while. I had had a breakdown—a nervous collapse, that was it—while on a delicate mission to Louisiana—the details were vague—and now I was resting at a nursing home in Harrow, run by kindly Mrs. Rogers. . . .

I sat up, felt a dizziness that reminded me of the last time I had spent a week flat on my back after a difficult surveillance job in . . . in . . . I had a momentary half-recollection of a strange city, and many faces, and . . .

It was gone. I shook my head, lay back. I was here for a rest; a nice, long rest; then, with my pension—a sudden, clear picture of my passbook showing a balance of 10,000 gold Napoleons on deposit at the Banque Crédit de Londres flashed across my mind—I could settle somewhere and take up gardening, the way I'd always wanted to. . . .

The picture seemed to lack something, but it was too much trouble to think about it now. I looked around the room. It was small, cheery with sunlight and bright-painted furniture, with hooked rugs on the floor and a bedspread decorated with a hunting scene that suggested long winter nights spent tatting by an open fire. The door was narrow, paneled, brown-painted wood, with a light brass knob. The knob turned and a buxom woman with grey hair, cheeks like apples, a funny little hat made of lace, and a many-colored skirt that brushed the floor came in, gave a jump when she saw me, and beamed as though I'd just said she made

75

apple pie like Mother's.

"Mr. Bayard! Ye're awake!" She had a squeaky voice as jolly as the whistle on a peanut stand, with an accent I couldn't quite place.

"And hungry, too, I'm guessing! Ye'd like a lovely bowl of soup, now would't ye, sir? And maybe a dab of pudding after."

"A nice steak smothered in mushrooms sounds better," I said. "And, uh . . ." I had meant to ask her who she was, but then I remembered: kindly Mrs. Rogers, of course. . . .

"A glass of wine, if it's available," I finished, and lay back, watching little bright spots dance before me.

"Of course, and a nice hot bath first. That'll be lovely, Mr. Bayard. I'll just call Hilda . . ." Things were a little hazy then for a few minutes. I was vaguely aware of bustlings and the twitter of feminine voices. Hands plucked at me, tugged gently at my arms. I made an effort, got my eyes open, saw the curve of a colored apron over a girlish hip. Beyond her, the older woman was directing two husky, blonde males in maneuvering something heavy below my line of sight. The girl straightened, and I caught a glimpse of a slim waist, a nicely rounded bosom and arm, a saucy face under straight-cut hair the color of clover honey. The two men finished and left, the motherly type with them. The girl fussed about for a minute, then followed the others, leaving the door open. I got up on one elbow, saw a six-foot-long enameled bathtub half full of water placed neatly on the oval rug, a big fluffy towel, a scrub brush, and a square cake of white soap on a small stool beside it. It looked inviting. I sat up, got my legs over the side of the bed, took deep breaths until the dizziness went away, then pulled off the purple silk pajama bottoms and stood, shakily.

"Oh, ye shouldn't try to walk yet, sir!" a warm contralto voice said from the doorway. Honey-hair was back, coming toward me with a concerned look on her pert features. I made a halfhearted grab for my pants, almost fell, sat down heavily on the bed. She was beside me now, with a strong hand under my arm.

"Gunvor and I've been worried about ye, sir. The

doctor said ye'd been very sick, but when ye slept all day yesterday . . ."

I wasn't following what she said. It's one thing to wake up in an unfamiliar room and have a little trouble getting oriented; it's considerably different to realize that you're among total strangers, and that you have no recollection at all of how you got there. . . .

With her assistance, I made the three steps to the tub, hesitated before tackling the climb in.

"Just put your foot in, that's right," the girl was saying. I followed orders, stepped in and sat down, feeling too weak even to wince at the hot water. The girl perched on the stool beside me, tossed her head to get her hair back, reached for my arm.

"I'm Hilda," she said. "I live just along the road. It was exciting when Gunvor phoned and told me about yer coming, sir. It isn't often we see a Louisianan here—and a diplomat, too. Ye must lead the most exciting life! I suppose ye've been in Egypt and Austria and Spain—and even in the Seminole Nation." She chattered and sudsed me, as unconcernedly as a grandmother bathing a five-year-old. What little impulse to resist I may have had faded fast; I was as *weak* as a five-year-old, and it felt good to have this lively creature briskly massaging my back with the brush while the sun shone through the window and the breeze flapped the curtain.

". . . yer accident, sir?" I realized Hilda had asked a question—an awkward one. I had a powerful reluctance to admit that I had—or appeared to have—some sort of mild amnesia. I hadn't forgotten everything, of course. It was just that the details were hazy. . . .

"Hilda—the man that brought me here—did he tell you anything about me—about the accident? . . ."

"The letter!" Hilda jumped up, went across to a table decorated with red, yellow, blue, and orange painted flowers, brought back a stiff square envelope.

"The doctor left this for ye, sir. I almost forgot!"

I reached for it with a wet hand, got the flap open, pulled out a single sheet of paper on a fancy letterhead, formally typed:

"Mr. Bayard,
It is with deep regret and expressions of the highest personal regard that I confirm herewith your retirement for disabililty from the Diplomatic Service of His Imperial Majesty, Napoleon V . . ."

There was more—all about my faithful service and devotion to duty, regrets that I hadn't recovered in time for a personal send-off, and lots of hopes for a speedy convalescence. Included was the name of the lawyer in Paris who would answer all my questions, and if at any time could be of assistance, etc. etc. The name at the end was unfamiliar—but then, of course, everybody knew Count Regis de Manin, Deputy Foreign Minister for Security. Good old Reggie. . . .

I read the letter twice, then folded it and crammed it back into the envelope. My hands were quivering.

"Who gave you this?" my voice came out hoarse.

"T'was the doctor, sir. They brought ye in the carriage, two nights since, and he was most particular about ye. A pity about yer friends having to hurry to catch the steam packet for Calais—"

"What did he look like?"

"The doctor?" Hilda resumed her scrubbing. "He was a tall gentleman, sir, handsomely dressed, and with a lovely voice. Dark he was, too. But I saw him only for a moment or two, and in the gloom of the stable-yard I couldn't make out more." She giggled. "But I did mark his eyes were close together as two hazelnuts in an eggcup."

"Was he alone?"

"There was the coachmen, sir—and I think another gentleman riding inside, but—"

"Did Mrs. Rogers see them?"

"Only for a few moments, sir. They were in a shocking hurry. . . ."

Hilda finished with the bath, dried me, helped me into clean pajamas, helped me stagger back to bed and tucked me in. I wanted to ask questions, but sleep came down over me like a flood from a broken dam.

The next time I woke up, I felt a little more normal. I got out of bed, tottered to the closet, found a suit of strange-looking clothes with narrow trousers and wide lapels, a shirt with ruffles at collar and wrist, shoes with tiny buckles.

But of course they weren't really strange, I corrected myself. Very stylish, in fact—and new, with the tailor's tag still in the breast pocket.

I closed the closet, went to the window for a look. It was still open, and late-afternoon sun glowed in the potted geraniums on the sill. Below was a tidy garden, a brick wall, a white picket fence, and in the distance, a tall openwork church spire. There was an odor of fresh-cut hay in the air. As I watched, Hilda came around the corner with a basket in her hand and a shawl over her head. She had on a heavy, ankle-length skirt and wooden shoes painted in red and blue curlicues. She saw me and smiled up at me.

"Hello there, sir! Have you had yer sleep out, now?" She came over, lifted the basket to show me a heap of deep red tomatoes.

"Aren't they lovely, sir? I'll slice ye some for dinner."

"They look good, Hilda," I said. "How long have I been asleep?"

"This last time, sir?"

"Altogether."

"Well, ye came about midnight. After we tucked ye in, ye slept all through the next day and night, and woke this morning about ten. After yer bath ye went back, and slept till now—"

"What time is it?"

"About five—so that's another six hours and more." She laughed. "Ye've slept like one drugged, sir. . . ."

I felt a weight slide off me like thawed snow off a steep roof. Drugged! I wasn't sick—I was doped to the eyebrows.

"I've got to talk to Gunvor," I said. "Where is she?"

"In the kitchen, plucking a fine goose for yer dinner, sir. Shall I tell her—"

"No, I'm getting dressed. I'll find her."

"Sir, are ye sure ye're feeling well enough—"

"I'm fine." I turned back to the closet, fighting the drowsiness that washed around me like thick fog. I got out the clothes, donned underwear, a loose-sleeved silk shirt and tight black pants of heavy cavalry twill, eased my feet into the slippers. Out in the narrow not-quite-straight passage papered in woodland scenes and decorated with framed tintypes, I followed the sounds of clattering crockery, pushed through a swinging door into a low-ceilinged, tile-floored room with a big black coal range, stainless steel sinks where a teen-age girl soaped dishes before a window with a flower box just outside, a glass-paneled door, a display of copper pots on the wall, and a big scrubbed-looking wooden table where Gunvor stood, working over the goose.

"Why, it's Mr. Bayard!" She blew a feather off her nose, looking flustered.

I leaned on the table for support, trying not to think about the buzzing in my head.

"Gunvor, did the doctor give you any medicine for me?"

"He did indeed, sir. The little drops for yer soup, and the white powders for yer other dishes—though since ye've taken no solid food as yet—"

"No more medicine, Gunvor." Everything was blacking out around me. I planted my feet, tried to will away the dizziness.

"Mr. Bayard, yer not strong enough yet—ye shouldn't be on yer feet!"

"Not . . . going back to bed. Need to . . . walk." I got out. "Get me outside . . ."

I felt Gunvor's arm under mine, heard her excited voice. I was vaguely aware of stumbling up steps, then the coolness of out-of-doors. I tried again, drew a couple of deep breaths, blinked away the fog.

"Better," I said. "Just walk me . . ."

Gunvor kept a running string of clucks and suggestions that I lie down right away. I ignored her, kept walking. It was a nice garden, with brick walls curving and meandering among the vegetable plots, past a rose bed along the side, under fruit trees at the far end, by a tempting bench under a thick-boled oak, and back to the kitchen door.

"Let's go around again." I tried not to lean on Gunvor this time. I was stronger; I could feel faint stirrings of appetite. The sun was sinking fast, throwing long, cool evening shadows across the grass. After the third lap, I waited by the kitchen door while Gunvor fetched a pitcher from the brown wooden icebox and poured me a glass of cool cider.

"Now ye'll sit and wait for yer dinner, Mr. Bayard," Gunvor suggested anxiously.

"I'm all right now." I patted the hand she had laid on my arm.

She watched me anxiously as I started off. I breathed deep and tried to sort out my thoughts. Someone had brought me here, drugged, arranged to keep me that way—for how long I didn't know, but I could check that by examining Gunvor's medicine supply. Someone had also been tinkering with my memory. The question of who—and why—needed answering.

I made an effort to cut through the fog, place an authentic recollection. It was June here, I judged, from the tender leaves and the budding roses. Where had I been in May, or last winter? . . .

Icy streets, tall buildings grim in the winter night, but inside, warmth, cheer, color, the laughing faces of friendly people and the smile of a beautiful redhead, named . . . named . . .

I couldn't remember. The almost-recollection slipped away like a wisp of smoke in a sudden breeze. Someone had done a good job—using deep hypnotics, no doubt—of burying my recollections under a layer of false memories. Still, they hadn't done as well as they thought. It had taken me only a few hours to throw off the nebulous impressions of a dubious past. Perhaps—

I turned, hurried back to the house. Gunvor was hesitating over a plate of fresh-baked pastries. She ducked something under her apron as I stepped into the room.

"Oh! Ye startled me, sir . . ."

I went across and removed a saltshaker half-filled with a coarse white powder from her hand, tossed it into the wastebasket.

"No more medicine, I said, Gunvor;" I patted her reassuringly. "I know the doctor gave you instructions, but I don't need it any more. But tell me, is there a . . ." I groped for a word. I didn't want to alarm her by asking for a brain doctor, and she wouldn't understand "psychiatrist." "A hypnotist?" I waited for signs of comprehension. "Someone who talks to troubled people, soothes them—"

"Ah, ye mean a mesmerist! But there's none here in the village, alas. . . . Only Mother Goodwill," she added doubtfully.

"Mother Goodwill?" I prompted.

"I've nothing against her, mind ye, sir—but there's those that talk of witchcraft. And I was reading just the other day in the Paris *Match* that ye can develop serious neuroses by letting unqualified practitioners meddle with yer psyche."

"You're so right, Gunvor," I agreed. "But it's only a little matter of a faulty memory—"

"Are ye troubled with that too, sir?" Her face lit up. "I'm that forgetful meself, sometimes I think I should have something done—but then a regular mesmerist's so dear, and as for these quacks—"

"What about Mother Goodwill? Does she live near here?"

"At the other end of the village, sir. But I wouldn't recommend her—not for a cultured gentleman like yerself. Her cottage is very plain, and the old woman herself is something less than a credit to our village. Dowdy, she is, sir—no sense of style at all. And as for clothes—"

"I won't be overly critical, Gunvor. Will you take me to her?"

"I'll summon her here, sir, if ye're determined—but there's a licensed master mesmerist in Ealing, just an hour by coach—"

"Mother Goodwill will do, I think. How soon can you get her here?"

"I'll send Ingalill—but if it's all the same to ye, sir, let me have her up after dinner. I've just popped me goose in, and the pies are browning even now—"

"After dinner will be fine. I'll take a few more turns around the garden and develop an appetite worthy of your cooking."

After a second slab of blackberry pie buried in cream too thick to pour, a final mug of ground-at-the-table coffee, and a healthy snort of brandy with the flavor of a century in a dark cellar safely under my belt, I lit up a New Orleans cigar and watched as Hilda and Gunvor lit the oil lamps in the sitting room. There was a timid tap at the door, and Ingalill, the kitchen slavey, poked her face in.

"The old witch is here," she piped. "Gunvor, she's smoking a pipe. I think it's got ground-up salamander innards in it—"

"She'll hear ye, ye wretch," Hilda said. "Tell her to wait until her betters summon her—"

Ingalill yelped and jumped aside, and a bent-backed ancient in a poke bonnet pushed in past her, one gnarled hand gripping a crooked stick on which she leaned. Bright black eyes darted about the room, lit on me. I stared back, taking in the warty nose, toothless gums, out-thrust chin, and wisp of white hair hanging beside one hollow cheek. I didn't see a pipe, but as I watched she snorted a last wisp of smoke from her nostrils.

"Who has need of Mother Goodwill's healing touch?" she quavered. "But, of course, it'd be ye, sir, who's come such a strange, long way—and with a stranger, longer path still ahead. . . ."

"Phooie, I told you it was the new gentleman," Ingalill said. "What's in the basket?" She reached to lift a corner of the red and white checked cloth covering the container, yelped as the stick cracked across her knuckles.

"Mind yer manners, dearie," Mother Goodwill said sweetly. She shuffled to a chair, sank down, put the basket on the floor at her feet.

"Now, Mother Goodwill," Gunvor said, sounding agitated. "The gentleman only wants a little help with—"

"He'd draw aside the veil of the past, the future to read more clearly," the crone piped. "Ah, he did well to call on old Mother Gee. Now . . ." her tone became more brisk. "If ye'll pour me a dram, Gunvor, to restore me strength a mite—and then ye'll all have to clear out—except m'lord, the new gentleman, o' course." She grinned at me like a meat-eating bird.

"I'm not interested in the future," I started—

"Are ye not, sir?" the old woman nodded as though agreeing. "Then it's a strange mortal ye are—"

". . . But there are some things I need to remember," I bored on, ignoring the sales pitch. "Maybe under light hypnosis I can—"

"So . . . then it's the past ye'd glimpse, as I thought,"
she commented imperturbably. Gunvor was clicking
glasses at the sideboard. She came over and handed the
old woman a glass, then got busy clearing dishes from
the table, with Ingalill and Hilda working silently beside
her.

Mother Goodwill smacked her lips over the brandy,
then waved an oversized brown-spotted hand.

"Away with ye, now, me chicks!" she quavered. "I feel
the spirit coming over me! The power's flowing in the
celestial field-coil! Strange visions are stirring, like
phantom vipers in a pot! What's this! What's this! Ai,
curious indeed, the things the spirits whisper to me
now. . . ."

"Hmmmp! Ye can skip the spirits routine," Hilda
said. "All Mr. Bayard wants from ye—"

"Get along with ye, girl," the old woman snapped, "or
I'll send a cramp that'll lock yer knees together that
tight the fairest swain this side o' Baghdad'll not unlock
'em! All o' ye! Off, now!"

They went. Then the hag turned to me.

"Now, down to business, sir." She used a wheedling
tone. "What were ye thinking o' giving the old woman
for a handful of lost recollections? Is it a lover ye've
forgot, the raptures of youth, the key to happiness once
glimpsed and now forever gone a-glimmering?"

I was grinning at her. "You'll be well paid, but let's
skip the rest of the routine. I'll get straight to the point. I
have reason to believe I'm suffering from induced
amnesia, probably the result of post-hypnotic
suggestion. I'd like you to put me under and see if you
can counter the block."

Mother Goodwill leaned forward, looked at me keenly.

"There's a strangeness about ye—something I can't
put me finger on. It's as though yer eyes was focused on
a horizon that other men can't see. . . ."

"Granted I'm a strange character, but not so strange
you can't hypnotize—or mesmerize me, I hope."

"Ye say ye've been tampered with, yer memories
taken from ye. Who'd've done a thing like that to ye,
lad—and why?"

"Maybe if you're successful, I'll find out."

She nodded briskly. "I've heard of such things. Spells of darkness, cast by the light of a bloodred moon—"

"Mother Goodwill," I cut in. "Let's get one thing straight: every time you mention spells, magic, dark powers, or geese, the fee goes down. I'm interested in straight scientific mesmerism. Okay?"

"What, good sir? Would ye tell the Mistress of Darkness how to ply her trade?"

The routine was beginning to get tiresome. "Maybe we'd better forget the whole thing." I reached in my pocket for a coin. "My mistake...."

"Are ye saying Mother Goodwill's a fraud, then?" Her voice had taken on a suspiciously mild note. I looked at her, caught a glint of light from an eye as black and bright as a polished opal. "D'ye think the old woman's out to trick ye, to play ye false, to gull ye fer a new fledged chick, to ..." her voice droned on, coming from far away now, booming like surf in a sea cave echoing, echoing ...

"...ten!"

My eyes snapped open. A woman with a pale, almost beautiful face sat, leaning pensively on one elbow, a cigarette in her hand, watching me. Her dark hair was done up in a tight bun. Her plain white blouse was open at the collar, showing a strong, graceful neck. There was one dark curl against her forehead.

I looked around the room; it was dark outside now; a clock was ticking loudly somewhere.

"What happened to the old beldame?" I blurted.

The woman smiled faintly, waved a well-manicured hand toward a black cape on the chair beside her, a gnarled stick leaning on it.

"Rather warm for working in," she said in a low voice. "How are you feeling?"

I considered. "Fine. But—" I caught a glimpse of a wisp of stringy grey hair under the edge of the cloak. I got out of my chair, went over and lifted it. There was a warty rubber mask, a pair of gnarly gloves.

"What's the idea of the getup?"

"I find it helpful in my ... business. Now—"

"You fooled me in a bad light," I said. "I take it Gunvor and the others are in on the gag?"

She shook her head. "No one ever sees me in a good light, Mr. Bayard—and no one wishes to approach too close, even then. They're simple people hereabouts. In their thoughts, warts and wisdom go together—so I fit their image of a village mesmerist, else none would seek my skill. You're the only one who shares my little secret."

"Why me?"

She looked at me searchingly. "You are a most unusual man, Mr. Bayard. A true man of mystery. You talked to me—of many things. Strange things. You spoke of other worlds, like this our own familiar plane, but different, alien. You talked of men like animals, clothed in shaggy hair—"

"Dzok!" I burst out. My hands went to my head as though to squeeze the recollections from my brain like toothpaste from a tube. "The Hagroon, and—"

"Calmly, calmly, Mr. Bayard," the woman soothed. "Your memories—if true memories they are, and not fever fancies—are there, intact, ready to be recalled. Rest, now. It was not easy for either of us, this stripping away of veils from your mind. A master mesmerist indeed was he who sought to bury your visions of strange paradises and unthinkable hells—but all lies exposed now." I looked down at her and she smiled.

"I am no journeyman practitioner myself," she murmured. "But all my skill was challenged this night." She rose, went to a framed mirror on the wall, gracefully tucked back a strand of hair. I watched her without seeing her. Thoughts of Barbro, the flaming figure in the dark storeroom, the escape with Dzok from the Hagroon cell were jostling each other, clamoring to be remembered, thought about, evaluated.

Mother Goodwill plucked her cape from the chair, swirled it about her shoulders, hunching into the posture of the hag she had been. Her white hands slipped the mask in place, fitting it to her nose and mouth. The gloves and wig followed, and now the bright eyes gazed at me from the wrinkled face of age.

"Rest, sir," the ancient face cackled. "Rest, sleep, dream, and let those restless thoughts seek out and know their familiar places once again. I'll attend ye on the morrow—there's more than Mother Goodwill would learn of the universes ye've told me lurk beyond the threshold of this drab world."

"Wait," I said. "I haven't paid you . . ."

She waved a veined hand. "Ye've paid me well in the stuff visions are wrought on, sir. Sleep, I say—and awake refreshed, strong, with your wits keened to razor's edge. For ye'll be needing all yer strength to face what waits ye in the days yet undawned."

She went out then. I went along the hall to my dark room, threw my clothes on a chair, fell into the feather-mattressed bed, and sank down into troubled dreams.

CHAPTER SEVEN

It was three days before I felt strong enough to pay my call on Mother Goodwill. Her cottage was a thatch-roofed rectangle of weathered stone almost lost under a tangle of wrist-sized rose vines heavy with deep red blossoms. I squeezed through a rusted gate, picked my way along a path overhung with untrimmed rhododendron, lifted the the huge brass knocker, clanked it against the low black oak door. Through the one small, many-paned window, I caught a glimpse of the corner of a table, a pot of forgetmenots, a thick leather-bound book. There was a humming of bees in the air, a scent of flowers, and a whiff of fresh-brewed coffee. Not the traditional setting for calling on a witch, I thought. . . .

The door opened. Mother Goodwill, looking neat in a white shirt and peasant skirt, favored me with a sad smile, motioning me in.

"No Halloween costume today," I commented.

"You're feeling better, Mr. Bayard," she said drily. "Will you have a mug of coffee? Or is't not customary in your native land?"

I shot her a sharp look. "Skeptical already?"

Her shoulders lifted and dropped. "I believe what my senses tell me. Sometimes they seem to contradict each the other." I took a chair at the table, glanced around the small room. It was scrupulously clean and tidy, furnished with the kind of rustic authenticity that would have had the ladies of the DAR back home oohing and aahing and overworking the word "quaint." Mother Goodwill brought the pot over, poured two cups, put cream and sugar on the table, then sat.

"Well, Mr. Bayard, is your mind clear this morning,

your remembrance well restored?"

I nodded, tried the coffee. It was good.

"Don't you have some other name I could call you?" I asked. "Mother Goodwill goes with the fright wig and the warts."

"You may call me Olivia." She had slim, white hands, and on one finger a fine green stone twinkled. She sipped her coffee and looked at me, as though making up her mind to tell me something.

"You were going to ask me questions," I prompted her. "After I've answered them, maybe you'll clear up a few matters for me."

"Many were the wonders you babbled of in your delirium," she said. I heard a tiny clatter, glanced at her cup; a fine tremor was rattling it against the saucer. She put it down quickly, ducked her hands out of sight.

"Oft have I sensed that there was more to existence than this . . ." she waved a hand to take in everything. "In dreams I've glimpsed enchanted hills and my heart yearned out to them, and I'd wake with the pain of something beautiful and lost that haunted me long after. I think in your wild talk, there was that which made a certain hope spring up again—a hope long forgotten, with the other hopes of youth. Now tell me, stranger, that talk of other worlds, like each to other as new-struck silver pieces, yet each with a tiny difference—and of a strange coach, with the power to fly from one to the next—all this was fancy, eh? The raving of a mind sore vexed with meddling—"

"It's true—Olivia," I cut in. "I know it's hard to grasp at first. I seem to recall I was a bit difficult to convince once. We're accustomed to thinking we know everything. There's a powerful tendency to disbelieve anything that doesn't fit the preconception."

"You spoke of trouble, Brion . . ." she spoke my name easily, familiarly. I suppose sharing someone's innermost thoughts tends to relax formalities. I didn't mind. Olivia without her disguise was a charming woman, in spite of her severe hairdo and prison pallor. With a little sunshine and just a touch of makeup—

I pulled myself back to the subject at hand.

She listened attentively as I told her the whole story, from Richthofen's strange interrogation to my sentencing by the Xonijeelians.

"So I'm stuck," I finished. "Without a shuttle, I'm trapped here for the rest of my days."

She shook her head. "These are strange things, Brion, things I should not believe, so wild and fantastic are they. And yet—I do believe. . . ."

"From what little I've learned of this world line, it's backward technologically—"

"Why, we're a very modern people," Olivia said. "We have steam power—the ships on the Atlantic run make the crossing in nine days—and there are the balloons, the telegraph, and telephone, our modern coal-burning road cars which are beginning to replace the horse in many parts of the colonies, even—"

"Sure, I know Olivia—no offense intended. Let's just say that in some areas we're ahead of you. The Imperium has the M-C drive. My own native world has nuclear power, jet aircraft, radar, and a primitive space program. Here you've gone in other directions. The point is, I'm stranded here. They've exiled me to a continuum I can never escape from."

"Is it so ill then, Brion? You have a whole world here before you—and now that the artificial barriers have been cleansed from your mind, you'll freely recall these wonders you left behind!" She was speaking eagerly now, excited at the prospect. "You spoke of aircraft. Build one! How marvelous to fly in the sky like a bird! Your coming here could mean the dawn of a new Age of Glory for the Empire!"

"Uh-huh," I said ungraciously. "That's great. But what about *my* world? By now the Hagroon have probably launched their attack—and maybe succeeded with it! My wife may be wearing chains now instead of pearls!" I got up, stamped over to the window and stared out. "While I rot here, in this backwater world," I snarled.

"Brion," she said softly behind me. "You find yourself troubled—not so much by the threat of your beloved friends as by the quality of remoteness these matters have taken on. . . ."

I turned. "What do you mean, remote? Barbro, my friends, in the hands of these ape-men—"

"Those who tampered with your mind, Brion, sought

to erase these things from your memory. True, my skill availed to lift the curse—but 'tis no wonder that they seem to you now as old memories, a tale told long ago. And I myself gave a command to you while yet you slept, that the pain of loss be eased—''

"The pain of loss be damned! If I hadn't been fool enough to trust Dzok—''

"Poor Brion. Know you not yet it was he who gulled you while you slept, planted the desire to go with him to Xonijeel? Yet he did his best for you—or so your memory tells.''

"I could have taken the shuttle back," I said flatly. "At least I'd have been there, to help fight the bastards off.''

"And yet, the wise ones, the monkey-men of Xonijeel, told you that this Zero-zero world did not exist—''

"They're crazy!" I took a turn up and down the room. "There's too much here I don't understand, Olivia! I'm like a man wandering in the dark, banging into things that he can't quite get his hands on. And now—" I raised my hands and let them fall, suddenly inexpressibly weary.

"You have your life still ahead, Brion. You will make a new place for yourself here. Accept that which cannot be changed.''

I came back and sat down.

"Olivia, I haven't asked Gunvor and the others many questions. I didn't want to arouse curiosity by my ignorance. The indoctrination Dzok and his boys gave me didn't cover much—just enough to get me started. I suppose they figured I'd get to a library and brief myself. Tell me something about this world. Fill me in on your history, to start with.''

She laughed—an unexpectedly merry sound.

"How charming, Brion—to be called upon to describe this humdrum old world as though it were a dreamer's fancy—a might-have-been, instead of dull reality.''

I managed a sour smile. "Reality's always a little dull to whoever's involved in it.''

"Where shall I begin? With Ancient Rome? The Middle Ages?''

"The first thing to do is establish a Common History date—the point at which your world diverged from mine. You mentioned 'The Empire.' What empire? When was it founded?"

"Why, the Empire of France, of course . . ." Olivia blinked, then shook her head. "But then, nothing is 'of course'," she said. "I speak of the Empire established by Bonaparte, in 1799."

"So far so good," I said. "We had a Bonaparte, too. But his empire didn't last long. He abdicated and was sent off to Elba in 1814—"

"Yes—but he escaped, returned to France, and led his armies to glorious victory!"

I was shaking my head. "He was free for a hundred days, until the British defeated him at Waterloo. He was sent to St. Helena and died a few years later."

Olivia stared at me. "How strange . . . how eerie, and how strange. The Emperor Napoleon ruled in splendor at Paris for twenty-three years after his great victory at Brussels, and died in 1837 at Nice. He was succeeded by his son, Louis—"

"The Duke of Reichstadt?"

"No; the Duke died in his youth, of consumption. Louis was a boy of sixteen, the son of Emperor and the Princess of Denmark."

"And his Empire still exists," I mused.

"After the abdication of the English tyrant George, the British Isles were permitted to enter the Empire as a special ward of the Emperor. After the unification of Europe, enlightenment was brought to the Asians and Africans. Today, they are semiautonomous provinces, administered from Paris, but with their own local Houses of Deputies empowered to deal with internal matters. As for New France—or Louisiana—this talk of rebellion will soon die down. A royal commission has been sent to look into the complaints against the Viceroy."

"I think we've got the C. H. date pretty well pinned down," I said. "Eighteen-fourteen. And it looks as though there's been no significant scientific or technological progress since."

This prompted questions which I answered at length. Olivia was an intelligent and well-educated woman. She was enthralled by my picture of a world without the giant shadow of Bonaparte falling across it.

The morning had developed into the drowsy warmth

of noon by the time I finished. Olivia offered me lunch
and I accepted. While she busied herself at the wood-
burning stove, I sat by the window, sipping a stone mug
of brown beer, looking out at this curious, anachronistic
landscape of tilled fields, a black-topped road along
which a horse pulled a rubber-tired carriage, the white
and red dots of farmhouses across the valley. There was
an air of peace and plenty that made my oddly distant
recollection of the threat to the Imperium seem, as
Olivia said, like a half-forgotten story, read long
ago—like something in the book lying on the table. I
picked up the fat, red leather-bound volume, glanced at
the title:

THE SORCERESS OF OZ, by Lyman F. Baum.

"That's funny," I said.

Olivia glanced over at the book in my hands, smiled
almost shyly.

"Strange reading matter for a witch, you think? But
on these fancies my own dreams sometimes love to
dwell, Brion. As I told you, this one narrow world seems
not enough—"

"It's not that, Olivia. We've pretty well established
that our C. H. date is early in the nineteenth century.
Baum wasn't born until about 1855 or so—nearly half a
century later. But here he is. . . ."

I flipped the book open, noted the publisher—Wiley &
Cotton, New York, New Orleans, and Paris—and the
date: 1896.

"You know this book, in your own strange world?"
Olivia asked.

I shook my head. "In my world he never wrote this
one. . . ." I was admiring the frontispiece by W. W.
Denslow, showing a Glinda-like figure facing a group of
gnomes. The next page had an elaborate initial "I" at the
top, followed by the words: " '. . . summoned you here,'
said Sorana the Sorceress, 'to tell you . . .' "

"It was my favorite book as a child," Olivia said. "But
if you know it not, how then do you recognize the
author's name?"

"He wrote others. THE WIZARD OF OZ was the first
book I ever read all the way through."

"The Wizard of Oz? Not The Sorceress? How
enchanting it would be to read it!"

"Is this the only one he wrote?"

"Sadly, yes. He died the following year—1897."

"Eighteen ninety-seven; that could mean . . ." I trailed off. The fog that had been hanging over my mind for days since I had awakened here was rapidly dissipating in the brisk wind of a sudden realization: Dzok and his friends had relocated me, complete with phony memories to replace the ones they'd tried to erase, in a world-line as close as possible to my own. They'd been clever, thorough, and humane. But not quite as clever as they thought, a bit less thorough in their research than they should have been—and altogether too humane.

I remembered the photogram the councillors had shown me—and the glowing point, unknown to Imperial Net cartographers, which represented a fourth, undiscovered world lying within the Blight. I had thought at the time that it was an error, along with the other, greater error that had omitted—the Zero-zero line of the Imperium.

But it had been no mistake. B-I Four existed—a world with a Common History date far more recent than the 15th century—the C. H. date of the closest lines beyond the Blight.

And I was there—or here—in a world where, in 1897 at least one man known in my own world had existed. And if one, why not another—or two others: Maxoni and Cocini, inventors of the M-C drive.

"Could mean what, Brion?" Olivia's voice jarred me back to the present.

"Nothing. Just a thought." I put the book down. "I suppose it's only natural that even fifty years after a major divergence, not everything would have been affected. Some of the same people would be born. . . ."

"Brion," Olivia looked at me across the room. "I won't ask you to trust me, but let me help you."

"Help me with what?" I tried to recapture the casual expression I'd been wearing up until a moment before, but I could feel it freezing on my face like a mud pack.

"You have made a plan; I sense it. Alone, you cannot succeed. There is too much that is strange to you here, too many pitfalls to betray you. Let me lend you what help I can."

"Why should you want to help me—if I were planning something?"

She looked at me for a minute without answering, her dark eyes wide in her pale, classic face.

"I've spent my life in search for a key to some other world . . . some dreamworld of my mind. Somehow, you seem to be a link, Brion. Even if I can never go there, it would please me to know I'd helped someone to reach the unattainable shore."

"They're all worlds, just like this one, Olivia. Some better, some worse—some much, much worse. They're all made up of people and earth and buildings, the same old natural laws, the same old human nature. You can't find your dreamworld by packing up and moving on; you've got to build it where you are."

"And yet—I see the ignorance, the corruption, the social and moral decay, the lies, the cheats, the treachery of those who hold the trust of the innocent—"

"Sure—and until we've evolved a human society to match our human intelligence, those things will exist. But give us time, Olivia—we've only been experimenting with culture for a few thousand years. A few thousand more will make a lot of difference."

She laughed. "You speak as though an age were but a moment."

"Compared with the time it took us to evolve from an amoeba to an ape—or even from the first Homo sapiens to the first tilled field—it *is* a moment. But don't give up your dreams. They're the force that carries us on toward whatever our ultimate goal is."

"Then let me lend that dream concrete reality. Let me help you, Brion. The story they told me—that you had fallen ill from overwork as an official of the Colonial Office, that you were here for a rest cure—'tis as thin as a Parisian nightdress! And, Brion . . ." She lowered her voice. "You are watched."

"Watched? By whom—a little man with a beard and dark glasses?"

" 'Tis no jest, Brion! I saw a man last night lurking by the gate at Gunvor's house—and half an hour since, a man well muffled up in scarves passed in the road yonder, as you supped coffee."

"That doesn't prove anything—"

She shook her head impatiently. "You plan to fly, I know that. I know also that your visit to me will arouse the curiosity of those who prison you here—"

"Prison me? Why, I'm as free as a bird—"

"You waste time, Brion," she cut me off. "What deed you committed, or why, I know not; but in a contest between you and drab officialdom, I'll support your cause. Now, quickly, Brion! Where will you go? How will you travel? What plan will—"

"Hold on, Olivia! You're jumping to conclusions!"

"And jump you must, if you'd evade the hounds of the hunter! I sense danger, closing about you as a snare about the roebuck's neck!"

"I've told you, Olivia—I was exiled here by the Xonijeelian Council. They didn't believe my story—or pretended not to. They dumped me here to be rid of me—they fancy themselves as humane, you know. If they'd meant to kill me, they had every opportunity to do so—"

"They sought to mesmerize your knowledge of the past away; now they watch, their results to judge. And when they see you restive, familiar of a witch—"

"You're no witch—"

"As such all know me here. 'Twas an ill gambit that brought you here by daylight, Brion—"

"If I'd crept out at midnight, they'd have seen me anyway—if they're watching me as you seem to think—and they'd have known damned well I wasn't satisfied with their hand-painted picture of my past."

"In any case, they'll like it not. They'll come again, take you away, and once again essay to numb your knowledge of the worlds, and of your past."

I thought that over. "They might, at that," I said. "I don't suppose it was part of their relocation program to have me spreading technical knowledge among the primitives."

"Where will you go, Brion?"

I hesitated; but what the hell, Olivia was right. I had to have help. And if she intended to betray me, she had plenty on me already.

"Rome," I said.

She nodded. "Very well. What is the state of your purse?"

"I have a bank account—"

"Leave that. Luckily, I have my store of gold Napoleons buried in the garden."

"I don't want your money—"

"Nonsense. We'll both need it. I'm going with you."

"You can't—"

"Can, and will!" she said, her dark eyes alight. "Make ready, Brion! We leave this very night!"

"This is crazy," I whispered to the dark, hooded figure standing beside me on the shadowed path. "There's no reason for you to get involved in this . . ."

"Hush," Olivia said softly. "Now he grows restless. See him there? I think he'll cross the road now, more closely to spy us out."

I watched the dense shadows, made out the figure of a man. He moved off, crossed the road a hundred yards below the cottage, disappeared among the trees on our side. I shifted my weight carefully, itching under the wild getup Olivia had assembled for me—warty face, gnarly hands, stringy white hair, and all. I looked like Mother Goodwill's older brother—as ill-tempered an old duffer as ever gnashed his gums at the carryings-on of the younger generation. Olivia was done up like Belle Watling in three layers of paint, a fancy red wig, a purple dress that fit her trim figure like wet silk, and enough bangles, rings, beads and tinkly earrings to stock a gyfte shoppe.

"Hist—he steals closer now," my coconspirator whispered. "Another half minute . . ."

I waited, listening to the monotonous chirrup of crickets in a nearby field, the faraway *oo-mau* of a cow, the yapping of a farm dog. After dark, the world belonged to the animals.

Olivia's hand touched mine. "Now . . ." I followed as she stepped silently off. I had to crouch slightly to keep below the level of the ragged hedge. There was no moon, only a little faint starlight to help us pick a way along the rutted dirt road. We reached the end of the hedge, and I motioned Olivia back, stole a look toward the house. A head was clearly silhouetted against the faint light from the small side window.

"It's okay," I said in a low voice. "He's at the

window—"

There was a crunch of gravel, and a light snapped on, played across the ruts, flashed over me, settled on Olivia.

"Here, woman," a deep voice growled. "What're ye doing aboard after bell-toll?"

Olivia planted a hand on her hip, tossed her head, not neglecting to smile archly.

"Aoow, Capting," she purred. "Ye fair give me a turn! It's only me old gaffer, what oi'm seein orf to the rile-trine."

"Gaffer, is it?" The light dwelt on me again briefly, went back to caress Olivia's sequinned bosom. "Haven't seen ye about the village before. Where ye from?"

"I float about, as ye might say, Major. A tourist, like, ye might call me—"

"On shank's mare, in the middle of the night? Queer idea o' fun, I call it—and with yer gaffer, too. Better let me see yer identity papers, ducks."

"Well, as it 'appears, I come away in such a rush, they seem to 'ave got left behind. . . ."

"Like that, is't?" I heard a snort from the unseen man behind the light—one of the roving security police who were a fixture of this world, I guessed. "Run off with a fistful o' spoons, did ye? Or maybe lifted one purse too many—"

"Nofink o' that sort! What cheek! I'm an honest, licensed tart, plying 'er profession and keeping her old gaffer, what oi'm the sole support of!"

"Never mind, love. I won't take ye in. A wee sample of yer wares, and I'll forget I ever saw ye." He came close, and a big hand reached out toward Olivia. She let out a sharp squeak and jumped back. The cop brushed past me. I caught a glimpse of a tricorn hat, a beak nose, loose jowls, a splash of color on the collar of the uniform. I picked my spot, chopped down hard across the base of his neck with the side of my hand. He yelped, dropped the light, stumbled to hands and knees. The stiff collar had protected him from the full force of the blow. He scrambled, trying to rise; I followed, kicked him square under the chin. He back-flipped and sprawled out, unconscious. I grabbed up the light and found the switch, flicked it off.

"Is he . . . badly hurt?" Olivia was staring at the smear of blood at the corner of the slack mouth.

"He'll have trouble asking for bribes for a few weeks." I pulled Olivia back toward the hedgerow. "Let's hope our snooper didn't hear anything."

We waited for a minute, then started off again, hurrying now. Far away, a spark of wavering, yellowish light moved across the slope of the hill beyond the village.

"That's the train," Olivia said. "We'll have to hurry!"

We walked briskly for fifteen minutes, passed the darkened shops at the edge of town, reached the station just as the puffing coal-burner pulled in. A severe-looking clerk in a dark uniform with crossed chest straps and coattails accepted Olivia's money, wrote out tickets by hand, pointed out our car. Inside we found wide seats upholstered in green plush. We were the only passengers. I leaned back in my seat with a sigh. The train whistle shrilled, a lurch ran through the car.

"We're on our way," Olivia breathed. She looked ecstatic, like a kid at the fair.

"We're just going to Rome," I said. "Not the land of Oz."

"Who can say whither the road of the future leads?"

CHAPTER EIGHT

At the Albergo Romulus, Olivia and I had adjoining rooms well up under the eaves, with ceilings that slanted down to a pair of dormer windows opening onto a marketplace with a handsome Renaissance fountain, the incessant flutter of pigeons' wings, and a day and night shrilling of excited Italian voices. We were sitting at the small table in my room, eating a late breakfast of pizzas, washed down with a musty red wine that cost so little that even the local begging corps could afford to keep a mild buzz on most of the time.

"The two men I'm interested in were born somewhere in northern Italy about 1850," I told Olivia. "They came to Rome as young men, studied engineering and electronics, and in 1893 made the basic discovery that gave the Imperium the Net drive. I'm gambling that if Baum managed to get himself born, and in the nineties was writing something pretty close to what he did in my world—and in the Zero-zero A-line too—then maybe Maxoni and Cocini existed here too. They didn't perfect the M-C drive, obviously—or if they did, the secret died with them—but maybe they came close. Maybe they left something I can use."

"Brion, did you not tell me that all the worlds that lie about your Zero-zero line are desolate, blasted into ruin by these very forces? Is it safe to tamper with such fell instruments as these?"

"I'm a fair shuttle technician, Olivia. I know most of the danger points. Maxoni and Cocini didn't realize what they were playing with. They stumbled on the field by blind luck—"

"And in a thousand million other worlds of might-have-been they failed, and brought ruin in their wake. . . ."

"You knew all this when we left Harrow," I said shortly. "It's my only chance—and a damned poor chance it is, I'll admit. But I can't build a shuttle from scratch—there's a specially wound coil that's the heart of the field-generator. I've installed 'em, but I never tried to wind one. Maybe—if there was a Maxoni here, and a Cocini—and they made the same chance discovery—and they wrote up their notes like good little researchers—and the notes still exist—and I can find them—"

Olivia laughed—a charming, girlish laugh. "If the gods decree that all those *ifs* are in your favor—why then 'tis plain, they mean you to press on. I'll risk it, Brion. The vision of the Sapphire City still beckons me."

"It's the Emerald City, where I come from," I said. "But we won't quibble over details. Let's see if we can find those notes first. We'll have plenty of time then to decide what to do with them."

An hour later, at the local equivalent of a municipal record center, a tired-looking youth in a narrow-cut black suit showed me a three-foot ledger in which names were written in spidery longhand—thousands of names, followed by dates, places of birth, addresses, and other pertinent details.

"*Sicuro, Signore*," he said in a tone of weary superiority, "the municipality, having nothing to hide, throws open to you its records—among the most complete archives in existence in the Empire—but as for reading them . . ." he smirked, tweaked his hairline mustache. "That the Signore must do for himself."

"Just explain to me what I'm looking at," I suggested gently. "I'm looking for a record of Giulio Maxoni, or Carlo Cocini—"

"Yes, yes, so you said. And here before you is the registration book in which the names of all new arrivals in the city were recorded at the time identity papers were issued. They came to Rome in 1870, you said—or was it 1880? You seemed uncertain. As for me . . ." he spread his hands. "I am even more uncertain. I have never heard of these relatives—or friends—or ancestors—or whatever they might be. In them, you, it appears, have an interest. As for me—I have none. There is the book, covering the decade in question. Look all you wish. But do not demand miracles of me! I have duties to perform!" His voice developed an irritated snap on the last words. He strutted off to sulk somewhere back in the stacks. I grunted and started looking.

Twenty minutes passed quietly. We worked our way through 1870, started on 1871. The busy archivist peered out once to see what we were doing, withdrew after a sour look. Olivia and I stood at the wooden counter, poring over the crabbed longhand, each taking one page of about two hundred names. She was a fast reader; before I had finished my page, she had turned to the next. Half a minute later she gave a sharp gasp.

"Brion! Look! Giulio Maxoni, born 1847 at Paglio; trade, artificer—"

I looked. It was the right name. I tried not to let myself get too excited—but my pulse picked up in spite of the voice of prudence whispering in my ear that there might be hundreds of Giulio Maxonis.

"Nice work, girl," I said in a cool, controlled voice that only broke twice on the three words. "What address?"

She read it off. I jotted it down in a notebook I had thoughtfully provided for the purpose, added the other data from the ledger. We searched for another hour, but found no record of Cocini. The clerk came back and hovered, as though we'd overstayed our welcome. I closed the book and shoved it across the counter to him.

"Don't sweat it, Jack," I said genially. "We're just making up a sucker list for mailings on budget funerals."

"Mailings?" He stared at me suspiciously. "Municipal records are not intended for such uses—and in any event—these people are all long since dead!"

"Exactly," I agreed. "A vast untapped market for our line of goods. Thanks heaps. I'll make a note to give you special treatment when your time comes."

We walked away in a silence you could have cut into slabs with a butter knife.

Maxoni had lived at number twelve, Via Carlotti, fourth floor, number nine. With the aid of a street map purchased from an elderly entrepreneur in a beret and a soiled goatee who offered us a discount on racy postcards, which I declined with regret, we found it—a narrow alley, choked with discarded paper cartons, vegetable rinds, overflowing garbage barrels, and shoeless urchins who dodged madly among the obstacles, cheerfully exchanging badinage which would have made Mussolini blush. Number twelve was a faded late Renaissance front of rusticated granite wedged between sagging, boarded-up warehouses no more than a hundred or so years old. Maxoni, it appeared, had started his career in the most modest quarters available. Even a century ago, this had been a slum. I pushed open the caked door, stepped into a narrow hall reeking of garlic, cheese, decay, and less pleasant things.

"It looks terrible, Brion," Olivia said. "Perhaps we'd best make enquiries first—"

A door opened and a round, olive face set in cushions of fat looked out, and launched into a stream of rapid Italian.

"Your pardon, Madam," I replied in the courtly accents I had learned from the Roman Ambassador to the Imperial court. "We are but foreigners, visiting the Eternal City for the first time. We seek the apartment where once our departed relative dwelt, long ago, when the gods favored him with the privilege of breathing the sweet air of sunny Italy."

Her jaw dropped; she stared; then a grin the size of a tenlira pizza spread across her face.

"*Buon giorno, Signore e Signorina!*" She squeezed out into the hall, pumped our hands, yelled instructions back into her flat—from which a mouth-watering aroma of ravioli emanated—and demanded to know how she could serve the illustrious guests of fair Italy. I gave her the number of the apartment where Maxoni had lived, ninety-odd years before, and she nodded, started up the narrow stair, puffing like the steam-engine that we had ridden across Europe for two days and nights. Olivia followed and I brought up the rear; admiring the deposits of broken glass, paper, rags and assorted rubbish that packed every step and landing, with a trail winding up through the center worn by the feet of

centuries of tenants. I would have given odds that the
bits Maxoni might have contributed were still there,
somewhere.

At the top, we went along a narrow hall, past battered-
looking doors with white china knobs, stopped at the
one at the end.

"There is a tenant, Signore," the landlady said. "But
he is away now, at his job in the fish market that I,
Sophia Gina Anna Maria Scumatti, procured for him!
Believe me, if I hadn't given him an ultimatum that the
rent must be paid or out he'd go, he'd be sleeping now,
snoring like a serviced sow, while I, Sophia Gina—"

"Undoubtedly the Signora has to endure much from
ungrateful tenants," I soothed. I had a hundred lira note
ready in my jacket pocket—the same oddly cut jacket
that had been in the closet at Gunvor's house. I fished
the bill out, tendered it with an inclination of the head.

"If   the   Signora   will   accept   this   modest
contribution—"

Mama Scumatti puffed out her cheeks, threw out her
imposing bosom.

"It is my pleasure to serve the guest of Italy," she
started; I pulled the bill back.

". . . but let it not be said that I, Gina Anna Maria
Scumatti, was ungracious—" Fat fingers plucked the
note from my hand, dropped it into a cleavage like the
Grand Canyon. "Would the Signore and Signorina care
to enter?" She fumbled a three-inch key from a pocket,
jammed it into a keyhole you could have put a finger
through, twisted it, threw the door wide.

"*Vidi!*"

I looked in at a collapsed cot snarled with dirty
blankets, a broken-down table strewn with garishly
colored comics, empty coffee cups, stained, finger-
greased glasses, and a half-loaf of dry-looking bread.
There was a bureau, a broken mirror with racing tickets
tucked under the frame, a wooden Jesus dangling on the
wall, and an assortment of empty wine and liquor
bottles bearing the labels of inferior brands, scattered
about the room. The odor of the place was a sour blend
of unlaundered bedding, old socks, and a distillery
infested with mice.

I looked at Olivia. She gave me a cool smile, turned to

our hostess.

"May we go in?"

Sophia Gina wrinkled her brow at me. "My sister would like to go inside and . . . ah . . . commune with the spirit of our departed progenitor," I translated freely.

The black, unplucked eyebrows went up. "But, as the Signore sees, the room is occupied!"

"We won't touch a thing; just look at it. A very emotional moment for us, you understand."

A knowing look crept over the round face. She gave Olivia, still wearing her makeup and rings, an appraising once-over, then looked me in the eye; one eyelid dipped in an unmistakable wink.

"Ah, but naturally, Signore! You and your . . . sister . . . would of course wish to commune—in private. Another hundred lira, please." She was suddenly brisk. I forked over silently, trying to look just a little hangdog.

"I dislike to hurry the Signore," the concierge said as she shook the second note down into the damp repository. "But try to finish in say two hours, *si*? There is the chance that Gino will be back for lunch." An elbow the size and texture of a football dug into my side. Two fat, broken-nailed hands outlined an hourglass in the air; two small black eyes rolled; then Mama Scumatti was waddling off, a hippo in a black skirt.

"What said the fat scroundrel?" Olivia demanded.

"Just admiring your figure," I said hastily. "let's take a look around and see what clues we can turn up."

Half an hour later Olivia stood in the center of the room, still wrinkling her nose, hands on hips, a lock of hair curling down over her damp forehead.

" 'Twas a hopeless quest from the first," she said. "Let's be off, before my stomach rebels."

I dusted off my hands, grimy from groping on the backs of shelves and under furniture. "We've looked in all the obvious places," I said. "But what about the unlikely spots? We haven't checked for loose floorboards, secret panels, fake pictures on the wall—"

" 'Tis a waste of time, Brion! This man was not a conspirator, to squirrel away his secrets in the mattress! He was a poor young student, no more, living in a rented room—"

"I'm thinking of little things he might have dropped; a bit of paper that could have gotten stuck in the back of a drawer, maybe. Nobody ever cleans this place. There's no reason something like that couldn't still be here, even after all these years."

"Where? You've had the drawers out, rooted in the base of the chest, lifted that ragged scrap of rug, probed behind the baseboard—"

She trailed off; her eyes were on the boxed-in radiator set under the one small window. The wooden panels were curled, split, loose-fitting. We both moved at once. Olivia deftly set aside the empty Chianti bottles and the tin can half full of cigarette butts. I got a grip on the top board, lifted gingerly. The whole assembly creaked, moved out.

"Just a couple of rusty nails holding it," I said. "I'll lever it free. . . ."

A minute later, with the help of a wooden coat hanger lettered "Albergo Torino, Roma," I had eased the housing away from the wall, revealing a rusted iron radiator, a few inches of piping, enough dust devils to fill a shoe box—and a drift of cigarette butts, ticket stubs, bits of string, hairpins, a playing card, paper clips, and papers.

"It was a good idea," I said. "Too bad it didn't pan out." Silently, I replaced the cover, put the bottles and ashtray back. "You were right, Olivia. Let's get back out in the street where we can get a nice wholesome odor of fresh garbage—"

"Brion, look!" Olivia was by the window, turning the blank scrap of paper at an angle to catch the sun. "The ink has faded, but there was something written here. . . ."

I came over, squinted at the paper. The faintest of faint marks were visible. Olivia put the paper on the table, rubbed it gently over the dusty surface, then held it up to the mirror. The ghostly outline of awkward penmanship showed as a grey line.

"Rub it a little more," I said tensely. "Careful—that paper's brittle as ash." She complied, held it to the mirror again. This time I could make out letters:

Instituzione Galileo Mercoledi Giugno 7. 3 P.M.

"Wednesday, June 7th," I translated. "This just might be something useful. I wonder what year that was?"

"I know a simple formula for calculating the day on which a given date must fall," Olivia said breathlessly. " 'Twill take but a moment . . ."

She nibbled at her lip, frowning in concentration. Suddenly her expression lightened. "Yes! It fits! June 7, 1871 fell on a Wednesday!" She frowned. "As did that date in 1899, 1911—"

"It's something—that's better than nothing at all. Let's check it out. The Galileo Institute. Let's hope it's still in business."

A dried-up little man in armbands and an eyeshade nibbled a drooping yellowed mustache and listened in silence, his veined hands resting on the counter top as though holding it in place as a barrier against smooth-talking foreign snoopers.

"Eighteen seventy-one. That was a considerable time in the past," he announced snappishly. "There have been many students at the Institute since then. Many illustrious scientists have passed through these portals, bringing glory to the name of Galileo." An odor of cheap wine drifted across from his direction. Apparently we had interrupted his midmorning snort.

"I'm not applying for admission," I reminded him. "You don't have to sell me. All I want is a look at the record of Giulio Maxoni. Of course, if your filing system is so fouled up you can't find it, you can just say so, and I'll report the fact in the article I'm writing—"

"You are a journalist?" He straightened his tie, gave the mustache a twirl, and eased something into a drawer out of sight behind the counter, with a clink of glass.

"Just give me the same treatment you'd accord any humble seeker after facts," I said loftily. "After all, the public is the owner of the Institute; surely it should receive the fullest attention of the staff whose bread and vino are provided by the public's largesse. . . ."

That got to him. He made gobbling sounds, hurried away, came back wheezing under a volume that was the twin to the municipal register, slammed it down on the counter, blew a cloud of dust in my face, and lifted the cover.

"Maxoni, you said, sir. 1871 . . . 1871 . . ." he paused, popped his eyes at me. "That wouldn't be *the* Maxoni?" His natural suspicious look was coming back.

"Ahhh . . ." a variety of sudden emotions were jostling each other for space on my face. "*The* Maxoni?" I prompted.

"Giulio Maxoni, the celebrated inventor," he snapped. He turned and waved a hand at a framed deguerrotype, one of a long, sombre row lining the room. "Inventor of the Maxoni churn, the Maxoni telegraph key, the Maxoni Improved Galvanic Buggy Whip—it was that which made his fortune, of course—"

I smiled complacently, like an inspector who has failed to find an error in the voucher files. "Very good. I see you're on your toes here at the Institute. I'll just have a look at the record, and then . . ." I let it trail off as Smiley spun the book around, pointed out a line with a chewed fingernail.

"Here it is, right here. His original registration in the College of Electrics. He was just a lad from a poor farming community then. It was here at the Institute that he got his start. We were one of the first, of course, to offer lectures in electrics. The Institute was one of the sponsors of the Telegraphic Conference, later in that same year . . ." He rattled on with the sales pitch that had undoubtedly influenced many an old alumnus or would-be patron of the sciences to fork over that extra bundle, while I read the brief entry. The address in the Via Carlotti was given, the fact that Maxoni was twenty-four, a Catholic, and single. Not much help there. . . .

"Is there any record," I inquired, "as to where he lived—after he made his pile?"

The little man stiffened. "Made his pile, sir? I fear I do not understand. . . ."

"Made his great contribution to human culture, I mean," I amended. "Surely he didn't stay on at the Via Carlotti very long."

A sad smile twitched at one corner of the registrar's tight mouth.

"Surely the gentleman jests? The location on the Museum is, I think, well known—even to tourists."

"What museum?"

The gnome spread his hands in a gesture as Roman as

grated cheese.

"What other than the museum housed in the former home and laboratory of Giulio Maxoni? The shrine wherein are housed the relics of his illustrious career."

Beside me, Olivia was watching the man's face, wondering what we were talking about. "Pay dirt," I said to her. Then:

"You don't have the address of this museum handy, by any chance?

This netted me a superior smile. A skinny finger pointed at the wall beside him.

"Number twenty-eight, Strada d'Allenzo. One square east. Any child could direct you."

"We're in business, girl," I said to Olivia.

"Ah . . . what was the name of the paper you . . . ah . . . claim to represent?" the little man's voice was a nice mixture of servility and veiled insolence. He was dying to be insulting, but wasn't quite sure it was safe.

"We're with the Temperance League," I said, and sniffed loudly. "The Maxoni questions were just a dodge, of course. We're doing a piece entitled: 'Drinking on Duty, and What it Costs the Taxpayer.'"

He was still standing in the same position, goggling after us, when we stepped out into the bright sunshine.

The Maxoni house was a conservative, stone-fronted building that would have done credit to any street in the East Seventies back home. There was a neglected-looking brass plate set above the inner rail beside the glass-paneled door, announcing that the Home and Laboratories of the Renowned Inventor Giulio Maxoni were maintained by voluntary contributions to the Society for the Preservation of Monuments to the Glory of Italy, and were open 9—4, Monday through Saturday, and on Sundays, 1—6 P.M. A card taped to the glass invited me to ring the bell. I did. Time passed. A dim shape moved beyond the glass, bolts rattled, the door creaked open, and a frowzy, sleep-blurred female blinked out.

"It's closed. Go away," said the voice like the last whinny of a dying plow horse. I got a foot into the narrowing space between the door and the jamb.

"The sign says—" I started brightly.

"Bugger the sign," the blurry face wheezed. "Come back tomorrow—"

I put a shoulder against the door, bucked it open, sending the charming receptionist reeling back. She caught her balance, hitched up a sagging bra strap, and raised a hand, fingers spread, palm facing her, opened her mouth to demonstrate what was probably an adequate command of Roman idiom—

"Ah—ah, don't say it," I cautioned her. "The Contessa here is unaccustomed to the vigor of modern speech. She's led a sheltered life, tucked away there in her immense palazzo at Lake Constance. . . ."

"Contessa?" A hideous leer that was probably intended as a simper contorted the sagging face. "Oh, my, if I only would've known her Grace was honoring our little shrine with a visit—" She fled.

"A portal guarded by a dragon," Olivia said. "And the fair knight puts her to rout with but a word."

"I used a magic spell on her. You're promoted to Contessa now. Just smile distantly and act aloof." I looked around the room. It was a standard entry hall, high-ceilinged, cream-colored, with a stained-glass window shedding colored light across a threadbare, once-fine rug, picking up highlights on a marble-topped table in need of dusting, twinkling in the cut-glass pendants of a rather nice Victorian chandelier. A wide, carpeted stairway led up to a sunlit landing with another stained-glass panel. A wide, arched opening to the left gave a view of a heavy table with pots of wax flowers and an open book with a pen and inkpot beside it. There were rows of shelves sagging under rows of dusty books, uncomfortable looking horsehair chairs and sofas, a fireplace with tools under a mantel on which china gimcracks were arranged in an uneven row.

"Looks like Maxoni went in for bourgeois luxury in a large way, once he got onto the buggy-whip boom," I commented. "I wonder where the lab is?"

Olivia and I wandered around the room, smelling the odor of age and dust and furniture polish. I glanced over a few of the titles on the shelves.

Experiments with Alternating Currents of High Potential and High Frequency by Nikola Tesla caught my eye, and a slim pamphlet by Marconi. Otherwise the collection seemed to consist of good, solid Victorian novels and bound volumes of sermons. No help here.

The dragon came back, looking grotesque in a house-coat of electric green—a tribute to Maxoni's field of research, no doubt. A layer of caked-looking makeup had been hastily slapped across her face, and a rose-bud mouth drawn on by a shaky hand. She laced her fingers together, did a curtsey like a trained elephant, gushed at Olivia, who inclined her head an eighth of an inch and showed a frosty smile. This example of aristocratic snobbishness delighted the old girl; she beamed so hard I thought the makeup was going to crack like plaster in an earthquake. A wave of an economical perfume rolled over me like a dust storm.

"Her Grace wishes to see the laboratories where Maxoni did his great work," I announced, fanning. "You may show us there at once."

She shouldered in ahead of me to get a spot nearer the duchess and with much waving of ringed hands and trailing of fringes, conducted us along a narrow hall beside the staircase, through a door into a weedy garden, along a walk to a padlocked shed, chattering away the whole time.

"Of course, the workrooms are not yet fully restored," she uttered, hauling a key from a baggy pocket. She got the lock open, stopped as she groped inside, grunted as she found the light switch. A yellowish glow sprang up. Olivia and I stared in at dust, lumpy shapes covered with tarpaulines, dust, heaped cartons, dust, grimed windows, and more dust.

"He worked *here*?"

"Of course it was not so cluttered then. We're short of funds, you see, your Grace," she got the sell in. "We haven't yet been able to go through the items here and catalogue them, dispose of the worthless things, and restore the laboratory to its original condition. . . " She chattered on, unabashed by Olivia's silence. I poked around, trying to look casual, but feeling far from calm. It was in this shed—or a near facsimile—that Maxoni had first made the breakthrough that had opened the worlds of alternate reality. Somewhere here, there might be . . . something. I didn't know what I was looking for: a journal, a working model not quite perfected . . .

I lifted the corner of the dust cover over a heaped table, glanced at the assortment of ancient odds and ends: awkward, heavy-looking transformers, primitive vacuum tubes, bits of wire—

A massive object at the center of the table caught my eye. I lifted the cover, reached for it, dragged it to me.

"Really, sir, I must insist that you disturb nothing!" my guardian hippo brayed in my ear. I jumped, let the tarp fall; dust whoofed into the air. "This is just as the professor left it, that last, fatal day."

"Sorry," I said, holding my face in what I hoped was a bland expression. "Looks like a collection of old iron to me."

"Yes, Professor Maxoni was a bit eccentric. He saved all sorts of odd bits and pieces—and he was forever trying to fit them together. He'd had a dream, he used to tell my departed Papa—when he was alive, of course—the professor, I mean—and Papa too, of course—"

"Your father worked for Maxoni?"

"Didn't you know? Oh, yes, he was his assistant, for ever so many years. Many's the anecdote he could tell of the great man—"

"I don't suppose he's still living?"

"Papa? Dear Papa passed to his reward forty-three—or is it forty-four . . .?"

"He didn't leave a journal, I suppose—filled with jolly reminiscenses of the professor?"

"No—Papa wasn't what you'd call a lit'ry man." She paused. "Of course, the professor himself was most diligent about his journal. Five big volumes. It's one of the great tragedies of the Society that we've not yet had sufficient funds to publish."

"Funds may yet be forthcoming, Madam," I said solemnly. "The Contessa is particularly interested in publishing just such journals as you describe."

"Oh!" The painted-on mouth made a lopsided O to match the exclamation. "Your Grace—"

"So if you'd just fetch it along, so that her Grace can glance over it . . ." I left the suggestion hanging.

"It's in the safe, sir—but I have the key—I know I have

the key, somewhere. I had it only last year—or was it the year before . . .?"

"Find it, my good woman," I urged. "Her Grace and I will wait patiently here, thrilling to the thought that it was in this very room that the professor developed his galvanic buggy-whip."

"Oh, no, that was before he took this house—"

"No matter; the journals, please."

"Wouldn't you rather come back inside? The dust here—"

"As I said, we're thrilling to it. Hurry back. . . ." I waved her through the door. Olivia looked at me questioningly.

"I've sent her off to find Maxoni's journals," I said. She must have noticed something in my voice.

"Brion, what is it?"

I stepped to the table, threw back the cover. The heavy assembly I had moved earlier dominated the scattering of articles around it.

"That," I said, letting the note of triumph come through, "is a Moebius-wound coil, the central component of the M-C drive. If I can't build a shuttle with that and the old boy's journals, I'll turn in my badge."

CHAPTER NINE

The workshop I rented was a twelve-by-twenty space under a loft opening off a narrow alleyway that wound from the Strada d' Allenzo to a side-branch of the Tiber, a trail that had probably been laid out by goats, back before Rome was big enough to call itself a town. The former occupant had been a mechanic of sorts. There were rusty pieces of steam-engine still lying in the corners, a few corroded hand tools resting among the dust-drifts on the sagging wall shelves at one side of the room, odds and ends of bolts and washers and metal shavings trodden into the oil-black, hard-as-concrete dirt floor. The old fellow who leased the premises to me had grumblingly cleared away the worst of the rubbish, and installed a large, battered metal-topped table. This, plus the Moebius coil, which I had bribed the Keeper of the Flame into letting me borrow, and the journals, constituted my lab equipment. Not much to start moving worlds with—but still, a start.

Olivia had gotten us rooms nearby, cheaper and better quarters than the Albergo Romulus. There was a small hot plate in her room, charcoal-fired; we agreed to husband our meager funds by having two meals a day in, and the other at one of the small neighborhood pasta palaces where the carafes of wine were put on the table as automatically as salt and pepper back home.

I started my research program by reading straight through all five journals, most of which were devoted to bitter comments on the current political situation—the capital had just been moved to Rome from Florence, and it was driving prices up—notes on some seemingly pointless researchers into magnetism, the details of a

114

rather complicated but strictly Platonic affair with a Signora C., and worried budgetary computations that enlisted my fullest sympathy.

Only in the last volume did I start to strike interesting passages—the first, tentative hints of the Big Secret. Maxoni had been experimenting with coils; winding them, passing various types and amounts of electric current through them, and attempting to detect results. If he'd known more modern physics, he'd never have bothered, but in his ignorance, he persevered. Like Edison trying everything from horsehair to bamboo splints as filaments for his incandescent bulb, Maxoni doggedly tried, tested, noted results, and tried again. It was the purest of pure research. He didn't know what he was looking for—and when he found it, he didn't know what it was—at least not in this world. Of course, there had been no Cocini here. I didn't know what the latter's role had been back in the Zero-zero world line. It would be an interesting piece of reading for me when I got back—if I got back—if there were any place to get back to—

I let that line of thought die. It wasn't getting me anywhere. The last volume of the journal yielded up its secrets, such as they were—a few scattered and fragmentary mentions of the coil-winding, and a line or two regarding strange manifestations obtained with the goldleaf electroscope when certain trickle currents were used.

A week had gone by, and I was ready to start the experimental phase. There were a few electrical supply houses in the city, mostly purveyors to the Universities and research institutes; electricity was far from the Reddy Kilowatt state in this world. I laid in a variety of storage batteries, oscillators, coils, condensers, vacuum tubes as big and clumsy as milk bottles, plus whatever else looked potentially useful. Then, at Olivia's suggestion, I let her mesmerize me, take notes as I repeated everything my subconscious had retained of the training I'd had in Net Shuttle technology—which turned out to be twice as valuable as Maxoni's notes.

They were pleasant days. I rose early, joined Olivia for breakfast, walked the two blocks to the shop, and toiled until lunch, recording my results in a book not much different from the ones Maxoni had used a century earlier. This was not a world of rapid change.

Olivia would come by at noon or a little after, looking fresh and cool, and healthier now, with the Roman sun giving her face the color it had lacked back in Harrow. The basket on her arm would produce sandwiches, pizzas, fruit, a bottle of wine. I had a couple of chairs by this time, and we'd spread our lunch on the corner of my formidable workbench, with the enigmatic bulk of the coil lying before us like some jealous idol in need of placating.

Then an afternoon of cut and fit and note, with curious passersby pausing at the open door to look in and offer polite greetings and shy questionings. By the time a month had passed, I was deferred to by all the local denizens as a mad foreigner with more than a suggestion of the sorcerer about him. But they were friendly, often dropping off a casual gift of a bottle or a salami or a wedge of pungent cheese, with a flourish of Roman compliments. Each evening, by the time the sun had dropped behind the crooked skyline across the way, and the shop had faded into deep shadow hardly relieved by the single feeble lamp I had strung up, my eyes would be blurring, my head ringing, my legs aching from the hours of standing hunched over the table. I would solemnly close the door, attach the heavy padlock, ignoring the fact that the door was nothing but a few thin boards hung from a pair of rusted hinges held in place by bent nails. Then walk home past the shops and stalls, their owners busy closing up now, up the stairs to the flat for a quick bath in the rust-stained tub down the hall, then out with Olivia to the evening's treat. Sitting at the wobbly tables on the tile floors, often on a narrow terrace crowded beside a busy street, we talked, watched the people and the night sky, then went back to part at the flat door—she to her room, I to mine. It was a curious relationship, perhaps—though at the time, it seemed perfectly natural. We were coconspirators, engaged in a strange quest, half-detectives, half-researchers, set apart from the noisy, workaday crowd all around us by the fantastic nature of the wildly impractical quest we were embarked on. She, for reasons of romantic fulfillment, and I, driven by a compulsion to tear through the intangible prison walls that had been dropped around me.

My estimate of Olivia's age had been steadily revised downward. At first, in the initial shock of seeing Mother Goodwill unmasked, I had mentally assigned her a virginal fortyishness. Later, bedizened in her harlot's finery—and enjoying every minute of the masquerade—she had seemed younger; perhaps thirty-five, I had decided. Now, with the paint scrubbed away, her hair cut and worn in a casual Roman style, her complexion warm and glowing from the sun and the walks, her figure as fine as ever in the neat, inexpensive clothes she had bought in the modest shops near our flat, I realized with a start one day, watching her scatter bread crumbs for the pigeons behind the shop and laughing at their clumsy waddle, that she was no more than in her middle twenties.

She looked up and caught me staring at her.

"You're a beautiful girl, Olivia," I said—in a wondering tone, I'm afraid. "What ever got you off on that Mombi kick?"

She looked startled, then smiled—a merrier expression than the Lady Sad-eyes look she used to favor.

"You've guessed it," she said, sounding mischievous. "The old witch in the *Sorceress of Oz*—"

"Yes, but *why?*"

"I told you: my business. Who'd patronize a Wise Woman without warts on her chin?"

"Sure—but why haven't you married?" I started to deliver the old saw about there being plenty of nice young men, but the look on her face saved me from that banality.

"Okay, none of my business," I said quickly. "I didn't mean to get personal, Olivia . . ." I trailed off, and we finished our walk in a silence which, if not grim, was certainly far from companionable.

Three weeks more, and I had assembled a formidable compilation of data—enough, I told Olivia when she came to the shop at ten P.M. to see what had kept me, to warrant starting construction of the secondary circuits—the portion of the shuttle mechanism with which I was most familiar.

"The big job," I said, "was to calibrate the coil—find out what kind of power supply it called for, what sort of field strength it developed. That part's done. Now all I have to do is set up the amplifying and focussing apparatus—"

"You make it sound so simple, Brion—and so safe."

"I'm trying to convince myself," I admitted. "It's a long way from simple. It's a matter of trying to equate a complicated assemblage of intangible forces; a little bit like balancing a teacup on a stream of water, except that I have a couple of dozen teacups, and a whole fire department's worth of waterworks—and if I threw full power to the thing without the proper controls . . ."

"Then what?"

"Then I'd set up an irreversible cataclysm—of any one of a hundred possible varieties. A titanic explosion, that keeps on exploding: an uncontrolled eruption of matter from another continuum, like a volcano pouring out of the heart of a sun—or maybe an energy drain like Niagara, that would suck the heat away from this spot, freeze the city solid in a matter of minutes, put the whole planet under an ice cap in a month. Or—"

" 'Tis sufficient. I understand. These are fearsome forces you toy with, Brion."

"Don't worry—I won't pour the power into it until I know what I'm doing. There are ways of setting up auto-timed cutoffs for any test I run—and I'll be using trickle power for a long time yet. The disasters that made the Blight, happened because the Maxonis and Cocinis of those other A-lines weren't forewarned. They set her up and let her rip. The door to Hell has well-oiled hinges."

"How long—before you'll finish?"

"A few days. There isn't a hell of a lot to the shuttle. I'll build a simple box—out of pine slabs, if I have to—just something to keep me and the mechanism together. It'll be a big, clumsy setup, of course—not compact like the Imperial models—but it'll get me there, as long as the power flows. The drain isn't very great. A stack of these six volt cells will give me all the juice I need to get me home."

"And if the Xonijeel were right," she said softly, "if

the world you seek lies not where you expect—what then?"

"Then I'll run out of steam and drop into the Blight, and that'll be the end of another nut," I said harshly. "And a good thing too—if I imagined the whole Imperium—"

"I know you didn't, Brion. But if, somehow, something has . . . gone wrong. . . ."

"I'll worry about that when I get to it," I cut her off. I'd been plowing along, wrapping myself up in my occupational therapy. I wasn't ready yet to think about the thousand gloomy possibilities I'd have to face when I stepped into my crude makeshift and threw the switch.

It was three evenings later, and Olivia and I were sitting at a window table in one of our regular haunts, having a small glass of wine and listening to the gentle night sounds of a city without neon or internal combustion. She'd been coming by the shop for me every evening lately; a habit that I found myself looking forward to.

"It won't be long now," I told her. "You saw the box. Just bolted together out of wood, but good enough. The coil's installed. Tomorrow I'll lay out my control circuitry—"

"Brion . . ." her fingers were on my arm. "Look there!"

I twisted, caught a fleeting glimpse of a tall, dark figure in a long, full-skirted coat with the collar turned up, pushing past through the sparse pedestrian traffic.

"It was—him!" Olivia's voice was tight with strain.

"All right, maybe it was," I said soothingly. "Take it easy, girl. How sure are you—"

"I'm sure, Brion! The same terrible, dark face, the beard—"

"There are plenty of bearded men in Rome, Olivia—"

"We have to go—quickly!" She started to get up. I caught her hand, pulled her gently back.

"No use panicking. Did he see us?"

"I—think—I'm not sure," she finished. "I saw him, and turned my face away, but—"

"If he's seen us—if he *is* our boy—running won't help.

If he didn't see us, he won't be back."

"But if we hurried, Brion—we need not even stop at the flat to get our things! We can catch the train, be miles from Rome by daylight—"

"If we've been trailed here, we can be trailed to the next town. Besides which, there's the little matter of my shuttle. It's nearly done. Another day's work and a few tests—"

"Of what avail's the shuttle if they take you, Brion?"

I patted her hand. "Why should anyone want to take me? I was dumped here to get rid of me—"

"Brion, think you I'm some village goose to be coddled with this talk? We must act—now!"

I chewed my lip and thought about it. Olivia wasn't being soothed by my bland talk—any more than I was. I didn't know what kind of follow-up the Xonijeelian Web Police did on their deportees, but it was a cinch they wouldn't look kindly on my little home workshop project. The idea of planting me here had been to take me out of circulation. They'd back their play; Olivia was right about that. . . .

"All right." I got to my feet, dropped a coin on the table. Out in the street, I patted her hand.

"Now, you run along home, Olivia. I'll do a little snooping, just to satisfy myself that everything's okay. Then—"

"No. I'll stay with you."

"That's silly," I said. "If there *is* any rough stuff, you think I want you mixed up in it? Not that there will be. . . ."

"You have some madcap scheme in mind, Brion. What is it? Will you go back to the workshop?"

"I just want to check to make sure nobody's tampered with the shuttle."

Her face looked pale in the light of the carbide lamp at the corner.

"You think by hasty work to finish it—to risk your life—"

"I won't take any risks, Olivia—but I'm damned if I'm going to be stopped when I'm this close."

"You'll need help. I'm not unclever in such matters."

I shook my head. "Stay clear of this, Olivia. I'm the one they're interested in, but you could get hurt—"

"How close are you to finishing your work?"

"A few hours. Then some tests—"

"Then we'd best be starting. I sense danger close by this night. 'Twill not be long ere they close their noose.

I hesitated for just a moment, then took her hand. "I don't know what I've done to earn such loyalty," I said. "Come on, we've got work to do."

We went to the flat first, turned on lights, made coffee. Then, with the rooms darkened, took the back stairs, eased out into a cobbled alley. Half an hour later, after a circuitous trip which avoided main streets and well-lit corners, we reached the shop, slipped inside. Everything looked just as I'd left it an hour earlier: the six-foot-square box, its sides half-slabbed up with boards, the coil mounted at the center of the plank floor, the bright wire of my half-completed control circuits gleaming in the gloom. I lit a lamp, and we started to work.

Olivia was more than clever with her hands. I showed her just once how to attach wire to an insulator; from then on she was better at it than I was. The batteries required a mounting box; I nailed a crude frame together, fitted the cells in place, wired up a switch, made connections. Every half hour or so, Olivia would slip outside, make a quick reconnaissance—not that it would have helped much to discover any spy sneaking up on us. I couldn't quite deduce the pattern of their tactics—if any. If we had been spotted, surely the shop was under surveillance. Maybe they were just letting me finish before they closed in. Perhaps they were curious as to whether it was possible to do what I was trying to do with the materials and technology at hand. . . .

It was well after midnight when we finished. I made a final connection, ran a couple of circuit checks. If my research had been accurate, and my recollection of M-C theory correct, the thing *should* work. . . .

"It looks so . . . fragile, Brion." Olivia's eyes were dark in the dim light. My own eyeballs felt as though they'd been rolled in emery dust.

"It's fragile—but a moving shuttle is immune to any external influence. It's enclosed in a field that holds the air in, and everything else out. And it doesn't linger long enough in any one A-line for the external temperature or vacuum or what have you to affect it."

"Brion!" She took my arm fiercely. "Stay here! Risk not this frail device! 'Tis not too late to flee! Let the evil men search in vain! Somewhere we'll find a cottage, in some hamlet far from this scheming . . ."

My expression told her she wasn't reaching me. She stared into my eyes for a moment, then let her hand fall and stepped back.

"I was a fool to mingle dreams with drab reality," she said harshly. I saw her shoulders slump, the life go from her face. Almost, it was Mother Goodwill who stood before me.

"Olivia," I said harshly, "For God's sake—"

There was a sound from the door. I saw it tremble, and jumped for the light, flipped it off. In the silence, a foot grated on bricks. There was a sound of rusty hinges, and a lesser darkness widened as the door slid back. A tall, dark silhouette appeared in the opening.

"Bayard!" a voice said sharply in the darkness—an unmistakably Xonijeelian voice. I moved along the wall. The figure advanced. There was a crowbar somewhere near the door. I crouched, trying to will myself invisible, reached—and my fingers closed around the cold, rust-scaled metal. The intruder was two yards away now. I straightened, raised the heavy bar. He took another step, and I jumped, slammed the bar down solidly across the back of his head, saw a hat fly as he stumbled and fell on his face with a heavy crash.

"Brion!" Olivia shrieked.

"It's all right!" I tossed the bar aside, reached for her, put my arms around her.

"You have to understand, Olivia," I rasped. "There's more at stake here than anyone's dream. This is something I have to do. You have your life ahead. Live it—and forget me!"

"Let me go with you, Brion," she moaned.

"You know I can't. Too dangerous—and you'd halve my chances of finding the Zero-zero line before the air gives out." I thrust my wallet into her cloak pocket. "I have to go now." I pushed her gently from me.

"Almost . . . I hope it fails," Olivia's voice came through the dark. I went to the shuttle, lit the carbide running light, reached in and flipped the warm-up switch. From the shadows, I heard a groan from the creature I had stunned.

"You'd better go now, Olivia," I called. "Get as far away as you can. Go to Louisiana, start over—forget the Mother Goodwill routine. . . ."

The hum was building now—the song of the tortured molecules as the field built, twisting space, warping time, creating its tiny bubble of impossible tension in the massive fabric of reality.

"Goodby, Olivia. . . ." I climbed inside the fragile box peered at the makeshift panel. The field strength meter told me that the time had come. I grasped the drive lever and threw it in.

CHAPTER TEN

There was a wrenching sensation, a sputter of arcing current through untried circuits. Then the walls flicked from view around me, and I was looking out on the naked devastation of the Blight. No need for viewscreens here. The foot-wide gaps between the rough slats gave me a panoramic view of a plain of rubble glowing softly under the light of the moon; a view that shifted and flowed as I watched, blackening into burned ruins, slumping gradually into a lava-like expanse of melted and hardened masonry and steel.

I unclenched my fists, tried a breath. Everything seemed all right. I was riding an egg crate across Hell, but the field was holding, leashed by the mathemetical matrices embodied in a few hundred strands of wire strung just so from nail to nail around my wooden cage. The massive Moebius coil bolted to the floor vibrated nervously. I made an effort to relax; I had a long ride ahead.

My half-dozen jury-rigged instruments were obediently giving readings. I looked at the trembling needles and tried to think about what they represented. The only map I had was a fuzzy recollection of the photogram the Xonijeelians had showed me. If this *was* a fourth island in the Blight—and I had already decided not to question that assumption—then I was driving in what ought to be close to the correct "direction." Navigation in the Net depended on orientation with an arbitrary set of values—measurements of the strength of three of the seemingly infinite number of "fields" which were a normal part of the multiordinal continua. A reading of any three of these values should give a location. Noting the progressive changes in the inter-relation of the values provided a pilot across the Net—maybe. There was the little matter of calibrating my instruments, estimating my A-entropic velocity, testing my crude controls to see how much steering I could do, and determining how to bring the shuttle into identity square on target when and if I had a target—and all of this before the air became too foul to breathe. There was no problem of food, water, or a place to sleep: I'd be dead long before any such luxuries became necessary.

My first rough approximation from the data on the dials told me that I was moving along a vector at least 150 degrees off the calculated one. I made a cautious adjustment to one of my crude rheostats, winced as the sparks flew, watched the dials to see the results.

They weren't good. Either I was misinterpreting my readings, or my controls were even worse than I'd thought. I scribbled down figures, made some hasty interpolations, and came up with the discovery that I was blasting along at three times my calculated Net velocity, on a course that seemed to be varying progressively. My hastily rigged untested circuitry was badly out of balance—not far enough out to spill the leashed entropic force in a torrent of destruction, but too far out to be soothing.

I made another haphazard adjustment, checked readings. The needles wavered, one back-tracking down the scale, two others moving steadily upward. I made a herculean effort to recall all I'd ever known about emergency navigation, and concluded that I had described most of a full circle and was now headed back in the opposite direction. There wasn't much play left in my controls. I pushed the lever which served as rudder all the way to the left, watched as instruments responded—not enough.

Another ten minutes passed. My watch was ticking away, measuring off some unimaginable quality in my timeless, headlong plunge across the alternate realities. It was like the tooth-gritting wait while the lab technician probes around with his needle, looking for a vein. One second seemed to last forever.

Another reading. No doubt about it now, I was following a roughly spiral course—whether descending or ascending, I couldn't tell. The control circuits were sparking continuously; the stresses induced by the unnatural entropic loads were rapidly overheating the inadequate wiring. A junction box tacked to a two-by-four was glowing a dull red, and the wood under it was smoking, turning black. As I watched, pale flames licked, caught, ran up the wood. I pulled off my jacket, slapped at the fire uselessly. A wire melted through, dropped, spattered fire as it crossed other naked wires, then hung, welded into a new position.

For a heart-stopping instant, I braced myself for the lurching drop into identity with the towering pillars of fire thundering silently outside—then realized that, miraculously, the shuttle was still moving. I rubbed smoke-stung eyes, checked dials; the coarse had changed sharply. I tried to reconstruct the erratic path I had taken, work out a dead reckoning of my position. It was hopeless. I could be anywhere.

The scene beyond the shuttle walls was strange, not like anything I remembered from Blight exploration films I'd seen. A row of steep-sided black cones stretched away to the horizon, each glowing dull red about its crater rim, over which continuous wellings of lava spilled, while vast bubbles burst, sending up dense belches of brown smoke that formed a cloud obscuring the moon. Here, it appeared, a new fault-line had been created in the planet's crust, along which volcanoes sprouted like weeds in a new-ploughed field.

I had been on my way for about forty minutes now. With a pang of homesickness I pictured Olivia, back at the flat, alone. Suddenly I was remembering the days, the evenings we'd spent together, her unfailing spirit, her gentle touch, the line of her throat and cheek as we sat at a table, raising glasses in the long Roman twilight. . . .

I had had everything there a man needed for a good life. Maybe I'd been a fool to exchange it for this—a doomed ride on a hell-bound train to nowhere. Maybe. But there hadn't really been any choice. There were things in life a man had to do, or the savor was gone forever.

I was lost now, that was clear enough. For the last hour the shuttle had been charging across the continua blindly, describing an erratic course which varied every time a connection fused and created a new pattern in the control circuits. The post was still smouldering and smoking.

I had stretched out on the floor some time earlier, trying to find cleaner air. It was about gone now. I coughed with every breath, and my head kept up a steady humming, like a wornout transformer. I was picking up some interesting observations on the effects of modifying shuttle circuitry at full gallop—and observing some new country, never before explored by our Net Scouts—but the chances of my surviving to use it were dwindling with each passing minute. I had scratched a few lines of calculations on the floor with a fragment of charred wood. At the rate I was moving, I was deep in the Blight by now. Outside the ruined worlds flowed past, a panorama of doomsdays. The volcanoes were gone, shrunken to fiery pits that sparked and hurled fountains of fire into the black sky. I blinked, peering through shrouding mists of steam and smoke. Far away, a line of dark hills showed—new hills, created by the upheavals of this world's crust. The smoke thinned for a moment, gave me a clearer glimpse of the distant landscape—

Was that a hint of green? I rubbed at my eyes, stared some more. The hills, dim in the moonlight, seemed to show a covering of plant life. The nearby fire pits seemed quieter now, stilling to glowing pools of molten lava, glazing over into dullness. And there—!! A scraggly bush, poking up at the rim of a crater—and another . . .

I drew a breath, coughed, got to hands and knees. The glow was fading from the scene. Unmistakable pinpoints of bright green were showing up everywhere. A shoot poked through the back soil, rose, twisted, unfurled a frond, shot up higher, extending leaf after leaf, in a speeded-up motion-picture sequence of growth, each frame a glimpse of a different A-line, varying by a trifle from the next, creating a continuous drama of change—a change toward life.

In its erratic wandering, it appeared, the shuttle had

turned back toward the edge of the Blight. I watched, saw new shoots appear, spring up, evolve into great tree-ferns, giant cattails, towering palm-like trunks, along whose concrete-grey surfaces vines crept like small snakes, to burgeon suddenly, embrace the vast tree in a smothering outburst of green, clamber over the crown, then sink down as the tree died and fell, only to turn on themselves, mound high, reach, capture a new host . . .

A jungle grew around me, nourished in the volcanic soil. Orchids as big as dinner plates burst like popcorn, dropped, were replaced by others as big as washtubs. In the bright moonlight, I saw a flicker of motion—a new kind of motion. A moth appeared, a bright speck, grew until he was two feet across. Then the vast flower on which he perched closed over him in a frantic flurry of gorgeous wings and flamboyant petals.

Nearby, a wall of foliage bulged, burst outward. A head thrust through—gaping jaws like those of an immense rat closed on vines that coiled, choking. . . . The head changed, developed armor which grew out, blade-like, slicing through the ropes of living plant-fiber. Juice oozed, spilled; thorns budded, grew hungrily toward the animal, reached the furred throat—and recoiled, blunted, from armored hide. Then new leaves unfolded, reached to enfold the head, wrapping it in smothering folds of leathery green. It twisted, fought, tearing free only to be entoiled again, sinking down now, gone in a surging sea of green.

I coughed, choked, got to my feet, reached for the control panel—missed, and fell. The crack on the head helped for a moment. I tried to breathe, got only smoke. It was now or never. The worlds outside were far from inviting, but there was nothing for me in the shuttle but death by asphyxiation. I could drop into identity, make hasty repairs, study the data I had collected, decide where I was, and try again. . . .

Back to hands ane knees; a grip on a board; on my feet now, reaching for the switch, find it in the choking smoke, pull—

There was a shock, a whirling, then a blow that sent me flying against shattering boards, into rubbery foliage and a gush of fresh air. . . .

I finished coughing, extricated myself from the bed of vines I found myself in, half expecting to see them reach for me; fortunately, however, the strange cause-and-effect sequences of E-entropy didn't apply here, in normal time.

In the gloom, I made out the shape of the flimsy box that had brought me here. It was canted against a giant tree trunk, smashed into a heap of scrap lumber. Smoke was boiling from under the heaped boards, and bright flames showed, starting along a wrist-thick vine, casting flickering lights and shadows on surrounding trees and underbrush. There was a board under my foot, still trailing a festoon of wires. I grabbed it up, struggled through to the fire, beat at the flames. It was a mistake—the bruised stems oozed an inflammable sap which caught with bright poppings and cracklings. The main chassis of the broken shuttle was too heavy for me to try to drag back from the blaze. I tried to reach the coil, with some vague idea of salvage, but the fire was burning briskly now. The dry wood flamed up, sending fire high along the tree trunk, igniting more vines. Five minutes later, from a distance of a hundred yards, I watched a first-class forest fire getting underway.

The rain started then, too late to salvage anything from the shuttle, but soon enough to save the forest. I found shelter of sorts under a wide-leafed bush, listened for awhile to the drumming of the rain, then sank into exhausted sleep.

Morning dawned grey, wet, chilly, with water dripping from a billion leaves all around me. I crawled out, checked over assorted bruises, found everything more or less intact. I still had a slight rawness in the throat from the smoke, and somewhere I'd gotten a nice blister on the heel of my left hand, but that seemed a modest toll for the trip I had had.

The fire had burned out a ragged oval about a hundred feet across. I walked across the black stubble to the remains of the shuttle, surveyed the curled and charred boards, the blackened lump that had been the coil. The last, faint hope flickered and died. I was stranded for good, this time, with no handy museum to help me out.

There was a vague sensation in my belly that I recognized as hunger. I had a lot of thinking to do, some vain regrets to entertain, and a full quota of gloomy reflections on what was happening now back in the Imperial capital. But first, I had to have food—and, if my sketchy knowledge of jungles was any guide, a shelter of some sort against other inhabitants of the region that might consider me to be in that category.

And even before food, I needed a weapon. A bow and arrow would be nice, but it would take time to find a suitable wood, and I'd have to kill something for gut for the string. A spear or club was about all I'd be able to manage in my present state of technological poverty. And even for those, I'd need some sort of cutting edge—which brought me back to the stone age in two easy steps.

The ground had a slight slope to what I suspected was the east. I pushed my way through the thick growth—not as jungle-like as what I'd seen from the shuttle minutes before my crash landing, but not a nice picnicky sort of New English wood either. I kept to the down-slope, stopping now and then to listen for gurgling streams or growling bears. The Boy Scout lore paid off. I broke through into a swampy crescent hugging a mud flat, with a meandering current at its center, fifty feet distant. Tight-packed greenery hung over the far side of the watercourse, which curved away around a spit of more grey mud. There were no stones in sight. Still, there was plenty of clay—good for pottery making, perhaps. I squatted, dipped up a sample. It was thin and sandy muck—useless.

There was ample room to walk beside the stream. I followed the course for several hundred yards, found a stretch of higher ground where the water came close to a bank of grassy soil. This would make as good a campsite as any. I pulled off my shoes, eased over the edge into the water, sluiced the worst of the soot and mud from myself and clothes. Turning back, I noticed a stratum of clean yellowish clay in the bank. It was the real stuff: smooth, pliable, almost greasy in texture. All I needed was a nice fire to harden it, and over which to cook my roasts, chops, fish fillets, et cetera—as soon as I had acquired the latter, using the weapons I would make as soon as I had an axe and a knife. . . .

It was almost sunset. The day's efforts had netted me one lump of flint, which I had succeeded in shattering into a hand axe and a couple of slicing edges that any decent flint worker would have tossed into the discard pile for archaeologists to quarrel over a few thousand years later. Still, they had sufficed to hack off two twelve-foot lengths of tough, springly sapling, remove the twigs and leaves, and sharpen the small ends to approximate points. I had also gathered a few handfuls of small blackberry-like fruits which were now giving me severe stomach pains, and several pounds of the pottery clay which I had shaped into crude bowls and set aside for air drying.

The skies had cleared off in the afternoon, and I had built a simple shelter of branches and large leaves, and dragged in enough nearly-dry grass for a bed of sorts. And using a strip of cloth torn from my shirt, I had made a small fire-bow. With a supply of dry punk from the interior of a rotted tree, and a more or less smooth stone with a suitable hollow, I was now preparing to make a fire. My hardwood stick was less hard than I would have liked, and the bow was a clumsy makeshift, but it was better than just sitting and thinking. I crumbled the wood powder in the hollow, placed the pointed end of the stick against it with the bow string wrapped around it, and started in.

Ten minutes later, with the bow twice broken and replaced, the stick dulled, and the punk and my temper both exhausted, I gave it up for the night, crawled into my cosy shelter. Two minutes later, a bellow like a charging elephant brought me bolt upright, groping for a gun that wasn't there. I waited, heard a heavy body crashing through underbrush nearby, then the annoyed growl that went with the kind of appetite that preferred meat. There were a number of large trees in the vicinity. I found one in the dark with amazing speed and climbed it, losing a trifling few square feet of skin in the process.

I wedged myself in a high crotch and listened to stealthy footsteps padding under my perch until dawn.

I found the tracks the next morning when I half-climbed, half-fell from the tree. They were deeply imprinted, too big to cover with my spread fingers, not counting the claws—on the prints, that is. Some kind of cat, I guessed. Down at the water's edge were more tracks: big hoof-marks the size of saucers. They grew 'em big in these parts. All I had to do was bag one, and I'd have meat for as long as I could stand the smell.

I was getting really hungry now. Following the stream, I covered several miles to the south, gradually working my way into more open country. There were plenty of signs of game, including the bare bones of something not quite as big as a London bus, with condor-like birds picking over them half-heartedly. I had my two spears and my stone fragments, and I was hoping to spot something of a size and ferocity appropriate to my resources—say a half-grown rabbit.

There was a sudden rattle of wings just in front of me, and a grousey-looking bird as big as a turkey took to the air. I advanced cautiously, found a nest with four eggs in it, speckled brown, three inches long. I squatted right there and ate one, and enjoyed every scrap. It would have been nice to have scrambled it but that was a minor consideration. The other three I distributed in various pockets, then went on, feeling a little better.

The country here was higher, with less underbrush and more normal-looking trees in place of the swampy jungle growth I'd started from. During high water, I imagined, the whole area where the shuttle lay would be submerged. Now I had a better view, off through the open forest, to what seemed like a prairie to the south. That's where the game would be.

Another half hour's walk brought me to the edge of a vast savannah that reminded me of pictures I'd seen of Africa, with immense herds grazing under scattered thorn trees. Here the trees were tall hardwoods, growing in clumps along the banks of the stream—and the animals were enough to make any zoo-keeper turn in his badge and start keeping white mice. I saw bison, eight feet at the shoulder; massive, tusked almostelephants with bright pink trunks and pendulous lower lips; deer in infinite variety; and horses built like short-necked giraffes, ten feet high at the shoulder with sloping withers. There they were—and all I had to do was to stick them with my spear.

There was a low snort from somewhere behind me. I whirled, saw a head the size of a rhino's, set with two rows of huge, needlesharp teeth in a mouth that gaped to give me a view of a throat like the intake duct on a jet fighter. There was a body behind the head—ten feet or more of massively muscled tawny cat, with a hint of mane, faint stripes across the flanks, snow white throat, belly and feet. I took all these details in as the mighty carnivore looked me over, yawned, and paced majestically toward me, frowning across at the distant herds like a troubled politician wondering who to pay the bribe to.

He passed me up at a distance of thirty feet, moved out into the area, head high now, looking over the menu. None of the animals stirred. King Cat kept on, bypassed a small group of mastodons who rolled their eyes, switching their trunks nervously. He had his eye on the bison, among whom were a number of cuddly calves weighing no more than a ton. They moved restlessly now, forming up a defensive circle, like the musk-ox of the Arctic. The hunter changed his course, angling to the left. Maybe he was thinking better of it—

With the suddenness of thought, he was running streaking across the grass in thirty-foot bounds, leaping now clear over the front rank of tossing horns to disappear as the herd exploded outward in all directions. Then he reappeared, standing over the body of a calf, one paw resting affectionately on the huddled tan corpse. The herd stampeded a short distance, resumed feeding. I let out a long breath. *That* was a hunter.

I jumped at a sound, spun, my hand with my trusty spear coming up automatically—

A brown rabbit the size of a goat stood poised on wiry legs, snuffling the air, showing long yellow rat-teeth. I brought the spear back, threw, saw it catch the creature in mid-leap as he whirled to flee, knocking him head over long white heels. I came pounding up, swung the second spear like a farmer's wife killing a snake, and laid him low.

Breathing hard, I gingerly picked up the bloody carcass, noting the gouge my spear had made. I looked around for a place to hole up and feast. Something black moved on my arm. A flea! I dropped the rabbit, captured the parasite, cracked him with a satisfying report. There were plenty more where that one came from, I saw, stirring around in the sparse hair on the foot-long ears. Suddenly I didn't want raw rabbit—or overgrown rat—for lunch.

As suddenly as that, the adrenalin I'd been getting by on for the past thirty-six hours drained away, left me a hungry, sick battered castaway, stranded in a hell-world of raw savagery, an unimaginable distance from a home which I knew I'd never see again. I had been bumbling along from one fiasco to the next, occupying my mind with the trivial, unwilling to face reality: the chilling fact that my life would end, here, in solitude and misery, in pain and fear—and that before many more hours had passed.

I lay under a tree, staring up at the sky, resting—I told myself—or waiting for another cat, less choosy, to happen along. I had had my chances—more than one—and I'd muffed them all. I'd gotten away clean in the Hagroon shuttle—then let it carry me helplessly along to their den-city, permitted myself to be captured without a struggle, thinking I'd learn something from the gorilla men. And after a combination of the enemy's stupidity and my luck had given me a new chance, a new shuttle—I'd guessed wrong again, let Dzok beguile me along to be sentenced to life in exile. And a third time—after my wild guesses had paid off—I had panicked, run from the enemy without waiting to test my homebuilt shuttle—and ended here. Each time I had made what seemed like the only possible choice—and each time I'd gotten farther from my starting point. Not farther in terms of Net distance, perhaps, but infinitely farther from any hope of rescue—to say nothing of my hope of warning the Imperial authorities of what was afoot.

I got to my feet, started back toward where I'd left the

wreckage of the shuttle, with some half-formed idea of
searching through the wreckage again—for what, I
didn't know. It was the blind instinct of one who had
absorbed all the disaster he can for a while, and who
substitutes aimless action for the agony of thought.

It was harder now, plodding back over the ground I'd
already covered. Following the course of the river, I
passed the huge skeleton—abandoned now by the
birds—reached the mud flat where the trampled
remains of my crude hut gave a clear indication of the
inadequacies of my choice of campsites.

I had an idea of sorts then. Back at the shuttle there
was a lump of metal—the remains of the original
Maxoni coil. I might be able to use the material in some
way—pound it out into spear-heads, or make a flint-and-
steel for fire starting purposes. . . .

The impulse died. My stomach ached, and I was tired.
I wanted to go home now, have a nice hot bath, crawl
into bed, and be joined there by someone soft and
perfumed and cuddly who'd smooth my fevered brow
and tell me what a hell of a guy I was. . . .

It was easy to see the mechanics of schizophrenia at
work here. From wishing, it was an easy jump to
believing. I took a couple of deep breaths, straightened
my back, and headed for the burn site. I'd try to retain
my grip on reality a little longer. When it got
unbearable, I knew the sanctuary of insanity would be
waiting.

There were animal tracks across the blackened
ground, hoof marks, paw prints, and—

I bent over, squinting to be sure. Footprints, human,
or near enough. I knew how Robinson Crusoe had felt;
the evidence of a fellow man gave me a sudden feeling of
exposure along my backbone. I made it to the
surrounding unburned wall of jungle in three jumps,
slid down flat on the ground, and scanned the landscape.
I tried to tell myself that this was a lucky break, the first
real hope I'd had—but an instinct older than theories of
the Brotherhood of Man told me that I had encountered
the world's most deadly predator. The fact that we
might be of the same species just meant competition for
the same hunting ground.

My spear wasn't a handy weapon, and my skill with it wasn't anything to strike a medal in praise of. I checked my pocket for one of my stones, found a smashed egg. For a moment, the ludicrousness of the situation threatened to start me snickering. Then I heard a sound from nearby—in what direction, I wasn't sure. I eased back, rose up far enough to scan the woods behind me. I saw nothing. I tried to think the situation through. If I was right—if it was a man who'd visited here—it was important to establish contact. Even a primitive would have some sort of culture—food, fire, garments of sorts, shelter. I had skills: pottery making, basket weaving, the principle of the bow. We could work out something, perhaps—but only if I survived the first meeting.

I heard the sound again, saw a deer-like creature making its way across the burn. I let out a breath I didn't know I'd been holding. There was no way of knowing how long ago the man prints had been made. Still, I couldn't lie here forever. I emerged, made a quick check of the burned-out shuttle. Everything was as I'd left it.

I took another look at the footprints. They seemed to be made not by a bare foot, but by a flat sandal of some sort. They came across the burn, circled the shuttle, went away again. On the latter portion of the trail, they clearly overlay my own booted prints. Whoever my visitor had been, he was following me—or had started out on my trail. It was a thought that did nothing for my peace of mind.

I tried to calm the instinct that told me to get as far from the spot as possible. I needed to meet this fellow—and on terms that I could control. I didn't want to kill him, of course—but neither did I want to try the palm outward "I friend" routine. That left—capture.

It was risky business, working out in the open. But then being alive was a risky business. If the man tracking me had followed my trail, then lost it somewhere on the high ground, it might be a matter of many hours before he came back here to cast about again—and I was sure, for some reason, that he'd do that. And when he did—

I had been working hard for two hours now, setting up

my snare. It wasn't fancy, and if my proposed captive were any kind of woodsman—which he had to be, to survive here—it wouldn't fool him for a moment. Still, it was action of a sort—occupational therapy, maybe, but better than hiding under a bush and waiting—and it was helpful to my morale to imagine that I was taking the initiative.

The arrangement consisted of a shallow pit excavated in the soft soil, covered over with a light framework of twigs and leaves, and camouflaged with a scattering of blackened soil. I had done the digging with my bare hands, helped out by a board from the wreck, and the dirt had been heaped under the brush, out of sight behind the wall of foliage. The hole was no more than four feet deep, but that was sufficient for my purpose—to throw the intruder off-balance, and give me the drop on him sufficiently to open negotiations.

I was hungry enough now to scrape one of the smashed eggs from the lining of my pocket and eat it. But first I had to select my hiding place and get ready to act when the victim stepped into the trap. I picked a spot off to the left, arranged myself so as to be able to jump out at the psychological moment, and settled down to wait.

The pit was dug just in front of the wreckage, at the point where the opening to the interior would lead an inquisitive victim. I had dropped a lacy-edged hanky just inside the opening as an added attraction. It was one Olivia had lent me to mop my forehead during that last all-night session, and it still held a whiff of a perfume that would attract a primitive more surely than a scattering of gold coins. I had done all I could. The next step was up to the opposition.

I awoke from a light doze to see that it was late evening. The trees were black lacework against a red-gold sky, and the chirruping of crickets and the shrill *tseet! tseet!* of a bird were the only sounds against an absolute stillness—

And then the crackle of underbrush, the snap of broken twigs, the sound of heavy breathing. . . . I froze, trying to see through the gloom. He was coming. Hell, he was here! And making no effort at stealth. He was sure of himself, this native—which probably meant that here in his own stamping ground he was top carnivore. I tried to picture the kind of man who could stand up to the King Cat I'd seen, and gave it up as too discouraging. And this was the fellow I was going to trip up and then threaten with a broom handle. . . .

I swallowed the old corn husks that had gotten wedged in my throat, squinted some more. I made out a tall figure coming across the burned ground, stooping, apparently peering around—looking for me, no doubt. The thought gave me no comfort. I couldn't see what kind of weapon he had. I gripped my spear, tried to hold my breathing to a deep, slow rhythm. He was close now, pausing to glance over the shuttle, then turning toward the entrance hold. The handkerchief would be visible in the dim light, and the scent. . . . He took a step, another. He was close now, a vague, dark shape in deep shadow—

There was a choked yell, a crashing, a thud, and I was out of my hidey-hole, stumbling across a tangle of roots, bringing my spear up, skidding to a halt before the pale torso and dark head of the man who struggled, scrabbling for a handhold, hip deep in my trap.

"Hold it right there!" I barked through clenched teeth, holding the spear ready with both hands, poised over the man who stood frozen now, a narrow-shouldered, long-armed figure, his face a dark blob under a white headpiece—

"I say, Bayard," Dzok's voice came. "You've led me a merry chase, I must say!"

CHAPTER ELEVEN

"It wasn't easy, old boy," Dzok said, offering me a second cup of a coffee-like drink he had brewed over the small fire he had built. "I can assure you I was in bad odor with the Council for my part in bringing you to Xonijeel. However, the best offense is a good defense, as the saying goes. I countered by preferring charges against Minister Sphogeel for compromise of an official TDP position, illegal challenge of an Agent's competence, failure to refer a matter of Authoritarian security to a full Board meeting—"

"I don't quite get the picture, Dzok," I interrupted. "*You* conned me into going to Xonijeel by promising me help against the Hagroon—"

"Really, Bayard, I promised no more than that I'd do my best. It was a piece of ill luck that old Sphogeel was on the Council that week. He's a notorious xenophobe. I never dreamed he'd go so far as to consign you to exile on the basis of a kangaroo hearing—"

"You were the one who grabbed my gun," I pointed out.

"Lucky thing, too. If you'd managed to kill someone, there'd have been nothing I could do to save you from being burned down on the spot. And I'm not sure I'd have wanted to. You *are* a bloodthirsty blighter, you know."

"So you followed me to B-I Four. . . ."

"As quickly as I could. Managed to get myself assigned as escort to a recruitment group—all native chaps, of course—"

"Native chaps?"

"Ahhh. . . Anglics, like yourself, captured as

139

cubs . . . er . . . babies, that is. Cute little fellows, Anglic cubs. Can't help warming to them. Easy to train, too, and damnably human—"

"Okay, you can skip the propaganda. Somehow it doesn't help my morale to picture human slaves as lovable whities."

Dzok cleared his throat. "Of course, old chap. Sorry. I merely meant—well, hang it, man, what can I say? We treated you badly! I admit it! But—" he flashed me a sly smile. "I neglected to mention your rather sturdy hypnotic defenses against conditioning. I daresay you'd have had a bit more trouble throwing off your false memories if they'd known, and modified their indoctrination accordingly. And to make amends I came after you, only to find you'd flown the coop—"

"Why so mysterious? Why not come right up and knock on the door and say all was forgiven?"

Dzok chuckled. "Now, now, dear boy, can you imagine the reaction of a typical Anglic villager to *my* face appearing at the door, inquiring after a misplaced chum?"

I scratched at my jaw, itchy with two day's stubble. "All right, you had to be circumspect. But you could have phoned—"

"I could have remained hidden in the garret until after dark, then ventured out to reconnoiter, which is precisely what I did," Dzok said firmly. "I was ready to approach you at Mrs. Rogers' house, when you slipped away from me. I located you again at the cottage at the edge of the woods, but again you moved too quickly—"

"We spotted you creeping around," I told him. "I thought it was the Xonijeelian Gestapo getting ready to revise the sentence to something more permanent than exile."

"Again, I was about to speak to you on the road, when that fellow in the cocked hat interfered. Then you fooled me by taking a train. Had a devil of a time learning where you'd gone. I had to return to Xonijeel, travel to Rome, reshuttle to your so-called B-I Four line, then set about locating you. Fortunately, we maintain a permanent station in Italy, with a number of trusties—"

"More natives, I presume?"

"Quite. I say, old man, you're developing something of

a persecution complex, I'm afraid—"

"That's easy, when you're persecuted."

"Nonsense. Why, you know I've always dealt with you as an equal . . ."

"Sure, some of your best friends are people. But to hell with that. Go on."

"Umm. Yes. Of course, I had to operate under cover of darkness. Even then, it was far from easy. The Roman police are a suspicious lot. I turned you up at last, waited about outside your flat, then realized what you were about, and hurried to your shop. You know what happened there. . . ." He rubbed his round skull gingerly. "Still tender, you know. Fortunately for me I was well wrapped up—"

"If you'd just said something . . ." I countered.

"Just as I opened my mouth, you hit me."

"All right, I'm sorry—sorrier than you know, considering what I went through after that. How the hell did you trail me here?"

He grinned, showing too many even white teeth. "Your apparatus, old boy. Fantastically inefficient. Left a trail across the Web I could have followed on a bicycle."

"You came to B-I Four ostensibly on a recruitment mission, you said?"

"Yes. I could hardly reveal what I had in mind—and it seemed a likely spot to find some eager volunteers for Anglic Sector duty—"

"I thought you had plenty of trusties you'd raised from cubs."

"We need a large quota of native recuited personnel for our Special Forces, chaps who know the languages and mores of the Anglic lines. We're able to offer these lads an exciting career, good pay, retirement. It's not a bad life, as members of an elite corps—"

"Won't it look a little strange when you come back without your recruits?"

"Ah, but I have my recruits, dear boy! Twenty picked men, waiting at the depot at Rome B-I Four."

I took a breath and asked The Question: "So you came to make amends? What kind of amends? Are you offering me a ride home?"

"Look here, Bayard," Dzok said earnestly. "I've

looked into the business of Sphogeel's photogram—the one which clearly indicated that there is no normal A-line at the Web coordinates you mentioned—"

"So you think I'm nuts too?"

He shook his head. "It's not so simple as that. . . ."

"What's that supposed to mean?" My pulse was picking up, getting ready for bad news.

"I checked the records, Bayard. Three weeks ago—at the time you departed your home line in the Hagroon shuttle—your Zero-zero line was there, just as you said. Less than twelve hours later—nothing."

I gaped at him.

"It can mean only one thing. . . . I'm sorry to be the one to tell you this, but it appears there's been an unauthorized use of a device known as a discontinuity engine."

"Go on," I growled.

"Our own technicians devised the apparatus over a hundred years ago. It was used in a war with a rebellious province. . . ."

I just looked at him, waiting.

"I can hardly play the role of apologist for the actions of the previous generation, Bayard," Dzok said stiffly. "Suffice it to say that the machine was outlawed by unanimous vote of the High Board of the Authority, and never used again. By us, that is. But now it seems that the Hagroon have stolen the secret—"

"What does a discontinuity engine do?" I demanded. "How could it conceal the existence of an A-line from your instruments?"

"The device," Dzok said unhappily, "once set up in any A-line, releases the entropic energy of that line in random fashion. A ring of energy travels outward, creating what we've termed a probability storm in each A-line as the wave front passes. As for your Zero-zero line—it's gone, old man, snuffed out of existence. It no longer exists. . . ."

I got to my feet, feeling light-headed, dizzy. Dzok's voice went on, but I wasn't listening. I was picturing the Hagroon stringing wire in the deserted garages of the Net Terminal; quietly, methodically preparing to destroy a world . . .

"Why?" I yelled. "Why? We had no quarrel with them. . . ."

"They discovered your Net capabilities. You were a threat to be eliminated—"

"Wait a minute! You said *your* bunch invented this discontinuity whatzit. How did the Hagroon get hold of it?"

"That, I don't know—but I intend to find out."

"Are you telling me they just put on false whiskers and walked in and lifted it when nobody was looking? That's a little hard to swallow whole, Dzok. I think it's a lot easier to believe you boys worked along with the Hagroon, hired them to do your dirty work—"

"If that were the case, why would I be here now?" Dzok demanded.

"I don't know. Why *are* you here?"

"I've come to help you, Bayard. To do what I can—"

"What would that be—another one-way ticket to some nice dead end where I can set up housekeeping and plant a garden and forget all about what might have been, once, in a world that doesn't exist anymore because some people with too much hair decided we might be a nuisance and didn't want to take the chance—" I was advancing on Dzok, with ideas of seeing if his throat was as easy to squeeze as it looked. . . .

Dzok sat where he was, staring at me. "You don't have to behave like a complete idiot, Bayard, in spite of your race's unhappy reputation for blind ferocity—besides which, I happened to be stronger than you. . ." He took something from the pocket of his trim white jacket, tossed it at my feet. It was my slug gun. I scooped it up.

"Still, if you actually are a homicidal maniac, go ahead. Don't bother to listen to what I have to say, or to wonder why I came here."

I looked at him across the fire, then thrust the gun into my pocket and sat down. "Go ahead," I said. "I'm listening."

"I gave the matter considerable thought, Bayard," Dzok said calmly. He poured himself another cup of coffee, sniffed at it, balanced it on his knee. "And an idea occurred to me. . . ."

I didn't say anything. It was very silent; even the night

birds had stopped calling. Somewhere, far away, something bellowed. A breeze stirred the trees overhead. They sighed like an old man remembering the vanished loves of his youth.

"We've developed some interesting items in our Web Research Labs," Dzok said. "One of our most recent creations has been a speical, lightweight suit, with its Web circuitry woven into the fabric itself. The generator is housed in a shoulder pack weighing only a few ounces. Its design is based on a new application of plasma mechanics, utilizing nuclear forces rather than the conventional magneto-electronic fields—"

"Sure," I snapped. "What does it have to do with me?"

"It gives the wearer Web mobility without a shuttle," Dzok continued. "The suit is the shuttle. Of course, it's necessary to attune the suit to the individual wearer's entropic quotient—but that in itself is an advantage: it creates an auto-homing feature. When the field is activated, the wearer is automatically transferred to the continuum of minimum stress—namely, his A-line of origin—or whatever other line his metabolism is attuned to."

"Swell. You've developed an improved shuttle. So what?"

"I have one here. For you." Dzok waved toward the bubble-shape of his standard Xonijeel model Web traveler—a far more sophisticated device than the clumsy machines of the Imperium. "I smuggled it into my cargo locker—after stealing it from the lab. I'm a criminal on several counts on your behalf, old fellow."

"What do I do with this suit? Go snark hunting? You've already told me my world is gone—"

"There is another development which I'm sure you'll find of interest," Dzok went on imperturbably. "In our more abstruse researches into the nature of the Web, we've turned up some new findings that place rather a new complexion on our old theories of reality. Naturally, on first discovering the nature of the Web, one was forced to accept the fact that the totality of all existence; that in a Universe of infinities, all possible things exist. But still, with the intellectual chauvinism inherent in our monolinear orientation, we assumed that the wavefront of simultaneous reality advanced everywhere at the same rate. That 'now' in one A-line was of necessity 'now' in every other—and that this was an immutable quality, as irreversible as entropy. . . ."

"Well, isn't it?"

"Yes—precisely as irreversible as entropy. But now it appears that entropy can be reversed—and very easily, at that." He smiled triumphantly.

"Are you saying," I asked carefully, "that you people have developed time travel?"

Dzok laughed. "Not at all—not in the direct sense you mean. There is an inherent impossibility in reversing one's motion along one's own personal time track. . . ." He looked thoughtful. "At least, I think there is—"

"Then what are you saying?"

"When one moves outward from one's own A-line, crossing other lines in their myriads, it is possible, by proper application of these newly harnessed subatomic hypermagnetic forces I mentioned to you, to set up a sort of—tacking, one might call it. Rather than traveling across the lines in a planiform temporal stasis, as is normal with more primitive drives, we found that it was possible to skew the vector—to retrogress temporally, to levels contemporaneous with the past of the line of origin—to distances proportional to the distance of normal Web displacement."

"I guess that means something," I said. "But what?"

"It means that with the suit I've brought you, you can return to your Zero-zero-line—at a time prior to its disappearance!"

It was nearly daylight now. Dzok and I had spent the last few hours over a chart laid out on the tiny navigation table in his shuttle, making calculations based on the complex formulation which he said represented the relationships existing between normal entropy, E-entropy, Net displacement, the entropic quotient of the body in question—me—and other factors too numerous to mention, even if I'd understood them.

"You're a difficult case, Bayard," the agent said, shaking his head. He opened a flat case containing an instrument like a stethoscope with a fitting resembling a phonographic pickup. He took readings against my skull, compared them with the figures he had already written out.

"I think I've corrected properly for your various wanderings in the last few weeks," he said. "Since it's been a number of years since your last visit to your original A-line—B-I three—I think we can safely assume that you've settled into a normal entropic relationship with your adopted Zero-zero line—"

"Better run over those manual controls with me again—just in case."

"Certainly—but let's hope you have no occasion to use them. It was mad of you, old chap, to set out in that makeshift shuttle of yours, planning to navigate by the seat of your pants. It just won't work, you know. You'd never have found your target—"

"Okay, but I won't worry about that until after I find out if I'm going to survive this new trip. What kind of margin of error will I have?"

Dzok looked concerned. "Not as much as I'd like. My observations indicated that your Zero-zero line was destroyed twenty-one days ago. The maximum displacement I can give you with the suit at this range is twenty-three days. You'll have approximately forty-eight hours after your arrival to circumvent the Hagroon. How you'll do that—"

"Is my problem."

"I've given it some thought," Dzok said. "You observed them at work in null time. From your description of what they were about, it seems apparent that they were erecting a transfer portal linking the null level with its corresponding aspect of normal entropy—in other words, with the normal continuum. They'd need this, of course, in order to set up the discontinuity engine in the line itself. Your task will be to give warning, and drive them back when they make their assault."

"We can handle that," I assured him grimly. "The trick will be convincing people I'm not nuts. . . ." I didn't add the disquieting thought that in view of the attitude of the Imperial authorities—at our last meeting—my own oldest friends included—it was doubtful whether I'd get the kind of hearing that could result in prompt action. But I could worry about that later too, after I'd made the trip—if I succeeded in finding my target at all.

"Now to fit the suit." Dzok lifted the lid of a wall

locker, took out a limp outfit like a nylon diver's suit, held it up to me.

"A bit long in the leg, but I'll soon make that right. . . ." He went to work like a skilled seamstress, using shears and a hot iron, snipping and re-sealing the soft woven plastic material. I tried it on, watched while he shortened the sleeves, and added a section down the middle of the back to accommodate my wider shoulders.

"Doesn't that hand-tailoring interfere with the circuits?" I asked, as he fussed over the helmet-to-shoulder fit.

"Not at all. The pattern of the weave's the thing—so long as I make sure the major connecting links are made up fast. . . ."

He settled the fishbowl in place, then touched a stud on a plate set in the chest area of the suit, looked at the meters mounted on a small test panel on the table. He nodded, switched off.

"Now, Bayard," he said seriously. "Your controls are here . . ."

It was full daylight now. Dzok and I stood on the grassy bank above the river. He looked worried.

"You're sure you understand the spatial maneuvering controls?"

"Sure—that part's easy. I just kick off and jet—"

"You'll have to use extreme care. Of course, you won't feel the normal gravitational effects, so you'll be able to flit about as lightly as a puff of smoke—but you'll still retain normal inertia. If you collide with at tree, or rock, it will be precisely as disastrous as in a normal entropic field."

"I'll be careful, Dzok. And you do the same." I held out my hand and he took it, grinning.

"Goodbye, Bayard. Best of luck and all that. Pity we couldn't have worked out something in the way of an alliance between our respective governments, but perhaps it was a bit premature. At least now there'll be the chance of a future rapprochement."

"Sure—and thanks for everything."

He stepped back and waved. I looked around for a last glimpse of the morning sun, the greenery, Dzok's transparent shuttle, and Dzok himself, long-legged, his shiny boots mud-spattered, his whites mud-stained. He raised a hand and I pressed the lever that activated the suit. There was a moment of vertigo, a sense of pressure on all sides. Then Dzok flickered, disappeared. His shuttle winked out of sight. The strange, abnormal movement of normally immobile objects that was characteristic of Net travel started up. I watched as the trees waved, edged about in the soil, putting out groping feelers toward me as though sensing my presence.

A hop, and I was in the air, drifting ten feet above the surface. I touched the jet-control and at once a blast of cold ions hurled me forward. I took a bearing, corrected course, and settled down for a long run.

I was on my way.

CHAPTER TWELVE

It was a weird trip across the probability worlds, exposed as I was to the full panoramic effects of holocausts of planetary proportions. For a while, I skimmed above a sea of boiling lava that stretched to the far horizon. Then I was drifting among fragments of the crust of a shattered world, and later I watched as pale flames licked the cinders of a burnt-out continent. All the while I sped northward, following the faint *be-beep!* of my autocompass, set on a course that would bring me to the site of Stockholm after four hours' flight. I saw great seas of oily, dead fluid surge across what had once been land, their foaming crests oddly flowing backwards, as I retrogressed through time while I hurled across A-space. I watched the obscene heaving and groping of monstrous life-forms created in the chaotic aftermath of the unleashed powers of the M-C field, great jungles of blood red plants, deserts of blasted, shattered stone over which the sun flared like an arc-light in a black, airless sky. Now and again there would be a brief uprising of almost normal landscape, as I swept across a cluster of A-lines which had suffered less than the others. But always the outré element intruded: a vast, wallowing animal form, like a hundred-ton dog, or a mountainous, mutated cow, with extra limbs and lolling heads placed at random across the vast bulk through which bloodred vines grew, penetrating the flesh.

Hours passed. I checked my chronometer and the navigational instruments set in the wrist of the suit. I was close to my target and, according to the positional indicator, over southern Sweden—not that the plain of riven rock below me resembled the warm and verdant plains of Scania I had last seen on a hiking trip with Barbro, three months earlier.

I maneuvered close to the ground, crossed a finger of the sea that marked the location of Hykoping in normal space. I was getting close now. It was time to pick a landing spot. It wouldn't do to land too close to the city. Popping into identity on a crowded street would be unwise. I recognized the low, rolling country south of the capital now; I slowed my progress, hovered, waiting for the moment. . .

Abruptly, light and color blazed around me. I threw the main control switch, dropped the last few feet to a grassy hillside. It took me a moment to get the helmet clear; then I took a deep breath of cool, fresh air—the air of a world regained from twenty-two days in the past.

Down on the road, with the suit bundled under my arm, I flagged a horse-drawn wagon, let the driver ramble on with the assumption that I was one of those crazy sky-diver fellows. He spent the whole trip into town telling me how you'd never get him up in one of those things, then asked me for a free ride. I promised to remember him next time I was up, and hopped off at the small-town post office.

Inside, I gave a rambling excuse for my lack of funds to an ill-tempered looking man in a tight blue uniform, and asked him to put through a call to Intelligence HQ in Stockholm. While I waited, I noticed the wall calendar—and felt the sweat pop out on my forehead. I was a full day later than Dzok had calculated. The doom that hung over the Imperium was only hours away.

The plump man came back, with a thin man in tow. He told me to repeat my request to his superior. I began to get irritated.

"Gentlemen, I have important information for Baron Richthofen. Just put my call through—"

"That will not be possible," the slim fellow said. He had a nose sharp enough to poke a hole through quarter-inch plywood. It was red on the end, as though he'd been trying.

"You can charge the call to my home telephone," I said. "My name is Bayard, number 12, Nybrovagen—"

"You have identity papers?"

"I'm sorry; I've lost my wallet. But—"

"You place me in a difficult position," the thin fellow said, with a smile that suggested that he was enjoying it. "If the Herr is unable to identify himself—"

"This is important!" I rapped. "You have nothing to lose but a phone call. If I *am* on the level, you'll look like a damned fool for obstructing me!"

That got to him. He conferred with his chubby chum, then announced that he would check with the number I had given him in Stockholm, supposedly that of Herr Bayard. . . .

I waited while he dialed, talked, nodded, waited, talked some more in an undertone, placed the receiver back on the phone with a triumphant look. He spoke briefly to the other man, who hurried away.

"Well?" I demanded.

"You say that *you* are Herr Bayard?" he cooed, fingertips together.

"Colonel Bayard to you, Buster," I snapped. "This is a matter of life and death—"

"Whose life and death, ah. . .*Colonel* Bayard?"

"To hell with that . . ." I started around the counter. He leaned on one foot and I heard a distant bell sound. The fat man reappeared, looking flushed. There was another man behind him, a heavy fellow in a flat cap and gunbelt, with cop written all over him. He put a gun on me an ordered me to stand clear of the wall. Then he frisked me quickly—missing the slug gun which Dzok had restored—and motioned me to the door.

"Hold on," I said. "What's this farce all about? I've got to get that call through to Stockholm—"

"You claim that you are Colonel Bayard, of Imperial Intelligence?" the cop rapped out.

"Right the first time," I started.

"It may interest you to know," the thin postal official said, savoring the drama of the moment, "that Herr Colonel Bayard is at this moment dining at his home in the capital."

CHAPTER THIRTEEN

The cell they gave me wasn't bad by Hagroon standards, but that didn't keep me from pounding on the bars and yelling. I had my slug gun, of course—but since they wouldn't recognize it as a weapon even if I showed it, there was no chance of bluff. And I wasn't quite ready yet to kill. There were still several hours to go before the crisis and my call wouldn't take long—once they saw reason.

The fat man had gone away, promising that an official from the military sub-station at Sodra would be along soon. Meantime I pounded and demanded that another call be put through—but nobody listened. Now my chance to use the gun was gone. The man with the keys kept to the outer office.

A slack-looking youth in baggy pants and wide blue and yellow suspenders brought me in a small smorgasbord about noon. I tried to bribe him to make the call for me. He gave me a crooked smile and turned away.

It was well after dark when there was a sudden stir in the outer room of the jail. Then the metal door clanged open and a familiar face appeared—a field agent I had met once or twice in the course of my duties with Intelligence. He was a tall, worried-looking man, wearing drab civvies and carrying a briefcase. He stopped dead when he saw me, then came on hesitantly.

"Hello, Captain," I greeted him. "We'll all have a good chuckle over this later, as the saying goes, but right now I need out of here fast . . ."

The cop who had arrested me was behind him, and the fat man from the post office.

"You know my name?" the agent asked awkwardly.

"I'm afraid not—but I think you know me. We've met once or twice—"

"Listen to the fellow," the fat man said. "A violent case—"

"Silence!" the agent snapped. He came up close, looked me over carefully.

"You wished to place a call to Intelligence HQ," he said. "What did you wish to speak about?"

"I'll tell them myself," I snapped. "Get me out of here, Captain—in a hell of a hurry! This is top priority business!"

"You may tell me what it is you wished to report," he said.

"I'll report directly to Baron Richthofen!"

He lifted his shoulders. "You place me in an awkward position—"

"To hell with your position! Can't you understand plain Swedish? I'm telling you—"

"You will adress an officer of Imperial Intelligence with more respect!" the cop broke in.

The agent turned to the two men behind him. "Clear out, both of you!" he snapped. They left, looking crestfallen. He turned back to me, wiped a hand across his forehead.

"This is very difficult for me," he said. "You bear a close resemblance to Colonel Bayard—"

"Resemblance! Hell, I *am* Bayard!"

He shook his head. "I was assured on that point, most specifically," he said. "I don't know what this is all about, my friend, but it will be better for you to tell me the whole story—"

"The story is that I have information of vital importance to the Imperium! Every minute counts, man! Forget the red tape! Get me a line to Headquarters!"

"You are an imposter. We know that much. You asked to have a call placed. A routine check at Colonel Bayard's home indicated that he was there—"

"I can't try to explain all the paradoxes involved. Just put my call through!"

"It is not possible to route every crank call to the Chief of Intelligence!" the man snapped. "What is this message of yours? If it seems to warrant attention, I will personally—"

"Let me talk to Bayard, then," I cut in.

"Ah, then you abandon your imposture?"

"Call it what you like. Let me talk to him!"

"That is not possible—"

"I didn't know we had anyone in the service as stupid as you are," I said clearly. "All right, I'll give you the message—and by all you hold sacred, you'd better believe me."

He didn't. He was polite, and heard me all the way through. Then he signaled for the jailer and got ready to leave.

"You can't walk out of here without at least checking my story!" I roared at him. "What kind of intelligence man are you? Take a look at the suit I had with me, damn you! That will show you I'm not imagining the whole thing!"

He looked at me, a troubled look. "How can I believe you? Your claim to be Bayard is a lie, and the story you tell is fantastic! Would *you* have believed it?"

I stared back at him.

"I don't know," I said, honestly. "But I'd at least have checked what I could."

He turned to the cop, who was back, hovering at the door.

"You have this . . . shuttle suit?"

The cop nodded. "Yes sir. I have it here on my desk. I've checked it for . . ." his voice faded as he and the agent went out and the door shut behind them. For another half hour I paced the cell, wondering whether I should have shot a couple of them and tried to scare the cop into unlocking me; but from what I knew of the men of the Imperium, it wouldn't have worked. They were too damned brave for their own good.

Then the door clanged open again. A stranger was there this time—a small man with a runny nose and eyes, and glasses as thick as checkers.

". . . very odd, very odd," he was saying. "But meaningless, of course. The circuitry is quite inert . . ."

"This is Herr Professor Doctor Runngvist," the agent said. "He's checked your . . . ah . . . suit, and assures me that it's crank work. A homemade hoax of some sort, incapable of any—"

"Damn you!" I yelled. "Sure the suit's inert—without me in it! I'm part of the circuitry! It's attuned to me!"

"Eh? Tuned to you? A part of the circuitry?" The old man adjusted his glasses at an angle to get a better view of me.

"Look, pops, this is a highly sophisticated device. It utilizes the wearer's somatic and neural fields as a part of the total circuitry. Without me inside, it won't work. Let me have it. I'll demonstrate it for you—"

"Sorry, I can't allow that," the agent said quickly. "Look here, fellow, hadn't you better drop this show now, and tell me what it's all about?" You're in pretty deep water already, I'd say, impersonating an officer—"

"You know Bayard, on sight, don't you?" I cut in.

"Yes . . ."

"Do I look like him?"

He looked worried. "Yes, to an extent. I presume it was that which inspired this imposture, but—"

"Listen to me, Captain," I said as levelly as I could through the bars. "This is the biggest crisis the Imperium has faced since Chief Inspector Bale ran amok. . . ."

The captain frowned. "How did you know of that?"

"I was there. My name's Bayard, remember? Now get me out of here—"

There was a shrilling of a telephone bell in the outer room. Feet clumped. Voices rumbled. Then the door flew open.

"Inspector! It's a call—from Stockholm. . . ."

My inquisitors turned. "Yes?"

"That fellow—Colonel Bayard!" an excited voice said. Someone shushed him. They stood in the hall, conversing in whispers. Then the intelligence captain came back with the cop behind him.

"You'd better start telling all you know," he snapped, looking grimmer than ever.

"What happened?"

"Stockholm is under attack by an armed force of undetermined size!"

It was close to midnight now. I had been looking for a

chance for a break for the past hour, but Captain Burman, the agent, was taking no chances. He had locked the outer door to the cell block and nobody was allowed even to come close to my cell. I think he was beginning to suspect that everything wasn't as simple as it appeared.

I watched the door across the aisle as a key clattered in it and it swung wide. It was Burman, white-faced, and two strangers, both in civilian clothes. My wrist tensed, ready to flip the gun into my palm, but they kept their distance.

"This is the man." Burman waved at me like a tenant complaining about a prowler. "I've gotten nothing from him but nonsense—or what I thought was nonsense, until now!"

The newcomers looked me over. One was a short, thick-set, hairless man in wide lapels and baggy-kneed pants. The other was trim, neat, well set up. I decided to make my pitch to the former. No underling could afford to look that messy.

"Listen, you," I started. "I'm Colonel Bayard, of Imperial Intelligence—

"I will listen, of that you may be assured," the little man said. "Start at the beginning and repeat what you have told the Captain."

"It's too late for talk." I flipped the gun into my hand. All three of them jumped, and a heavy automatic appeared in the snappy dresser's hand.

"Ever seen one of these before?" I showed the slug gun, keeping the armed man covered.

The thick man jerked his head in a quick nod.

"Then you know they're only issued to a few people in Net Surveillance work—including me. I could have shot my way out of here when I first arrived, but I thought I'd get a fair hearing without killing anybody. Now its too late for humanitarianism. One of you open up, or I start shooting—and I'm faster than you are, Buster," I added for the benefit of the tall man with the gun.

"Here, you're only making it worse—"

"It couldn't be worse. Get the key. Call that dumb flatfoot out front."

The thick man shook his head. "Shoot then, sir. Major Gunnarson will then be forced to return your fire, and so two men will die. But I will not release you."

"Why not? You can watch me. All I want to do is call Intelligence—"

"I do not know what set of signals you may have worked out, or with whom, and I do not intend to find out at the expense of the Imperial security."

"There's not any Imperial security, as long as you keep me here. I've told my story to Burman! Take action! Do something!"

"I have already attempted to relay your statement to Baron Richthofen at Stockholm," the rumpled man said.

"What do you mean, attempted?"

"Just that. I was unable to get through. All telephonic connection is broken, I found. I sent a messenger. He failed to return. Another messenger has reached me but now. He was dispatched an hour ago, and heard the news over his auto radio set just before . . ."

"Just before what?"

"Before the gas attack," he said in a harsh voice. Abruptly there was a gun in his hand—a heavy revolver. He had drawn it so quickly that I couldn't even say where he'd gotten it.

"Now, tell me all you know of these matters, Mr. Bayard, or whatever your name might be! You have ten seconds to begin!"

I kept my gun on his partner. I knew that if I moved it as much as a millimeter, the baggy man would gun me down. I tried to match the steely look in his eye.

"I told Burman the whole story. If you choose not to believe it, that's not my fault. But there may still be time. What's the situation in the city?"

"There is *no* time, Mr. Bayard. No time at all. . . ." To my horror I saw a tear glisten at the corner of the thick man's eye.

"What . . ." I couldn't finish the question.

"The invaders have released a poisonous gas which has blanketed the city. They have erected barricades against any attempt at relief. Strange men in helmeted suits are shooting down every man who approaches . . ."

"But what about . . . the people . . . What about my wife? What—"

He was shaking his head. "The Emperor and his family, the government, everyone, all must be presumed dead, Mr. Bayard, inside the barricaded city!"

There was a shattering crash from the outer room.
The thick man whirled from me, jumped to the door,
shot a look out, then went through at a dead run,
Burman at his heels. I yelled at Major Gunnarson to stop
or I'd shoot, but he didn't and neither did I. There was a
clatter of feet, a crash like breaking glass, a couple of
shots. Someone yelled "The ape-men!" There were more
shots, then a heavy slam like a body hitting the floor. I
backed into the corner of my cell, cursing the fatal
mistake I'd made in letting myself get cornered here. I
aimed at the door, waited for the first Hagroon to come
through—

The door flew open—and a familiar narrow-
shouldered figure in stained whites sauntered into view.

"Dzok!" I yelled. "Get me out of here—or—" A
horrible suspicion dawned. Dzok must have seen it in
my face.

"Easy, old fellow!" He shouted as my gun covered
him. "I'm here to give you a spot of assistance, old
chap—and from the looks of things, you can jolly well
use it!"

"What's going on out there?" I yelled. There was
someone behind Dzok. A tall young fellow in a green
coat and scarlet knee pants came through the door,
holding a long-barrelled rifle with a short bayonet fixed
to the end of it. There were white facings on the coat,
wide loops of braid, and rows of bright gold buttons.
There was a wide cocked hat on his head, with a gold
fringe and a crimson rosette, and he wore white
stockings and polished black shoes with large gilt
buckles. The owner of the finery flashed me a big smile,
then turned to Dzok and gave a sloppy salute with the
palm of his hand out.

"I reckon we peppered 'em good, sor. Now what say ye
we have a look about out back here for any more o' the
gossoons as might be skulkin' ready to do in a honest
man?"

"Never mind that, sergeant," Dzok said. "This is a jail
delivery, nothing more. Those chaps out there are our
allies, actually. Pity about the shooting, but it couldn't

be helped." He was talking to me now. "I attempted to make a few inquiries, but found everyone in a state of the most extreme agitation. They opened fire with hardly a second glance, amid shouts of 'hairy ape-men'! Disgraceful—"

"The Hagroon have hit the capital," I cut him off. "Laid down a gas attack, barricaded the streets, everybody presumed dead...." I wasn't thinking now—just reacting. The Hagroon had to be stopped. That was all that mattered. Not that anything really mattered any more, with Barbro gone with the rest—but she was a fighter. She'd have expected me to go on fighting, too, as long as I could still move and breathe.

Dzok looked stricken. "Beastly, old fellow! I can't tell you how sorry I am..." He commiserated with me for awhile. Then the sergeant came back from the outer room with a key, opened my cell door.

"And so I came too late," Dzok said bitterly. "I had hoped..." He let the sentence trail off, as we went into the outer room.

"Who are these fellows?" I gaped at the half-dozen bright-plumaged soldiers posted about the jail covering the windows and the door.

"These are my volunteers, Bayard—my Napoleonic levies. I was on a recruiting mission, you'll recall. After I left you, I went back and loaded these chaps into my cargo shuttle, and returned to Zaj—and found—you'll never guess, old fellow!"

"I'll take three guesses," I said, "and they'll all be 'the Hagroon.'"

Dzok nodded glumly. "The bounders had overrun Authority headquarters, including the Web terminal, of course. I beat a hasty strategic retreat, and followed your trail here..." he paused, looking embarrassed. "Actually, old chap, I'd hoped to enlist the aid of your Imperium. We Xonijeelians are ill-equipped to fight a Web war, I'm sorry to say. Always before—"

"I know. They caught us off-guard too. I wondered all along why you figured you were immune—"

"the audacity of the blighters! Who'd have expected—"

"You should have," I said shortly.

"Ah, well, what's done is done." Dzok rubbed his hands together with every appearance of relish. "Inasmuch as you're not in a position to assist me, perhaps my chaps and I can still be of some help here. Better start by giving me a complete resumé of the situation. . . ."

After ten minutes' talk, while the troops kept up a sporadic fire from the jail windows, Dzok and I had decided on a plan of action. It wasn't a good one, but under the circumstances it was better than nothing. The first step was to find the S-suit. We wasted another ten minutes searching the place before I decided to try the vault. It was open, and the suit was laid out on a table.

"Right," Dzok said with satisfaction. "I'll need tools, Bayard, and a heat source and a magnifying glass. . . ."

We rummaged, found a complete tool kit in a wall locker and a glass in the chief's desk drawer. I made a hasty adaptation of a hot plate used for heating coffee, while Dzok opened up the control console set in the chest of the suit.

"We're treading on dangerous ground, of course," he said blandly, while he snipped hair-fine wires, teased them into new arrangements. "What I'm attempting is theoretically possible, but it's never been tried—not with an S-suit."

I watched admiring the dexterity of his long grayish fingers as he rearranged the internal components of the incredibly compact installation. For half an hour, while guns cracked intermittently, he made tests, muttered, tried again, studying the readings on the miniature scales set on the cuff of the suit. Then he straightened, gave me a wry look.

"It's done, old chap. I can't guarantee the results of my makeshift mods, but there's at least an even chance that it will do what we want."

I asked for an explanation of what he had done, followed closely as he pointed out the interplay of circuits that placed stresses on the M-C field in such a way as to distort its normal function along a line of geometric progression leading to infinity . . .

"It's over my head, Dzok," I told him. "I was never a really first-class M-C man, and when it comes to your Xonijeelian complexities—"

"Don't trouble your head, Bayard. All you need to know is that adjusting this setting . . ." he pointed with a pin drill at a tiny knurled knob—"controls the angle of incidence of the pinch-field—"

"In plain English, if something goes wrong and I'm not dead, I can twiddle that and try again."

"Very succinctly put. Now let's be going. How far did you say it is to the city?"

"About twelve kilometers."

"Right. We'll have to commandeer a pair of light lorries. There are several parked in the court just outside. Some sort of crude steam-cars, I think—"

"Internal combustion. And not so crude; they'll do a hundred kilometers an hour."

"They'll serve." He went into the guard room, checked the scene from the windows.

"Quiet out there at the moment. No point in waiting about. Let's sally at once." I nodded, and Dzok gave his orders to the gaily costumed riflemen, five of whom quietly took up positions at the windows and door facing the courtyard, while the others formed up a cordon around Dzok and me.

"Hell, we may as well do our bit," I suggested. There were carbines in the gun locker. I took one, tossed one to Dzok, buckled on a belt and stuffed it with ammo.

"Tell your lads to shoot low," I said. "Don't let anybody get in our way, but try not to kill anybody. They don't know what's going on out there—"

"And there's no time to explain," Dzok finished for me, looking at his men. "Shoot to wound, right, lads? Now, Sergeant, take three men and move out. Cover the first lorry and hold your fire until they start something. Mr. Bayard and I will come next, with ten men, while the rest of you lay down a covering fire. Those in the rear guard stand fast until number two lorry pulls up to the door, then pile in quickly and we're off."

"Very well, sor," the sergeant said. He was working hard on a plug of tobacco he'd found in the police chief's desk drawer. He turned and bawled instructions to his men, who nodded, grinning.

"These boys don't behave like recruits," I said. "They look like veterans to me."

Dzok nodded, smiling his incredible smile. "Former

members of the Welsh regiment of the Imperial Guard. They were eager for a change."

"I wonder what you offered them?"

"The suggestion of action after a few months changing of the guard at Westminster was sufficient."

The sergeant was at the door now, with two of his men. He said a quick word, and the three darted out, sprinted for the lorry, a high-sided dark blue panel truck lettered FLOTTSBRO POLIS. A scattering of shots rang out. Grass tips flew as bullet clipped the turf by the sergeant's ankle. The man on his left stumbled, went down, rolled, came up limping, his thigh wet with a dark glisten against the scarlet cloth. He made it in two jumps to the shelter of the truck, hit the grass, leveled his musket and fired. A moment later, all three were in position, their guns crackling in a one-round-per-second rhythm. The opposing fire slackened.

"Now," Dzok said. I brought the carbine up across my chest and dashed for the second truck. There was a white puff of smoke from a window overlooking the courtyard, a whine past my head. I ducked, pounded across the grass, leaped the chain at the edge of the pavement, skidded to a halt beside the lorry. Dzok was there ahead of me, wrenching at the door.

"Locked!" he called, and stepped back, fired a round into the keyhole, wrenched the door open. I caught a glimpse of his shuttle, a heavy passenger-carrying job, parked across a flowerbed. He followed my gaze.

"Just have to leave it. Too bad . . ." He was inside then, staring at the unfamiliar controls.

"Slide over!" I pushed in beside him, feeling the vehicle lurch as the men crowded in behind me, hearing the *sprang*! as a shot hit the metal body. There were no keys in the ignition. I tried the starter; nothing.

"I'll have to short the wiring," I said, and slid to the ground, jumped to the hood, unlatched the wide side panel, lifted it. With one hand jerk, I twisted the ignition wires free, made hasty connections to the battery, then grabbed the starter lever and depressed it. The engine groaned, turned over twice, and caught with a roar. I slammed the hood down as a bullet cut a bright streak in it, jumped for the seat.

"Who's driving the second truck?"

"I have a chap who's a steam-car operator—"

"No good. I'll have to start it for him. . . ." I was out again, running for the other lorry, parked twenty feet away. A worried-looking man with damp red hair plastered to a freckled forehead was fumbling with the dash lighter and headlight switch. There was a key in the switch of this one; I twisted it, jammed a foot against the starter. The engine caught, ran smoothly.

"You know how to shift gears?"

He nodded, smiling.

"This is the gas pedal. Push on it and you go faster. This is the brake . . ." He nodded eagerly. "If you stall out, push this floor button. The rest is just steering."

He nodded again as glass smashed in front of him, throwing splinters in our faces. Blood ran from a cut across his cheek, but he brushed the chips away, gave me a wave. I ran for it, reached my truck, slammed it in gear, watched a moment to see that the redhead picked up the rear guard. Then I gunned for the closed iron gates, hit them with a crash at twenty miles an hour, slammed through, twisted the wheel hard left, and thundered away down the narrow street.

It took us twenty minutes to cover the twelve kilometers to the edge of the city. For the last hundred yards, we slowed, steered a course among bodies lying in the street, pulled up at a rough barricade of automobiles turned on their sides and blackened by fire, bright tongues of flame still licking over the smouldering tires. A church tower clock was tolling midnight—a merry sound to accompany the cheery picture.

I looked at the dark towers of the city behind the barrier, the dark streets. There were at least a dozen men in sight, sprawled in the unlovely attitudes of violent death. None was in uniform or armed; they were bystanders, caught in the clouds of poison that had rolled out from the city's streets. There were no Hagroon in sight. The streets were as still as a grave-yard.

There was a sound to the left. I brought my carbine

up, saw a hatless man in a white shirt.

"Thank God you've got here at last," he choked. "I got a whiff—sick as a dog. Pulled a couple back, but . . ." he coughed, retched, bending double. "Too late. All dead. Gas is gone now, blown away . . ."

"Get farther back," I said. "Spread the word not to try to attack the barricades." There was another man behind him, and a woman, her face soot-streaked.

"What do you want us to do?" someone called. They clustered around the car, a dozen battered survivors, thinking we were the police, and ready to do whatever had to be done to help us.

"Just stay back, keep out of harms' way. We're going to try something—"

Someone yelled then, pointing at Dzok. A cry went through the crowd.

"Everybody out—fast!" I barked to the men in the rear of the truck. Then: "This is a friend!" I yelled to the crowd. I jumped down, ran around to the side where the man had raised his first outcry, caught him by the arm as he jerked at the shattered door handle.

"Listen to me! This isn't the enemy! He's an ally of the Imperium! He's here to help! These are his troops!" I waved at the ten costumed soldiers who had formed a rough circle around the truck. The headlights of the second truck swung into view then. It growled up beside the first, chugged to a stop and stalled out. The doors flew open and men swarmed out.

"He's got hair on his face—just like the others—"

"You saw them?"

"No—but I heard—from the man I pulled back from the barricade—before he died—"

"Well, I don't have hair on my face—unless you want to count three day's beard. This is Commander Dzok! He's on our side. Now, spread the word! I don't want any accidents!"

"Who're you?"

"I'm Colonel Bayard, Imperial Intelligence. I'm here to do what I can—"

"What can we do?" several voices called. I repeated my instructions to stay back.

"What about you?" the man who had spotted Dzok

asked me. "What's your plan, Colonel?"

Dzok was out of the car now. He handed the modified S-suit to me, turned and bowed in courtly fashion to the crowd.

"Enchanted, sirs and madams, to make your acquaintance," he called. Someone tittered, but Dzok ignored it. "I have the honor, as Colonel Bayard has said, to offer my services in the fight against the rude invader. But it is the Colonel himself who must carry out our mission here tonight. The rest of us can merely assist . . ."

"What's he going to do?"

I had the suit halfway on now. Dzok was helping me, pulling it up, getting my arms into the sleeves, settling the heavy chest pack in place, zipping long zippers closed.

"Using this special equipment," Dzok said in his best theatrical manner, "Colonel Bayard will carry out a mission of the utmost peril . . ."

"Skip the pitch and hand me the helmet," I interrupted him.

"We want to help," someone called.

"I'd like to go along," another voice said.

"Our chief need at the moment," Dzok's voice rang above the rest, "is a supply of coffee. My brave lads are a trifle fatigued, not having rested since leaving their home barracks. For the rest, we can only wait—"

"Why can't some of us go along, Colonel," a man said, stepping close. "You could use an escort   and not those overdressed fancy dans, either!"

"The Colonel must go alone," Dzok said. "Alone he will carry out a spy mission among the enemy—on the other side of time!" He turned to me, and in a lower voice said: "Don't waste any time, old fellow. It's after midnight now—in about two hours the world ends. . . ."

The transparent helmet was in place, all the contacts tight. Dzok made a couple of quick checks, made me the O sign with his fingers that meant all systems were go. I put my hand on the "activate" button and took my usual deep breath. If Dzok's practice was as good as his theory, the rewired S-suit would twist the fabric of reality in a different manner than its designers had intended, stress the E-field of the normal continuum in a way that would expel me, like a watermelon seed squeezed in the fingers, into that curious non-temporal state of null entropy—the other side of time, as he poetically called it.

If it worked, that was. And there was only one way to find out. I pressed the button—

CHAPTER FOURTEEN

There was a moment of total vertigo; the world inverted itself around me, dwindled to a pinhole through which all reality flowed, to expand vastly, whirling . . .

I was standing in the street, looking across at the black hulks of burned-out cars glowing with a bluish light like corpses nine days under water. I turned, saw the empty police lorries, the dead bodies in the street, the stark, leafless trees lining the avenue, the blank eyes of the houses behind them. Dzok, the soldiers, the crowd—all of them had vanished in the instant that the suit's field had sprung into being—or, more correctly, I had vanished from among them. Now I was alone, in the same deserted city I had seen when I awakened after my inexplicable encounter with the flaming man in the basement of Imperial Intelligence Headquarters.

I looked again at the clock on the church tower: the hands stood frozen at twelve twenty-five. And the clock I had seen in the office just after the encounter had read twelve-o-five. I was already too late to intercept the flaming man before he did whatever he had been there to accomplish.

But I wasn't too late to spy out the Hagroon position, discover where the discontinuity engine was planted, then return, lead an assault force . . .

There were too many variables in the situation. Action was the only cure for the hollow sensation of foredoomed failure growing in the pit of my stomach.

A pebble hopped suddenly, struck the toe of my shoe as I took a step. Small dust clouds rose, swirled toward my feet as I crossed the dry, crumbling soil where grass had grown only moments before. The eerie light that

seemed to emanate from the ground showed me a
pattern of depressions in the soil that seemed to form
before my foot reached them. . . .

I looked behind me. There were no prints to show
where I had come, but a faint trail seemed to lead ahead.
A curious condition, this null time. . . .

I crossed the sidewalk, skirted a dead man lying
almost on the barricade. I clambered over the burned
wreck of a car, a boxy sedan with an immense spare tire
strapped to the rear. There were more bodies on the
other side—men who had died trying to climb the wall,
or who had chosen that spot to make a stand. Among
them a lone Hagroon lay, the bulky body contorted in
the heavy atmosphere suit, a bloody hole in the center of
his chest. Someone on the Imperial side had drawn
enemy blood. The thought was cheering in this scene of
desolation. I went on, glanced up at the tower clock as I
passed—

The hands stood at one minute after twelve. As I
watched, the minute had jerked back, pointed straight
up.

And suddenly I understood. Dzok's changes to the
S-suit had had the desired effect of shifting me to null
time. But both of us had forgotten the earlier
adjustment he had made to the suit's controls—the
adjustment that had caused the suit to carry me in a
retrograde direction, back along the temporal profile,
during my trip from the jungle world. Now, with the suit
activated, holding me in my unnatural state of anti-
entropy, the retrograde motion had resumed. I was
traveling backward through time!

I walked on, watching the curious behavior of objects
as they impinged on the E-field of the suit, or crossed
from the field to the external environment. A pebble
kicked by me took up a motion, flew from the
field—where it resumed its natural temporal direction,
sprang back, seemed to strike my foot, then dropped
from play. The air around me whispered in constant
turmoil as vagrant currents were caught, displaced
backward in time, only to be released, with the resultant
local inequalities in air pressure. I wondered how I
would appear to an outside observer—or if I could be
seen at all. And my weapon; what effect would—or *could*

it have, fired in the future, dealing death in the past—

Soundlessly, a figure backed into view around a corner two blocks away, walked briskly toward me, the feet moving back, the arms swinging—like a movie in reverse. I flattened myself against a wall, watched as the walker came closer. A Hagroon! I felt my hackles rise. I flipped the slug gun into my hand, waited . . .

He stepped past me, kept going, his head turning as though scanning the sidewalk for signs of life—but he paid no attention to me. I looked around. There were none of his fellows in sight. It was as good a time as any to make a test. I stepped boldly out, aimed the gun at his retreating chest at a distance of twenty feet, twenty-five . . .

There was no reaction. I was invisible to him, while he, somehow, remained visible to me. I could only assume that light rays striking me were affected by the field, their temporal progression reversed, with the effect of simply blanking them off, while normal light emanating from the scene to me . . .

But how could I see, with light traveling *away* from my eyes. . . .

I remembered a statement made by an Imperium Net physicist, explaining why it was possible to scan the continua through which a moving shuttle passed in an immeasurably short instant of time: "Light is a condition, not an event. . . ."

Whatever the reason, the Hagroon couldn't see me. A break for our side at last. Now to see what I could accomplish on the strength of one small advantage and whatever luck I could find along the way.

It was half an hour's walk to the Net Garages. There were few corpses in the street along the way. Apparently the people had been caught in their beds by the attack. Those few who had been abroad had fallen back toward the barricades—and died there. I passed a pair of Hagroon, walking briskly backward, then a group of a half dozen, then a column of twenty or thirty, all moving in the opposite direction from my own course, which meant that, in normal progression, they were headed for the area of the Net Garages, coming from the direction of the Imperial HQ.

Two blocks from there, the crowd of Hagroon almost filled the street.

Moving with the stream—which seemed to part before me, to the accompaniment of perplexed looks on the Hagroon faces I glimpsed through the dark faceplates—I made my way across the North Bridge, through the dim-glowing wrought-iron gates before the looming bulk of the headquarters building. The mob of Hagroon here was tight-packed, a shoving, sullen mass of near-humanity—jostling their way backward through the wide doors, overflowing the gravel walks and the barren rectangles of dry dirt that were immaculately manicured flower beds in normal times. I caught a glimpse of a clock in the front of a building across the plaza—eleven fifteen.

I had moved back through time three-quarters of an hour, while thirty subjective minutes passed.

I made my way through the streaming crowd of suited Hagroon, reached the door, slipped through into the same high-ceilinged foyer that I had left, alone, six weeks earlier. Now it was crowded with silent Hagroon masses, overseen by two heavily brassed individuals who stood on the lower steps of the flight leading to the upper floors, waving their arms and grimacing. Sound, it appeared, failed to span the interface between "normal" null time and my reversed field effect.

The stream pressed toward a side corridor. I made my way there, reached a small door set in the hall with the sign SERVICE STAIR beside it—

I remembered that door. It was the one through which I had pursued the flaming man, so many weeks before. I pushed through it, felt the ghostly jostle of Hagroon bodies that seemed to slip aside an instant before I touched them, descended one flight, followed the direction of the stream of aliens along to a door—the one beyond which the fiery man had turned at bay. . . .

The stream of Hagroon was smaller now, less tightly packed. I stood aside, watched as the creatures shuffled backward through the narrow entry into the small room—and more and more, packing into the confined space. . . .

It wasn't possible. I had seen hundreds of the brutes in the streets, packing the entryway, crowding the corridors, all streaming here—or *from* here in the normal time sequence—from this one small room. . . .

There were only a few Hagroon in the hall now, standing listening to a silent harangue from a brass-spangled officer. They shuffled back, almost eagerly passed into the room. The officers appeared from above, joined in a brief huddle, backed through the door into the gloom. I followed—and stopped dead.

A glistening, ten-foot disk of insubstantiality shimmered in the air, floating an inch or two above the dull stone floor, not quite grazing the dusty beamed ceiling of the abandoned storeroom. As I watched, one of the remaining Hagroon officers backed quickly to it, crouched slightly, leaped backward through the disk—and disappeared as magically as a rabbit into a magician's hat. There were only two Hagroon left now. One of them backed to the disk, hopped through. The last spoke into a small hand-held instrument, stood for a moment gazing about the room, ignoring me utterly. Then he too sprang through the disk and was gone.

I was seeing wonders, which, by comparison, the shuttles of the Imperium were as prosaic as wicker baby buggies, but there was no time to stand in awe, gaping. This was an entry portal from some other space to null-time Stockholm. The Hagroon had entered through it; from where, I didn't know. There was a simple empirical method of answering that question. . . .

I went to the disk—like the surface of a rippled pond, upended in gloom. There was another visible beyond that mysterious plane. I gritted my teeth, took an instant to hope I was guessing right, and stepped through.

I knew at once that I was back in normal time—still running backwards, doubtless, still in the same room—but I was standing in honest darkness, away from the pervasive death light of null time. There were Hagroon all about me, bulky, suited figures, almost filling the confined space of the room, overflowing into the corridor, seemingly unbothered by the lack of illumination. I recognized the officers I had seen moments before, the last to pass through the portals—or the first, in normal time: the pioneers sent through ahead of the main body to reconnoiter—before the

horde poured through, to stream back to the Net
Garages. Six weeks earlier—or tonight; either way of
looking at it was equally valid—I would meet them
there, embarking in their shuttles to return to the
Hagroon world line, their job here finished. But now,
because of the miracle of my retrograde. motion in the
time stream, I was seeing the play acted out in reverse;
watching the victorious troops, flushed from their
victory over the sleeping city, about to back out into the
streets, and re-enact their gas attack.

Many of the Hagroon, I noted, carried heavy canisters.
Others, as I watched, took empty containers from a heap
in the corridor, hitched them into place on their backs.
They were filing away now, by two's and three's,
backing out into the corridors, up the stairs, back into
the dead streets. I started to follow—then checked
myself. There was something tugging at the edge of my
awareness. Something I must do, now—quickly—before
my chance slipped away. Events were flowing
inexorably toward their inevitable conclusion, while I
hesitated, racking my brain. It was hard to think, hard
to orient my thoughts in the distorted perspective of
reversed time; but I had to stop now, force myself to
analyze what I was seeing, reconstruct the attack.

The Hagroon had arrived at the Net Garages. I had
seen their shuttles there. It was the perfect spot for an
assault in force via shuttle, and due to the characteristic
emanations of the Net communicator carriers, easy to
pinpoint for navigation purposes.

Once there, they had marched across the empty null-
time city to Intelligence Headquarters, a convenient
central location from which to attack, and with plenty of
dark cellar rooms—and perhaps there was also an
element of sardonic humor in their choice of staging
areas. . . .

Then the troops had poured through the portal,
emerged into the midnight streets of the real-time city,
spewing gas—the attack the end of which I was now
witnessing.

Then they had returned through the portal, crossed to
their shuttles again in null time—the exodus I had just
witnessed. . . .

But why the gas attack on a city about to suffer

annihilation along with the rest of the planet?

Simple: The Hagroon needed peace and quiet in which to erect the discontinuity engine—and they needed the assurance that the infernal machine would remain undisturbed for the necessary time to allow them to pass back through their portal into null time, regain their shuttles, and leave the doomed A-line. By gassing the city, they had ensured their tranquillity while they perpetrated the murder of a universe.

Because it was more than a world they killed. It was a planet, a solar system, a sky filled with stars, to the ends of conceivable space and beyond—a unique, irreplaceable aspect of reality, to be wiped forever from the face of the continuum, because one world, one tiny dust-mote in that universe posed a possible threat to Hagroon safety. It was an adominable plot—and the moments during which I could take action to thwart it were fast slipping away. Somewhere, at this moment, a crew was at work, preparing the doomsday device. And if I delayed, even for minutes, in finding it—it would be too late or (too early!). The machine would be separated into its component parts, carried away to the shuttles by backward-walking men, transported out of range—

I had to find the engine—now!

I looked around. Hagroon laden with empty canisters were still backing away along the corridor. Their officers waved their arms, mouths moving behind faceplates. One individual, helmetless, caught my attention. He came from the opposite direction along the narrow hall, stepping briskly up to the Hagroon directing the canister operation. Two rank-and-file Hagroon preceded him. They turned away, joined a group plucking empty canisters from a heap and fitting them on their backs. The helmetless one talked to the officer; both nodded, talked some more; then the former backed away down the dark hall—away from the stair. I hesitated a moment, then followed.

He backed off fifty feet, turned into a storeroom much like the one in which the portal had been erected. There were four other Hagroon there, crouching around a heavy tripod on which a massive construction rested, its casing lying on the floor to one side.

Luck was with me. I had found the discontinuity engine.

The next step was clear to me in the same instant that I saw the engine. As two of the Hagroon paused, staring with comically puzzled expressions, I went to the stand, planted my feet, gripped the massive casing, and lifted. It came away easily. My slightly accelerated time rate, although reversed, gave me an added quota of brute strength. I stepped back, hugging the horror device to my chest, feeling the buzz of its timer—and to my blank amazement, saw it still resting where it had been—while I held its counterpart in my hands. The Hagroon technicians were working away, apparently undisturbed. But then, I hadn't yet appeared, to create paradox before their startled eyes. . . .

I turned to the door, made my way along the corridor, climbed the steps, set off at the fastest dog trot I could manage for the Net Garages.

I made it in twenty minutes, in spite of the awkward burden, forcing myself to ignore the gas attack going on all around me. Suited Hagroon clumped backward through the well-lit streets under a vague cloud of brownish gas that seemed to slowly coalesce, drawing together as I watched. I half-ran, half-walked, shifting my grip on the heavy casing, sweating heavily now inside the suit. The gas was all around me, and I hoped the seals of my garment were as secure as Dzok had assured me they were.

At the garages, a few morose-looking Hagroon loitered about the parked shuttles, peering out through the wide doors toward the sounds of action in the city streets. I passed them unnoticed, went to the last shuttle in line—the same machine I had ridden once before. I knew it had preset controls, which would automatically home it on its A-line of origin—the Hagroon world. I pulled open the door, lowered my burden to the grey metal floor, pushed it well inside, then checked the wall clock. Dzok and I had calculated that the engine had gone into action at two A.M. precisely. It was now ten forty-five; three hours and fifteen minutes until M minute.

And the transit of the shuddle from the Zero-zero line to the Hagroon line had taken three hours and twenty-five minutes.

I had ten minutes to kill. . . .

The discontinuity engine was already counting down toward its moment of cataclysmic activity—the titanic outpouring of energy which would release the stasis which constituted the fabric of reality for this line of alternate existence. I had plucked it from the hands of its makers just as they were completing their installation. When the time came, it would perform. The shuttle was the problem now. I climbed inside, looked over the controls. They, at least, were simple enough. A trip wire, attached to the main field switch . . .

I went back out, found a length of piano wire on a workbench at one side of the garage, secured it to the white painted lever that controlled the shuttle's generators, led the wire out through the door. Five minutes to go, now. It was important to get the timing as exact as possible. I watched the hands of the clock move back: ten thirty-four; ten thirty-three; ten thirty-two; ten thirty-one. There was a faint vibration from the shuttle. . . .

I closed the door carefully, checked to be sure the wire was clear, then gripped it, gave it a firm pull. The shuttle seemed to waver. It shimmered, winked for an instant—then sat, solid and secure, unmoving. I let out a breath; the example of the engine had forewarned me. The results of my actions on external objects weren't visible to me, but I had sent the shuttle on its way. This was its past reality I saw before me now.

CHAPTER FIFTEEN

Back in the street, the attack was in full swing. I saw a man lying in the gutter rise, like a dummy on a rope, clutch at his throat, run backwards into a building—a corpse risen from the dead. The brown cloud hung low over the pavement now, a flat stratum of deadly gas. A long plume formed, flowed toward a Hagroon, whipped into the end of the hand-held horn of his dispenser. Other plumes shaped up, flowed toward other attackers. I was watching the gas attack in reverse—the killers, scavenging the streets of the poison that would decimate the population. I followed them as the poisonous cloud above gathered, broke apart, flowed back into the canisters from which it had come. I saw the invaders, laden now, slogging in their strange reverse gait back toward the dark bulk of Intelligence HQ. And I followed, crowding with them along the walk, through the doors, along the corridor, down the narrow steps, back to the deserted storeroom where they poured in a nightmare stream through the shining disk, back to null time and their waiting shuttles.

There was a paralyzing choice of coures of action open to me now—and my choice had to be the right one—with the life of a universe the cost of an error.

The last of the Hagroon passed through the portal, returning to null time, to march back to the Net Garages, board their shuttles and disappear back toward their horrendous home world. The portal stood deserted in the empty room, in a silence as absolute as deafness. I stood by it, waiting, as minutes ticked past—minutes of subjective time, during which I moved

176

inexorably back, back—to the moment when the Hagroon had first activated the portal—and I saw it dwindle abruptly, shrink to a point of incredible brilliance, wink out.

I blinked my eyes against the darkness, then switched on a small lamp set in the suit's chest panel, intended as an aid in map and instrument reading during transit through lightless continua. It served to show me the dim outlines of the room, the dusty packing cases, the littered floor—nothing else. The portal, I was now certain, required no focusing device to establish its circle of congruency between null and real time.

I waited a quarter of an hour to allow time for the Hagroon to leave the vicinity of the portal, studying my wrist controls and reviewing Dzok's instructions. Then I twisted the knob that would thrust me back through the barrier to null time. I felt the universe turn inside out while the walls whirled around me; then I was standing in null time, alone, breathing hard, but all right so far.

I looked around, and saw what I was looking for—a small, dull metal case, perched on a stand, half-obscured behind a stack of cases—the portal machine. I went to it, put a hand on it. It was humming gently, idling, ready to serve its monstrous owners when they arrived, minutes from now in normal time.

There were tools in a leather case clipped to the arm of my suit. I took out a screwdriver, removed the screws. The top of the case came off, showed me a maze of half-familiar components. I studied the circuits, recognized an analog of the miniature moebius-wound coil that formed the heart of my S-suit. The germ of an idea was taking shape—a trick probably impossible, certainly difficult, and very likely impractical, even if I had the necessary technical knowledge to carry it out—but an idea of such satisfying scope that I found myself smiling down in Satanic anticipation at the machine in my hands. Dzok had told me a little about the working of the S-suit—and I had watched as he had modified the circuits on two occasions. Now it was my turn to try. If I could bring it off . . .

Twenty minutes later I had done what I could. It was simple enough in theory. The focusing of the portal was controlled by a simple nuclear-force capacitor, tuned by a cyclic gravitational field. By reversing contacts, as Dzok had done when adjusting the suit to carry me backward in time as I crossed the continua, I had modified the orientation of the lens effect. Now, instead of establishing congruency at a level of temporal parity, the portal would set up a contact with a level of time in the future—perhaps as much as a week or two. I could go back now, reverse the action of the suit, and give my warning. With two weeks or more to convince Imperial Intelligence that I was something other than a madman with a disturbing likeness to one B. Bayard. I could surely make them see reason. True, there would be a number of small problems, such as the simultaneous existence of two battered ex-diplomats of that name—but that was a minor point, if I could avert the total destruction that waited in the wings.

I replaced the cover, for the first time feeling a throb of hope that my mad gamble could pay off—that in moving back through time to a point before the Hagroon attack, I might actually have changed the course of coming events. If I was right, it meant that the invaders I had seen pouring through the portal would never come—had never come; that the gas attack was relegated to the realm of unrealized possibilities; and that the city's inhabitants sleeping peacefully now would wake in the morning, unaware of the death they had died and risen from. . . .

It was a spooky thought. I had done what I could here. Now it was time to go. I braced my stomach against the wrench of the S-suit's null-time field, reversed the control. . . .

I blinked, letting my senses swim back into focus. I was back in real time, in the dark, deserted storeroom. There was no sign of the portal—and now, if my guesses were right, there wouldn't be for many days—and then the startled Hagroon would emerge into a withering fire from waiting Imperial troops.

Back in the hall, I licked my lips, suddenly as dry as a mummy's. The next step was one I didn't like. Tampering with my suit was dangerous business, and I'd had my share of daring experimentation for the night. But it had to be done.

The light here was dim—too dim for fine work. I went up the stairs to the ground floor corridor, saw a group of men back across the entry hall, walk backwards up the stairs that led to the second floor. I stifled the impulse to rush out with glad cries; they wouldn't hear me. They were as impervious to sounds coming from the past as the Hagroon. I was a phantom, moving in an unreal world of living memories, unrelled in reverse like a glimpse of an old album, riffled through from back to front. And when I had reversed the action of the S-suit, I'd still have the problem of making someone believe me.

It was hard, admittedly, for anyone to take my story seriously when my double—another me—was available to deny my authenticity. And nothing would have changed. I—the "I" of six weeks ago, minus the scars I had collected since then, was at home—now—dining in my sumptuous villa, with the incomparable Barbro, about to receive a mysterious phone call—and I would appear—a dirt-streaked man in torn clothing of outlandish cut, needing a shave and a bath, and talking nonsense. But this time at least I'd have a few days to convince them.

I stepped back into the cross corridor, found an empty office, closed and locked the door and turned on the light. Then, without waiting to consider the consequences of a miscalculation, I switched off the suit's power-pack. I unzipped, lifted the light helmet off, pulled the suit off, looked around the room. Everything seemed normal. I reached to the desk, gingerly lifted the black-handled paper knife that lay there—and with a sinking sensation saw it, still lying on the desk—the duplicate of the one in my hand. I tossed the knife back to the desk—and it winked out of existence—gone along the stream of normal time.

It was what I had been afraid of: even with the suit off, I was still living backwards.

Again, I got the miniature tool kit, used it to open the chest control pact. I knew which wires to reverse. With infinite care, I shifted the hair-fine filaments into new positions, guessing, when my recollection of Dzok's work failed. If I had known I'd be doing this job alone, I could have had Dzok run through it with me, even made notes. But both of us, in the excitement of the moment, had forgotten that I would slide away into past time as soon as the suit was activated. Now he was out of reach, hours in the future.

I finished at last, with a splitting headache, and a taste in my mouth like an abandoned rat's nest. My empty stomach simultaneously screeched for food and threatened violence if I so much as thought about the subject. I had been operating for the best part of forty-eight hours now without food, drink, or rest.

I pulled the suit back on, zipped up, too tired now even to worry, flipped the control—and knew at once that something was wrong—badly wrong.

It wasn't the usual nauseous wrench that I had come to expect; just a claustrophobic sense of pressure and heat. There was a loud humming in my ears, and a cloying in my throat as I drew a breath of scalding air.

I stepped to the desk, my legs as sluggish as lead castings. I picked up the paperweight—strangely heavy—

It was hot! I dropped it, watched it slam to the desk top. I dragged in another breath—with a sensation of drowning. The air was as thick as water, hot as live steam . . .

I exhaled a frosty plume of ice crystals. The sleeve of the suit caught my eye. It was glazed over with a dull white coating. I touched it with a finger, felt the heat of it, the slickness. It was ice—hot ice, forming on my suit! Even as I watched, it thickened, coating my sleeve, building up on my faceplate. I bent my arm to wipe it clear, saw crusts break, leap toward the floor with frantic speed. I managed to get one finger-swipe across the plastic visor. Through the clear strip, I saw a mirror across the room. I started for it—my legs strained uselessly. I was rooted to the spot, enchased in ice as rigid as armor!

My faceplate was frosted over solidly now. I tried to move an arm; it was rigid too. And suddenly, I understood. My tinkering with the suit's circuits had been less than perfect. I had re-established my normal direction of temporal progression—but my entropic rate was only a fraction of normal. I was an ice statue—an interesting find for the owner of the office when he broke the door down in the morning, unless I could break free fast!

I tensed my legs, threw my weight sideways—and felt myself toppling, whipping over to slam stunningly against the floor. My ice-armor smashed as I hit, and I moved quickly, brought one numbed arm up, groped for the control knob, fumbled at it with half-frozen fingers, twisted—

There was a sudden release of pressure. The faceplate cleared, dotted over with water droplets that bubbled, danced, disappeared. A blinding cloud was boiling up from me as the ice melted, flashed away as steam. I thrust against the floor, felt myself bound clear, rise halfway to the ceiling, then fall back as leisurely as an inflated balloon. I landed on one leg, felt the pressure build as the ankle twisted. I got my other foot under me, staggered, regained my balance, cursing between clenched teeth at the agony in the strained joint. I grabbed for the control, fumbled over the cold surface—

The control knob was gone. The twist I had given with numbed fingers had broken if off short!

I limped to the door, caught the knob, twisted—

The metal tore; pain shot through my hand. I looked at my palm, saw ripped skin. I had the strength of a Gargantua without the toughness of hide to handle it. I had overcontrolled. Now my entropic rate was double or triple the normal one. My body heat was enough to boil water. The friction of my touch bubbled paint! Carefully I twisted the door's lock, pulled at the crushed knob. The door moved sluggishly, heavy as a vault. I pushed it into the hall—and lurched to a stop.

A seven-foot specimen of the Hagroon species stood glowering from a dark doorway ten feet across the corridor.

I backed away, flattened myself against the wall. This boy was a factor I hadn't counted on. He was a scout, probably, sent through hours ahead of the main column. I had seen the last of his fellows leave, and watched the portal blink out. On the strength of that, I had assumed they were all gone. But if the portal had been activated briefly, an hour earlier, as a test . . .

Another academic question. He was here, as big as a grizzly and twice as ugly, a broad, thick troll in a baggy atmosphere suit, raising an arm slowly, putting a foot forward, heading my way—

I jumped aside, almost fell, as the Hagroon slammed heavily against the wall where I'd been standing—a wall charred black by the heat of my body. I moved back again, carefully this time. I had the speed on him, but if he caught me in that bonecrusher grip . . .

He was mad—and scared. It showed in the snarling expression I could dimly see through the dark faceplate. Maybe he'd already been down to the portal room, and found his escape hatch missing. Or maybe the follow-up invasion force was behind schedule now. . . .

I felt my heart take a sudden leap as I realized that I'd succeeded. I had worked over the suit for an hour, and perhaps another half-hour had gone by while I floundered in my slow-time state, building up a personal icecap—and they hadn't appeared on the scene. I could answer the theorists on one point now: a visitor to the past *could* modify the already-seen future, eliminate it from existence!

But the Hagroon before me was unaware of the highly abnormal aspects of his presence here. He was a fighter, trained to catch small hairless anthropos and squeeze their necks, and I fitted the description. He jumped again—a curiously graceless, slow-motion leap—hit and skidded, whirling ponderously to grab again—

I misjudged my distance, felt his hand catch at my sleeve. He was fast, this hulking monster. I pulled away, tore free—and stumbled as I skidded back, felt my feet go out from under me—

He was after me, while I flailed the air helplessly. One huge hand caught my arm, hauled me in, gathered me to his vast bosom. I felt the crushing pressure, almost heard the creak of my ribs as blood rushed blindingly to my face—

The fabric of his suit was bubbling, curling, blackening. His grip relaxed. I saw his face, his mouth open, and distantly, through his helmet and mine, I heard his scream of agony. His hands came up, fingers outspread, blistered raw by the terrible heat of my body. Even so, he ripped with them at his suit, tearing the molten plastic from his shaggy chest, exposing a bleeding second degree burn from chin to navel.

I continued my fall, took the shock on my outstretched hands, felt the floor come up and grind against my chin, felt the skin break, the spatter of hot blood. Then there was only the blaze of stars and a soft bottomless blackness. . . .

I lay on my back, feeling an Arctic chill that gripped my chest like a cold iron vise. I drew a wheezing breath, pressed my hands against the floor. They were numb, as dead as a pair of iceman's tongs, but I managed to get my feet under me, stagger upright. There were blackened footprints burned against the polished wood of the floor, and a larger black area where I had lain—and even as I burned the surfaces I touched, they bled away my heat, freezing me.

The Hagroon was gone. I saw a bloody hand-print on the wall, another farther along. He had headed for the service stair, bound no doubt for the storage room where the portal had been. He'd have a long wait. . . .

I leaned against the wall, racked with shivering, my teeth clamped together like a corpse in rigor. I had had enough of lone world-saving missions. It was time for someone else to join the party, share the honor—and incidentally, perform a delicate operation on my malfunctioning S-suit before I froze solid, fell on my face, and burned my way through to the basement.

I turned toward the front hall with a vague idea of finding someone—Richthofen, maybe. He was here tonight. Sure, good old Manfred, sitting at his desk upstairs, giving the third degree to a poor slob named Bayard, hauled on the carpet because some other poor slob of the same name was in jail a few miles away, claiming he was Bayard, and that the end of the world was nigh!

I reached the corner, staggered, feeling the hot flush of fever burning my face, while the strength drained from my legs, sucked away by the terrible entropic gradient between my runaway E-field and the normal space around me.

Bad stuff, Mr. B, tinkering with machines you don't understand. Machines made by a tribe of smart monkeymen who regard us sapiens as little better than homicidal maniacs—and with good reason, good reason . . .

I had fallen, and was on hands and knees watching the smoke curl up from between my numbed fingers. It was funny, that. Worth a laugh in anybody's joke book. I clawed at the wall, bubbling paint, got to my feet, made another yard toward the stair. . . .

Poor old Bayard; me. What a surprise he'd get, if he walked into that little room down below, and encountered one frightened, burned, murder-filled Hagroon—a pathetic leftover from a so-carefully-planned operation that had gotten itself lost along the way because it had overlooked a couple of small factors. The Hagroon, self-styled tough guys. Ha! They didn't know what real bloodthirstiness was until they ran up against good old Homo sap. Poor little monsters, they didn't have a chance . . .

Down again, and a mouthful of blood. Must have hit harder that time, square on the face. A good thing, maybe. Helps to clear the head. Where was I going? Oh, yes. Had to go along and warn poor old B. Can't let the poor fellow walk in all unsuspecting. Have to get there first . . . still have the slug gun . . . finish off bogie man. . . .

I was dimly aware of a door resisting as I leaned against it, then swinging wide, and I was falling, tumbling down stairs, bouncing, head over heels, slow and easy like a pillow falling—a final slam against the gritty, icy floor, the weight, and the pain. . . .

A long trip this. Getting up again, feeling the cold coming up the legs now like slow poison . . . cloud of brown gas, spreading up the legs, across the city. Have to warn them, tell them . . .

But they don't believe. Fools. Don't believe. God, how it hurts, and the long dark corridor stretching away, and the light swelling and fading, swelling again—

There he is! God, what a monster. Poor monster, hurt, crouched in the corner, rocking and moaning. Brought it on himself, the gas-spreading son of a bearskin rug! Sees me now, scrambling up. And look at those teeth! Makes old Dzok look like a grass-eater. Coming at me now. Get the gun out, feel it slap the palm, hold it, squeeze—

The gun was falling from my numbed hand, skidding on the floor, and I was groping for it, feeling with hands like stumps, seeing the big shape looming over me—

To hell with the gun. Can't press the firing stud anyway. Speed, that's all you've got now, m' lad. Hit him low, let his weight do the job, use your opponent's strength against him, judo in only five easy lessons, class starts Monday—

A blow like a runaway beer truck and I was skidding across the floor, and even through the suit I heard the sickening *crunch!* as the massive skull of the Hagroon struck the corner of a steel case, the ponderous *slam!* as he piled against the floor. I was on hands and knees again, not feeling the floor anymore, not feeling anything—just get on your feet once more and make sure . . .

I pulled myself up with the help of a big box placed conveniently beside me, took three wavering steps, bent over him. I saw the smear of blood, the thin ooze of fluid from the gaping wound above the ear, the black-red staining the inside of the helmet. Okay, Mr. Hagroon. You put up a good scrap, but that low block and lady luck were too much for you, and now—

I heard a noise from the door. There was a man there, dim in the wavering light of fading consciousness. I leaned, peering, with a strange sense of *déjà vu*, the seen-before . . .

He came toward me in slow-motion, and I blinked, wiped my hand across the steamed-over faceplate. He was in midair, in a dream leap, hands reaching for me. I checked myself, tried to back away, my hand outflung as though to hold back some unspeakable fate—

Long, pink sparks crackled from his hand to mine as he hung like a diver suspended in midair. I heard a noise like fat frying, and for one unbelievable instant glimpsed the face before me—

Then a silent explosion turned the world to blinding white, hurling me into nothingness.

CHAPTER SIXTEEN

It was a wonderful bed, wide and cool and clean, and the dream was wonderful too. Barbro's face, perfect as an artist's conception of the goddess of the hunt, framed by her dark red hair in a swirl of silken light. Just behind the rosy vision there were a lot of dark thoughts clamoring to be dragged out and reviewed, but I wasn't going to get hooked on that one. No sir, the good old dream was good enough for me, if only it wouldn't go away and leave me remembering dark shapes that moved in foul tunnels—and pain, and loss, the sickness of failure and dying hope—

The dream leaned closer and there were bright tears in the smoke-grey eyes, but the mouth was smiling, and then it was against mine, and I was kissing warm, soft lips—real lips, not the dream kind that always elude you. I raised a hand, felt a weight like an anvil stir, saw a vast bundle of white bandage swim into view.

"Barbro!" I said, and heard my voice emerge as a croak.

"Manfred! He's awake! He knows me!"

"Ah, a man would have to be far gone indeed to fail to know you, my dear," a cool voice said. Another face appeared, less pretty than the other, but a good face all the same. Baron von Richthofen smiled down at me, looking concerned and excited at the same time.

"Brion, Brion! What happened?" Barbro's cool fingertips touched my face. "When you didn't come home, I called, and Manfred told me, you'd gone—and then they searched the building, and found footprints, burned—"

"Perhaps you'd better not press him now," Manfred murmured.

"No, of course not." A hot tear fell on my face, and Barbro smiled and wiped it away. "But you're safe now, that's all that matters. Rest, Brion. You can think about it later. . . ."

I tried to speak, to tell her it was all right, not to go . . .

But the dream faded, and sleep washed over me like warm, scented soapsuds, and I let go and sank down in its green depths.

The next time, I woke up hungry. Barbro was sitting by the bed, looking out the window at a tree in full spring leaf, golden green in the afternoon sun. I lay for a while, watching her, admiring the curve of her cheek, the line of her throat, the long, dark lashes—

She turned, and a smile like the sun coming out after a spring rain warmed me all the way to my bandaged heels.

"I'm okay now," I said. This time the voice came out hoarse but recognizable.

There was a long, satisfying time then, of whispered words and agreeable nonsense, and as many feather-soft kisses as we could fit in. Then Manfred came in, and Hermann, and Luc, and things got a bit more brisk and businesslike.

"Tell me, Brion," Manfred said mock-sternly. "How did you manage to leave my office, disappear for half an hour, only to be discovered unconscious beside some sort of half-ape, and dressed like a wanderer from a fancy dress ball in a variety of interesting costumes, wearing a three-day beard, with twenty-seven separate and distinct cuts, abrasions, and bruises, to say nothing of second-degree burns, frostbite, and a broken tooth?"

"What day is it?" I demanded.

He told me. I had been unconscious for forty-eight hours. Two days since the scheduled hour for the invasion—and the Hagroon hadn't appeared.

"Listen," I said. "What I'm going to tell you is going to be a little hard to take, but in view of the corpse you found beside me, I expect you to do your best. . . ."

"A truly strange creature, Brion," Hermann said. "It attacked you, I presume, which would account for some of the wounds, but as for the burns . . ."

I told them. They listened. I had to stop twice to rest, and once to eat a bowl of chicken broth, but I covered everything.

"That's it," I finished. "Now go ahead and tell me I dreamed it all. But don't forget to explain how I dreamed that dead Hagroon."

"Your story is impossible, ridiculous, fantastic, mad, and obviously the ravings of a disordered mind," Hermann said. "And I believe every word of it. My technicians have reported to me strange readings on the Net Surveillance instruments. What you have said fits the observations. And the detail of your gambit of readjusting the portal, so as to shun the invading creatures into a temporal level weeks in the future; I find that of particular interest—"

"I can't know how far I deflected them," I said. "Just be sure to station a welcoming party down there to greet them as they arrive."

Hermann cleared his throat. "I was about to come to that, Brion. You yourself have commented on the deficiencies in your qualifications for the modification of sophisticated MC effect apparatus—and by the way, I am lost in admiration of the suit you have brought home from your travels. A marvel—but I digress.

"You adjusted the portal, you said, to divert the Hagroon into the future. Instead, I fear, you have shunted them into a past time-level of our Zero-zero line. . . ."

There was a moment of silence. "I don't get that," I said. "Are you saying they've already invaded us—last month, say?"

"The exact temporal displacement, I cannot yet state. But it seems clear, Brion, that they went back, not forward. . . ."

"Never mind that," Barbro said. "Wherever they are, they are not troubling us now—thanks to your bravery, my hero!"

Everybody laughed and my ears got hot. Manfred stepped in with a comment on the fiery figure.

"A strange sensation, my friend, to meet yourself face to face. . . ."

"Which reminds me," I said in the sudden silence.

"Where's the . . . ah . . . other me?"

Nobody said anything. Then Hermann snapped his fingers.

"I think I can tell you the answer to that! It is an interesting problem in the physics of the continuum—but I think it can be accepted as axiomatic that the paradox of a face-to-face confrontation of identities is intolerable to the fabric of simultaneous reality. Hence, when the confrontation occurs—something must give! In this case, the intolerable entropic stress was relieved by the shunting of one aspect of this single ego into the plane you have called null time—where you encountered the Hagroon, and embarked on your strange adventure."

"Your friend, Dzok," Barbro said. "We must do something, Manfred, to help his people in their fight against these shaggy monsters. We can send troops—"

"I fear the implications of what Brion said regarding the disposition of the discontinuity engine have escaped you, my dear," Hermann said. There was a glint of ferocious amusement in his eyes. "From the care with which he timed his operation, I should imagine that the Hagroon shuttle bearing the apparatus of destruction arrived on schedule in the Hagroon world-line—just as the timer actuated it. The Xonijeelians have nothing to fear from invading Hagroons. Our Brion has neatly erased them from the roster of the continuum's active menaces."

"Dzok was right," Manfred said sadly. "We *are* a race of genocides. But perhaps that is a law of the nature that produced us. . . ."

"And we must help the poor peoples of these sub-technical A-lines," Barbro said. "Poor Olivia, dreaming of a brighter world, and never to know it, because we selfishly reserve its treasures for ourselves—"

"I agree, Barbro," Manfred said. "There must be a change in policy. But it is not an easy thing to bring what we think of as enlightenment to a benighted world. Whatever we do, there will be those who oppose us. This Napoleon the Fifth, for example. How will he regard a proposed status as vassal of our Emperor?"

Barbro looked at me. "You were half in love with this Olivia, Brion," she said. "But I forgive you. I am not such a fool as to invite her to be our houseguest, but you must arrange to bring her here. If she is as lovely as you say, there will be many suitors—"

"She wasn't half as gorgeous as you are," I said. "But I think it would be a nice gesture."

There was a clatter of feet at the door. A young fellow in a white jacket came in, breathing hard.

"A call for you, Herr Goering," he said. "The telephone is just here along the hall."

Hermann went out, and we talked—asking lots of questions and getting some strange answers.

"In a way," Manfred said, "it is a pity that these Hagroon were so thoroughly annihilated by your zeal, Brion. A new tribe of man only remotely related to our own stock, but having high intelligence, a technical culture—"

Hermann came back, pulling at his earlobe and blinking in a perplexed way.

"I have spoken to the Net Laboratory just now," he said. "They have calculated the destination of your unhappy party of invading Hagroon, Brion. They worked from the brief traces recorded by our instruments over the period of the last five years—"

"Five years?" several voices echoed.

"From the date on which our present improved Net instrumentation was installed," he said, "there have been a number of anomalous readings, which in the past we were forced to acept as a normal, though inexplicable deviation from calculated values. Now, in the light of Brion's statements, we are able to give them a new interpretation."

"Yes, yes, Hermann," Manfred urged. "Spare us the dramatic pause-for-effect. . . ."

"The Hagroon, to state it bluntly, Barbro and gentlemen, have been plunged over fifty thousand years into past time by our clever Brion's adjustment to their portal!"

There was a moment of stunned silence. I heard myself laugh, a wild-sounding cackle.

"So they made it—just a little early. And if they tried to go back—they jumped off the deep end into an A-line that had been pulled out from under them. . . ."

"I think they did not do that latter," Hermann said. "I

believe that they safely reached the Neolithic era—and remained there. I think they adapted but poorly to their sudden descent to a sub-technical status, these few hundreds of cast-aways in time. And I think, never did they lose their hatred of the hairless hominids they found there in that cold northland of fifty millenia past.

"No, they were safely marooned there in the age of mammoths and ice. And there they left their bones, which our modern archaeologists have found and called Neanderthal. . . ."

THE END
OF BOOK I

BOOK II:

THE OTHER SIDE OF TIME

PROLOGUE

He sat astride the great war-horse, in the early morning, looking across the field toward the mist-obscured heights where the enemy waited. The chain-mail coif and hauberk weighed heavy on him; and there was another weight within him: a sense of a thing undone, a duty forgotten, of something valuable betrayed.

"The mist clears, my lord," Trumpington spoke at his side. "Will you attack?"

He looked up at the sun, burning through the mist. He thought of the green vales of home, and the sense grew in him that death waited here on this obscure field.

"No. I'll not unsheathe Balingore this day," he said at last.

"My lord—is all well with you?" There was concern in the young squire's voice.

He nodded curtly. Then he turned and rode back through the silent, staring ranks of his panoplied host.

Chapter One

At Molly's place, the jukebox was breaking its heart over a faithless woman, but there was nobody listening but a few conchs sitting out on the rickety porch under the yellow bug lights, nursing beers and catching the breeze moving in off the gulf. It was after nine P.M. and the heat of the day was gone from the beach, and the surf coming up on the sand sounded lonesome and far away, like an old man's memories.

I took a stool at the bar and Molly put a bottle of wine in front of me, with the seal still intact.

"Johnny, it happened again today," she said. "I found a platter I swear I broke last month, right there in the sink, not a chip out of it. And the whiskey stock is different—stuff I never ordered there, and not a sign of the Red Label—and you know I know my stock. And three heads of cabbage, fresh yesterday—rotten in the cooler!"

"So—your last order was mixed up—and the vegetables weren't as fresh as they looked," I said.

"And toadstools growing in the corners?" she said. "I guess that's natural too? You know better'n that, John Curlon! And how about this?" She brought a heavy cut-glass cup up from behind the bar. It was about one-quart capacity, rounded on the bottom, with a short stem.

"This was here when I came in this evening. It's worth money. How'd it get here?"

"Impulse shopping," I suggested.

"Don't kid me, Johnny. There's something happening—something that scares me! It's like the world was shifting right under my feet! And its not just here! I see things all around—little things—like trees are in different places than they used to be—and a magazine I started reading; when I came back to it—there wasn't any such story in the book!"

I patted her hand and she caught my fingers. "Johnny—tell me what's happening—what to do! I'm not losing my mind, am I?"

"You're fine, Molly. The glass was probably the gift of some secret admirer. And everybody loses things sometimes, or remembers things a little differently than they really were. You'll probably find your story in another magazine. You just got mixed up." I tried to make it sound convincing, but it's hard to do when you're not sure yourself.

"And Johnny—what about you?" Molly was still holding my hand. "Have you talked to *them* yet?"

"Who?" I asked.

She gave me a hot look from a pair of eyes that had probably been heartbreakers back before the Key West sun had bleached the fire out of them. "Don't act like you don't know what I mean! There was another one in today asking for you—a new guy, one I never saw before."

"Oh—them. No, I haven't had time—"

"Johnny! Smarten up! You can't buck that crowd. They'll smash you so flat you could slide under the linoleum without making a bump."

"Don't worry about me, Molly—"

"Sure, grin! Johnny Curlon, six foot three of bone and muscle, the fellow with the bullet proof hide! Listen, Johnny! That Jakesy's a mean one—especially since they put the wire in his jaw. He'll chop you into cutbait—" she broke off. "But I guess you know all that. I guess nothing I can say is going to change you." She turned and picked a Remy Martin bottle from the back bar.

"Like you said, it's just a glass. Might as well use it." She poured brandy into the chalice and I picked it up and looked into the glint of amber light inside it. The glass was cool and smooth and heavy against my palms. . . .

Seated in my great chair, I looked down at the narrow, treacherous face of him I had loved so well, saw hope leap up in those crafty eyes.

"My lord kind," he started, and shuffled toward me on his knees, dragging the chains that he bore. "I know not why I was cajoled to embark on such rude folly. 'Twas but a fit of madness, meaning naught—"

"Three times ere now have you sought my throne and crown," I cried, not for his ears alone, but for all those who might murmur against that which I knew must be. "Three times have I pardoned thee, lavished anew my favor on thee, raised thee up before loyal men."

"Heaven's grace descend on thy Majesty for thy great mercy," the glib voice babbled, and even in that moment I saw the hunger in his eyes. "This time, I swear—"

"Swear not, thou who are forsworn!" I commanded him. "Rather think on thy soul, to tarnish it no more in these thy final hours!"

And I saw fear dawn at last, driving out the hunger and all else save lust for life itself. And I knew that lust to be foredoomed.

"Mercy, brother," he gasped, and raised his manacled hands to me as to a god. "Mercy, out of memory of past joys shared! Mercy, for love of our mother, the sainted Lady Eleanor—"

"Foul not the name of her who loved thee!" I shouted, hardening my heart against the vision of her face, pale under the hand of approaching death, swearing me to the eternal protection of him who knelt before me.

He wept as they bore him away, wept and swore his true allegiance and love for me. And later in my chambers, drugged with wine, I wept, hearing again and ever again the jail of the headsman's ax.

They told me that at the end, he found his manhood, and walked to the block with his head held high, as befits the son of kings. And with his last words, he forgave me.

Oh, he forgave me. . . .

A voice was calling my name. I blinked and saw Molly's face as through a haze of distance.

"Johnny—what is it?"

I shook my head and the hallucination faded. "I don't know," I said. "Not getting enough sleep, maybe."

"Your face," she said. "When you took the glass in your hands and held it up like that, you looked—like a stranger. . ."

"Maybe it reminded me of something."

"It's getting to you too, isn't it, Johnny?"

"Maybe." I drank the brandy off in a gulp.

"The best thing for you would be to go away," she said softly. "You know that."

"And if they don't?"

"You can't have everything," I said.

She looked at me and sighed.

"I guess I knew all along you'd go your own way, Johnny," she said.

I felt her eyes following me as I pushed through the screen door and out into the cool evening air.

A heavy fog had rolled in from the gulf, and down at the pier the big merc lamps were shining through the mist like a bridge out into nowhere. At the end of it, my boat floated in fog. She was a sweet forty-footer, almost paid for, riding low in the water with full loads in her four hundred-gallon tanks. The pair of 480 Supermarine Chryslers under her hatches were old, but in top condition; I'd rebuilt them myself. They'd always gotten me where I was going, and back again.

I went up past the gear locker by the pole and two men separated themselves from the shadows and stepped out to block my way. One of them was the big ex-pug, the one they call Jakesy. The other was a foxy little bird in race-track clothes. He flipped a cigarette away and pinched the knot in his tie and shook out his cuffs like a card shark getting set for a fast shuffle.

"This here is Mr. Renata, Curlon," Jakesy said. Somebody had hit him in the throat once and his voice was a foghorn whisper. "He came down from Palm special to talk to ya."

"A pleasure, Mr. Curlon," the foxy man put out a long narrow hand like a monkey's. I didn't look at it.

"I told you not to hang around my boat," I said.

"Don't get tough, Curlon," Jakesy said. "Mr. Renata's a big man, he come a long way—"

"The Fishermen's Protective Association's an important organization, fella," Renata spoke up. "A man can save hisself a lot of trouble by signing up."

"Why would I want to save myself trouble?"

He nodded, as if I'd said something reasonable. "Tell you what, Curlon," he said. "To show our good will, we'll waive the three hundred initiation fee."

"Just stay out of my way," I said, and started past him.

"Wait a minute, conch," Jakesy growled. "Mugs like you don't talk to Mr. Renata that way."

"Take it easy, Jakesy," Renata said softly. "Mr. Curlon's too smart a man to start any trouble."

I looked the way his eyes had flicked and saw the car that had eased up across the street. Two men had gotten out and were leaning against the front fender with their arms folded.

"You got to move with the times, Curlon," Renata said, and showed me some teeth that needed work. "A guy on his own ain't got a chance nowadays. The competition is too tough." He took some papers out of an inside pocket and held them out. "Sign 'em, fella. It's the smart thing to do."

I took the papers and tore them across the middle and tossed them away. "Anything else before you go?" I asked him. His face got nasty, but he put out a hand to hold Jakesy back.

"That's too bad, Curlon. Too bad." He took out his show hanky and flapped it and I stepped in fast past him and left-hooked Jakesy before his hand had time to finish its sweep up from his hip. The blackjack went flying and Jakesy took two off-balance steps back and went over the side and hit with plenty of splash. I grabbed for Renata, and a small automatic fell out of his clothes; he dived for it and ran into the toe of my shoe. He flopped out on his back, spitting blood and mewling like a wet kitten. The two back-up men were coming at a run. I grabbed up the gun and started to say something to Renata about calling them off, but a gun flashed and coughed through a silencer and a slug cut air past my right ear. I fired twice from the hip and a man skidded and went down and the other hit the planks. I caught Renata's collar and hauled him to his feet.

"Any closer and you're dead," I said; he kicked and tried to bite my hand, then squalled an order.

"The lousy punk got Jimmy," the yell came back.

Renata yelled again and one of the gunnies got to his feet, slowly.

"Jimmy, too," I said. Renata passed the word. The

man on his feet tried to lift his partner, couldn't make it, settled for getting a couple of handfuls of coat and dragging him. After a minute or two I heard the car start up, gun away into the fog.

"OK—now gimme a break," Renata said. I pushed him away. "Sure," I said, and hit him hard in the stomach, and when he bent over, I slammed a solid one to the chin. I left him on the dock and went on out and started up. I used my old knife to cut her stern line; in two minutes I was nosed out into the channel, headed for deep water. I watched the beach lights sliding away into the mist that covered the decay and the poverty and just left the magic of a harbor at night. And the smell of corruption; it couldn't cover that.

I ran due west for five hours, then switched off and sat on deck and watched the stars for an hour, listening for the sound of engines, but nobody was chasing me.

I put out a sea anchor and went below and turned in.

There was a low mist across the water when I rolled out just before dawn. My shoulder was aching, and for a minute that and the feel of the clammy fog against my face almost reminded me of something: the glint of light on steel and a pennon that fluttered in the breeze, and the feel of a big horse under me; and that was pretty strange, because I've never been on a horse in my life.

The boat was dead still on the flat sea, and even through the mist the sun already had some heat in it. It looked like another of those wide, blue days on the gulf, with the sea and sky empty to the far horizon. Out here, Jakesy and his boss Renata seemed like something out of another life. I started for the galley to rustle some ham and eggs, noticed a curious thing: little clumps of funguslike stuff, growing on the mahogany planking and on the chrome rail. I kicked it over the side and spent half an hour swabbing her down and polishing her brass, listening to a silence as big as the world. Afterward, I lifted the hatch and checked the engines over, screwed the grease cups on the stuffing boxes down a turn or two. When I came back up on deck, there was a man standing by the port rail, looking at me over the sights of a gun.

He was dressed in a tight white uniform with little twists of gold braid at the cuffs. His face was lean, hard, not sunburned; a city man. The thing in his hand wasn't like any gun I had ever seen, but it had that functional look; and the hand that pointed it at my face was as steady as it needed to be. I looked past him, all around the boat. There was no other boat in sight—not even a rubber raft.

"Smooth," I said. "How did you manage it?"

"This is a neurac—a nerve-gun," he said in a matter-of-fact tone. "It is indescribably painful. Do exactly as I tell you and I won't be forced to use it." He motioned me back toward the hatch. He had a strange accent—British, and yet not quite British. I moved back a step or two and he followed, keeping the distance between us constant.

"There is a fuel-pump valve located at the left of the water manifold," he said, in the same tone you might ask to have the sugar passed. "Open it."

I thought of things to say then, but the gun was the answer to all of them. I climbed down and found the valve and opened it; diesel fuel gushed out, making a soft splashing sound hitting the water on the port side. Three hundred gallons of number two, spreading out oily on the flat water.

"Open the forward scuttle valve," the man with the gun said.

He moved with me as I lifted the hatch, watched me open the valve to let the green water boil in. Then we went aft and opened the other one. The water made a cool, gurgling sound coming in. I could see it in the open engine hatch, rising beside the big cylinder blocks, with bits of flotsam swirling on the dark surface. In two minutes she was down by the stern, listing a little to port.

"It's a cumbersome way to commit suicide," I said. "Why not just go over the side?"

"Close the aft valve," he said. He was braced against the side of the cockpit, cool and calm, a technician doing his job. I wondered what the job might be, but I went aft fast and closed the valve. Then the forward one. By then, she was riding low, her gunwales about six inches out of the water. The smell of the oil was thick in the air.

"If the wind comes up, under we go," I said. "And with no fuel, that means no pumps—"

"Lie down on the deck," he cut me off.

I shook my head. "I'll take it standing up."

"As you wish." He dropped the gun muzzle and I tensed and shifted my weight to make my try and the gun made a sharp humming noise and liquid fire smashed into me and tore my flesh apart.

. . . I was lying with my face against the deck, quivering like a freshly amputated leg. I got my knees under me and got to my feet.

The man in the white uniform was gone. I was alone on the boat.

I went over her from bow to transom—not that I thought I'd find him hiding in the bait locker. It was just something to do while I got used to the idea of what had happened. I finished that and leaned against the deckhouse while a spell of pain-nausea passed. The spot I'd picked to ride out the night hours was sixty miles south of Key West, about forty north of the Castillo del Morro. I was afloat, as long as the wind didn't rise enough to put a riffle on the water. I had plenty of food, and water for two days—maybe three if I stretched it. The man with the gun had fixed my radio before he left; I checked and found a tube missing. There was no spare. That meant my one chance was to stay afloat until somebody happened past who could put a line on me. It would mean losing the boat—but she was as good as lost now, unless I could save her fast.

There wasn't much I could do in that direction: the hand pump in the bilge was under two feet of water. I spent an hour rerigging it on deck, and put in another hour working the handle before it broke. I may have lowered the level an eighth of an inch—or maybe it was just the light. I bailed for a while with a bait bucket, doing math in my head: at six buckets a minute, figuring three gallons to a bucket, how long to pour ten thousand gallons over the side? Too long, was the answer I came up with. By noon, the wind was starting to stir, and the level was down about an inch. I fished a canned ham and a bottle of beer out of the water sloshing around in the galley, then sat on the shady side of the cockpit and watched the pale clouds piling up far away across the brassy water, and thought about sitting in the cool dimness of Molly's bar, telling her about how a mysterious man in a dapper white suit had aimed something he called a nerve-gun at me and told me to dump her fuel and scuttle her, and then disappeared while I was lying down . . .

I got up and checked the spot where he'd been standing. There was nothing there to prove he hadn't been an illusion. He'd walked me forward, and then aft again, but that hadn't left a trail, either. I had opened the dump valve myself, flooded her myself. There was still the missing radio tube, but maybe I'd sneaked in and done that, too, while I wasn't looking. Maybe the hot tropical sun had finally crisped my brains, and the shot from the nerve-gun, which I could still feel every time I moved, had been the kind of fit people have after they've lost their grip on reality.

But I was just talking to myself. I knew what I'd seen. I remembered that hard, competent face, the way the light had glinted along the barrel of the gun, the incongruously spotless whites with the shiny lapel insignia with the letters TNL in blue enamel on them. I got my bucket and went back to work.

A breeze sprang up at sunset, and in ten minutes she had shipped more water than I had bailed in ten hours. She wallowed in the swells, logy as a gravid sea cow. She'd swamp sometime in the night, and I'd swim for a while, and after that. . . .

There wasn't any future in that line of thought. I stretched out on my back on top of the deckhouse and closed my eyes and listened to her creak, as she moved in the water with all that weight in her. . . .

. . . And came awake, still listening, but to a new sound now. It was full dark, with no moon. I slid down to the deck and solid water came over the gunwale and soaked me to the knees.

I heard the sound again; it came from forward—a dull *thunk*! like something heavy bringing up solid against the decking. I reached down inside the cockpit and brought out the big six-cell flash I keep clamped to the wall beside the chart board and flicked it on and shone it up that way, and a voice out of the dark said, "Curlon—kill that light!"

I went flat against the house and flashed the beam along the rail and found his feet, raised it and put it square in his eyes. It wasn't the man who'd used the pain-gun on me. He was tall, gray-haired, wearing a trim gray coverall. His hands were empty.

"Put the light out," he said. "Quick! It's important!"

I switched off the flash. I could still see him faintly.

"There's no time to explain," he said. "You'll have to abandon her!"

"I don't suppose you brought a boat with you?" More water came over the side. She shuddered under me.

"Something better," he said. "But we'll have to make it fast. Come on forward!"

I didn't answer because I was halfway to him. I tried to find his silhouette against the sky, but it was all the same color.

"She's sinking fast," he said. "Jumping me won't change that."

"Her fuel and water tanks are dry," I said. "Maybe she'll float." I gained another yard.

"We don't have time to wait and see. There are only a few seconds left."

He was standing on the forehatch, half turned to the left, looking out into the dark as though there were something interesting out there he didn't want to miss. I followed the way he was looking and saw it.

It was a platform, about ten feet on a side, with a railing around it that reflected faint highlights from what looked like a glowing dish perched on a stand in the center. It was about a hundred yards away, drifting a few feet above the water. There were two men on it, both in the white suits. One of them was the man who'd scuttled my boat. The other was a little man with big ears: I couldn't see his face.

"What's the hurry?" I said. "I see a man I need to have a talk with."

"I can't force you," the man in gray said. "I can only tell you that this time they're holding all the cards. I'm offering you a chance at a new deal. Look!" He hooked a thumb over his shoulder. At first I didn't see anything; then I did: a rectangle, six feet high, two feet wide, like an open doorway into a room where a dim candle burned.

"I can't afford to be caught," the man in gray said. "Follow me—if you decide to trust me." He turned and stepped up into the ghost-door hanging in the air and was gone.

The platform was coming up fast now; the lean man was standing at the forward edge with the nerve-gun in his hand. "Give me ten seconds" I said to the hole in the air.

I went back along the pilot-house, dropped down into hip-deep water in the cockpit. I felt around up above the dead binnacle light, found the leather belt and sheath, strapped it on. As I swung back up. I felt her start to go. White water churned up around my waist, almost broke my grip on the rail. The glowing doorway was still there, hanging in the air six feet away. I jumped for it as she slid under. There was a sensation like needles against my skin as I crossed the line of light; then my feet struck floor, and I was standing in the strangest room I ever saw.

Chapter Two

It was about eight feet by ten, carpeted with curved white-painted walls lined with the glitter of screens, dials, instrument faces, more levers and gadgets than the cockpit of a Navy P2V. The man in gray was sitting in one of two contoured bucket seats in front of an array of colored lights. He flashed me a quick glance, hit a button at the same time. A soft humming sound started up; there was an indefinable sense of motion, in some medium other than space.

"Close, but I don't think they saw us," he said tensely. "At least there's no tac-ray on us. But we have to move out fast, before he sets up a full-scale scan pattern." He was looking into a small, green-glowing screen, the size of a flight-deck radarscope, flipping levers at the same time. The scanning line swept down from top to bottom, about two cycles per second. I'd never seen one like it. But then I'd never seen anything like any of what had happened in the last few minutes.

"Who are they?" I said. "What are they?"

He gave me a fast up-and-down look. "For the moment, suffice it to say they're representatives of someone who seems to have taken a dislike to you." He flipped a switch and the lights dimmed down almost to nothing. On a big screen, six feet square, a picture snapped into sharp focus. It was the platform, hovering above the choppy water about fifty feet away, receding. The view was as clear as though I were looking out through a picture window. One of the men in white was playing a powerful beam of bluish light across the waves. My boat was gone. There was nothing in sight but a few odds and ends of gear, bobbing on the black water.

"You dropped off his tracer cold," the man in gray said. "He won't like that very well—but it couldn't be helped. By picking you up, I've put myself in what one might call an impossible position." He eyed me as if he were thinking over how much more to tell me.

"After what's already happened, that's not a word I'd use lightly," I said. "What are you—FBI? CIA? Not that they'd have anything like this." I nodded at that fantastic control panel.

"My name is Bayard," he said. "I'm afraid you're going to have to take me on trust for a while, Mr. Curlon."

"How do you know my name?"

"I've been following them," he nodded at the screen. "I've learned a number of things about you."

"Why did you pick me up?"

"Curiosity is as good a word as any."

"If you were tailing them, how did you manage to get here first?"

"I extrapolated their route and got ahead of them. I was lucky; I spotted you in time."

"How? It's a dark night, and I was showing no lights."

"I used an instrument which responds to . . . certain characteristics of matter."

"Make that a little plainer, will you, Bayard?"

"I'm not being intentionally mysterious," he said. "but there are regulations."

"Whose regulations?"

"I can't tell you that."

"So I just ask you to drop me at the next corner, and go on home and have a couple of drinks as if nothing had happened. By tomorrow the whole thing will seem silly—except for my boat."

He stared at the screen. "No, you can't do that, of course." He gave me a sharp stare. "Are you sure you're not holding something back? Something that would shed some light on all this?"

"You're the man of mystery, not me. I'm just a fisherman—or was until today."

"Not just any fisherman. A fisherman named Richard Henry Geoffrey Edward Curlon."

"I didn't think there was anyone alive who knew I had three middle initials."

"He knows. He also knows something that makes you important enough to be the object of a full-scale Net operation. I'd like to know what it is."

"It must be a case of mistaken identity. There's nothing about me to interest anyone except a specialist in hard-luck cases."

Bayard frowned at me. "Do you mind if I run a few tests on you? It will only take a minute or two. Nothing unpleasant."

"That will be a nice change," I said. "What kind of tests, for what purpose?"

"To find out what it is about you that interests them," he nodded at the screen. "I'll tell you the results—if any." He took out a gadget and ran it over me like a photographer checking light levels.

"If the word hadn't already been overworked," he said, "I'll call these readings impossible." He pointed to a green needle that wavered, hunting around a luminous dial, like a compass at the North Pole. "According to this, you're in an infinite number of places at the same time. And this one—" he indicated a smaller dial with a glowing yellow arrow, "says that the energy levels concentrated in your area are of the order of ten thousand percent of normal."

"Your wires are crossed," I suggested.

"Apparently," he went on thinking out loud, "you represent a nexus point in what is known as a probability stress pattern. Unless I miss my guess, a major nexus."

"Meaning what?"

"That great affairs hinge on you, Mr. Curlon. What, or how, I don't know. But strange things are happening—and you're at the center of them. What you do next could have a profound effect on the future of the world—of many worlds."

"Slow down," I said. "Let's stick to reality."

"There is more than one reality, Mr. Curlon," Bayard said flatly.

"Who did you say you were again?" I asked him.

"Bayard. Colonel Brion Bayard of Imperial Intelligence."

"Intelligence, eh? And Imperial at that. Sounds a little

old-fashioned—unless you're working for Haile Selassie."

"The Imperium is a great power, Mr. Curlon. But please accept my word that my government is not inimicable to yours."

"Nowadays, that's something. How is it you speak American without an accent?"

"I was born in Ohio. But let's leave that aside for the moment. I've bought some time by whisking you out from under his nose, but he won't give up. And he has vast resources at his disposal." I still had the feeling he was talking to himself.

"All right, you've bought time," I prompted him. "What are you going to do with it?"

Bayard pointed to a dial with a slim red needle that trembled over a compass face. "This instrument is capable of tracing relationships of a high order of abstraction. Given a point of fixture, it indicates the position of artifacts closely associated with the subject. At the moment, it indicates a distant source, to the east of our present position."

"Science, Mr. Bayard? Or witchcraft?"

"The wider science ranges, the more it impinges on the area of what was once known as the occult. But after all, occult merely means hidden."

"What does all this have to do with me?"

"The instrument is attuned to you, Mr. Curlon. If we follow it, it may lead us to the answers to your questions and mine."

"And when we get there—then what?"

"That depends on what we find."

"You don't give away much, do you, Colonel?" I said. "I've had a long day. I appreciate your picking me off my boat before she went under—and I suppose I owe you some thanks for saving me from another taste of that nerve-gun. But the question-and-no-answer game is wearing me down."

"Let's reach an understanding, Mr. Curlon," Bayard said. "If I could explain, you'd understand—but the explanation would involve telling you the things I can't tell you."

"We're talking in circles, Colonel. I suppose you know that."

"The circle is tightening, Mr. Curlon. I'm hoping it isn't a noose that will choke us all."

"That's pretty dramatic language, isn't it, Colonel? You make it sound like the end of the world."

Bayard nodded, holding his eyes. In the varicolored light from the instrument panel, his face was hard, set in lines of tension.

"Precisely, Mr. Curlon," he said.

The moon rose, painting a silver highway across the water. We bypassed Bermuda, saw the lights of the Azores in the distance. Two more hours passed, while the ocean unrolled under us, until the shore of France came into view dead ahead.

"The proximity sensors are registering in the beta range now," Bayard said. "We're within a few miles of what we're looking for."

He moved a lever and the moonlit curve of the shore dropped away under us. It was swift, noiseless, smooth. We leveled off at a height of a couple of hundred feet over tilled fields, swung over the tiled rooftops of a small village, followed a narrow, winding road that cut through a range of wooded hills. Far ahead, a wide river glittered against the black land.

"The Seine," Bayard said. He studied the illuminated chart that unrolled on a small screen before him, with a red dot in the center that represented our position.

"The indicator is reading in the red now. Not much farther."

Ahead, the river curved between high banks. At the widest point, there was a steep, tree-covered island.

"Does any of this look familiar to you?" Bayard asked. "Have you ever been here before?"

"No. It doesn't look like much. A river, and an island."

"Not just an island, Mr. Curlon," Bayard said. "Take a closer look." There was a note of suppressed excitement in his voice.

"There's a building," I said. I could make it out now: a massive pile of stone, topped by castellated towers.

"A rather famous building—known as Chateau Gaillard," Bayard said. He glanced at me. "Does the name mean anything to you?"

"I've heard of it. Pretty old, isn't it?"

"About eight hundred years." All the while we talked,
the shuttle was gliding in across the river, toward the
stone walls and towers of the fortress Bayard adjusted
levers and we stopped, hanging in empty air about fifty
feet from the face of the high wall. There was ivy
growing there, and in the spaces between the dark
leaves the stone looked as old as the rocks below.

"We're within five hundred feet of the center of
resonance." Bayard said. "It's somewhere below us."
The wall in front of us slid upward as the shuttle
dropped vertically. There were narrow loopholes in the
stonework, between weathered buttresses that gripped
the rockface like talons. We leveled off at the base of the
wall.

"Our target is some twelve feet below this point, and
approximately sixteen feet to the north-northeast,"
Bayard said.

"That puts it somewhere in the foundations," I said.
"It seems we're out of luck."

"You're about to have another unusual experience,
Mr. Curlon," Bayard said. "Hold on to your
equanimity." He flipped a switch. The view on the
screen faded into a sort of luminous blue, the color of a
gas flame, and about as solid-looking. He moved the
controls, and the ghost-wall slid upward. The line of
rubble that was the surface slid past, like water rising
over a periscope, and the screen went solid blue, with
clearly defined stratum lines running across it at an
angle. There were a few embedded stones, a darker
shade of blue, like lumps of gelatin floating in an
aquarium, some gnarled roots, pale and transparent,
pieces of broken pottery. The screen went darker,
almost opaque.

"We're into the solid rock now," Bayard said in a tone
as calm as if he were pointing out movie stars' homes.
We stopped, and I felt a few million tons of the planet
pushing in at me. It gave me a strange, insubstantial
feeling, as if I were nothing but a pattern drawn in
smoke, like the gaseous granite just beyond the thin
hull.

"As I said, quite a machine," I grunted. "What else
will she do?"

Bayard showed me a faint smile and touched the

controls. The texture of the rock swirled around us like muddy water with a dim light shining through it. We eased forward about ten feet, and slid out through a wall and were in a small room, stone walled and floored, windowless, thick with dust. It was almost bright here, after the trip through the rock. There were things in the room: the tattered shreds of a rotted tapestry on the wall, a wooden bench, crudely made from rough planks, heaped with dust; some metal plates and mugs ornately decorated with colored stones, pieces of gaudy jewelry, lumps of rusted iron.

"I think maybe we've found something, Mr. Curlon," Bayard said, and now he didn't sound quite so calm. "Shall we step out and have a closer look?"

Bayard did things with his levers and a soft hum I'd forgotten I was hearing ran down the scale, and the scene on the viewplate faded, as if a projector had been switched off. He snapped another switch and a harsh white light glared against the bleak walls, casting black shadows in the corners. The panel slid back and I stepped out after him. The dust was a soft carpet underfoot; the odor of age in the air was like all the musty books in all the forgotten libraries.

"An old storeroom," Bayard said in the kind of hushed voice that went with a disturbed grave. "Sealed up, probably centuries ago."

"It could do with a sweeping," I said.

"The cloth and wood and leather have rotted away, except for the heavier pieces. And most of the metal has oxidized."

I stirred a heap of rust with my foot. A flake the size of a saucer crumbled off. Bayard went to one knee, poked at the corrosion, lifted the curved piece clear.

"This is a *genouillère*," he said. "A knee guard; part of a suit of chain armor."

He had an instrument like a Geiger counter in his hand, with a pointer on a cable that he aimed around the room.

"There are extraordinary forces at work here," he said. "The Net tension reading is off the end of the scale."

"Meaning?"

"The fabric of reality is stretched to the breaking point. It's almost as if there were a discontinuity in the continuum—a break in the entropic sequence. Forces like these can't exist, Mr. Curlon—not for long—not without neutralization!"

He changed the settings on the gadget he was holding, swung around to point it at me.

"You seem to represent the focus of a strongly polarized energy flow," he said. He came closer, pointed the instrument at my face, waved it down across my chest, stopped with the thing aimed at my left hip.

"The knife," he said. "May I see it?"

I took it out and handed it over. It was nothing much to look at: a wide, thick blade, about a foot long, ground to a rather crude point, with a stubby cross-guard and an oversized, leather-wrapped handle. It wasn't the handiest scaling knive in the world, but I'd had it a long time. Bayard held the metal pointer against it and looked incredulous.

"Where did you get this, Mr. Curlon?"

"I found it."

"Where?"

"In a trunk, in an attic, a long time ago."

"Whose trunk? Whose attic? Think carefully, Mr. Curlon. This may be of vital importance."

"It was my grandfather's attic, the day after he died. The trunk had been in the family a long time; the story was it belonged to a sea-faring ancestor, back in the eighteen hundreds. I was rummaging in it and turned the knife up. I kept it. I don't know why. It's not much, as knives go, but it seemed to fit my hand pretty well."

Bayard looked closely at the blade. "There's lettering here," he said. "It looks like Old French: *Dieu et mon droit.*"

"We didn't come all this way just to study my knife," I said.

"Why keep calling it a knife, Mr. Curlon?" Bayard said. "We both know better." He gripped the hit of the weapon and hefted it. "It's much too massive for a knife, too clumsy."

"What would you call it?"

"It's a broken sword, Mr. Curlon. Didn't you know?" He offered it to me, hilt first. As I took it, Bayard looked at his dials. "The reading went up into the blue when you took it in your hand," he said in a voice that was as taut as a tow-cable.

In my hand, the hilt of the knife seemed to tingle. It tugged, gently, as if invisible fingers were pulling at it. Bayard was watching my face. I felt sweat trickle down across my left eyebrow. Hackles I didn't know I had were trying to rise. I took a step and the pull became stronger. A vivid blue spark, like static electricity, played across a lump of rusted iron on the bench. Another step, and a faint blue halo sprang up around the end of the knife. From the corner of my eye, I saw that objects all around the room were glowing softly in the gloom. Dust trickled from the bench; something stirred there, rotated a few inches, stopped. I took a step sideways; it pivoted, following me.

Bayard stirred the dust with his finger, lifted a piece of pitted steel about three inches by six, beveled along both edges, with a groove along the central ridge.

"Just a piece of scrap iron," I said. "What made it move?"

"Unless I'm mistaken, Mr. Curlon," Bayard said, "it's a piece of your broken sword."

Chapter Three

"I don't believe in magic, Colonel," I said.

"Not magic," Bayard said. "There are subtle relationships between objects, Mr. Curlon; affinities between people and the inanimates that play a role in their lives."

"It's just old iron, Bayard. Nothing else."

"Objects are a part of their environment," Bayard said flatly. "Every quantum of matter-energy in this Universe has been here since its inception. The atoms that make up this blade were formed before the sun was formed; they were there, in the rock, when the first life stirred in the seas. Then the metal was mined, smelted, forged. But always, the matter itself has been a part of the immutable sum total of this material plane of reality. Complex inter-relationships exist among the particles of a given world-line—relationships which are affected by the uses to which the matter they comprise are put. Such a relationship exists between you and this ancient weapon."

Bayard was grinning now—the grin of an old gray wolf who smells blood. "I'm beginning to put two and two together: you—with that red mane, that physique —and now this. Yes, I think I'm beginning to understand who you are, Mr. Curlon—*what* you are."

"And what am I?"

Bayard made a motion that took in the room, and the massive pile above it. "This chateau was built in the year 1196 by an English king," he said. "His name was Richard—known as the Lion-Hearted."

"That's what *he* was. What am I?"

216

"You're his descendant, Mr. Curlon. The last of the Plantagenets."

I laughed aloud at the letdown. "I suppose the next move is to offer me a genuine hand-painted reconstruction of the family coat of arms, suitable for framing. This must be your idea of humor, Colonel. And even if it were true, after thirty generations, any connection between him and a modern descendant would be statistically negligible."

"Careful, Mr. Curlon; your education is showing," Bayard's smile was grim. "Your information is correct—as far as it goes. But a human being is more than a statistical complex. There are linkages, Mr. Curlon—relationships that go beyond Mendel and Darwin. The hand of the past still reaches out to mold the present—and the future—"

"I see. The lad with the nerve-gun is running me down to collect a bill that Richard the First owed his tailor—"

"Bear with me a moment, Mr. Curlon. Accept the fact that reality is more complex than the approximations that science calls the axioms of physics. Every human action has repercussions that spread out across a vast continuum. Those repercussions can have profound effects—effects beyond your present conception of the exocosm. You're not finished with all this yet. You're involved—inevitably, like it or not. You have enemies, Mr. Curlon, enemies capable of aborting every undertaking you attempt. And I'm beginning to get a glimmering of an idea why that might be."

"I'll admit somebody sank my boat," I said. "But that's all. I don't believe in vast plots, aimed at me."

"Don't be too sure, Mr. Curlon. When I discovered that missions were being carried out in B-I Three—the official designation of this area—I looked into the matter. Some of those missions were recent—within the last few weeks. But others dated back over a period of almost thirty years."

"Which means someone has been after me since I was a year old? I ask you, Colonel: Is that reasonable?"

"Nothing about this affair is reasonable, Mr. Curlon. Among other curiosa is that fact that the existence of B-I Three wasn't officially known to Intelligence HQ until ten years ago—" He broke off, shook his head as though irritated. "I realize that everything I say only compounds your confusion—"

"Am I the one who's confused, Colonel?"

"Everything that's happened has a meaning—is a part of a pattern. We must discover what that pattern is, Mr. Curlon."

"All this, on the basis of a fishknife and a piece of rusty metal?"

I put out my hand and he put the piece of iron in it. The upper end was broken in a shallow V. There was a gentle tugging, as if the two pieces of metal were trying to orient themselves in relation to each other.

"If it's all my imagination, Mr. Curlon," Bayard said softly, "why are you fighting to hold the two pieces apart?"

I let the smaller shard turn, brought it slowly across toward the point of the knife. When it was six inches away, a long pink spark jumped across the gap. The pull increased. I tried to hold them apart, but it was no use. They moved together and touched . . . and a million volts of lightning smashed down and lit the room with a blinding glare.

The rays of the late sun shone fitfully from a cloud-serried sky, and shadows fled across the sward, across the faces of those who stood before me, swelled up in arrogance, petty men who would summon a king to an accounting. One stood forth among them, a-glitter in rich stuff, and made much of flourishing the scrolls from which he spelled out those demands by which they thought to bind my royal power.

To the end I let him speak his treason, for all to hear. Then I gave my answer.

From the dark forest roundabout my picked archers stepped forth, and in a dread silence bent their bows. And my heart sang as their shafts sang, finding their marks in traitors' breasts. And under my eyes were the false barons slain, every one, and when the deed was done I walked forth from my pavilion and looked on their dead faces and spurned with my foot that scrap of parchment they called their Charter.

The voices and the faces faded. The shadowed walls of

the old storeroom closed in around me. But it was as though years had passed, and the room was a forgotten memory from some distant life, lived long ago.

"What happened?" Bayard's voice rasped in the silence.

"I . . . know not," I heard myself say, and my own voice sounded strange in my ears. " 'Twas some fit took hold on me." I made an effort and shook the last of the fog out of my brain. Bayard was pointing at me—at what I held in my hand.

"My God, the sword!"

I looked—and felt time stop while my pulse boomed in my ears. The broken blade, which had been a foot long, was half again that length now. The two pieces of metal had welded themselves together into a single unit.

"The seam of the joining is invisible," Bayard said. "It's as though the two parts had never been separated."

I ran my fingers over the dark metal. The color, the pattern of oxidation was unbroken.

"What did you experience while it was happening?" Bayard asked.

"Dreams. Visions."

"What kind of visions?"

"Not pleasant ones."

Bayard's eyes went past me to the wall beyond.

"The sword wasn't the only thing that was affected," he said in a tight voice. "Look!"

I looked. Against the stones, where only tatters had been, a faded tapestry hung. It showed a dim, crudely worked design of huntsmen and hounds. There was nothing remarkable about it—except that it hadn't been there five minutes ago.

"Notice the pattern," Bayard said. "The big figure in the center is wearing a cloak trimmed in ermine tails—a symbol of royalty. My guess is that's Richard himself." He looked around the room, bent and picked up the *genouillere*. The metal was dark with age, but there was no rust on it now.

"What happened here had an effect on the fabric of the continuum itself," Bayard said. "Reality is being reshaped as the Net tensions resolve themselves. There are fantastic powers in balance, Mr. Curlon, ready for a

touch to send them tumbling one way—or another." His
eyes held on mine. "Someone is working to upset that
balance. I think we can take it as axiomatic that we must
oppose him."

As he finished speaking, a bell clanged from the
shuttle. Bayard leaped to the panel, hit the switches.

"There's a tracer locked on us at close range!" he
snapped. "They followed us here! The energy discharge
must have given them a fix to home on." The familiar
humming sound started up, but this time it had a
groaning note, as if it was working under an overload. I
smelled hot insulation, and smoke curled up from
behind the panel.

"Too late," Bayard said. "He's holding a suppressor
beam on us. We can't shift out of identity with this line.
It looks like we're trapped!"

A deep thrumming sound started up somewhere. I
could feel it vibrating through the floor of the room.
Dust floated from the cracks in the walls, rose from the
floor. A metal ornament made a soft thump falling off
the bench.

"He's right above us," Bayard said. "He doesn't have
half-phase capability; he'll use a force probe to dig his
way down to us."

"All right," I said. "Let him. Two against two is fair
odds."

"I can't take the chance," Bayard said. "It's not just
you and me—it's the machine. It's unique, a special
model. And if what I'm beginning to suspect is true,
letting it fall into Renata's hands would be a major
disaster."

"Renata?" I started to ask all the questions, but
Bayard pulled a ring from his finger, handed it to me.
"This is a control device governing the half-phase unit.
With it, you can hold the machine clear until he's gone.
You'll know, when the red light goes off—"

"Where will you be?"

"I'll meet him, try to steer him away from you. If he
has any suspicion of what's happened, he'll be able to
detect the shuttle, and grapple it."

"I'll stay, Bayard," I said. "I have a bone to pick with
Mr. Renata."

"No—there's no time to argue! Do as I ask, Curlon, or

he'll take both of us!" He didn't wait for an answer; he stepped out of the shuttle and the entry snapped shut behind him. His image appeared on the screen.

"Now, Mr. Curlon!" his voice came through the speaker. "Or it will be too late for both of us!"

A crack had already appeared in the wall he was facing. The time for talk had all run out. I pressed the stone set in the ring and heard a soft *click*! and felt space twist between my bones.

A soft, high-pitched whine started up, went up and off into the supersonic. Bayard's outline turned transparent blue, like the wall behind him. To him, the shuttle was invisible now.

"Good man," he said. His voice had a whispery quality but it was clear enough. He turned and faced the wall. A section of it bulged and fell in. A beam of dazzling light played through the opening. A man stepped through. It was Renata, the foxy man I'd left unconscious on the dock at Key West a couple of short lifetimes ago; there was no doubt about it: the sharp eyes, the narrow jaw, the slick black hair. But now he was in a swank white uniform that he wore as if he'd been born to it. But it was his face that bothered me most. I'd hit him hard, but there was no mark on him to prove it. He looked around the room, then at Bayard.

"You seem to be a long way from home, Colonel," he said, in a casual drawling voice—nothing like Renata's throaty whine.

"About the same as you, Major," Bayard said.

"Why did you come here—to this particular spot? And how did you get in? I see no entrance from the outside—other than the one I used."

Bayard glanced at the broken wall. "Your tactics seem a little rough for use in an interdicted area, Major. Are you acting on orders—or have you gone in business for yourself?"

"I'm afraid for the present you'll answer the questions, Colonel. You're under arrest, of course. Where have you left your shuttle?"

"I lent it to a friend."

"Don't fence with me, Bayard. It dropped completely off my screens less than half a minute ago—just as it did

earlier, in the Gulf of Mexico. It seems you have
equipment in your possession unknown to Imperial
Intelligence. I shall have to ask you to lead me to it.''

"I can't help you.''

"You realize I must use force, if necessary. I can't
permit the subject Curlon to slip out of my hands.''

"I'm afraid you already have.''

The little man half turned his head. "Lujac,'' he called.
Another man came in through the hole in the wall. It was
the fellow who'd used the nerve-gun on me. He had it in
his hand now.

"Level three,'' the major said. Lujac raised the gun
and pressed the firing stud on the side. Bayard
staggered and doubled over.

"Enough,'' the little man said.

"Colonel, you're in considerable difficulty: absence
from your post of duty without leave, interference with
an official Net operation, and so on. All this will be
dealt with in due course—but if you'll cooperate with
me now, I think I can promise to make it easier for you.''

"You don't know . . . what you're doing,'' Bayard got
the words out. It wasn't easy; I knew what he was going
through then. "There are forces . . . involved . . .''

"Never mind what's involved,'' the major snapped. "I
don't mean to let the man slip through my fingers. Speak
up, now! How did you do it? Where is he hidden?''

"You're wasting . . . your breath,'' Bayard said. "You
know damned well you can't break my conditioning.
Face it, Major; he got away from you. What are you
going to do about it?''

"Don't be a fool, Bayard! You know the Imperium
faces a crisis—and you're well aware that I'm acting on
orders from a very high ranking official! You're
throwing away not only your career, but your life, if you
oppose me! Now—I want an explanation of why you
came to this spot, what you expected to accomplish
here—and where you've sent the man I want!''

"I'll bet you do,'' Bayard said. "Try and get it.''

"Let me deal with the swine,'' Lujac said, and took a
quick step forward, but Renata waved him back.

"I'm taking you in to Stockholm Zero-zero,'' he told
Bayard. "You'll face a firing squad for this night's
work—I promise you that!'' He put cuffs on him and

they went out through the hole in the wall. Half a minute later the red telltale light went off, meaning Renata's shuttle was gone. I flipped the switch that shifted me back to full-phase identity, waited for the color to come back into things, then stepped out and switched the machine back to half-phase. It shimmered like a mirage and winked out. The air was still swirling from that when the tunnel mouth exploded. When the dust cleared, it was packed solid with broken rock. The major had taken the precaution of closing the route behind him.

Chapter Four

It took me four hours of shifting sharp-edged rock fragments before I pushed aside the last slab and poked my head out into the open air beside the old stone wall rising up from a tangle of untrimmed shrubbery. I climbed out and breathed some fresh night air and tried to shake off the feeling that I was dreaming the whole thing. The Occam principle told me that the simplest explanation was that I was strapped into a jacket in some quiet rest home, living out a full-fledged delusional system. But if I was dreaming it, the dream was still on. Ten feet from the hole I'd crawled out of, I found a set of booted footprints which led a few yards to the imprint of a set of skids. That would be where the major's shuttle had been parked—if there had been a major, and he had a shuttle, and it had been parked.

And while I was still following that one through, I got the proof I'd been wanting: The man called Lujac stepped out from black shadows and for the second time I felt the bone-crushing agony of the nerve-gun sweep over me.

I came to lying on the floor in front of the control panel of a shuttle with my arms clamped behind me. It wasn't Bayard's machine, but there was no mistaking the sweep of unfamiliar dials and the big pink-glowing screen, or the hum that went between my bones until it rose out of the audible range. On the screen, things were happening. The old walls rising on the left of the screen flickered and sank down into heaps of rubble, with weeds poking out from between the stone slabs. The weeds withered and the rubble blackened into cokelike ash, then glowed blue and slumped into puddled lava. The river was rising, it welled out over its banks and became an oily black sea that stretched away to a row of volcanic cones that shed red light on the far horizon. Green slime crawled up on the rocks that showed above the surface. It changed into moss that grew into toadstools fifty feet high that jostled and thrust for footing. The water receded, and new plants swarmed up out of the sea; a vine-thing like writhing snakes threw itself over the jungle and tiny black plants sprang up along its tendrils, eating at it like acid. Broad leaves poked out from under the rotted vegetation and wrapped themselves around the black vine-eaters. I saw all this through a sort of purple haze of pain that did nothing to brighten the nightmare.

Animal life appeared: Strange creatures with deformed limbs and misshapen bodies like melting wax statues posed among the cancerous plants. The leaves grew huge and curled and fell away, and scaly, deformed trees rose up, and all the while the creatures didn't move. They swelled, twisted, flowed into new shapes. A forty-foot lizard was locked in the clutch of a plant with rubbery, spike-studded branches that wound around the bossed hide until the hide grew its own spikes that impaled the thorn tree, and it shriveled and fell away and the lizard dwindled into a crouching frog-thing that bloated into a stranded tadpole the size of a cow and sank into the ooze.

For a while, night glowed like day under a radioactive moon; and then the ground dissolved and the shuttle was hanging in black space, with the glare of the sun coming from behind to illuminate the undersides of the dust and rock fragments that arched up and over in a pale halo that must have dwarfed Saturn's rings. Then land appeared again: a dusty plain where small plants sprouted and grew thicker and turned into tangled underbrush dotted with small, cancerous trees. They grew taller and developed normal bark and green leaves, and slowly the atmosphere cleared and the moon was riding high and white in a dark sky full of luminous clouds.

Lujac switched off and the sound of the drive dwindled down to a low growl and died. He pointed the nerve-gun at me, gestured toward the exit. I made it to my feet, stepped out onto a trimmed green lawn beside a high stone wall that was the same one we'd started from. But now there was ivy growing there, and lighted windows, up high. There were flowerbeds along the base, and a tended path led off down the slope toward the moonlit water of the river below. The trees were gone, but other trees grew in places where there had been no trees. Across the river, the lights of a town glowed, not quite where the town had been before.

We went along the path to a broad, paved walk, rounded the front of the building. Light blazed from a wide entry with glass doors set in the old stone. Two sharp-looking troopers in white jodhpurs snapped to and passed us into a high marble hall. Nobody seemed to think there was anything exceptional about a prisoner in cuffs being gun-walked here. We went along a corridor to an office where neat secretaries sat at typewriters with only three rows of keys. A lean, worried-looking man exchanged a few words with Lujac, and passed us into an inner office where Major Renata sat at a desk, talking into a recorder microphone. He twitched his sharp mouth into a foxy smile when he saw me and motioned Lujac out of the room.

This wasn't the same man I'd known back at Key West, I saw that now. It was his twin brother, better fed, better bred, but with the same kind of mind behind the same sly face. Not a man I'd ever really take a liking to.

"You led me quite a chase, Mr. Curlon," he said. "It's unfortunate that events fell out as they did; I had hoped to handle matters more subtly. You understand that I require certain information from you as the first order of business. Let's begin with the matter of Colonel Bayard's involvement. When did he first contact you, and what was his proposition?"

"Where is he now?"

"Never mind that!" Renata rapped. "Don't be confused by any false sense of misguided loyalty, Mr. Curlon. You owe him nothing! Now—answer my questions fully and promptly, and I give you my assurance that you will be in no way held accountable for his crimes."

"Why did you sink my boat?"

"It was necessary. You will be reimbursed, Mr. Curlon. As a matter of fact, you are an extremely lucky man. When this matter is finished up to the satisfaction of, ah, Imperial authorities, you'll find yourself in a most comfortable situation for the rest of your life."

"Why me?"

"I'm acting on instructions, Mr. Curlon. As to precisely why you were selected for this opportunity, I can't say. Merely accept your good fortune and give me your cooperation. Now, kindly begin by telling me precisely how Bayard contacted you and what he told you of his plans."

"Why not ask him?"

"Mr. Curlon, please limit your comments to answering questions for the present. Later, all your questions will be answered—within the limits of Imperial security requirements, of course."

I nodded. I was in no hurry. What came next probably wouldn't be as much fun.

"I know about your good intentions," I said. "I've met your lieutenant, the fellow with the nerve-gun."

"It was necessary to insure there'd be no unfortunate accident, Mr. Curlon. You're a powerful man, possibly excessively combative. There was no time for explanations. And you've suffered no permanent injury. Oh, by the way: where did Bayard secrete the shuttle?"

"You mean the amphibious car he picked me up in?"

"Yes. It's Imperial property, of course. By helping me to recover it, you'll be reducing the charges against Bayard."

"He must have parked it out of sight."

"Mr. Curlon . . ." Renata's face tightened. "Perhaps you don't understand the seriousness of your situation. Cooperate, and your rewards will be great. Fail to cooperate, and you'll live to regret it."

"It seems you're always offering me a proposition, and I'm always turning it down," I said. "Maybe you and I just weren't meant to get together, Renata."

He took a breath as though he were about to yell, but instead he thumbed a button on his desk, savagely. The door opened and a couple of the armed troops were there.

"Place this subject in a Class Three quarters, MS

block," he snapped. He favored me with a look like a poison dart. "Perhaps a few days of solitary contemplation will assist you in seeing the proper course," he snapped, and went back to his paper work.

They marched me along halls, down steps into less ornately decorated halls, down more steps, along a passage with no pretensions of elegance at all, stopped before a heavy iron-bound door. A boy with blond fuzz on his chin opened up. I stepped through into the dim light of a shielded bulb and the door closed behind me with a solid sound. I looked around and put my head back and laughed.

I was back in the underground room I'd started from all those hours before.

It was the same, and yet not quite the same. The floor was swept, and the litter of dust and rusty junk was gone. But the tapestry was still on the wall, more complete now than it had been.

I prowled around the room, but aside from a chair and a cot, I didn't find anything that hadn't been there before. I rapped on the walls, but no sliding panels opened up on hidden stairways with daylight showing at the top of them. I looked at the tapestry, but it didn't tell me anything. The central figure was a tall, red-bearded man with a bow slung at his back, a sword at his side. His horse was pawing the air with one hoof and the hounds were leaping up, as if they were eager to be off. I knew how they felt. I was ready to travel myself. But this time there was no convenient tunnel waiting to be dug out. It was too bad Renata hadn't tossed Bayard in the same VIP cell. Maybe he'd have had another trick ring up his sleeve. I looked at the one wedged on my little finger and felt a prickling along my scalp line at the thoughts I was thinking. I wondered if I was missing some angle that was too obvious to see, but if I was, it was still invisible.

I pushed the stone and got ready for nothing to happen. For five seconds, nothing did. Then air *whooshed* around me and the shuttle winked into existence, with the door open and the soft light gleaming from inside.

I stepped into the shuttle and sat in the chair facing all those dials, packed in the panel like chrome and glass anchovies. I tried to remember which ones Bayard had used, and a trickle of sweat went down the side of my face when I thought about all the things that could go wrong if I made a mistake. But thinking at a time like this was a mistake. It would be too bad if I cross-controlled and stalled out in the middle of the solid rock, but chances like this didn't come along every day. I pushed the half-phase switch and the walls faded to electric blue. The first lever I pushed did nothing that was visible. I worked another one and had a short heart attack when the shuttle started to sink through the floor. I moved it the other way and moved up like a balloon rising through dense blue fog. Seconds later, I popped through the surface. I was behind a dense clump of trees, just a few feet from the spot where I'd seen the runner-marks. Just a few feet, and at the same time, in some way I wasn't ready to try to put into words yet, as far away as you could get. And that brought me to the question of my next move.

For the moment, I was in the clear. If my operating the shuttle had registered on any meters in the vicinity, it wasn't apparent. The obvious thing for me to do was to return the machine to half-phase, get off the premises as fast as I could, and forget about a stranger named Bayard and his story of a probability crisis coming that would turn the world into bubbling chaos.

On the other hand, I was sitting on a device which, according to its previous owner, was something out of the ordinary, even among the men in the white Imperial uniforms. And those same high-powered operators owed me a few things, including one boat of which I'd been rather fond. I had an advantage now; they didn't know where the shuttle was, where I was. And I could watch them, without being seen.

There was just one catch: It meant operating a machine that was more sophisticated than a jet fighter, and potentially more dangerous. I'd watched Bayard at the controls; I had a rough idea of how he had maneuvered it. The big white lever marked DR-MAIN was the one that started everything working. It had a nice feel to it under my hand: smooth and cool, a lever that wanted to be pulled.

I was still sitting there, looking into the screen and thinking these thoughts when lights came on over a side entry fifty feet along the wall. The door·opened and Major Renata stepped out, carrying a briefcase and talking over his shoulder to a harassed-looking adjutant with a notebook. My reaction was automatic: I punched the half-phase switch and the scene faded out to the transparent blue that meant I was invisible.

A big, boxy staff-car pulled up along the drive and Renata and four others got in and the car pulled away. I remembered the controls Bayard had used to maneuver on half-phase. I tried them; the shuttle glided away as smoothly as oil spreading out on water. I followed the car down the winding drive through parklike grounds, past a gate where a sentry yawned as I slid by two feet from him, across a bridge and through the village. On the open highway, he opened up, but I had no trouble staying with him.

I trailed the car for half an hour, until it pulled through a gate in a wire fence around a small grassed airstrip. Renata got out and his aides scuttled around, readying a big, fabric-covered prop-driven airplane with wings the size of barn roofs. There were handshakes and some heel-clicking from a couple of Germanic-looking fellows; then Renata and one other climbed in and the plane taxied out and headed into the wind.

I'd spent the time looking over the controls, and was ready when the plane revved up and started its run. It took me three tries to match my rate of ascent to the airplane's, but I managed it, then maneuvered into a spot a quarter of a mile astern. So far, it had been easy; all I'd had to do was steer. For all I knew, the instruments were indicating ten different critical overloads, but I'd worry about that when I had to. The theory of a shuttle was a complex thing, but straight-line operation was simple enough.

It was a three-hour flight over rolling farmland straight into the rising sun, then out across water that had to be the English Channel. The plane began letting down toward a city that had to be London, circled a field a few miles out from the center of the city, landed and taxied up to a small operations building with RBAF-NORTHOLT lettered across it. I had a bad few seconds when the pavement washed up around me like muddy water, but I managed to level the shuttle out a foot above the pavement.

Renata climbed down, and a car pulled out and collected him. By now I was getting used to the capabilities of my little machine; I didn't bother with the gate, just slid across through the fence and fell in behind the car as it picked up speed along a broad parkway that led straight toward the towers of the city.

It was a fast twenty-minute trip. Renata's car, with a few touches of a siren that sounded like a ghost wailing through the audio pickup, cleared traffic, making speed through narrow, twisting streets, crossed the Thames on a bridge with a fine view of the House of Commons, swung into a stone-walled courtyard behind a big, grim fortress. Renata stepped out and headed for a small door under a big wrought-iron lantern, and I followed him through the wall. The sun winked out and I was in a wide, well-lit corridor lined with open doors where people in uniform did what people do in government offices. Renata took a sudden corner, and I over-corrected, found myself in solid rock that must have been five feet thick. By the time I'd maneuvered back into the open, he was out of sight.

For the next hour, I cruised through the building like a mechanized ghost, looking into big offices with ranks of filing cabinets and desks under banks of flourescents, into smaller offices with deep carpets and solemn-looking bureaucrats admiring their reflections in the picture windows, into storerooms, a message center. I tried the lower levels, found dead-record storage, a mechanical equipment room, a small theater, and lower still, some grim-looking cells. There was nothing for me there. I took a shortcut through a wall and was in an eight-foot-square room with rusty manacles and a hole in the floor for plumbing. It had everything a medieval dungeon needed except a couple of human skeletons chained to the wall.

I slid through the wall and was in a hollow in the masonry with rough steps leading up. It didn't look like a much-traveled way. I followed the route, found an intersecting passage above. It led to another. The walls of the old building were riddled with hideaways, it seemed. I found exits into a dozen rooms, a hidden door into the gardens at the bottom. But none of this was getting me any closer to Renata.

Back on the upper level, I checked out more VIP offices, and in the tenth or twelfth one found my quarry, sitting on the edge of a chair across from a big-shouldered, gray-haired man with career military written all over him. He didn't look pleased.

". . . difficult to explain to the Baron just how it was this subject was able to appear and disappear at will," he was growling. "No one outside Operation Rosebush was aware of the existence of the sub-HQ at the chateau. Yet Bayard was found there; and later, the subject pops up—from nowhere! This is an unacceptable report, Major." He slammed a piece of paper to the desk in front of him and stared at Renata with less than a friendly look.

"My report is factual, Colonel," the little man said. He didn't seem to be much intimidated by the eyebrow treatment. "The fact that I have no hypothesis to offer in explanation doesn't alter my observations."

"Tell me more about the security arrangements you made for holding the subject," the colonel rapped.

"The man is under close guard in a maximum security cell under the chateau," Renata said crisply. "I'll stake my career on that."

"Better not," the colonel said.

Renata shifted in the chair. "Would the colonel care to explain?"

"He's gone. Half an hour after your departure, a routine check showed the cell empty."

"Impossible! I—"

"You're a fool, Renata," the colonel snapped. "The man had already demonstrated that he had unusual resources at his command. Yet you persisted in dealing with him in a routine way."

"I followed service procedures to the letter," Renata came back. Then a thought hit him. "What about Colonel Bayard? He's not . . .?"

"He's here. I've taken the precaution of cuffing him to

his bedstead, and posting two armed guards in the room with him."

"He must be questioned! His conditioning will have to be broken—"

"I'll make that decision, Major! Bayard enjoys a rather special status with top headquarters—"

"Break him, Colonel! He'll confirm what I've told you—and I think he can also offer an explanation of this subject's apparently miraculous powers!"

The colonel picked up a cigar, rolled it between his fingers, then snapped it in two.

"Renata, what the devil is behind this? What's Baron von Roosevelt planning? How does Bayard tie in—and just how much bearing does Richthofen's sudden illness have to do with it?"

"I'm not at liberty to discuss Baron van Roosevelt's plans," Renata said, and returned the colonel's look with interest.

"I'm still your superior officer," the colonel barked. "I demand to know what's going on under my nose!"

"I showed you my report out of courtesy," Renata stood. "I'll make further report to Baron General van Roosevelt, and no one else."

"We'll see about that, Major!" As the colonel jumped to his feet, a red telephone on his desk clanged. He grabbed it up, listened. His expression changed. He looked around the room.

"Right," he said. "I understand."

I moved the shuttle closer, until half of the desk was inside with me, turned up the audio to maximum. Among the crackling and hissing static, I caught the words from the telephone:

"*. . . as though you suspected nothing! It will take us another thirty seconds to bring the suppressor into focus . . .*"

That was enough for me. I backed off, sent the shuttle out through the side wall, shot through another office where a fat man was kissing a girl, on out through the exterior wall and was hovering over a city park, with hedges, a fountain, winding paths. There was a sharp crackling from the panel, and all my meters jumped at once. The hum of the drive faltered, took on a harsh note. I dropped the shuttle to ground level in a hurry; a power failure in mid-air would be messy. When I tried to head across the park, the shuttle moved six feet and halted with a jolt. The smell of hot wiring was strong now. Flames spouted from behind the panel. I slammed the drive switch off; I was caught but there still might be time to accomplish some denial to the enemy. I switched to full phase, and the color flooded back into the scene on the screen. It took me another five seconds to cycle the door open, jump clear, and thumb the ring switch. The shuttle wavered and faded from view, and dry leaves swirled where it had been a moment before. Then there were white uniforms all around me, closing in with drawn nerve-guns.

The building looked different in normal light. My escort walked me along a white-floored hall, up a wide staircase to a big white door flanked by sentries.

Everything in sight was smooth and efficient, but I could feel the tension in the air: a sort of wartime grimness, with lots of hurrying feet in the middle distance. And in the midst of all that spit-and-polish, a curious anomaly caught my eye: a patch of what looked like yellow toadstools, growing in a corner where the marble floor met the wall.

A fellow with a bundle of silver braid looped under his epaulet popped out of the door and we went in. It was a big office with dark-paneled walls and gold-framed paintings of tough-looking old birds in stiff uniform collars, and a desk the size of a bank vault. I looked at the man sitting behind it and met a pair of eyes that literally blazed power.

"Well, Mr. Curlon," he said in a voice like the dirge notes on an organ. "We meet at last."

He was a big man, black-haired, with a straight nose and a firm mouth and eyes with a strange, dark shine. He motioned with one finger and the men who had brought me in disappeared. He stood and came around the desk and looked me up and down. He was as tall as I was, which made him over six three, and about the same weight. Under the smooth gray uniform he wore, there was plenty of muscle. Not the draft-horse kind; more like an elegant tyrannosaurus in tailored silk.

"Major Renata made a number of mistakes," he said. "But in the end—you're here, safe and sound. That's all that counts now."

"Who are you?" I asked him.

"I am Baron General van Roosevelt, Chief of Imperial Intelligence—Acting Chief, I should say, during the temporary indisposition of Baron Richthofen." He gave me one of the those from-the-neck-up bows and a smile that was like the sun coming through a black cloud. He clapped me on the shoulder and laughed.

"But between you and myself, Mr. Curlon, formalities are unnecessary." He looked me in the eye, and the smile was gone, but a merry glint still burned there. "I need you, Curlon. And you need me. Between us, we hold the destiny of a world—of many worlds—between our fingers. But I'm being obscure—and I don't mean to be." He waved me to a chair, went to a liquor cabinet and poured two drinks, handed me one, and sat behind the desk.

"Where to begin?" he said. "Suppose I start by assuming that Colonel Bayard has told you nothing—that you have guessed nothing. Listen, then, and I'll tell you of the crisis we face now, you and I . . ."

Chapter Five

"The continuum of multi-ordinal reality is a complex structure, but for purposes of simplicity we can consider it as a bundle of lines stretching from the remote past toward the unimaginable future. Each line is a world, a universe, with its own infinitude of space and stars, separated from its sister worlds by the uncrossable barriers of energy that we know as entropy.

"Uncrossable, that is, until the year 1897, when two Italian scientists, Maxoni and Cocini, stumbled on a principle which changed the course of history—of a billion histories. They created a field in which the energy of normal temporal flow was deflected at what we may consider right angles to the normal direction. Objects and individuals enclosed in the field then moved, not forward in time as in nature, but across the lines of alternate reality. From that beginning grew the Imperium—the government claiming sovereignty over the entire Net of alternate worlds. Your world—which is known to us as Blight Insular Three—is but one of the uncountable parallel universes, each differing only infinitesimally from its neighbors. Like this world, it lies within the vast disaster area we call the Blight, a desert formed when an unfortunate miscarriage in early experimentation with the M-C principle led to the utter destruction of a vast complex of worlds, to the abortion of their destinies into the chaos which you no doubt saw as you crossed that area coming here.

"Among the relationships existing between parallel lines are those linking individuals, Mr. Curlon. Think for a moment: If two worlds differ by only the disposition of two grains of sand on a beach—or of two molecules within a grain of sand—then it follows that analogues of individuals will exist in all those world-lines whose date of common history—the date at which their histories diverged—is later than the birth date of the individual in question. Your case, Mr. Curlon, is an exception—and that fact is at the root of the problem. Your world is an island in the Blight, surrounded not by viable parallel worlds, but by a desert empty of normal life. You are unique, Mr. Curlon—which renders the present situation all the more poignant."

"That's a mild adjective, General," I said. "I'm still listening for what's going to make sinking my boat sound like a friendly move."

"As I said, Major Renata made a number of errors—but his intentions were good. He'd been working here with me, under great strain, for many weeks. As for his mission, consider, Mr. Curlon: You are a man destined for a role in great affairs—yet what did I know of you? Nothing. And time was short. It was necessary—unfortunate, but absolutely necessary—to put you to the test. I apologize for the Major's excessive zeal. Of course, he wasn't aware of the full ramifications of the situation—of your importance to the present contretemps."

"That makes a pair of us."

Roosevelt's expression flickered; there were emotions boiling under that bland facade, but he wasn't the man to show them.

"In the lost worlds of the Blight, your family loomed like a colossus, Mr. Curlon. Now, of all that mighty stock, only you remain." His eyes held me. "The destinies of many men died in the holocaust of the Blight—and human destiny is a force equal to the evolutionary pressure of the Universe itself. Remember: the vast energies choked off by the disaster were not destroyed, but instead shunted into the orgy of pattern-less vitality that characterizes the Blight. Now those energies seek to reorient themselves, to force a pattern on reality. Unless this power is channeled, guided, given form—our worlds will be engulfed in the cancer of the Blight. Already, signs of the coming plague are here!"

He waved a hand at the gold and blue royal seal on the wall behind him. There were flecks of green on the gilding, and at one corner a tiny crust of mold had formed.

"That crest was polished this morning, Mr. Curlon. And observe this." He pointed to the gold wire insignia on his collar: it was pitted by tarnish. "And this!" he pushed a leather-bound folder across the table. The regal coat of arms embossed on it in silver was bubbly with corrosion.

"Symbols—but symbols that represent the fixed parameters of our cosmos—and those parameters are being eroded, Mr. Curlon!" He leaned back, forced the fire out of his eyes, his voice.

"Unless something is done now, at once, to reinforce the present reality, existence as we know it is doomed, Mr. Curlon."

"All right, General," I said. "I've listened. I don't understand all this, but I've seen enough in the last few hours to keep me from calling you crazy to your face. What is it you want from me? What do you expect me to do about the toadstools growing in the corridors?"

He stood and walked the length of the room, turned and paced back, stopped beside me.

"My plan is a dangerous one; you may think it fantastic, Captain Curlon . . ." I looked the question at him; he nodded and smiled. "I've ordered that you be commissioned in the Imperial Service, and gazetted to my staff," he said casually.

"Thanks, General," I said. "But you can skip the fancies. I'll settle for facts."

He looked disturbed for an instant. "This isn't intended as a bribe," he said, and picked up a thick parchment from the desk. "It's already accomplished—"

"Not without some kind of commitment on my part, it isn't," I said. "Not in any army I ever heard of."

"The oath is required, of course," he said. "A mere formality—"

"A symbol, I believe you said, General. For what it's worth, I'm still a civilian."

"Very well," he tossed the fancy commission aside in a way that I sensed wasn't quite as casual as it looked. "As you wish. Perhaps something Colonel Bayard said has prejudiced you—"

"By the way, where is Bayard now? The last I saw of

him he was having a set of stomach cramps brought on
by Major Renata's itchy trigger finger."

"Colonel Bayard was misguided. His intentions were
good, no doubt, but he was uninformed. I don't wonder
that he formed a false impression of the operation on the
basis of the few facts he stumbled on."

"I'd like to see him."

"That won't be possible at present; he's in the
hospital. However, I contemplate no action against him
for breach of discipline, if that's what concerns you. He
has an excellent record—until now. He was merely
overzealous in this instance."

"You said something about working together. What is
it you want from me?"

He stood, came around the desk and clapped me on
the shoulder.

"Come along, Captain," he said. "I'll show you."

The room he took me to was an underground vault,
guarded by three relays of white-jacketed troopers with
guns in their hands. One high wall was filled by a
ground-glass screen, on which lines and points of light
twinkled.

"This is a chart of the Net, covering the area lying
within the hundred-thousand-year CH range," Roosevelt
said. He picked up a pointer, indicated a red light at the
exact center. "This is the Zero-zero world-line of the
Imperium. Here"— he showed me another glowing
point, not far away—"is your home-line, B I Three. Note
that all around these isolated lines, for a vast area, there
is nothing— a desert. This, Mr. Curlon, is the Blight.
Calculations by our physicists tell us that the
probability imbalance, dating from the original
cataclysm that formed the Blight some seventy years
ago, is now seeking equilibrium. Fantastic energies are
trapped there in a precarious stasis; energies of the kind
that generate reality instant by instant as normal
entropy progresses. I needn't tell you of the incon-
ceivable potency of such powers. Consider only that in
each instant of time the Universe is destroyed and
recreated—and that here, in this blighted region, that
process has been aborted, blocked like a choked
volcano. For seven decades the pressure has mounted.

Now it will not longer be denied. A great probability storm rages at the centroidal point of the Blight. When it blasts through, unless we take some action first, it will carry our world—and all other worlds within a vast range—with it into a limbo of probability disaster which beggars the imagination. Even now, probability waves are moving outward from the holocaust, with results that anyone can see—a mere hint of the holocaust to come."

He grounded the pointer, looked at me long and hard.

"Your destiny is interwoven with that of your world, Mr. Curlon—your fate, your history, are a part of the basic warp of the fabric of the reality we know. We have to seize on that thread—and every other thread we know of, few though they are—and from them, attempt to reweave a viable matrix into which the trapped energies can drain."

I had the feeling he was oversimplifying the problem; but even so, it was too dense for me.

"Keep talking, General," I said. "I'm trying to grope along with you."

"Our lives don't exist in a vacuum, Curlon. We have pasts, roots, antecedents. Actions of men of a thousand years ago affect our lives today, just as our actions of today will repercuss down the ages that come after. Napoleon, Hitler, Caesar, affected their times and all the times to follow. But we stand at a moment where the very texture of existence is strained to the breaking point. What we do, far beyond the ordinary measure of the potency of key individuals, will determine the shape of the world to come. We must act promptly, decisively, correctly. We can afford no weakness, no mistake."

"You're building up to something, General. Why not come to the point."

He pushed a button on a console and the map winked out and another diagram took its place. This one showed an amoeba of pink and red lines twitching and writhing over a grid dotted with glowing points.

"This is a close-range energy chart of the Blight," he said. "Here you see the shifting of the lines of quantum demarcation, as they seek to adjust to the abnormal pressures exerted by the probability storm. In every world-line adjoining the Blight, objective reality is in flux. Objects, people, landscapes, are shifting, changing from moment to moment, day to day. I need not detail for you the pandemonium thus produced. So far we've felt the effects less, here; the Zero-zero line is a stable one firmly rooted in past history by a series of powerful key events. The same is true of your line, B-I Three. For the Blight to engulf these lines would entail the obliteration of basics of human cultural development as powerful as the discovery of fire."

He switched again, this time to a view of a blazing roil like a close-up of the sun.

"This is the center of the probability storm, Mr. Curlon. We've pinpointed its location, in a world-line that was once the seat of a great culture. This is where the key to the crisis will be found. I propose to go there, Mr. Curlon, to find that key."

"It looks as though that would be a lot like jumping down the throat of a live volcano."

"This diagram represents the turmoil of probability energies," Roosevelt said. "On the surface, to an observer within the A-line itself, the storm is not directly apparent. Abnormalities, freaks, impossibilities, the suspension of natural law, the distortion of reality under your very eyes, yes; but the tempest itself rages at a level of energy detectible only to specialized instruments. A man can go there, Mr. Curlon; the dangers he faces will be beyond description—but not perhaps beyond overcoming."

"Once there, then what?"

"Somewhere in that line is a key object, an artifact so inextricably interwoven with the past and future of the line, and of the quantum it controls, that all major probability lines must pass through it, in the way that lines of magnetic force flow through the poles of a magnet. I propose to find and identify that object, and remove it to a safe place."

"Go ahead," I said. "Spell the rest of it out."

"What more is there to say, Mr. Curlon?" Roosevelt gave me the sunny smile again, and his eyes had that dangerous twinkle of a man in love with danger. "I want you with me. I need you—the powers you represent—at my side."

"What makes you think I'll go?"

"I ask you to go—I can't, wouldn't attempt to force you. That would be worse than useless. But remembering the greatness of your line, I believe you'll know where your duty lies."

"Now it's my duty, eh?"

"I think it is, Captain Curlon." He rose and gave me the smile again. This was a man I would have to love or hate; there'd be no middle ground.

"You needn't make your decision now," he said easily. "I've arranged for quarters for you here in my apartments. Get a night's rest; then we'll talk again." His eyes strayed down over my sweater and dungarees, fixed on the knife stuck through my belt.

"I shall have to ask that you leave the, er, weapon with me," he said. "Technically, you're under what is known as RIA—routine interrogational arrest. No point in causing talk."

"I'll keep it," I said. I don't know why. He had an army at his disposal to take it away from me if he felt like it. He leaned forward and frowned at me. His eyes were showing a little controlled anger now.

"Be kind enough to save unpleasantness by placing the knife on my desk," he said.

I shook my head. "It's a sentimental hang-up I have, General. I've carried it so long I'd feel naked without it."

His eyes locked on mine like electronic gun-pointers; then he relaxed and smiled.

"Keep it, then. Now go along and think over what I've said to you. And by tomorrow I hope you've decided to do as I ask."

The room they took me to was a little small for a diplomatic reception, but otherwise would have filled the bill OK. After my escort left I poked into a dressing room fit for a Broadway star, a closet that could have slept six with room left over for an all-night poker game, stuck a finger in a bed that looked like an Olympic wrestling mat with tassels. It was fancier than my usual style, but I had an idea I'd be able to sleep on it all right.

I took a shower in a bathroom full of gold faucets and pink marble, and put on the fresh clothes that were laid out for me, after which a waiter in black knee pants and a gold vest arrived with a cart loaded with pheasant on translucent china and wine and paper-thin glasses. While I tucked it away I thought about what I'd learned from Roosevelt. The surface part—the story about parallel worlds and the disaster hanging over them unless he and I did something about it—was all right; as all right as insanity ever is. I didn't understand it, would never understand it—but the evidence was here, all around me. It was the other parts of the general's presentation that bothered me.

Once, when time hung heavy on my hands in a flat-top ready room, I spent some time reading up on games theory. The present situation seemed susceptible to analysis in the light of what I learned then. Roosevelt had tried three gambits: First, when he'd eased the commission at me. Second, when he'd tried to get my agreement to go along with him, in the blind, on a mission into the Blight. And third, when he'd tried to separate me from the knife. I'd resisted all three moves, more by instinct than any logic or plan.

I walked over to the window and looked down at a wall and a cobbled street. The big trees threw shadow patterns over the grass strips and flowerbeds, and the wide sidewalks were full of pretty women and men in bright uniforms with horsetail plumes and buttons that sparked under the lights. Across the park there were shops with bright-lit windows full of plush merchandise, and cafés with open-air terraces and awnings and tables and an odor of fresh-ground coffee and fresh-baked bread. From a bandstand somewhere you could hear an orchestra playing a Straussy sort of waltz—one that had never been heard, back where I came from.

I wondered what Bayard was doing now and what he'd have to say about the latest developments. I'd accepted him at face value, mostly on the basis of the fact that he'd snatched me off my boat just before I started the long swim. But if Roosevelt was telling the truth—if the whole thing had been designed just to test my reactions before pulling me into a key role in world-shaking events . . .

In that case, I should tell Roosevelt all I'd seen at Chateau Gaillard. Maybe there was a clue there for someone who knew how to use it. Or misuse it.

Bayard had known a lot more about the situation than I did, and he hadn't trusted Renata, or Renata's boss. I wished he could have heard Roosevelt's pitch and given me the other side of the story.

What I needed now was information about Roosevelt, about Bayard, about what was going on and most of all, information about my place in all this—and the meaning of the old piece of steel with the magical property of pointing the other old pieces of steel.

I went to the door and eased it open; there was a guard in a white and gold uniform standing at a rigid parade rest at the far end of the passage. He looked my way and I gave him an offhand wave and he went back to eyes-front. I wasn't exactly under arrest, but they were keeping an eye on me. I started to close the door—and heard a scream like a gutted horse from the room next to mine. The sentry yanked a shiny chrome-plated gun from a polished holster and came on at a run. I took two jumps to the door the yell had come from and jerked at the knob, then stepped back and kicked it open and was looking at a white worm the size of a fire hose looped like a boa constrictor around the crushed body of a man.

He was an old man with a purple face and white hair and popped-out eyes and tongue. I was holding the broken sword in my hand; I didn't remember drawing it. It made a sound like an ax hitting a saddle when I brought it down on the worm. It cut through it like cheese, and the severed end whipped around, splattering foul-smelling juices. Something boomed like a cannon behind my ear, and a chunk of worm flew. A ten-foot piece was flapping across the floor and the gun boomed again and it flew up in the air, whipping, while I hacked at another loop that was weaving around on end like a charmed snake. There were four pieces of the thing now and more boiling out through the bathroom door. I heard a gun click on an empty chamber and the guard swore and ended on a gurgling note. I chopped my way through to him, but I was too late. He was wrapped like a mummy and his head was at an angle that meant he'd made his last formation. There were yells from the passage, and the sound of running feet and shots. I cut my way across and into the bathroom. The jade green marble tub was full of worm, writhing up through the drain. I hacked it off, grabbed up a long-handled bath brush and rammed it down the drain, then chopped my way back through the flopping sections and into the hall. What was there was worse than the worm. It looked like a mass of raw meat, bulging up from the stairwell halfway down the corridor. Two men were firing into it, but it didn't seem to mind that much. I came up on it from the side and carved a slice off, and the mass of rubbery stuff recoiled, oozing pink blood. It didn't like cold steel.

"Get knives and swords!" I yelled. "You're wasting time firing slugs in it!"

The mass had bulged along the hall far enough to half cover a door. I burst inward, and I got a glimpse of a woman standing there before it welled through and blocked the opening. I caught just a faint echo of her scream. It took a half a dozen good chops to amputate the mass in the door, but I was too late again. All I could see of the girl was a pair of slippered feet sticking out from under the thing like a careless mechanic under a slipped jack.

Back in the hall I saw Roosevelt, in his shirt-sleeves, his teeth bared in what might have been a grin, hewing away at the thing with a two-handed sword. He saw me and yelled, "Curlon, to me!"

Uniformed men were doing what damage they could with ceremonial short swords, but it was Roosevelt who was driving the thing back. It had bulged in to form a pocket, and he was wading into the pocket, while the rest of the thing bulged alongside, flanking him. I hit it on his left, hacked away a chunk the size of a Shetland pony just as the other side folded in, almost caught him. He stabbed at it, and I cut a swath through and got a stance back to back with him. He seemed to be trying to cut his way to a door that was two-thirds covered and starting to sag. We cleared it, and by then there were a dozen men working on the outer perimeter with swords they'd pulled off walls somewhere. We were ankle-deep in the thin pink blood that drained from every cut we made. I smelled smoke, and saw a pair of firemen in protective suits coming up the stair with oversized blowtorches. The thing flowed away ahead of them,

turning black and shriveling. In another minute or two
it was all over. I looked at Roosevelt through the smoke
and the stink, past him along the corridor that was
splashed to the ceiling and reeking like a slaughter-
house.

"Nice," I said, and discovered I was as winded as if I'd
just run the four-minute mile. "What was it?"

Roosevelt grinned at me. He was breathing hard, and
there was blood on his face, but incredibly, he looked
like a man having fun.

"A brisk hour and a quarter," he said. "I congratulate
you, Captain. You matched me blow for blow. Not many
could have done it." It was a brag, but somehow it didn't
sound arrogant. Just truthful.

"You didn't answer the question, General," I said.

His eyes went past me to the foul bulk spread across
the blue Oriental carpeting.

"I don't really know," he said. "This was the worst
attack so far. The periodicity has decayed to ninety-one
hours and the intensity is increasing logarithmically. It
doesn't seem to be an animal, in the normal sense of the
word—merely a mass of flesh, growing wild."

"What kind of flesh?" I growled. It made my skin
crawl to look at it.

His eyes met mine. "Human flesh, Mr. Curlon," he
said.

I nodded. "I'm still not sure about all this, General;
but if this is what you're fighting, I'm with you."

He gave me the smile, reached out and caught my
hand with a grip like a rock-crusher.

"With you behind me—"

"Beside you," I cut in.

He nodded, still smiling. "Beside me, then. Perhaps
we can yet prevail."

I didn't get much sleep for the next couple of nights.
When I wasn't busy bone-bending with an unarmed
combat master named Lind, I was listening to lectures
on field operation, and doing my napping with a
hypnotaper strapped to my skull, pumping me full of
background data on the history of the Blight.

There were a few other trainees around. One was a
beautiful Oriental-looking girl from an A-line where the

Chinese had settled America back in the ninth century, and had met the Romans head-on along the Mississippi in 1776. She was headed for a place where a horde of backward, matriarchal Mongols were getting ready to sweep across a fuedal Europe. It seemed that she fitted the bill of particulars for the incarnation of the goddess Chiu-Ki, a sort of celestial Dragon Lady. And a big coal-black man with a fierce look—maybe because of the stainless steel peg through his nose—had been recruited from a Zulu-ruled African empire to help organize a grass-roots resistance to a murder-suicide cult that was decimating the enslaved blacks in a line where the Greeks had developed science in the pre-Christian era and used it to conquer the known world before stagnation set in. I met one fellow who was a classic example of the Australian Bushman—but in his line his tribe had made it big on the mainland. He had a hard time not wrinkling his flat nose at the strange odors, but he was a gentleman. He treated us like equals.

During the week, I tried several times to see Bayard, but Roosevelt always put me off. The colonel was a sick man, he said. Pneumonia had set in, as if often did after a taste of the neurac. He was in an oxygen tent, and no visitors allowed.

Then the day came when the general came down and watched for half an hour while Lind tried to throw me on my ear; but I got lucky and threw him instead.

"You're ready," Roosevelt said. "We'll leave at midnight."

The shuttle terminus was a huge bright-lit room with a polished white floor marked off in orange lines, with shuttles ranked between the lines. There were little one-man scouts and big twenty-man passenger transports, some bare, functional boxes, some fancy VIP jobs, some armored, some fitted up to look like moving vans or delivery trucks. There was a steady, high-pitched whine, and a constant booming and buffeting from air displacement as shuttles came and went. I'd never seen any of it before, but it was all familiar from the sessions under the hypnotaper.

Technicians in white coveralls worked over machines, standing at little desks that were spaced along the aisles. Across the room I saw a party of men in costumes like Spanish conquistadores, and another group in Puritan black.

"Protective coloration," Roosevelt said. "Our agents always try to blend with the background. In our case, no disguises are necessary. As far as I know, there's no human life left where we're going."

The technicians fitted us into our suits—old-fashioned flyers' outfits with lightweight diving helmets. They checked us over with a minimum of formality, and we strapped in and closed the hatch. Roosevelt looked sideways at me and gave me the thumbs-up sign. "Ready?"

"It's your show, General," I said. He nodded and threw in the drive control. The whining hum started up; the light outside faded. The walls and roof quivered and disappeared, and we were perched two feet above a vacant lot full of weeds and blown dust under the open sky.

Chapter Six

We didn't talk much, crossing the Blight, following the *beep-beep*! of the tracer tuned to our target. I watched the blasted landscape flow past while Roosevelt monitored fifty dial faces at once and corrected the control settings from time to time for no reason I could make out. For a while we skimmed above a plain of shattered rock, where smoke boiled up from fumaroles and volcanic cones that threw a red glow across the sky. Then there was an ocean of oily, scummed fluid that broke in sluggish foamy waves. And then land again: cinder-black, with pale flames licking over it until it coalesced into a sea of lava, dull-red and bubble-pocked. All the while, the clouds over the moon never moved.

The lava darkened, hardened, turned to a dusty plain. Green appeared, and strange, scabbed trees shot up in clumps of two or three. Vines spread, and ruins poked up among them. A slab of rock came into view, tilted up by the roots of a fifty-foot dandelion with hooks all along the stem. "We're close," Roosevelt said. "That's the highway leading into the city of Fontrevrault."

He corrected course to bring us in over the old road leading off through the nightmare jungle, between fallen walls and rusted steel frameworks that were trellises now for ropes of flesh entwined with warty vines with leaves like rotted canvas curving over clusters of over-sized, blind rodent-heads like bunches of fruit. They had no eyes, but there were plenty of teeth showing, set in the husks of the plants that nourished them.

The forest opened out, thinned. Tall ochre and rust buildings loomed up on both sides, like jungle temples in Yucatan. Fungus grew on the granite and marble, and

the bronze statues of gods and goddesses were overgrown with cancerous-looking corrosion. The forest
retreated to expose a paved plaza, and a mountain of
marble chips and tiles and glass behind a set of hundred-
foot columns tangled in vines.

Some of the discolored blotches faded from the
marble; the wide sweep of the plaza smoothed minutely.
A fountain at the center that had been scattered slid
back into shape, all but the head of the mermaid at the
center. Then there was a sharp *be-beep*! and the amber
light went on on the panel. We had arrived in the eye of
the probability storm.

Roosevelt slung an instrument pack over his shoulder
and checked the dials on it.

"You and I will be the first men ever knowingly to set
foot in the Blight," he said. "And if we do anything
wrong—make the slightest error—we'll be the last. One
mistake here could send our entire cosmos tumbling."

"Fair enough," I said. "Just one question: How do we
know what might be a mistake?"

"Follow your instinct, Mr. Curlon," Roosevelt said
and gave me a smile that seemed to be loaded with
obscure significance. Then he opened up and we stepped
out into a nightmare fantasy.

All around, tall buildings reared up against a sky of
broken clouds over a yellow moon. The nearest was
made of polished crimson stone, carved into patterns
where huge vines clung, casting black shadows. From it,
white marble steps led down to a walk lined with giant
oaks on which green orchids grew. Vivid-colored birds
sang in branches that arched across the tiled avenue.
And behind this island of comparative order, the jungle
loomed like a besieging army.

"Amazing," Roosevelt said in a low voice. "It's almost
intact, Curlon—almost as it was in the days of its glory!
There is the Summer Palace—and there the
Cathedral—and the Académie des Artes—still standing,
in the midst of carnage!"

"Hard to believe we're in the center of a storm," I
said. "It's as peaceful as a graveyard."

"A mighty empire died here," Roosevelt said. "Where
we stand, triumphal armies marched, with kings at their

heads. The fairest women in any universe rode their carriages along these avenues. Here art and culture rose to their highest peak—to be dashed to the lowest depths. Grieve for it, Curlon; for magnificence, lost forever."

"For now I'll settle for finding what we came for."

"Quite right," Roosevelt said in a suddenly brisk tone. He checked the dials strapped to his wrist, then tilted back his helmet.

"The air is all right," he said. I tried it. It was hot, steamy, like a greenhouse at night. There was a steady surf-roar of sound: the rustle and scrape of leaves, the rasp and creak of stems bending in the breeze, the cluck and groan and hiss and whine and bleat of animal voices, as if we were in the middle of the world's biggest zoo, and all the inmates were having bad dreams. The tiled pavement under our feet was chipped and shattered, but navigable. Lichenous vines as big as your wrist snaked across it, and the moonlight glinted on spines like poinards that bristled along them.

"To protect the shuttle, I'm putting it on an oscillatory circuit that will prevent it from phasing into identity with any A-line," Roosevelt said. "When we're ready to leave, I can recall it with a remote signaler."

I watched as it winked out of sight with a boom of imploding air. As we started off, something moved among the greenery; a thing like a hairy snake dragged its length over a fallen tree-trunk, gaping a dog's head at us. At first I thought there were no legs, but then I saw them—dozens of them, all sizes, growing out of the ten-foot body at random angles. A vine hissed and struck at it, and the jaws snapped and another ten feet of body flopped into view, with more heads, all biting at once. The vine took a few more loops around the wormlike body and squeezed. Somewhere a cat yowled, and underbrush crashed and the yowl became a scream.

"Don't use your gun except in extremity," Roosevelt warned. "To take life here—any life—is to interfere with the probability equation. Even the slightest realignment could interfere with the shuttle recall signal."

There was an archway across the avenue ahead almost lost under its load of washtub-sized toadstools, but across the top carved figures and flowers were still visible. Roosevelt consulted his dials again.

"Our destination appears to be the Royal Archives,"
he said. "It's just ahead."

The side street faced a wall of foliage that had been a
park. On our side, there was a monumental facade,
festooned with ragged vines. Some of the windows still
had glass in them, but most of them were blind, like eyes
afflicted with green cataracts. Where the door had been,
there was a gap in the screen of vines.

"Something's been using that entrance," I said.
"Something the size of a rhinoceros."

"Still—that's where we must go," Roosevelt said, and
pushed through a screen of limp, yellow-spotted leaves
the size of garrison flags. There was a path through the
mat of moss on the floor, where tiles showed. We
followed it fifty feet to a dead end. Roosevelt unshipped
a handlight and played it over a wall of impacted vines.
"We'll have to cut through." He changed the torch
setting, and the beam dimmed to deep red, sliced
through the tangled growth. In half a minute he had cut
a hole big enough to climb through.

He clipped the torch to his belt and went ahead. I
started after him, and heard a rumble like a Bengal tiger
disturbed at his nap. I came through fast, grabbing for
my gun, and saw moonlight on low walls, black lawn, a
fountain with water. Roosevelt was backed against the
carved Neptune, facing something right out of the fairy-
tale books. It had a long, feline body, a maned neck, a
beak like an eagle—if eagles had beaks two feet long.
The legs were scaled from the midpoint down and ended
in talons like the big claw in a wrecking yard. It was a
griffin, half lion and half eagle, and both halves were
closing in for the kill.

I yelled and fired high to distract the thing. It reared
up and danced around on its hind legs to face me,
showing an expanse of snow-white underbody and
giving me a good look down the red throat behind the
beak. The eyes were the size of Dixie cups, three
concentric circles around yellow irises. The outer circle
was scales—iridescent silver ones. Darker scales ran
back across the face and ended where the white mane
began. A pointed black tongue licked out like a snake
between the halves of the knife-edged beak. I saw all this

in a couple of fast seconds while I backed away and wondered just what Roosevelt would call an extremity.

"Hold your fire!" he called. "It's tame!" I started to ask him what his idea of wild was, when I saw what he meant. There was a harness strapped around the thing's chest, almost hidden under the mane. Silver ornaments dangled from the black leather, jingled as it moved. It dropped down to all fours less than ten feet from me, gave a scream that ended in a yowl, and sat down on its haunches. Its timing was good; in another half second I'd have blown its chest open. Which would have been a serious mistake, because just then the owner came walking out of the shadows.

Chapter Seven

I'd gaped pretty hard at the snake-dog, and the griffin had held my attention, too; but neither of them was anything at all to what I saw now.

It was a girl: tall, high-bosomed, long-legged, with skin as white as the fallen marble columns, and dark copper hair piled up high over a face that was like the one you dream about, that smiles and is lost forever, and you wake up sick with yearning. She was dressed in a flimsy swath of white gauzy stuff that clung to her hips and thighs like wet tissue paper and floated when she moved. She came straight up to the thing that had me cornered and said, "Aroint thee, Vrodelix! An ill greeting for visitors!" It dropped its head and whined like an overgrown puppy.

The girl pushed the monster aside and looked at me. Her eyes were dark blue, and they glistened in the moonlight. I knew those eyes; I'd seen them in the dream.

"Are you a man?" she said. "Or a god?" Her tone indicated that both choices were equally likely. I told her and she nodded.

"I'm glad. I am a mortal woman." She looked across at Roosevelt, who had come up to us. He gave her a courtly bow and the smile.

"But *you* are a god," she said.

"Only a man, my dear," he said. "Pieter Roosevelt, at your service—and this is Richard Curlon."

She smiled up at him, and I felt a strange feeling that somehow I'd missed out on something rare and valuable.

"And I am Ironel, Pieter," she said.

"You live here alone?" Roosevelt was asking.

"Oh, no. Vrodelix is with me." She ran a hand along the sleek, curved neck of the nightmare animal. "And I have other friends—and now, two new ones!" She caught Roosevelt's hand and then mine and smiled from one to the other of us, and we grinned back.

"Tell me about your other, ah, friends, Ironel," Roosevelt said in the gentle, fatherly tone he had adopted with her.

"Of course, Pieter! There is Ronizpel the Climber, and Chazz the Dweller Below, and Arnq of the Spines—and many more!"

"All animals?"

She had to think that one over. "Mostly," she said. "Except for Chazz—I think. But you'll meet them soon. Oh, how glad they'll be you've come!" She stopped, as if she had just remembered something. "But Old Garff—I'm not sure *he'll* be pleased."

"How long have you lived here?" Roosevelt wanted to know.

"Why—forever." She sounded surprised at the silly question.

"Where are your parents?"

"What are parents?"

"The people who raised you—taught you to speak, to dress yourself so prettily?"

"Why . . . 'tis a novel thought, Pieter! Must one *learn* to talk as I taught Arnq to weave his nets o'er the Dark Places?" She touched the soft fold of the cloth she wore. "As for my garment—'tis made for me by Arnq, of course." She looked at Roosevelt's nylon suit, touched my sleeve. "I must show him your weaver's work; 'twill set him a task, to make stuff like it." She laughed, pleased by the idea.

"Are there no other people here—like you, and us?" Roosevelt persisted.

"But—we are not like!" Ironel laughed. "You are taller than I, and your hair is short, and your shoulders wide and your chest flat—not like me." She touched her body, ran her hand down her slim waist as if to sense the differences with her fingertips.

"We're men," Roosevelt said, smiling faintly. "You're

a woman. Are there other humans of either sex here?"

That seemed to puzzle her. "No, none," she said.

"What do you eat? How do you keep warm in winter?"

"Why—Chazz brings me roots from the deep earth, and Ronizpel knows where the grapes and melons ripen soonest. And when the whiteness falls, I dwell indoors, and Arnq swathes the windows with his finest weaving to hold back the cold."

Vrodelix whined, and while the girl was soothing him, Roosevelt stepped close to me.

"Are we to believe this poor natural maid lives all alone here as she says? Is it possible?"

"It looks that way. For some reason the Blight seems to stay clear of this little patch of ground. You said it was the eye of the storm. The eye of a hurricane is a dead calm."

Ironel was back beside us, smiling. "Come," she said. "Now I'll show thee my playthings!" She towed us across a flagstone walk between tended flowerbeds where black and gold fungus blossoms grew between roses and daisies. We went through an archway and across a tiled hall and up stairs into a wide, shadowy corridor that was blocked twenty feet away by fallen masonry; but the part that was clear was swept clean. She opened a door on a room with a deep black carpet and high, glassless windows with curtains of the same gauzy stuff as her clothing. There was a high bed with a white silk canopy over it, decorated with a floral design in gold thread. She knelt by a big chest with a carved lid and opened it and lifted out a bolt of scarlet cloth.

"Is it not pretty?" she said and stretched a length of it across her body. I had to agree it was pretty.

She took out a smaller box and poured gold coins out on the rug. I knelt to gather them up and discovered that the rug was a layer of moss, as smooth and even as black velvet.

"And these!" she dumped jewels among the coins; they sparkled like hot embers.

"And these are my dearest treasures!" she said, and spilled colored seashells out among them.

She laughed. "And now we must sort them, and put them away. Is it not a fine game?"

Roosevelt picked up a big square-cut ruby with an incised crest.

"Where did you get this?" his voice grated roughly. His eyes bored into hers. She didn't seem to notice the change of pace.

"In the Pretty Place," she said. "There are many more, but I liked these the best."

"Show me!" he snapped.

"Easy, General," I said. "We play the young lady's game first, then yours."

For a moment his eyes clashed with mine; then he relaxed, smiled, laughed aloud. He got down on his knees and started picking up seashells and placing them in a careful heap.

She led us down into a wide, moonlit avenue, almost roofed over by vines. Vrodelix paced beside her, making hissing sounds and acting increasingly nervous as we came closer to the fallen buildings at the far end.

"Poor beast, he remembers the Thing-with-eight-legs and the Fanged Ones," Ironel said. "They frightened him, ere he slew them."

She pointed to a tall, mold-blackened building nestled up against the barricade of rubble. "Vrodelix mislikes me to go there—but with you by me, naught can emperil us."

"The State Museum," Roosevelt said. He looked at the instrument strapped to the underside of his wrist, but if it told him anything he didn't say so.

We went through a weed-choked entrance, crossed a hall that was carpeted and walled with vines, went up a wide, curved staircase. The second floor was in better condition. There were glass-topped cases here, dusty but intact. Old paintings hung on the walls, mold-spotted faces in strange ruffs and plumed helmets peering down from leafy shadows, but their stiff expressions looked more frightened than arrogant. We went on into the next room, where formerly elaborate uniforms with knee-boots and capes with moth-eaten tiger-skin facings hung on decaying dummies with vacant, horrified faces. Fancy saddles and tattered regimental flags were displayed along with lances and dueling pistols and hand-tooled matchlocks, all draped with spiderwebs.

"Now—you must close your eyes," Ironel said, and took our hands. Her fingers were slim and cool and soft. She watched to make sure I followed instructions, then led the way up three steps, and across more floor, around obstructions, then down again. I was just beginning to wonder how long the blindman's buff went on when she stopped and said, "Open your eyes!"

Colored moonlight streamed down through a stained-glass window on a gray stone floor leading away to an altar with slim columns and a gold canopy and silver candlesticks. A silver-mounted reliquary box lay there. There was a stone sarcophagus before the altar, with the carved figure of a Crusader on it, dressed in full armor, his hands crossed over the hilt of his sword that lay on his chest like a crucifix.

"Dost like my Pretty Place?" Ironel asked in a breathless voice.

"We like it very much indeed," Roosevelt said softly. "Will you show me where you found the signet stone?"

"Here." Ironel turned to a brass-bound coffer sitting on wooden trestles to the left. Roosevelt lifted the lid. The soft light winked on rings and armlets and brooches—a magpie's trove of trinkets. Ironel lifted a chain of soft gold links and held it against her, then dropped it and took a tiny silver chain with a dangling amethyst.

"This is prettier," she said. "Do thee not think so, Pieter?"

"Much prettier, my dear." His eyes moved past her, roving over the details of the little chapel, back to the dial on his wrist. He started toward the altar, and Ironel made a distressed sound and caught at his hand.

"Pieter—no! Thou must approach no closer!"

He gave her a smile that was more grim than comforting.

"It's all right," he said in a soothing tone. "I mean only to have a look at it." He brushed her hand away.

"Pieter—you mustn't! Bad things will happen if we intrude there! Canst thou not feel it in the very air?"

He wasn't listening. He took another step—and stopped. Far away, something rumbled. The floor trembled, and a piece of glass cracked in the window. I stepped to his side.

"You're a guest here," I said. "Maybe you'd better play house rules."

He shot me a look like a harpoon. "I'll decide that," he said, and started on.

I caught his arm. It was like grabbing an oak rail. He strained to pull free and I strained to hold him back. Neither of us seemed to be gaining.

"The girl says 'no,' General," I said. "Maybe she has a reason."

"Come to your senses, Curlon," he said, still sounding calm. "Remember what we came here to find!"

"You said yourself the equation is in delicate balance," I said. "Take it slowly, until you know what you're doing."

There was another rumble, closer this time. I felt the floor move under my feet. The griffin raked his talons on the floor and yowled. Ironel whimpered; I heard a sound from above, looked up in time to see a safe-sized stone dropping at me. I dived to the side; the smash was like switch-engines colliding. Rock chips flew like shrapnel. Roosevelt whirled and ran for the altar. The griffin hissed and reared to strike at him, but Ironel shrieked and the animal crouched back, his ears flat and Roosevelt ran past him. I started after him and a marble pilaster crashed down between us. The floor was heaving like jelly, with broken stone and fragments of ceiling mosaic and stained glass and ironwork and chunks of statuary dancing on it like water drops in a hot skillet. Roosevelt ran into the thick of it; stones fell around him like bomb fragments. A small one hit him on the shoulder, but he stayed on his feet, staggering now but still trying to reach the altar. He was six feet from it when the canopy over it sagged and went down. One of the columns fell. It barely brushed him, but it threw him ten feet. He skidded in the dust and lay still, a broken doll. The rumble died away. A few stray pebbles clattered down into silence.

Ironel went to her knees beside Roosevelt. She touched his face. "Is he dead?" she whispered.

I checked him over. There was a nasty dent in his

skull. His breathing was shallow and rasping, but his pulse was solid.

"He's badly hurt," I said. "But not dead—yet."

With Ironel's help I got him on my back, carried him back to her sleeping room, and laid him out on the bed in the dark.

Chapter Eight

Daylight came after a long time. Ironel was asleep, her head on Roosevelt's bed. When I woke her, she smiled at me.

"He still lives, Richard," she said. I checked his pulse again. It was still there, but his breathing was shallow and ragged. I touched the depressed fracture over his eye.

"I've got to do something about this," I said. "Do you have any way to make fire?"

"Ronizpel fears the fire," she said. "But he will bring it to me."

I examined the wound. There was one main bone splinter, with some smaller fragments. Ironel came back with a shallow brass tray with glowing embers in it. I didn't ask questions, just added some wood to the coals and got a brisk fire going, and sterilized my knife blade in it.

I made an incision across the wound, crossed it with another, and folded back the flaps of skin. Ironel stepped in like a trained nurse, following every step, acting without even words from me. While she held the incision open, I used a hook bent from wire and heat-sterilized to lift the big splinter back into position, then probed for the others. After a while I was finished. I closed the wound and he was still breathing. Ironel used red silk thread to stitch up the cuts. She finished and then sat beside him, watching his face. I found a corner and went to sleep.

I woke up with light in my face; Ironel was beside me; her face was cameo-pale against the shadows.

"Richard—I am afraid for Pieter."

I got up and went to him. He lay on his back on the bed. His eyes were closed and sunken, his face drawn into a tortured rictus. He snarled between his locked teeth, and his hands raked at the coverlet.

"No," he ground out the words. "Never . . . bend the knee . . . better . . . eternal destruction . . ." His voice ran off into a mutter.

I put my fingers against his neck. He was hot as new-cast iron. The wound in his forehead was swollen and inflamed.

"I'm sorry," I said. "We need medicines we don't have."

"Richard," the girl said. "Chazz says we must bring Pieter to him."

I looked at her. Her eyes were big and dark, her hair red-black, a damp curl against her white skin.

"We shouldn't move him."

"But—Chazz cannot come here, Richard!"

I looked at Roosevelt. I didn't know much about medicine, but I'd seen a dying man before. I lifted him and the girl led the way down through the dark halls among the black vines and the fallen statuary and out into the perfumed night.

Stone mermaids cavorted in a dry fountain at the center of a weed-choked garden. Ironel pulled aside the leafy branch of a twisted bush that grew up through a crack in the basin, exposing an opening. Stone steps led down at a steep angle into an odor of mushrooms and wet clay. Ironel led the way. In a room at the bottom, she flashed my handlight on sagging shelves loaded with dusty wine bottles. At the far side the wall was broken away by what looked like a giant rat-hole. The odor that came from it was like the ape-house at the zoo.

Ironel didn't seem to notice. She went to the opening, called:

"Chazz—it's I, Ironel—and Richard, my friend. We've brought Pieter!"

A sound came back, like boulders grinding together under the earth. Ironel turned to me.

"Chazz says we may bring him in."

I went down through the opening; it was a smooth-walled tunnel cut through damp earth. It curved, dipped, ended at a complicated wall of lumpy wet leather that blocked the tunnel. Ironel put the light on the wall and I saw it was a face, six feet high, six feet wide, with a vast hooked nose, sunken eyelids that lifted to show the glint of eyes the size of basketballs. There was matted hair as coarse as mammoth fur on the cheeks and on the sloping, wrinkled forehead. Where there wasn't hair, the skin was black, scaled, and creased like a rhino's hide. The edges of broken teeth the size of bargain tombstones showed under the purple edge of the lip. The mouth opened and the voice rumbled forth.

"He says to put him down here," Ironel relayed. I did as she asked. Roosevelt lay like a corpse, death-pale now. The big eyes roved over him. A tongue like a pink feather blanket peered out from the vast mouth, tested the air, went in again.

"This one made the rocks fall," the big voice boomed out, clearer now—or maybe I was just getting used to hearing an earthquake talk.

"He didn't know, Chazz dear," Ironel said in a pleading tone. "He meant no harm."

"A stone hurt me," Chazz said. He rotated his huge skull, and the edge of a black-crusted cut big enough to lay an arm in came into view.

"Poor Chazz—did it hurt very much?"

"Not much, Ironel." The face came back up and a tear that would have filed a teacup splashed down across the leather face. "Don't feel bad for Chazz. Chazz is all right, Ironel."

"And—can you help Pieter?"

Again the incredible eyeballs rotated, stared at the unconscious man. The lids came down, half-covering them like wrinkled leather blinds.

"I can try," the monster rumbled. "I feel the hurt place . . . there. Bad, bad hurt—but it's not that which is killing Pieter. No—it's the things that pull—there and there! But I push . . . push against them . . ." his voice went into a mutter like a glacier breaking apart in a spring thaw. Roosevelt stirred, made vague sounds. Ironel put her hand on his forehead. I held the light and saw the color come slowly back into his face. He sighed and his hands moved restlessly, then lay still. His breathing eased.

"Ahhh," Chazz groaned. "Bad things still there, Ironel! I fix him—but I feel bad things stir there still! Better I kill him now—"

"Chazz—no!" Ironel threw herself half across Roosevelt. "You mustn't!"

"I feel things there, inside him," Chazz said. "Things that make me afraid!"

"He's only a man, Chazz—he said so himself. Like Richard! Tell him, Richard!" Ironel caught at my arm. "Tell Chazz that Pieter is our friend!"

"What kind of bad things do you feel inside him, Chazz?" I asked the big face. He rolled his whale's eyes at me.

"When the stones fell, I felt them," he said. "And when I reached into him—I felt them again. Black things prowl there, in the red caverns of his sleeping brain, Richard. He would mold all the world to an image he keeps secret there."

"Back home, he's an important man," I said. "He came here to try to save his world. He made a mistake, and it almost killed him. I don't think there's any harm in him now."

Chazz groaned. "I have known him in my dreams, as I slept here under the earth. Why does he come, Richard? And why you? For of you, too, I have dreamed, moving across the bright, restless pattern of the world. A doom hangs about your head, and about his. But I cannot tell which doom is the stronger." He groaned again. "I fear him, Richard. But for Ironel's sake, I give him his destiny. Now take him from me. His mind stirs and the pain of that stirring cuts to my heart."

I lifted Roosevelt and carried him back through the stinking tunnel and up to Ironel's room.

She woke me with half a golden melon on a gold plate and a cluster of red grapes the size of plums. Roosevelt was better, now, she said. I went over and looked at him, lying there on his back, still unconscious. He didn't look any different to me, but his temperature seemed to be normal, and his pulse and breathing too. Maybe I was a better brain surgeon than I thought.

Ironel took me for a tour of her kingdom: the lower floors of the building where she slept, the garden, what was left of the street the earthquake had shaken up. With the early morning light slanting down through the leaves that overgrew it, it had a sort of eerie, silent beauty. Ironel led me by the hand, showed me little clumps of flowers growing in hidden places, a clear pool in a basin that must have been a beautiful fountain once, led me to where there were pretty stones lying scattered in the rank grass—the fragments of an alabaster statue.

We went down chipped marble steps under huge old trees and bathed in a black pool, climbed up in a ruined tower, and looked out through a stone-filigreed window at the view of other towers thrusting up through the jungle. In the evening, we sat on a bench in the garden and listened to the hooting and screeching and hissing of night things that prowled just beyond the borders of the garden. Sometimes she talked, chattered away about her friends and her games; other times she sang strange little tuneless songs. And sometimes, she just smiled into the vague distance, like a flower, glad to be alive. There were a lot of questions I wanted to ask, but I didn't ask them. She was like a sleeping child; I didn't want to wake her. That night she came to my bed and slept with me, like a child.

The second day passed, and Roosevelt woke up, gave us a faint smile, and went back to sleep. The next day he stayed awake. He seemed to be his old self, assurance and all—except for the hollow-cheeked look. He professed to have no recollection of anything from the time we'd met the girl.

He mended fast then. On the fourth day, he was up and walking. On the fifth day, on my way back from an expedition to the edge of the jungle to gather fruit, I heard an angry yowl from the direction of the park, followed by shots. I knew that yowl—it was Vrodelix, and he was mad. I dropped the red and yellow mangoes I had collected and ran for the gates. Ten feet inside the park, I found the griffin, stretched beside the dolphin fountain, with three holes in him. He moaned and tried to get up, and fell back, dead, his beak gaping. I ran on across the park, up the steps. I shouted for Ironel, but there was no answer. Something made a soft sound behind me, and I turned to see Roosevelt come out of shadows with his nerve-gun aimed at my head.

"I'm sorry, Curlon," he said. "But there's no other way." He pulled the trigger and the world blew up in my face.

I was lying on my back, dreaming that Roosevelt was bending over me. His face was thin, hollow-cheeked, and the wound over his eye stood out like a big X marked in lipstick. His voice came from someplace as far away as the stars, but the words were clear enough.

"Get on your feet, Curlon. I've paralyzed your volitional centers, but you can hear me. We have a duty to perform."

I felt myself climbing to my feet. They seemed to be miles below my head, which floated all alone in a rarified level high above the clouds that drifted just at the edge of vision. My hands were wired together in front of me.

"That way," Roosevelt said. We went out across the garden, past the gentle, dead monster lying on the flagstones, into the ruined street. There was a high, humming noise inside my head, and the light was strange, as though there were an eclipse in progress. We entered the museum, went up the stairs littered with plaster and fragments of a skylight, into the big hall where the armored mannikins lay strewn around like disaster victims. In the chapel, the sun came through the broken window like a spotlight. The altar was still standing, with the ruins of the golden canopy around it. There was a feeling in the air as if the whole world was a bowstring, stretched to the breaking point.

"Go ahead of me," Roosevelt ordered. I picked my way through the rubble, stepped over the broken sarcophagus, brushed away the rotted strands of a velvet cape, stopped in front of the altar.

"Take the box," Roosevelt ordered. I picked it up awkwardly in my wired hands. It was heavy, and the surface tingled as though an electric current was running through it. I felt the current in my feet, too. The floor vibrated under me. There was a rumbling around, like distant thunder. Roosevelt's face was strained in a tight, bared-teeth look that wasn't a smile.

"Give it to me," he said. I handed it over as the rumble grew louder.

"Lo, the very heavens attend our enterprise," he said, sounding as though he meant it. "But we have what we want. Now we'll go."

He turned away and I followed. A section of carved stone toppled from up high, smashed down a few feet away from us. Other things fell, but none of them touched us. As we reached the door, the roof came down behind us. On the stair, I felt the stones breaking up under my feet, but they held until we were down in the big hall; then they came tumbling down.

Outside, the street was a sea of heaving rubble. The building across the way sagged and leaned and fell into the plaza.

We jumped across broken pavement slabs that tilted and ground together like an ice floe breaking up. A tree fell, trailing a snarl of vines, and back in the jungle something as massive as an apartment house loomed up, bellowing.

"The centroid of the probability storm is moving, following us," Roosevelt called to me. "It's success, Curlon—if we can reach the shuttle before this enclave of antiprobability collapses! Stay close to me!" He ran, and I ran with him, while the world came apart around us.

In the clearing where we'd left the shuttle on half-phase, Roosevelt took the signaler from the pouch clipped to his belt. I saw something moving in the trees just above him, but I made no effort to say anything. It eased out from under a spray of tent-sized leaves, a spider with a body as big as a bathtub, thick, bristly legs, faceted eyes the size of dinner plates. It swung out on a clotted, grayish cord, a pair of pinchers at its fore end cocked and ready.

"No, Ronizpel!" Ironel's voice cried out behind us, and the spider-thing checked just long enough for Roosevelt to draw his gun and fire a burst of mini-slugs into the swollen abdomen ten feet above him. The thing fell, thrashing its eight legs and Ironel screamed and rushed to it while Roosevelt pumped more rounds into the dying thing. He jumped past her, knocking her aside,

pressed the recall button of the signaler. I felt the
buzzing in the air around me, saw the light darken,
taking on a tarnished tinge like the light before a
thunderstorm. A gust of air whirled leaves up, and the
shuttle phased into identity, low, black, deadly-looking.
Its door slid open to spill white light out into the gloom.

"Curlon—get in!" Roosevelt shouted. The ground
shook under me as I walked past the weeping girl and
the gutted spider. To my left, the jungle crashed and
burst open and the ground rose up and split and the
head of Chazz rose up into view, squinting against the
light. His eyes went to the girl, and his mouth opened in
a howl of rage. Roosevelt brought the gun up and fired
into the big face, and chunks of flesh flew and black
blood welled out of the craters, and Chazz bellowed in
agony; then I was inside, and Roosevelt was behind me,
slamming the hatch. He produced handcuffs, chained
me to the contoured seat. The screen glowed pink, then
cleared to a view of the outside. Chazz had forced his
shoulders up through the earth, and his hands, huge and
gnarled with chipped black nails as big as coal scuttles,
groped out toward the girl. He touched her with one
finger, and then the giant head slumped, and Roosevelt
threw the drive switch in and the scene flowed like wax
in the sun, as the jungle closed in over the spot where
Ironel's garden had been.

Chapter Nine

I came up out of a drugged sleep to see early morning sunshine glowing through curtains at an open window. I had a headache like a cracked anvil. Roosevelt was sitting in a brocaded chair beside the bed, dressed in a fantastic outfit that somehow, on him, looked natural enough: a short, loose coat with a fur collar, tight breeches, slippers with jeweled pompons, a big gold chain across his chest, and jewels everywhere, stitched to his sleeves, sparkling in finger rings.

He said "Good morning" in a cheery tone and passed me a cup of coffee. "We've been through a difficult time," he went on. "But it's over now, Curlon. I regret the necessity for the things I was forced to do—but I had no choice. And we succeeded, you and I. Now the victory and all its fruits are ours." He said this in a low voice, but his black eyes glowed like a man looking at visions.

I tried the coffee. It was hot and strong, but it didn't help my head any.

"You understand, don't you?" His eyes probed mine. "A great new destiny is taking shape—for you as well as me. Think of it, Curlon! Who hasn't wished to seize the sorry scheme of things entire, and mold it nearer to his heart's desire? Well—we've done it—together! Out of the ashes of the old, a new world rises—a world in which our fates loom like colossi over the faceless mob! The world that should have been, Curlon, a world of might and glory, such as has never before been seen—spread at our feet like a carpet! We've turned back the clock of fate, set history back on a course that seemed doomed forever!"

"What about the girl?" I asked.

"I'm sorry; she was a shadow in a twilight world. And you, I'm afraid, were caught up in her spell. I did what I had to do. I would have brought her with us, but it was impossible. The fabric I'm weaving is too fragile at this stage to support the transfer of a key figure from a peripheral A-line."

"I don't know what you're doing, Roosevelt," I said. "But whatever it is, the price is too high."

"One day you'll understand, Curlon. Of all mankind you'll understand best. Because, out of all the millions of pawns on the board, you alone are my compeer; like mine, your destiny is entwined with that of the new world that's taking shape."

"Count me out, General," I said. "I want no part of your operations. If you'll tell me where my pants are, I'll be going now."

Roosevelt shook his head, smiling a little. "Curlon, don't talk like a fool. Do you have any idea where you are?"

I got out of the bed, shakily, and went to the window and looked down on lawns and flowerbeds that were almost familiar.

"This is a world-line far removed from the turmoil of the Blight," Roosevelt said as I dressed in the loose shirt and tight pants laid out for me. "Its common-history date with your world is 1199 A.D. We're in the city of Londres, capital of the province of New Normandy, an autonomous duchy under the French king, Louis Augustus. Great affairs are afoot here, Curlon. Rebels challenge the power of the Emperor, loyalists are charged with treason, and across the Channel, Louis waits, ready to land forces at Harwich and Dover and Newcastle if needed. A touch would send the situation crashing into war. It's that which we must prevent."

"And what's in it for you, General?"

"I'm known here; I enjoy the confidence of both Victory Garonne and important members of the rebellious faction. My hope is to prevent bloodshed, stablize the situation. A strongly established A-line is necessary to contain the vast energies I've channeled here. You'll recall what I told you of key objects, key lines. New Normandy will become the key line of its probability quantum, with the aid of the artifact we brought here. And with the rise of the new master-line, our stars too will ascend!"

"And where do I come in?"

"Ten days ago, Duke Richard fell dead at a public ceremony in full view of the populace. Murdered, they say. The rebels charge the loyalists with elminating the natural leader of the Britons; the loyalists in turn charge the rebels with killing a man they regarded as no more than a vassal of the French king. The tension has reached crisis level; it must be relieved."

"I still haven't heard anything illuminating."

"It's really quite obvious," Roosevelt said. "As a Plantagenet born and bred, you'll step forward to take up the role of the Duke of Londres."

"You're out of your mind, General," I told him.

"Nothing could be simpler," he said with a wave of the hand. "No one could deny that you look the part; you're enough like the departed Duke to be his brother. However, we shall present you in the role of a more distant relation, raised secretly north of the Scots border. Your appearance will satisfy the most fanatical rebel, and of course you'll make suitably defiant pronouncements to satisfy that clique. More discreetly, you'll engage in dialogues with Viceroy Garonne aimed at easing the crisis and restoring civil order."

"What's going to make me do all this?"

"This is the drama of life itself—and you were a part of it from the moment you were born—and before. Like me, you're the inheritor of a mighty dynasty. All that you might have been —that your analogs, those close to you might have done—all the vast repercussions across time and history of every act of that great clan, chopped down in the prime of their strength—all those aborted probability energies must find their expression in you—and in the world you help create!"

"What about my own world?"

"The new master-line will dominate the quantum," Roosevelt said flatly. "In the readjustment that accompanies its establishment, lesser lines must of necessity be sacrificed. The Imperium and the Blight Insular lines will go under. But that's a matter of no moment to you, Mr. Curlon—or to me. Our destinies lie elsewhere."

"You have it all figured out," I said. "There's just one weak point."

"Which is?"

"I won't play."

Roosevelt looked grim. "Understand me, Curlon: I want you as my willing ally; but willing or not, you'll help me."

"You're bluffing, Roosevelt. You need a walking, talking puppet, not a man with wires on his wrists."

He made an impatient gesture. "I told you I regretted that, and the need for drugging you to bring you here. But I'd do it again, ten thousand times, if that were the only way! The Old Empire *will* rise again! We're not discussing *if*, Curlon; only *how*. Meet this challenge—lend me your full support—and your future will be of a splendor unimaginable to you now. Defy me, and you'll walk like a corpse through what would have been your triumph. Which do you want, Curlon? Honors, or rotted rags? Majesty, or misery?"

"You've worked your story out pretty carefully, General. But it still doesn't make sense."

"The rebels are strong," Roosevelt said grudgingly. "They have all the strength on their side, if the truth were known. They could seize power any time they chose. They lack only one thing: leadership. They'll rally to you, Curlon—but instead of leading them to victory, you'll cool their revolutionary fervor. Because if they should rise up and cast out the French, a major branching of the line will result! Seven hundred years of stable history would be shattered, creating a whole new probability spectrum. I need not detail the effect this would have on my plans for New Normandy!"

I smiled a smile I didn't feel. "You're in trouble, aren't you, Roosevelt? You need me—and not just to carry a spear in the third act of some farce to fool the locals. What is it? What's the real reason for trying to drag me into this paranoid fantasy-system of yours?"

"I've told you! We're linked, you and I, all down through the corridors of past time, on every world within a thousand years of common history. As your fortunes wax, so do mine. I can force you, Curlon—but to the extent that I must break you to my will our joint stature is diminished. Join with me freely, lend your *mana* to mine—and anything we desire is within our grasp!"

"And if I don't?"

"I want your willing aid," he said in a steely voice. "But your broken mind and body, dangling from the strings, will serve if need be."

"Everything you say confirms the one clear idea I've gotten from all this, Roosevelt. Whatever this fight is, you're on one side, and I'm on the other."

"I can break you, Curlon. The stronger man can always break the weaker. A simple demonstration will suffice to prove my point." He took a stance with his feet apart and raised his arms until they were level with his shoulders, smiling.

"The first to drop his arms acknowledges the other man his superior—at least in one small way."

I put my arms out. The effort made my temples pound, but I didn't burst into tears. If Roosevelt wanted to play little games I was willing to go along. The hamburger machines could wait.

"In every world, in every time, the will of some man has shaped reality," Roosevelt said suddenly. "Here, now, that old rule is still in force—but made more potent by the existence of titanic new forces. Those forces are at the command of whoever can master them. Fate is a fragile thing, Curlon. A mindless thing, controlled by the whim of a strong man. Let an Alexander set out to conquer the world, the world becomes what he makes it. Without Alexander, there would have been no Caesar, no Atilla, no Muhammad, no Hitler in your world, no Guglielmo Maxoni in the Zero-zero line. Men make fate, Curlon, not the other way around. You saw that demonstrated when we fought together, back to back. We two form islands of stability about _____ ____ ____ ____ _____. ____ not because his will. ___ _____ ___ __y will never had any interest in shaping will. But I'm not willing to see it destroy a Darius." But because I shaped to yours. Home was never much to me, but I'm not ready to see it flushed down the drain to give you a roost to rule."

Roosevelt nodded. "I suppose it's a thing outside both of us, Curlon, written in the stars, as they say. For seven hundred years, your ancestors and mine fought to rule the quantum. Think of it, Plantagenet! In a thousand billion alternate world-lines, each differing from the others in some greater or lesser degree, your clan and mine, striving, down through the centuries, each to dominate his world, none knowing of the others, all driven by the common instinct to fulfill the potentiality inherent in them. And then—the day of cataclysm, when the Blight swept in to wipe them out, root, stem and branch—all but one man of my line, and one of yours."

It had been about ten minutes since the game had begun. Fiery pains were shooting along the backs of my arms and shoulders. Roosevelt was still standing as rigid as a statue. His arms hadn't quivered.

"They tell me the Blight dates back to the nineties," I said. "You're a little young to be remembering it—unless your Imperium has face-lift techniques that beat anything Hollywood's come up with."

"I'm telling you what I've learned—what my researchers have revealed, what I was told—" He cut himself off.

"I thought this was all your own idea, Roosevelt."

"Told—by my father," Roosevelt said. "He devoted his life to the conviction that somehow—somewhere—our time would come again. His world was gone—but how could such glory be forever vanished? He worked, studied, and in the end made his discovery. He was old then, but he passed the charge on to me. And I've made it good! I worked first to gain a powerful position within Imperial Intelligence—the one organization that knew whi~~~~ts of the Net. This gave me a platform from vessel its

Blight."
I had to conce~his line—New Normandy—to be the
level. Somehow, it ~he w~l shape the forces of the
Roosevelt's game. If he w~l shape the forces of the
"Are you tiring?" he ask~

"Poor Mother Nature, so blind in her efforts to protect the body. She sends pain as a warning, first. Then little by little, she'll numb the nerves. Your arms will begin to sag. You'll try, with all your will, to hold them high—to outdo me, your inevitable master. But you'll fail. Oh, the strength is there—but Nature forces you to husband your strength. So though you might be willing of yourself, to endure the torture of fatigue until death from exhaustion—she won't let you. You'll suffer—for nothing. A pity, Mr. Curlon."

I was glad he felt like talking. It kept my mind off the hot clamps set in the back of my neck. I tried to fan a little spark of anger alive—another of Mother Nature's tricks, this one on my side. I wanted to keep him chattering, but at the same time coax along the frustration I hoped he was beginning to feel.

"Seeing you drop will be worth waiting for," I said.

"But you won't. I'm stronger than you are, Mr. Curlon. Since childhood I've trained every day in these exercises—and the mental control that goes with them. At the age of seven I could hold a fencing foil across my palms at arm's length for a quarter of an hour. For me, this is literally child's play. But not for you."

"There's nothing to this," I said breezily. "I can stand here all day."

"So far, you've endured it for less than a quarter of an hour. How will you feel fifteen minutes from now, eh, Mr. Curlon? And half an hour after that?" He smiled—not quite the easy smile he'd have liked. "In spite of yourself, you'll have failed long before then. A simple demonstration, Curlon—but a necessary one. You must be brought to realize that in me you've met your superior."

"There must be a catch to it," I said. "Maybe this is supposed to keep my attention occupied while your pals aim a spy beam at my brains—or whatever it is mad scientists do."

"Don't talk like a fool, Curlon," Roosevelt almost snapped the words. "Or—why, yes, I see." He smiled and the strain went out of his face. "Very good, Mr. Curlon. You were almost beginning to irritate me. A well-designed tactic. Such distractions can appreciably sap endurance. By the way, how are your arms feeling? A trifle heavy?"

"Fine," I said in what I hoped was a light tone. "How about yours?" The lines of fire were lancing out into my trapezius muscles, playing around my elbows, tingling in my fingertips. My head ached. Roosevelt looked as good as new. He stared across at me, silent now. That bothered me. I wanted him to talk.

"Keeping up the patter's hard work, eh? But I'll tip you, Roosevelt. You picked the wrong man. I'm a fisherman. I'm used to fighting the big ones eight hours at a stretch. For me, this is a nice rest."

"A flimsy lie, Curlon. I expect better of you."

"The circulation is the weak point," I said. "Soldiers who could march all day in the sun under a full pack used to drop out in a dead faint on parade. Standing at attention, not moving, restricted the flow of blood to the brain—and all of a sudden—blackout. Some fellows couldn't take it. Nothing against them, just a peculiarity of the metabolism. It never bothered me. Good circulation, you know. How's yours?"

"Excellent, I assure you."

"But you're not talking." I gave him a grin that cost me a year off the end of my life.

"I've said what I intended."

"I don't believe you. You had canned lecture number three all ready to go. I can see it in your eyes."

Roosevelt laughed—a genuine laugh. "Mr. Curlon, you're a man after my own heart. I wish we could have met in another time at another place. We might have been friends, you and I."

Neither of us said anything after that. I discovered I was counting off the seconds. It had been about twenty minutes now, maybe a little more. I realized one hand was sagging and brought it back up. Roosevelt smiled a faint smile. More time passed. I thought about things, then tried not to think about things. It occurred to me that the ancient Chinese had wasted a lot of time and effort designing iron maidens and chipping bamboo splinters. Torture was a sport you could play without equipment. And Roosevelt's version was a double challenge, because the only one forcing me was me. I could quit now and laugh it off and call for the next round.

That was the catch. There'd be a next round—and one after that. And if I quit on the first, I'd quit sooner on the second, until I refused to meet his challenge—and that was what he wanted.

That was his swindle. To make me think that if I lost—I'd lost. But it wasn't true. Losing was nothing. Only surrender counted.

And once I understood that, I felt better. The pain was like flaying knives, but it was just pain, something to be endured until it ended. I hitched my arms back up into line and stared across at him through the fading light . . .

. . . and came to, lying on the floor. Roosevelt was standing over me. His face looked yellowish and drawn.

"A commendable effort, Curlon," he said. "One hour and twelve minutes. But as you see—you lost. As you must always lose—because it's your destiny to lose to me. Now—will you join with me willingly?"

I climbed back to my feet, feeling dizzy, and with slow fires still burning in my shoulders. I raised my arms to the crucifix position.

"Ready to try it again?" I said. Roosevelt's face twitched before he laughed.

I grinned at him. "You're afraid, aren't you, Roosevelt? You see your grand scheme coming apart at the seams—and you're afraid."

He nodded. "Yes, I'm afraid. Afraid of my own weakness. You see—incredible though it may seem to you—I truly wanted you to be a part of it, Plantagenet. A foolish sentimentality—but you, like me, are a man of the ancient stock. Even a god can be lonely—or a devil. I offered you comradeship. But at the first trial, you turned against me. I should have known then. And now I've learned the lesson. I have no choice left to me. My course is plain now."

"You're a flawed devil, Roosevelt," I said. "A devil with a conscience. I pity you."

He shook his head. "I want none of your pity, Plantagenet. As I can have none of your friendship. What I want from you, I'll take, though the taking will destroy you."

"Or you."

"That's a risk I'll run." He motioned to the waiting

guards; they closed in around me. "Spend these next hours in meditation," he said. "Tonight you'll be invested with the honors of a dukedom. And tomorrow you'll be hanged in chains."

The dungeons under the viceregal palace were everything that dungeons should be, with damp stone walls and iron doors and unshielded electric lights that were worse than smoky flamebeaux. The armed men in Swiss Guard uniforms that had herded me down the upper levels waited while a burly man with a round, oily, unshaven face opened a barrel grill on a six-by-eight stone box with straw. I didn't move fast enough for him; he swung a kick to hurry me along, but it never landed. Roosevelt showed up in time to slam the back of his hand across the fat face.

"You'd treat a royal duke like a common felon?" he barked. "You're not fit to touch the floor he stands on."

Another man grabbed up the fat man's keys, led the way along the narrow passage, opened an oak door on a larger cell with a bed and a loophole window.

"You'll meditate here in peace," Roosevelt told me, "until I have need of you."

I lay on the bed and waited for the pounding in my head to retreat to a bearable level.

. . . and woke up with a voice that wasn't in my head, whispering, "Plantagenet! Be of good cheer! Wait for the signal!"

I lay where I was and waited for more, but there wasn't any more.

"Who's that?" I whispered, but nobody answered. I got up and examined the wall by my head, and the bed itself. It was just a wall, just a bed. I went to the door and listened, pulled myself up and looked out the six-inch slit at a light-well. There were no lines dangling there with files tied to them; no trapdoors opened up in the ceiling. I was locked in a cell, with no way out, and that was that. The voices were probably courtesy of the management, another of Roosevelt's subtle moves to either wear me down or convince me I was crazy. He was doing pretty well on both counts.

I was having a fine dream about a place where flowers as big as cabbages grew on trees beside a still lake. Ironel was there, walking toward me across the water, and the water broke into a sea of glass splinters, and when I tried to reach her, the flowers turned to heads that shouted threats and the branches were arms that grabbed at me, and shook me—

Hands shook me awake; lights shone in my face. Men with neat uniforms and unholstered nerve-guns took me along passages and up stairs to a room where Roosevelt waited, rigged out in purple velvet and ermine and loops of gold cord. A jewel-covered sword as big as a cased garrison flag hung at his sides as if it belonged there. He didn't talk, and neither did I. Nobody was interested in the condemned man's last words.

Servants clustered around, fitting me with heavy garments of silk and satin and gold thread. A barber trimmed my hair, and poured perfume on me. Someone fitted red leather shoes to my feet. Roosevelt himself strapped a wide, brocaded baldric around my waist, and the tailor's helper attached a jeweled scabbard to it. The hilt that projected from it was unadorned and battered. It was my old knife, looking out of place in all this magnificence. The armorer complained, offered a shiny sword, but Roosevelt waved him away.

"Your sole possession, eh, Curlon?" he said. "It shares your aura strongly. You'll keep it by you—in your moment of glory."

A procession formed up in the wide corridor outside, with the gun-handlers sticking unobtrusively close to me. Roosevelt was beside me as we walked up a wide staircase into an echoing hall hung with spears and banners and grim-faced paintings. Wigged and spangled and beribboned people filled the room. Beyond an arched opening, I saw a high, stained-glass window above a canopied altar. I knew where I was then.

I was standing in the spot where I had stood with Ironel, with the griffin, Vrodelix, beside us, just before Roosevelt had tried the first time to reach the altar. Now the floor was carpeted in gold rose, and there was an odor of incense in the air, and the woodwork gleamed

with the dull shine of wax—but it was the same
room—and not the same. Not by a thousand years of
history.

We halted, and priests in red robes and dry-faced old
men in ribbons and fluffy little wigs went into action,
handing ritual objects back and forth, ducking their
heads at each other, mumbling incantations. I suppose it
was an impressive ceremony, there in the ancient room
under the damask-draped, age-blackened beams, but I
hardly noticed it. I kept remembering Ironel, leading
Roosevelt to her Pretty Place, so that he could destroy it.

The odor of incense was strong; strong enough to burn
my eyes. I sniffed harder and realized I was smelling
something more than scented smoke; it was the real
kind, that comes from burning wood and cloth and
paint. There was a faint, brassy haze in the air.
Roosevelt was looking back; the head priest interrupted
his spiel. The gun-handlers jostled in close to me,
looking worried. Roosevelt snapped off some orders,
and I heard yells from outside the big room. A wave of
heat rolled at us then, and the party broke up. Four guns
prodded me toward the archway. If this was a signal, it
was a dandy, but there wasn't much I could do about it.
The nerve-gun squad cut a path through the notables
who were dithering, coughing, half headed one way and
half the other. We reached the low steps, and two new
guards came in from the flank and there was some fast
footwork, and they were close to me, and the crowd was
closing around us, fighting for position. An old boy in
pink and gold, with his wig askew, thrust his face close
to mine.

"Favor the left, y'r Grace," he hissed in my ear. I was
still working on that one when I saw the nearest guard
put his nerve-gun in his partner's kidney and press the
button. Two more men in uniform came from somewhere; I heard a thud behind me, and then we were
clear, peeling off from the edge of the main crowd, heading right into the smoke.

"Only a few yards, y'r Grace," the little old man
squeaked. A door opened and we were in a cramped
stairway, leading down. On the landing, all four guards
stripped off their uniform jackets and tossed their caps
aside and pulled on workmen's coveralls from a stack

behind the door. The old fellow ditched his wig and cape and was in a footman's black livery. They handed me a long gray cloak. The whole operation was like a well-practiced ballet. It didn't take twenty seconds.

On the next floor down, we pushed out into a concourse full of spectators, firemen, a few belted earls and mitred priests, none of them looking at a repair crew in dirty overalls. The old man led the way to a passage where a lone sentry stood, looking anxious. He stepped in front of us, and the old boy raised a finger and drew him around to the right while one of the others expertly sapped him back of the ear. Then we were in the passage and running.

Two startled scrubwomen watched us cross the kitchen and duck out a door between garbage cans into an unlit alley. The truck parked there started up with a lot of valve click and black kerosene exhaust. I went over the tailgate and the old man scrambled up behind me and pulled the canvas flap down as the truck pulled away. Three minutes later, it slowed, stopped. I heard voices up front, the clatter of a gun, leather boots on cobbles. After a minute, gears clashed and we went on. On the bench opposite, my new friend let out a held breath and grinned from ear to ear.

"Worked like a charm," he said. He cackled and rubbed his hands together. "Like a bloody charm, beggin' y'r Grace's pardon."

The old man's name was Wilibald. "Our friends are waiting for y'r Grace," he said. "True Britons, they are, every man Jock o' 'em. Simple men, y'r Grace, but honest! Not like those treasonous palace blackguards in their silks and jewels!" He gnashed his gums and wagged his head.

"That was a neat play, Wilibald," I said. "How did you manage it?"

"There's true men among the Bluecoats, y'r Grace. The jailor was one. He tried to lodge y'r Grace in a safe cell—one we'd a tunnel to—but his high and mightiness the Baron would ha' none o't. So it took a little longer. But here y'r Grace be now, all the same!" He cackled and rasped his hands together like a cricket's wings.

"You're with the rebel party?"

"Some call us rebels, y'r Grace—but to honest men, we're patriots, pledged to rid these islands o' the French pox!"

"Why did you spring me?"

"Why? Why?" the old man looked astonished. "When word went abroad the Plantagenet was housed in the viceregal tombs, what other course could a loyal Briton follow, y'r Grace? Did y'r Grace deem we'd leave ye there to rot?"

"But I'm not—" I started and left it hanging.

"Not what, y'r Grace?" Wilibald asked. "Not surprised? Of course not. There's ten million Britons in this island, sworm to free the land o' tyranny!"

"Not going to waste any time," I finished. "We'll strike immediately."

The traffic on the road was a mixed bag of horse carts, big solid-tired trucks with open cabs, little droop-snoot cars that looked as if they came in cereal boxes and more than a sprinkling of blue-painted military vehicles. According to Wili, the viceroy was concentrating his forces around the fortified ports, ready to cover the landing of reinforcements if the talk of rebellion crystalized into action. The place we were headed for was the country seat of Sir John Lackland.

"A dark-avised gentleman," Wili said. "But moneyed, and of the ancient stock." He rambled on for the next hour, filling me in on the local situation. The rebels, he swore, were ready to move. And according to Roosevelt, if they moved, they'd win.

"You'll see," Wili told me. "Loyal Britons will rise to a man and flock to y'r Grace's standard!"

After an hour's run, we turned down a side road and swung in between brick pillars, went along a drive that led through tended woods into a cobbled yard fronting a three-story house with flower boxes and leaded windows and half-timbered gables that looked like the real thing. Steps went up to a broad veranda. An old man in a fancy vest and black pants and house slippers let us in. His eyes bugged when he saw me.

" 'Is Grace must see Sir John at once," Wili said.

"Sir John's been abed this twoday wi' a touch o' the ague. He's had no callers—"

"He has now," Wili cut him off.

The old fellow dithered, then led the way into a dark room full of books, and shuffled away.

I looked at the books on the shelves, mostly leather-bound volumes with titles like *Historic Courts* and *Campaigns Among the Quanecticott*. After five minutes or so the door opened and the old fellow was back, piping that Sir John would see us now.

The master of the house was in a bedroom on the top floor, a lean-faced sharp-nosed old aristocrat with a silky black eyebrow-moustache and a matching fringe of hair around a high bald dome. He was propped up in a bed no larger than a skating rink, half buried in a violet satin pillow with an embroidered monogram and more lace than a Hollywood bishop. He had a tan woolen bathrobe with satin lapels wrapped around him, and a knitted shawl over that, and even so, the end of his nose looked cold. When he saw me, he nearly jumped out of bed.

"What—now . . .?" he stared from me to Wili and back. "Why did you come here—of all places?"

"Where else would I be more likely to find friends?" I came back.

"Friends? I'd heard that the viceregent had declared a pretender heir to the dukedom, but I scarce expected to see him present himself *here* in that guise."

"How do you know I'm the man—or that I'm an imposter?"

"Why—why—who else would you be?"

"You mean you're accepting me as genuine? I'm glad, Sir John. Because the time has come for action."

"Action? What action?"

"The liberation of Briton."

"Are you mad? You'd bring destruction down on my house—on all of us! We Plantagenets have always lived on sufferance! The murder of Duke Richard shows us all how precarious our position is—"

"Who killed him?"

"Why—Garrone's men, of course."

"I wonder about that. From the viceroy's point of view, it was a foolish move. It aligned the Britons against him more solidly than Richard ever did alive."

"Conjecture. Idle conjecture," Sir John barked. "You

come here, unbidden, preaching treason! What do I know about you? You imagine I'll place our trust in an upstart, a stranger?

"Hardly that, Sir John," Wili said indignantly. "One glance at him—"

"What do you know of him, fellow? Is any oversized carrot-locked bumpkin who cares to lay claim to the dukedom to be accepted without question?"

"That's hardly fair, Sir John—"

"Enough! The matter will have to wait for resolution until I can summon certain influential men! In the meantime, I'll give you sanctuary. I can do no more." Lackland gave me a look like a dagger in the ribs and yanked at his bellcord. The old footman popped in with a speed that suggested he'd been standing by not far away.

"Show milord to his suite," Lackland got out between lips as stiff as a Hoover collar. "And quarter Master Wilibald below stairs."

I followed my guide along the corridor to a high-ceilinged, airy room with big windows and a sitting room and bath opening from it. The old fellow showed me the soap and towel and then paused at the door and gave me a sly look.

"It did me heart proud to hear y'r honor gi' a bit o' the rough to his Lordship," he cackled. "It's been a weary time since a real fighting duke put foot o' these old boards, beggin' y'r Honor's pardon."

"You listen at keyholes, eh?" But I grinned at him. "Wake me as soon as the clan's gathered. I wouldn't want to miss anything."

"Rely on me, y'r Grace," he said and went out and I pulled off my boots and lay in the dark and slid off into a dream about knights on horseback riding with leveled lances into the fire of massed machine guns.

I came back from somewhere a long way off with a hand shaking my shoulder and a thin old voice saying, "They're here, y'r Grace! Milord Lackland's wi' 'em i' the study this minute—and unless I mistake me, there's mischief afoot!"

"Does Lackland know you're here?"

"Not 'em, y'r Grace."

We went down the stairs and across the hall to a door that was standing ajar. When Wili got close he turned and gave me a quick jerk of the head, cupping his ear.

". . . imposter, gentlemen," Lackland was saying. "No true Briton, but a hireling of Garrone, bought with French gold and sent here to betray us all—"

I pushed the door open and walked in. The talk cut off as if a switch had been thrown. There were about a dozen men grouped around a long table with Lackland seated at the head. They were dressed in a variety of costumes, but all of them featured fur and brocades and a sword slung at the hip. The nearest was a big, wide-shouldered, neckless man with a curly black beard and ferocious eyes. He took a step back when he saw me, looked me up and down, surprised.

"Don't be beguiled by his face and stature!" Lackland spat the words. "He'd seize control of the rebellion, and turn coat, come to terms with Garrone! Can he deny it?" He was pointing at me with a finger that quivered with rage.

I didn't answer immediately. What he was saying was precisely what Roosevelt had proposed. There seemed to be a message for me in that somewhere, but it wouldn't come clear.

"You see?" Lackland crowed. "The treacher dares not deny it!"

The black-bearded man drew his sword with a skin-crawling rasp.

"A shrewd stroke!" he said in a high, rasping voice. "With a Plantagenet puppet to dance on his strings, he'd accomplish what the Louis have dreamed of for seven centuries! The total subjugation of Briton!" More swords were out now, ringing me in.

"Spit him, Tudor!" Lackland screeched.

"Stop!" Wilibald stood in the doorway with fire in his old eye. "Would you murder our Duke in cold blood? In the name of Free Briton, I say he deserves a better hearing at your Lordship's hands than this!"

For an instant, nobody moved—and in the silence I heard a droning sound, far away but coming closer. The others heard it, too. Eyes swiveled to stare at the ceiling as if they could see through it. A man rushed to the window, threw back the long drapes to stare out.

Another jumped for a wall switch. Tudor didn't move as the chandelier went dark, leaving just what light filtered in from the hall.

"An aircraft!" a man at the window called. "Coming straight in over us!"

"It was a trick to get us here together!" a lean man in yellow snarled, and drew back his sword for a cut. I saw this from the corner of my eye; it was Tudor I was watching. His jaw had set harder, and the tendons beside his neck tensed and I knew the thrust was coming.

I twisted sideways and leaned back and the point ripped through the ruffles on the front of my shirt; my back-handed swing caught him across the cheekbone, knocked him backward into the table as the room went pitch dark. The engines sounded as if they were right down the chimney. A piece of bric-a-brac fell from the mantle.

The *to-to! to-to!* marched across off to the right and the engine sound was deafening, and then receding. I heard glass tinkling, but the ceiling didn't fall in. I slid along the wall toward the door and heard feet break for it and a chair went over. Somebody slammed into me and I grabbed him and threw him ahead of me. I found the door and got through it, and could see the big hall faintly by the moonlight coming through the stained glass along the gallery. There was a lot of yelling that was drowned by the bomber's engines. Then a flash lit the room and the wall seemed to jump outward about a foot. When things stopped falling, I was bruised, but still alive. Wilibald was lying a few feet away, covered with dust and brick chips. There was a timber across his legs above the ankle; by the time I got it clear the plane was making its third run. With the old man over my shoulder, I reached the rear hall just as the front of the house blew in. I made it out through the kitchen door, went across grass that was littered with bricks. Blood from a cut on my scalp was running into my eyes. I made it to a line of trees before my legs folded.

The roof was gone from the house and flames were leaping up a hundred feet high and boiling into smoke clouds that glowed orange on their undersides. The shells of the walls that were still standing stood up in black silhouetted against the fire, and the windows were bright orange rectangles cut in the black.

Then there was a sound and I tried to get up and made it as far as my hands and knees, and three men with singed beards and torn finery and bare swords in their hands came out of the darkness to surround me.

One of the men was Tudor; he stepped in close and drew his arm back, and I was bracing myself for the thrust when all three of them turned and looked toward the house. Light flickered from among the trees lining the drive; pieces of bark jumped from the bole of the tree beside me and the man nearest it went over backward and the man beside him spun and fell, and Tudor turned to run, but it was the wrong reflex. I saw the bullets smack into him, throw him six feet onto his face.

There were men on the drive, coming up at a run—men in blue uniforms. I started to crawl and suddenly old Wilibald was there, his thin hair wild, soot on his face. He had been below the line of fire, like me; he was all right.

"Run, Wili!" I yelled. He hesitated for a moment, then turned and disappeared into the woods. Then the soldiers were all around me, grim and helmeted, smoking guns ready. And I waited for what came next.

Chapter Ten

This time, I got to ride up front. The countryside was pretty, but the towns were as deserted as Mexican villages at siesta time. You could feel in the air that a storm was about to break, and the populace had taken cover. If the rebels were as strong as Roosevelt said, it didn't show. The roads were full of military traffic in the blue paint of the French king. I wondered how much my short-lived escape had to do with that. I tried to pump the man beside me, but he didn't answer.

When we rolled into the outskirts of Londres, the town was carrying on some semblance of business as usual. The shops were open, and big canvas-topped buses rumbled along the streets, half full. We passed a big market square, lined with stalls with bright-colored awnings and displays of flowers and vegetables. At one side a raised platform was roped off. Half a dozen downcast-looking men and women in drab gray stood there, under a sign above the platform that said BULLMAN & WINDROW— CHATTELS. It was a slave market.

We swung into a cobbled courtyard ringed in by high walls. I was hustled inside, along a corridor full of the smell of government offices.

An officer in shirt-sleeves stepped out of a door ahead, swiveled hard when he saw me. He rattled off a question in strange-sounding French that sounded like "Where are you taking him?"

"*À la général, mon major.*"

"*No, c'est la province du demiregent. Laissez les cordes!*"

"*J'ai les ordeurs direct—*"

"A diable avec vos ordeurs! Fait que je dit, vite!"

The sergeant in charge of my detail put a hand on his holstered pistol. The major shouted to someone inside the room. Two sharp-looking lads in khaki with holstered side arms appeared behind him. That ended the argument. One of the new men cut the ropes off. Then they formed up a new procession and marched me off in a new direction.

We rode up in an elevator, went along a lushly carpeted hall, into a fancy outer office. A young fellow in a shiny blue uniform with aide's aglets ducked in through the inner door, came back and made an ushering motion to me. I walked through and was looking at Garonne, the French viceroy.

He was a pouch-eyed fellow in his late forties or early fifties, with thick gray hair, a large, rather soft-looking mouth with a quirk at one end registering benign intentions grown weary. He wore Ben Franklin glasses over a pair of sharp black eyes. His clothes were plain, his fingers lean and competent and without rings.

"I regret the discomfort you were forced to undergo, milord," he said, in straight New Norman without a trace of French accent. His voice was deep as a bullfrog's. "In view of the great importance of time just now, I asked that you be brought directly to me. A discussion between us might yet retrieve the unfortunate situation that now obtains."

"How does Baron General van Roosevelt feel about that?" I asked. It didn't mean anything. I was just probing.

"Some of my lieutenants are overzealous," he said cryptically. "It is a matter I must deal with. However, the business of the moment takes precedence. I am empowered, your Grace, by His Most Christian Majesty, to offer certain emoluments to loyal liegemen who support his efforts to calm the present unrest. Among them, greater internal autonomy for the island, with offices to deserving servants; various tax and import benefits, revised trade regulations, including issuance of import licenses to men of proven character. For yourself, a royal patent as Prince Imperial of the New Normandy

provinces, together with the grant of estates and
pensions appropriate to your station. And of course, full
recognition of your status as inheritor of the ancient
honors of your House."

"What do I do to earn all this?" I stalled.

"You will accept appointment, under his Majesty, as
emergency peace marshal of New Normandy. You will
appear on telescreen and wireless and instruct all loyal
New Normans to return to their homes, and exhort all
subjects of his Majesty to observe his laws regarding
assembly and bearing of arms. In short, only those acts
which I feel certain your own good judgment would
dictate, once freed from the pressures placed on you by
incendiary elements: the exercise of your influence
toward the achievement of civil stability and order."

"In other words, just sell out the Britons."

Garrone narrowed his eyes at me. He leaned across
the desk. "Don't waste my time. I'm sure you'll find my
offer preferable to a miserable death in the
interrogation section."

"You wouldn't murder me, Monsieur Garonne," I
said, trying to sound as if I believed it. "I'm the people's
hero, remember?"

"We can drop all that nonsense between us," Garonne
said in a flat tone. "I'm aware of your masquerade.
There was no Lady Edwinna, no secret hideaway in
Scotland, no long-lost heir of the bastard honors of
Plantagenet! Who are you? Where do you come from?
Who sent you here?"

"Whoever I am," I said, "you need me all in one
piece."

"Nonsense. Modern methods of persuasion don't rely
on thumbscrews. In the end you'll babble whatever I
choose for you to babble. But if you'll act as I
command—now—lives will be saved. His Majesty's offer
still stands. Now, again: Who are you? Who sent you?"

"If I'm a fake, what makes you think what I say will
help you?"

"Rumors of your presence are abroad here—a Plantagenet of the Old Mark, as Duke Richard was, but
without his shabby record of failure and compromise. If

word spreads that you've been killed, the countryside will rise—and I'll have no choice but to crush the revolt."

"That might not be easy. The guerrillas—"

"There are no guerrillas, no irregulars, no rebel organization. These are fictions, fabricated by myself." He nodded. "Yes, myself. Consider the facts: New Normandy has been the scene of increasing unrest for decades now, most particularly since the Continental War of 1917-1919, with its Prussian dirigible raids, and the less than glorious peace that ended it. The old cries of Saxon unity were revived—idiotic nonsense, of course, based on imaginary blood-ties. I needed a force which would bring the provinces back under tight control. Duke Richard was the perfect foil. By his loose living, he had discredited himself with the islanders, of course—but a rousing call to ancient loyalties served to unite popular sentiment behind him. Then—with all New Normandy pledged to follow him—the final stroke would have been the 'compromise,' granting the hollow honors he craved— and placating the revolutionary spirit with fancied autonomy. His murder destroyed a scheme ten years in the building."

"You murdered him yourself."

"No. It was not I who killed him! He was a valuable tool—and unless you—whoever you are, whatever your original intentions—can be brought to see the wisdom of cooperation—I foresee tragedy!

"You have proof of this?"

"I have Duke Richard's seal on the secret agreement between us. I have the records of payments to him, of subsidies to him and to various *agents provocateurs* working ostensibly for his underground organization. Of course, they might be counterfeit—how can I demonstrate otherwise? My best evidence is the inherent logic of my version of affairs, as opposed to the romantic nonsense you've been deluded into accepting! Face facts, man! You have the opportunity laid at your feet to spring from obscurity to princely rank overnight. Your best—your *only* interest lies in cooperation!"

"I don't believe you. The rebels can win."

"Nonsense!" He pointed to a wall map, showing blue

arrows aimed across the channel from Dunkirk to Brest.

"His Majesty's forces are overwhelmingly powerful. The only result of war would be a murderous guerrilla delaying action, profitable to no one."

"Why not give the Britons their independence and save all that?"

Garonne was wagging his head in a weary negative. "Milord, what you propose is, has always been, an economic and political fantasy. These islands, by their very nature, are incapable of pursuing an independent existence. Their size alone would preclude any role other than that of starveling dependent, incapable of self-support, at the mercy of any power which might choose to attempt annexation. A Free Briton, as the fanatics call it, is a pipe dream. No, milord: France will never give up her legitimate interests here. In conscience, she cannot. To discuss such fantasies is a waste of valuable time. You've heard His Majesty's most gracious offer. As we sit here, time is passing—time that takes us closer to the brink of tragedy with each instant. Accept His Majesty's generosity, and in an hour you'll be installed in your own apartments in the town, secure in your position as chief local magistrate of New Normandy, with all the honors and privileges appertaining thereunto; refuse your duty to your soverign, and your end will be a miserable one! The choice is yours, milord!"

He was staring across the desk at me, waiting. The ormolu clock on the marble mantel behind him ticked loudly in the silence. Things were coming at me too fast; there was something I was missing, or forgetting. I needed time to think.

The door opened; a small, dried-up footman with a little white peruke and ribbons on his knees came into the room. He doddered across to the table beside the big desk, put a tray down on it. There was a squat brown bottle, a pair of long-stemmed glasses, a big white napkin folded into a peak. The old fellow lifted the napkin, and scooped a small, flat automatic pistol from under it. He turned and fired three shots into Garonne's chest from a distance of six feet.

I saw the stiff black brocade of the viceroy's coat jump as the bullets hit, saw splinters of pinkish mahogany fly from the chair back, heard the dull smack of the slugs as they lodged in the plaster. The pistol had made a soft unimportant sound as it fired: a silencer, or maybe compressed gas. Garonne jerked and threw his arms up and flopped forward with his face on the fancy leather-bound blotter. The old man pulled off the peruke and I saw it was Wilibald. He shrugged out of the long-skirted coat, all gold and blue with little pink flowers. He was wearing plain gray under it, not too clean. He grinned a toothless grin and said, "We'd best be off direct, m'lord?" He tucked the gun away and went past me, around the end of the desk where a brilliant scarlet stain was growing, and pulled back the drapes gathered at the end of the big window. There was a dark opening in the paneled wall behind them. His flashlight beam showed me rough brickwork and time-blackened timber, a narrow passage leading off into darkness.

"This way, y'r Grace. No time to waste!" There was a sharp note in his voice; an impatient note. I hadn't moved since the shots were fired.

"What's your hurry, Wili?" I said. "No one's going to burst in on the viceroy, in conference—except maybe a trusted servant with his ten o'clock tea."

"How's that? Beggin' y'r Grace' pardon—but that's a dead man lying there! The penalty for murder is hanging! If y'r caught here—"

I went to him and instead of going past him into the passage I caught his wrist.

"What if we're both caught here, Wili? Would that spoil the scheme?"

"We'd hang!" He tried to jerk free, but I held him.

"They all know I was with him. When he's found dead, it will be an open-and-shut case, eh, Wili?"

"What matter if it is? Ye'll be far away by then—"

"Who are you working for, Wili? Roosevelt? He *let* me escape last time, didn't he? Why? So I could stir up the populace? Why did he bomb Lackland's house? But it was a fake raid, wasn't it? Just a flock of near misses—with the machine guns to clean up the witnesses, including Lackland."

"It was Lackland called the attack down on the house!" Wili croaked. "He was a creeping spy and tell-tale for the Louis, hoping to see y'r Grace killed—but he paid for his crimes! Aye, he paid—"

"Don't kid me—he was working for Roosevelt. I guess he'd outlived his usefulness."

"Shameful times we've fell on," Wili babbled on. "But what was he but a Black Plantagenet, eh? But now it's needful we make our escape. I've a car waiting—"

"Very convenient, you and your cars. It hardly fits in what I've seen of the Organization here. I suppose we'll breeze right through the police lines, just like we did last time, thanks to Roosevelt."

"The Organization—"

"Is a lot of hot air, Wili. Roosevelt sent you here to kill Garonne, and arranged for it to look as though I'd done the job—just as he killed Duke Richard and spread the word Garonne was guilty. Why? The situation was already balanced on a knife-edge. Why did he tell me the rebels had the winning hand? That was another lie. They're evenly matched at best. But he wants them to make their try, wants to see the country cut to pieces in a civil war that won't end until both factions are ruined. Why, again?"

"Y'r daft!" Wili yelped. "Let go, you fool! They'll be here at any instant—"

"Who tipped them this time, you? Better start talking, Wili—and it had better be good—"

I was watching his free hand; it dipped to his pocket and I grabbed it as it came out with the automatic. He was strong, but I was lots stronger.

"I'm going to spoil the play, Wili," I told him. "I'm a little slow, but after awhile even I catch on. Your boss has been dancing me on the strings from the beginning, hasn't he? Every move has been planned: getting me here on my own initiative, the dramatic escape complete with voices coming out of the walls, then letting Garonne's men have me. What's planned for me next? Maybe I'm supposed to get on a horse and lead the peasants into battle, is that it? But I'm breaking the chain, Wili. The moves are too subtle for me, but that doesn't matter. A fancy knot cuts as easy as a simple one—"

His knee came up, almost fast enough. As I took it on the thigh, he put everything he had into twisting the gun around. It wasn't enough. The muzzle was pointing to his own chest when it coughed. He went slack, fell backward into the room. He tried, tried hard to speak, but I couldn't make out the words. Then his eyes went dull and blank. I dragged the body into the passage, felt over the wall until I found the lever that closed the panel behind me.

"Good-bye, Wili," I said. "You were loyal to something, even if it was the wrong thing." I left him there and started off in what I hoped was the right direction.

It was different, picking my way in the dark through the network of hidden passages that I had traced out once before in the shuttle, on half-phase. I made a wrong turning, bumped my head and barked my shins, retraced my steps and tried again. It took me hours—I don't know how many—to find the passage I was looking for: the one that led to Roosevelt's quarters.

I found the lever and eased the panel back and was looking down from over the fireplace into the quiet luxury of the spacious study. It was empty. Roosevelt would be fully occupied elsewhere for a while, working out an explanation of the locked-door murder of the viceroy.

It was a difficult room to search. Every door and drawer was locked, and there were a lot of them. I levered them open one by one, looked at books and papers and boxed records, and drew a blank.

The next room was the Baron's sleeping chamber. I started in the closet, worked my way through two large bureaus and a wardrobe, and in the last drawer, found a flat, paper-wrapped bundle. It was my broken sword. I wondered what it meant to Roosevelt that had made him squirrel it away here, but that was a problem I could solve later—maybe. I buckled it on, and the weight of it felt good at my hip. It wasn't much of a weapon, but it was better than nothing, if they walked in and found me here.

Ten minutes later, in a cubicle almost hidden in a shadowy corner, I found what I was looking for: the silver-mounted reliquary box that Roosevelt had destroyed a world to get.

There was a silver lock on the silver hasp that closed the lid. I hated to destroy such a handsome piece of workmanship, but I put the edge of the sword under it and levered and it shattered. The lid came up; inside, in a bed of yellowed satin, lay a rusted slab of steel, a foot long, three inches wide, beveled on both edges. It was another piece of the broken sword.

I picked it up, felt the same premonitory tingle in my hand that I'd felt that other time, in the underground room beneath the old chateau. Like that time, I brought the scrap of metal to the broken blade, saw the long, blue spark jump between them as they came together—

The world exploded in my face.

I sat astride a great war-horse, in the early morning. I felt the weight of the chain armor on my back, the drag of the new-forged sword at my side. Beside me, Trumpington turned in his saddle to look across at me. He spoke, but I gave him no answer. A strange vision was on me. Though I was here, a part of me was elsewhere, observing. . . .

My vision widened, and I seemed to see myself riding away from the field of Chaluz, my mind unbloodied. More ghostly images flocked in my mind. I saw the lean face of John my brother, hungry-eyed, silky-bearded, as he knelt before me, pleading for his life. And the sudden look of fear, as I, who had always before been merciful of his treacheries, hardened my heart.

I heard the thunk of the headsman's ax . . .

Then it seemed I sat in my pavilion on the island of Runnymede, summoned there by my rebellious barons. They stood before me in their arrogance, and presented to me, their sovereign lord, the perfidious writing of their demands. And again, I saw their looks a triumph change to the knowledge of death as my hidden bowmen stepped forth and loosed their clothyard shafts into the false hearts of my forsworn vassals . . .

Scenes of warfare passed before my eyes. I saw the

*walls of Paris go down before me, saw the fires that
blazed up from the cathedrals of Madrid, saw the head of
him who once had been a king, impaled on a pike and
borne before me. Faces crowded around me, fair women
and ambitious men, praising me. There was revelry, and
riding behind the baying hounds, and roasted venison
before the roaring blaze; and tuns of wine broached, and
the passing of days, years of gluttony and lechery and
sloth, until the time when my hand no longer sought the
sword. Swollen with excess, rotten with disease, I
cowered in my palace while my picked retainers parleyed
with the invaders at my gates. Parleyed, and sold their
kingdom and its king for their own vile lives. But no viler
than mine, when I knelt, weeping, at the feet of the
stripling whose father I had hanged to his own gates, and
swore to him on my sword the eternal servility of all my
house . . .*

I swam back from across a gulf wider than the
Universe and was standing in the room I remembered
from an eon—or a second—before. The sword burned
hot in my hand—no longer an awkward stub, but a blade
four feet long, ending in a blunt, broken tip. The cross-
guard was different: longer, the quillons curving out
above carved knuckle-bows. There were traces of gold
on the grip, and a single jewel glinted in the pommel.
It was the same magic I'd seen before, all the talk in the
world about probability stresses and the reshaping of
reality couldn't make it anything else for me. I groped
after the dream that had filled my head a moment
before: a panorama of faces and sounds and vain
regrets; but it faded, as dreams do, and was gone. Then
my reverie was shattered into small pieces as the door
to the next room slammed open and feet came across the
rug toward the bedroom.

"Milord Baron," a familiar voice called. "An
emergency in the Net! The stasis has been broken! The
probability storm will strike within hours!"

His rush had carried him past me where I had
flattened myself to the wall beside the door. He halted
when he saw the room was empty, spun, saw me, yelled.

"Thanks for the information, Renata," I said, and laid

the flat of the sword against the side of his head with all
the power in my arm. I didn't wait to see if I had broken
his skull. I went across the study and was back inside
my private tunnel before the first of his men had gotten
up his nerve to enter without knocking.

An hour or two of exploring the tunnel system turned
up plenty of side-branches, some secret rooms with
tables and rotted bedding, a cramped stairway leading
down to ground level; but there seemed to be no direct
way into the other wing of the palace and the exit behind
the rhododendrons. I thought about coming out and
trying it in the open, but there were too many sounds of
activity beyond the walls to make that seem really
attractive. The whole building seemed to be in a state of
uproar. That wasn't too hard to understand. With a dead
viceroy to handle, and a probability storm coming on, it
looked like a busy day.

My break came when I found a shaft with a rusty
ladder bolted inside it.

The rungs were too close together, and scaled with
rust, and the bore was barely big enough to give me
operating space. It seemed to get smaller as I went
down. It ended on a damp floor that I recognized as
running behind the rank of cells where I'd once been a
guest. I started along the two-foot-wide passage, in near
pitch-dark. What light there was came from chinks in
the mortar between the stones. If night fell while I was
still here, the going would be rough.

I followed the passage fifty feet to a dead end. I turned
back, and after thirty feet, encountered an intersection
that I would have sworn hadn't been there two minutes
before. The right-hand branch led to an uncovered pit
that I discovered by almost falling in it. The other
spiraled down, debouched into a circular room lined
with dark openings. I turned my back, and when I
looked again, everything had changed. This time I was
sure; where the passage I had entered by had been there
was a solid wall of stone. I knew now what Roosevelt
meant by a probability storm. Subjective reality had
turned as insubstantial as a dream.

The next passage I tried ended in a blank wall of wet

clay. When I came back into the circular room it was square, and there were only two exits now. One led to a massive iron-bound door, locked and barred. I retraced my steps, but instead of a room I came into a cave with water trickling across its floor and a single dark opening on the far side. I went into it, and it widened and was a carpeted hall, faced with white doors, all locked. When I looked back, there was only a gray tunnel, cut through solid rock.

For a long time, I wandered through dark passages that closed behind me, looking for a way up. And then, in a tunnel so low that I had to duck my head, I heard the clank of chains, not far away.

I listened hard, heard heavy breathing, the rasp of feet on stone, another clank. It wasn't what would ordinarily be considered an inviting sound, but under the circumstances I was willing to take the risk. I pushed ahead ten feet and saw dim light coming through a crack in the wall. It was a loose stone slab, three feet on a side. I put my eye to the crack and looked into a cell with windowless walls, a candle on a table, a straw pallet. An old man stood in the center of the room. He was as tall as I was, wide through the shoulders, with big, gnarled hands, a weather-beaten complexion, pale blue eyes with a hunted look. He was dressed in tattered blue satin knee-pants, a wine and rose brocaded coat with wide fur lapels, a flowered vest, scuffed and worn shoes that had once been red. The chains were on his ankles. He looked around, scanning the walls as if he knew I was there.

"Geoffrey," he said, in a hoarse, old voice that I'd heard before, in a dream, "I feel you near me."

I got a grip on the stone and slid it aside and was looking through a barred opening. The old man turned slowly. His mouth opened and closed.

"Geoffrey," he said. "My boy . . ." He put out a hand, then drew it back. "But my boy is dead," he told himself. "Forever dead." A tear ran down the leathery cheek. "Who are you, then? His cousin, Henry? Or Edward? Name yourself, then!"

"Curlon is my name. I'm lost. Is there a way out of here?"

He ignored the question. "Who sent you here? The black-hearted rogues who slew Geoffrey?" He caught at the bars, and the sleeve of his coat fell back. There was a welted, two-inch-wide scar all the way around his wrist.

"No one sent me," I said. "I managed it on my own."

He stared at me and nodded. "Aye—you're of the blood—I see it in your face. Are you, too, caught in his traps?"

"It looks that way," I said. "Who are you? Why are you here?"

"Henry Planget is my name. I claim no other honor. But I'll not fall in with his schemes, though all the devils in hell come to haunt me!" He shook his fist at the wall. "Do your damnedest, rascals! But spare the boy!"

"Snap out of it, old man!" I said roughly. "I need your help! Is there a way out of here?"

He didn't answer. I drew the broken sword and levered at the bars. They were solid, an inch thick, set in barred sockets.

"My help?" His rheumy eyes held on mine. "A Planget never calls for help—and yet . . . and yet, perhaps it would have been better if we had, so long ago . . ."

"Listen, to me, Henry. There's a man called Roosevelt—Baron General Pieter van Roosevelt. He's crazy enough to think he can remake the Universe according to a private set of specifications and I'm crazy enough to believe him. I'd like to stop him, if I can. But first, I have to break out of this maze. If you know the way—tell me!"

"The maze?" The old man looked at me vaguely; then as if he were shaking off a weight, he straightened his back; his eyes cleared and vitality came into them.

"The maze of life," he said. "The maze of fate. Yes, we must break out!" He stopped, staring at the broken sword. His hand went out to it, but stopped, not touching it.

"You bear Balingore?" his voice quavered. His eyes met mine, and now fire flashed in them. "A miracle passes before my eyes! For these same eyes saw Balingore broken and cast into the sea! And now . . . he lives again!"

"I'm afraid it's just a broken sword," I said, but he wasn't listening.

"Balingore lives again!" he quavered. "His strength runs in you, lad! I sense it! And still the powers draw at you across the veils of the worlds! I've seen them—yes, he showed me, long ago, when he plied me with fine words and talk of glories vanished. There are more worlds than one, and they call to me—and to you, too! Can you feel them, the voices that cry out of darkness, summoning you? Go! Go to them! Break the ring of fate that forever doomed our house!"

"How do I do that, Henry?"

He clung to the bars and I could see the fight he was having to hold to the glimmer of sanity that had come to him—if that was what it was.

"I must speak quickly, before the veils descend again," he said. His voice was steadier now. "This is the tale that he told me:

"Long ago, a king of our line bore Balingore into battle, and with him built a mighty empire across the world. But in the end, he turned aside from honor. Balingore passed to the hands of another, and for seven centuries, served the cause of evil. But at last the usurper's greed undid him. His wise men built a strange machine in which a man might leave his proper frame of fate and walk in worlds of might-have-been. He sought to use this wonder as a weapon, to spread his black dream of empire—but he failed. And in his failure, he brought down the very skies about him!"

"The machine was called a shuttle," I said. "It used the MC-drive to move across the alternate world-lines. I've heard that the Blight was caused by the drive running out of control."

"Nay—it was no accidental havoc! Van Roosevelt knew what he did when he unleashed its power on the world! And now his spawn seeks again to mold the cosmos to his liking! But this is a task too great for him alone! He needs the might of Angevin beside him. This much he told me when he snatched me from my manor house in the far world of my birth. But I defied him! As you must!"

"Who is he, Henry? What is he?"

"A fallen angel; a man so evil that the world cannot contain his malice! Even now it melts and flows—as I have seen it melt and flow before! Run, lad! Flee this pit of horrors before you find yourself forever lost . . . as I was lost, so long ago . . ."

"You were telling me about the sword," I reminded him.

"Many things have I learned, strange beyond belief," Henry mumbled. "And yet you must believe them!" The fire came back into his tone. "There are many worlds, many lines of fate that grow across the walls of time like so many vines of ivy! Once there were many Balingores, each holding some fraction of the power that was once welded into one. But in the disaster that overtook the world, all were lost, save two: One, in the hands of the devil, Roosevelt. And another, which hung on the high wall of my house, in a far land I shall never see again!" Knuckles whitened as he gripped the bars. "Once, this was my house, these chambers my cellars. Then *he* came. His talk beguiled me, in my ignorance. At his behest, I took down the ancient blade of my ancestors, and would have put it in his hand. But at his touch, it shattered.

"He raged, blamed me for the miracle. But I took new pride from the sign given me. I defied him, then! Too late, I defied him! He brought me here, told me his tale—and his lies. He swore I was the key to his greatness, that together we would rebuild his world—that other world, so like mine, and yet so different. I would not listen. I saw the sword he bore—the other Balingore, so long ago dishonored—but I sensed that the true power flowed not in it. He needed me, in truth—but what he did not know was that I had saved one fragment of the true sword. I hid it away from him, and when he scattered the shards in the salt sea, there to corrode to nothing, one piece was left behind . . ."

"There were more than two Balingores," I said. "I have part of one. And I found another part, in a ruined city in the Blight—"

"Listen to me!" Henry's voice shook. "I feel the red darkness returning! Time is short! Go to my world,

Curlon! Find my house of the high stone walls and the red towers; and there, in the chapel dedicated to St. Richard, search beneath the altar-stone. But beware the False Balingore! Now go—before the world melts away into a tortured dream!"

"I'll try, Henry," I said. "But I can't leave you here. I'll try to find something—some way to release you." I went back along the passage, feeling the walls, with the vague idea I might find a ring of keys hanging there; but there was nothing.

When I came back to the barred window, the candle still burned on the table; but the room was empty. Only the rusted shackles lay on the floor among scattered bones.

For a long time, I stood in the dark, watching the candle burn down and gutter out. Then I went on. I don't know how many hours later it was that I came into a room where light filtered down from a heavy oak door, half-smashed from its hinges. I went up stone steps into late afternoon light in a kitchen that looked as though it had been fought through. There was shooting going on outside, not far away.

The door opened into a bricked alley under high walls. A dead man in a blue uniform lay on his back a few feet from it. I picked up his gun and moved up to cross the street without any unnecessary noise. In the distance, big guns rumbled and boomed, and flashes showed against the colors of early dusk. I knew where I was now. I had covered several city blocks, underground. The viceregal palace was in the next square, a hundred yards away.

A sudden burst of gunfire nearby made me flatten myself against the wall. I heard running feet, and three blue-uniformed Imperial guards dashed out of a doorway, heading across the street. There was more gunfire, from up high, and one of them fell. A shell shrieked, and a section of street blew up and blanketed the scene with dust. When it cleared, a dead civilian with a bandolier across his shoulders lay near the dead soldier. The revolution was in full swing, but somehow I had a feeling that in spite of that, things hadn't turned out the way Roosevelt had wanted them. The thought warmed me, and turned my mind to what I had to do next.

I left my cubbyhole, made it across the street, and into a narrow street that led to the delivery yard at the back of the palace. I went along it with the machine pistol ready; I didn't want to be gunned down, by either side. Near the gate, I heard feet coming up behind me. I threw the gun away and went over the wall and was in the vice-regal gardens, fifty feet from the spot where I had left the shuttle on half-phase.

The shadowy trees and bushes looked different some-how; wild flowers of a kind I'd never seen before sprouted in the tended beds. Somewhere a nightingale was singing his heart out, ignoring the gunfire.

I was still wearing the ring Bayard had given me, the one with the miniaturized shuttle recall signaler set inside the synthetic ruby. I had left the shuttle in another world-line, with Imperial suppressor beams holding it pinned down like a butterfly on a board, but this wasn't the time to pause and consider things like that. If the signaler worked, I was on the board for another round; if not, the game was finished now. I pressed the stone.

The bird sang. A breeze stirred the long grass. At the far side of the garden, a man stepped into view, capless, dressed in sweat-stained blues. He stopped when he saw me, shouted, and started for me at a run. He was halfway there when the shuttle shimmered and phased into solidity with a rush of displaced air. I stepped inside and flipped the half-phase switch. On the screens, the twilit garden faded to eerie blue. The man who had been running skidded to a stop, raised his gun and fired a full clip into the spot the shuttle occupied. The gun made a remote, flat sound. Then the man threw the gun down and laughed a wild laugh. He turned and wandered away. I could sympathize with him. I knew how he felt. The world had come apart around his ears, and there was no place to turn.

The telltale light on the panel was blinking on, off, on. It was the tracer that had been locked to Roosevelt's shuttle. It still was—and the target was moving.

Again, I didn't stop to calculate the odds. I threw in the drive lever and set off in pursuit.

I had seen it before, but it was a thing that could never lose its fascination. All around me, as the hours passed, the world changed and flowed. I knew now that what I was seeing was a simultaneous sequences of A-lines, each differing only slightly from the next, like the frames of a movie film. Nothing really moved; no normal time elapsed during a transdimensional crossing. But the eerie pseudo-activity of E-entropy went on; plants jostled each other for favorable positions; vines attacked trees; weeds swelled and crowded out other weeds. The ivy-covered walls of the palace shrank, broadened, became a fortress ringed with a moat. The walks shifted position, slid away, became footpaths. The trees moved back, gliding slowly through the turf that parted like water, until the shuttle was perched in an open field edged by an ancient forest. The fort had become a stone manor house, with mansard roofs and chimneys poking up into the unchanging sky; the chimneys drew together and merged, became towers of brick with castellated tops.

Suddenly, the hum of the drive whined down-scale and ceased. The scene stabilized. I was looking across a tilled field of grain toward the lone house occupying the top of a low rise among tall trees.

A high stone house with brick towers. Bricks would be red in normal light. Out of all the possible destinations in all the Universes, Roosevelt had led me to the house of Henry Planget.

I waited until full dark before I switched the shuttle back to full-phase and stepped out, then shifted it back. The soft *boom*! of imploding air had a lonely sound of finality.

For the past hour, a steady stream of men had come and gone around the big house. Couriers had galloped up on horseback, and others had ridden away down the unpaved road with full saddlebags slapping at their mounts' flanks. Lights burned in all the ground-floor windows. Sentries paced in front of the main door.

Everything about the place spelled military headquarters. Somewhere inside, Roosevelt would be
cooking up the last ingredients of his grand scheme for
the world.

I skirted the house, came up in the shelter of a row of
poplars until I could see through the nearest set of
casement windows. A group of men in ornate green
uniforms clustered around a table on which a map was
spread, under a gas-burning chandelier. Roosevelt
wasn't among them. It was the same in the next room,
except that the men wore plain khaki and were working
over what might have been manning documents or
supply lists. I worked my way halfway around the
house, using the hedges for concealment, before I found
my man. He was sitting alone at a table, writing rapidly
with a ball-point pen—a curious anomaly in the old-
fashioned setting. He was smiling a little as he wrote.
There was a small cut on his forehead. He was still
wearing the fancy outfit he had donned for the
ceremony back in New Normandy, now stained and
powder-burned. It seemed the general had seen some
close action before he had left the scene of battle.

He finished writing and left the room. I closed in and
checked the windows. It was a mild evening, and they
stood open half an inch. Ten seconds later, I was inside.

I listened at the door, heard nothing, opened it, and
took a look along the papered hallway glowing softly in
the light of a single gas jet. A sentry stood at the far end,
all shiny leather and brass, with a musket over his
shoulder. I tried to pretend I was a shadow moving
along the hall, sliding into the recess of a stairwell. He
never turned his head.

There was red carpeting on the stairs, a polished
mahogany rail. On the landing, I gave a listen, then went
on up into a dark corridor, door-lined. I was standing
there, waiting for instinct to whisper instructions in my
ear, when I felt a touch at the hip. I came around fast,
and my hand went to the sword-hilt before I understood.
The touch had been the sword, tugging gently at my side.
I drew it, following the direction of the pull.

At the end of the corridor, three steps led up to double

doors of carved oak. I pushed through them, stood in moonlight shining through a rose window. It wasn't a room that I had ever seen before—and yet it was. I knew, without knowing how I knew, that it was the analog of the chapel from which Roosevelt had stolen the reliquary box. This room was smaller, simpler, almost unadorned. But somehow, in the abstruse geography of the Net of alternate reality, it occupied the same position. The altar under the high window consisted of two heavy oak uprights with a flat slab of rough stone across them, but somehow, it was the same altar. In the dim light, it looked like an ancient sacrificial block. I started forward and the door made a soft sound behind me. I turned, and Roosevelt stood there. His black eyes seemed to blaze across the darkness at me, as armed men spread out behind him.

"You see, Plantagenet?" he said softly. "Struggle as you will, your fate must deliver you into my hands!"

"I misjudged you when we met," Roosevelt said. "And again, in New Normandy. You should have seized on the chance to escape, filled with the zeal to set a nation free. The countryside would have risen at your call; you'd have ridden into glory with your followers at your back and the bright sun overhead. Why didn't you?"

"You're a clever man, Roosevelt," I said. "But not clever enough to play God. Men aren't cardboard cutouts for you to arrange to suit yourself."

"Men are tools," Roosevelt said flatly. "As for you—you're a tool that turns in the hand, and your edges are surpassingly sharp." He shook his head. "You're supposed to be a man of emotion and action, Plantagenet, not thought!"

"Stop second-guessing me, Roosevelt. Your scheme's blown up in your face. You've failed—the way your father failed with Henry Planget." It was a shot in the dark, just something to say. For a moment, he looked startled. Then his teeth flashed in a smile.

"It was my grandfather," he said. "I wonder how you learned of that? But it doesn't matter now, does it? You've come here, to the one place you had to come to—and found me waiting and ready."

"Not so ready. I could have shot you while you were

writing at your desk."

"I fail to see the weapon." He was still smiling an almost gentle smile. "No, Plantagenet, it's not your destiny to shoot me in the back. We'll have our meeting face to face—and the fateful time is now." He drew the heavy longsword slung at his side. The light winked on the jewels that crusted the pommel and grip and *pas-d'âne*. The men behind him stood silent, drawn guns in their hands.

"You like to talk about fate, Roosevelt," I said. "It's a lot of hot air. A man determines his own fate." I was watching the long blade, ready to ward off a blow with the broken weapon in my hand. Roosevelt looked at it and laughed, a low chuckle.

"Like your blade, Plantagenet, you're incomplete! You know a little—though even that little surprises me—but not enough. Don't you recognize the weapon you face?"

"It's a fancy piece of iron," I said. "But a weapon is as good as the man behind it."

"Look on Balingore!" Roosevelt held the sword out so that the blade caught the light. It was a slab of edged and polished steel, six feet long, as wide as my hand, and Roosevelt's brawny arm held it as though it were a stick of wood. "It was forged for your once-great ancestor, Richard of the lion-heart. It served him well—but he was a greedy man. He went too far, grew fat on gold and wine. Richard Bombast, they called him in the end. He lay drunk in his chamber while the French attacked the walls of London and his people opened the gates to them. He bought his life with this. He handed it, hilt-first, to the Dutch mercenary who led the forces of Louis Augustus, and swore the submission of himself and his house, to the end of time!"

"Fairy tales," I said.

"But a fairy tale you believe in." Roosevelt tilted the sword, made light wink in my eyes. "I know why you're here, Plantagenet."

"Do you?"

He nodded somberly. "Somehow—and later you'll tell me how—you learned that Balingore was the key object through which the lines of power run. You imagined you could steal it, and win back all that you lost, so long ago." He shook his head. "But the weapon is mine, now! Its touch would shrivel your hand. All the probability energies built up in seven hundred years of history flow through this steel, and every erg of that titanic charge denies your claim. I offer you your last chance for life and its riches. Plantagenet! Submit to me now, and you'll stand first below the throne in the new order. Refuse, and you'll die in an agony beyond your comprehension!"

"Dead is dead," I said. "The method doesn't matter much. Why don't you go ahead, do it now? You've got the weapon in your hand."

"I should have killed you," he said between his teeth. "I should have killed you long ago!"

"You kept me alive for a reason," I said raggedly. "But it wasn't your reason, Roosevelt. All along, you've thought you were in charge, but you weren't. Maybe fate isn't as easy to twist as you thought it was—"

One of the men behind Roosevelt gave a muffled yell; a rat as big as a tomcat scuttled out between his feet. Roosevelt cut at it with the sword—and I whirled and sprinted for the altar.

I expected gunfire to racket, a bullet in the spine, a wash of agony from a nerve-gun; but Roosevelt shouted an order to his men to hold their fire. I jumped up on the low platform, gripped the altar-stone, and heaved at it. I might as well have tried to lift the columns of the Parthenon. Roosevelt was coming toward me at a run. I jammed the broken sword in under the rock, felt it clash on metal—

The Universe turned to white fire that fountained round me, then dwindled away to misty gray . . .

"My lord, will you attack?" Trumpington's voice came from beside. I looked up at the sun, burning through the mist. I thought of England's green fields, and the sunny vineyards of Aquitaine, of the empire I might yet win. I looked across toward the place where the enemy waited, where I knew death waited with a message for me.

"I will attack," I said.

"My lord," Trumpington's voice was troubled. "Is all

well with you?"

"As well as can be with mortal man," I said, and spurred forward toward the high gray walls of Chaluz.

The chapel of St. Richard swam back into solidity. Roosevelt was running toward me; behind him, his men were spreading out; one brought his gun up and there was a vivid flash and I felt a smashing blow in my shoulder that spun me back and down. . . .

Roosevelt was standing over me, the bared sword in his hand.

"You can't die yet, Plantagenet," he said in a voice that seemed to ring and echo like a trumpet. "Get on your feet!"

I found my hands and knees, dragged them under me. My body was one pulsating agony . . . like the other time, when Renata had shot me with the nerve-gun. Remembering Renata helped. I stood.

"You're a strong man and a proud one," Roosevelt said; his voice swelled and faded. My hand burned and tingled. I remembered the sword, blinked the haze away, saw it still projecting from under the altar-stone where I had jammed it just before somebody shot me. I wished I could get my hands on it.

"You've run a long way, Plantagenet," Roosevelt was saying. "I think you knew how it would end, but still you fought. I admire you for that—and soon I'll let you rest. But first—make your submission to me!"

"You're still afraid . . ." I got the words out. "You can't swing it . . . on your own."

"Listen to me," Roosevelt said. "The storm is all around us; it will reach us here, soon. You've seen it, seen what the Blight is! Unless we resolve the probability flaw now, it will engulf this world-line along with all the rest! You're holding the fault-line open with your stubbornness! In the name of the future of humanity, give up your false pride!"

"There's another solution," I said. "You can submit to me."

"Not though the pit should open to swallow me alive," Roosevelt said, and brought the sword up, poised—

I used the last ounce of strength in my legs to lunge

for his wrist, caught it, held him. I reached past him, toward the scarred hilt of my weapon. His hand closed on my wrist. We stood there, locked together, his black eyes inches from mine.

"Stand back!" Roosevelt shouted as his men came close. "I'll break him with my own hands!"

My fingers were six inches from the hilt of the sword. I could feel a current, not a physical pull, but a force as intangible as hate or love flowing from my hand to it.

"Strive, Plantagenet," Roosevelt hissed in my ear, and threw his weight against me. My hand was forced back, away from the sword . . .

"Balingore!" I shouted.

The sword moved, leaped across the intervening space to my hand.

There was a sensation as though fire poured through my arm, not burning, but scouring away the fatigue. I threw Roosevelt back, and swung six feet of scarred and rusted steel in my two hands. He backed away, his eyes fixed on the old sword, nicked and blunted, but complete now. An expression passed across his face like a man who's looked into the furnace doors of Hell. Then his eyes met mine.

"Again, I underestimated you," he said. "Now I begin to understand who you really are, Plantagenet, *what* you are. But it's far too late to turn back. We meet as we were doomed to meet, face to face, your destiny against mine!" He lunged, and the False Balingore leaped toward me, and the True Balingore flashed out to meet it. The two blades came together with a ring like a struck anvil and the sound filled the world . . .

. . . *I saw the shaft leap toward me out of the dust, felt the hammer blow in my shoulder that almost struck me from the saddle.*

"Sire—you're hit!" Trumpington shouted, and reined closer to me in the press of battle. For an instant weakness swept over me, but I kept my seat, spurred forward.

"My lord—you must retire and let me tend your wounds!" Trumpington's voice followed me; but I did

*not heed him. He galloped abreast, seeking to interpose
himself between me and the enemy.*

"Sire—turn back!" he shouted. "Even a king can die!"

*For a moment we faced each other among the plunging
mounts and struggling men.*

*"More than other men, a king knows how to die," I
said. "And when, as well." Then the charge of the enemy
host separated us, and I saw him no more. . . .*

I saw the change come into Roosevelt's eyes, locked on
mine as we strained together, chest to chest. He
staggered back, staring unbelievingly at his empty
hands. Under my eyes, his face withered, his cheeks
collapsed, his silks and brocades turned to gray rags
that dropped away to expose gaunt ribs, the yellow skin
of age. He fell, and his toothless mouth mumbled words,
and his hands, like the claws of a bird, scrabbled for a
moment at the stone floor. Then there were only bones
that dwindled to dust.

The sword burned in my hands. I looked at it and saw
how the light shone along the flawless length of the
perfect blade, how the jeweled hilt glittered. I sheathed
it and walked down the length of the empty chapel and
out into the sunlight.

Chapter Eleven

Colonel Bayard was waiting for me in the Imperial Shuttle Garages when I rode the homing beam back. I spent a week in a nice bed under the care of as pretty a nurse as ever raised a temperature. Bayard spent a lot of time with me, filling in the details.

"We've pieced together most of the story," he told me. "Seventy years ago, when the Blight wiped out most of our quantum of alternate world-lines, one man escaped from the general destruction. He was a high official in the government of the key world-line of the Blighted area. He'd been instrumental in the misguided shuttle experimentation that led to the disaster. He managed to coax a crude experimental machine across the Net to the Zero-zero line—one of the very few with a stable enough probability framework to survive the disaster.

"It wasn't a world to his liking. At home, he'd been a power behind the throne of Orange that ruled half the planet. Here he was a nobody—though not without ability. In time, he rose to a top position in the Imperial Trans-Net Liaison Service. But his heart was never in his work. His real ambition was to reestablish the old empire. In his lifetime, he didn't succeed, but he passed the charge on to his son and to his grandson after that.

"Obviously, it was impossible for one man to overthrow the Imperial government single-handed. The van Roosevelts needed another line, outside the Blight, in which to carry out their plan. They picked New Normandy. It was at an adequate technical level, was politically unstable and ripe for a strong hand—and it had a suitable historical base on which to build. Roosevelt's intention was to foment rebellion, play the

French against the Britons, and when both sides were exhausted and discredited, step in with a small but highly organized band of irregulars and take over.

"He soon learned the undertaking wasn't as easy as he had supposed. The Duke of Londres was a powerful key figure, not easy to manipulate. He killed him—and discovered that by his interference from outside the line, he'd created a massive probability imbalance with the results you saw here, and at home. He had to restore stability. That meant stamping out the power of the Plantagenets, once and for all, because as long as one of them was alive, anywhere, the probability forces would concentrate in him, force him into the theater of events, and create a probability subnucleus around him. Roosevelt couldn't have that: he needed all the probability energy he could command to make his chosen line stable enough to stand against the Blight.

"Just killing off the Plantagenets wouldn't do. He needed their strength, their *mana*, added to his. That was where you came in. He used some very special instruments that his grandfather had brought with him in his original shuttle from the Orange line to trace the affinities across the Net—and found you. I know you're just a fisherman, you know nothing about the Plantagenets. Buy the probability lines were concentrated around you. He intended to use you as a figurehead to restore the stability of the New Normandy line, let you destroy your power in a hopeless war, then offer you escape. The price would be your acknowledgment of him as master.

"He made his first mistake when he secretly arrested the Chief of Intelligence, Baron von Richthofen. Manfred has friends; we weren't content with Roosevelt's story of a sudden stroke. Either he was too soft-hearted, or he was afraid to break too many important life-lines in the Imperium. He should have killed him, and me, too. But he didn't.

"They broke me out of the cell I was in a few hours after he left with you on his mission into the Blight. We tried to follow, but the storm blew up, and we barely made it back. When Roosevelt didn't return, we started searching. Our instruments pinpointed him in New Normandy. When I arrived, it was all over—as you

know. We haven't found a trace of Roosevelt. I suppose
he was killed in the fighting. You're lucky to be alive
yourself."

There were a few holes in Bayard's version of what
had happened, but that was all right. It covered the main
points; it seemed to satisfy everybody. With Roosevelt's
death, the storm had blown itself out. There were no
more toadstools sprouting in the archives. And Imperial
umpires were rapidly pacifying New Normandy under a
free parliament.

But there was still something bothering Bayard.
When I left the hospital, he showed me the city, took me
to restaurants and concerts, fixed me up with a nice
little apartment for as long as I wanted it. He didn't
mention taking me back home, and neither did I. It was
as though we were both waiting for something
impending hanging over everything.

We were sitting at a table at a terrace restaurant in
Uppsala when I asked him about it. At first he tried to
pass it off lightly, but I caught his eyes and held them.

"You'll have to tell me sooner or later," I said, "It
concerns me, doesn't it?"

He nodded. "There's still an imbalance in the Net. It's
unimportant now, but in time it will grow until it
threatens the stability of the Imperium—and of B-I
Three, and New Normandy; of every viable line in the
quantum. The Blight is a cancer that can never be
contained permanently. There's an incompleteness
there, and like an electric circuit, it must complete
itself."

"Go on."

"Our instruments indicate that the aborted lines
center on you, and in the sword Balingore."

I nodded. "I'm not a part of the line, is that it? You'll
have to take me back to Key West, then, and let me get
on with my fishing."

"It's not as simple as that. Seven hundred years ago a
key figure in the ancestral line entered into a course of
action that ended by creating the holocaust. Stability
will never be attained until the probability lines that
were scattered then are led back to their source."

That was all he said, but I understood what he was
trying to tell me.

"Then I have to go back," I said. "Into the Blight."

"It's your decision," he said. "The Imperium won't try to force you."

I stood up. The sunset colors had never looked lovelier, the distant music more appealing.

"Let's go," I said.

The technicians who checked us into the shuttle worked silently and efficiently. They shook hands all around and we strapped in, Bayard and I.

"Our target is the former master-line of the quantum," Bayard said. I didn't tell him I'd been there before. The shapes and colors of the Blight flowed around us, but for once I didn't notice.

"What will happen afterward?" I asked.

"Our hope is when the Blight energies are canceled, the Blight itself will dissipate instantly. The ruined worlds will no longer exist in the Net."

We didn't talk any more after that. It seemed like only minutes before we clocked down and the hum of the drive died.

"We've arrived," Bayard said. He cycled the lock open and I looked out into shifting fog. It shifted and blew away and the jungle and the ruins were gone, and gleaming towers rose up into sunlight, above green lawns and the play of light in fountains. Far away, a woman was singing.

"I wish there was something I could say," Bayard said. "But there isn't. Good-bye, Mr. Curlon."

I stepped down onto the ground, and the door closed behind me. I waited until the shuttle had vanished in a shimmer of light. Then I walked forward along a flower-bordered path toward the sound of Ironel's voice.

EPILOGUE

Baron von Richthofen, Chief of Imperial Intelligence, looked at Bayard across the polished expanse of desk.

"Your mission was successful, Brion," he said quietly. "At the instant the subject entered the Blighted line, the stress indicators dropped to zero readings across the board. The peril to the Net is ended."

"I wonder," Bayard said, "what he felt, in those last seconds?"

"Nothing. Nothing at all. In one silent instant of re-adjustment, the continuum closed in to seal the scar. The probability equation is satisfied." Richthofen paused a moment. "Why? Did you see something there?"

"Nothing," Bayard said. "Just fog, as dense as concrete, silent as death."

"He was a brave man, Brion. He fulfilled his destiny."

Bayard nodded, frowning.

"Brion, is there something else—something that troubles you?"

"We've always held the theory that history is immutable," Bayard said. "Perhaps I'm just deluding myself. But I seem to remember a story of King Richard's massacre of the barons of Runnymede. I checked the references to make sure, and I was wrong, of course."

Richthofen looked thoughtful. "The idea has a certain feel of familiarity . . . but that's illusory, of course," he added. "It was King John who met with the barons—and signed their Magna Charta."

"Where did I get the idea that John was executed by Richard in 1201?"

Richthofen started to nod, then checked himself. "For a moment—but no, I recall now. Richard was no longer living then. He was killed by a cross-bow bolt in a minor skirmish at a place called Chaluz, in 1199." He looked thoughtful. "Curious . . . there was no need for him to have taken part in the engagement at all—and after he was wounded, he refused all medical aid. It was almost as though he sought death in battle."

"It was all so clear," Bayard said. "How he lived to a ripe old age—an overripe old age—lost his crown, died in disgrace. I'd swear I read it as a kid. But none of that's in the books. It never happened."

"No," Richthofen said. "It never happened. If it had, the worlds we know would never have existed."

"Still—it's strange."

"Every phenomenon in the space-time probability continuum is strange, Brion—one no more than another."

"I suppose it was just a dream," Bayard said. "A vivid dream."

"Life itself is a dream, they say," Richthofen sat up, suddenly brisk. "But this is the dream we're in, Brion. And we have work waiting for us."

Bayard returned his smile.

"You're right," he said. "One dream is enough for any man."

THE END

KEITH LAUMER

☐	54369-6	*The Monitors*	$2.75
	54370-X		Canada $3.25
☐	54373-4	*A Trace of Memory*	$2.95
	54374-2		Canada $3.50
☐	48503-4	*The Breaking Earth*	$2.50
☐	48509-3	*The House in November* and *The Other Sky*	$2.50
☐	54375-0	*Worlds of the Imperium*	$2.75
	54376-1		Canada $3.25
☐	48551-4	*Knight of Delusions*	$2.75
☐	48559-X	*The Infinite Cage*	$2.75
☐	54366-1	*The Glory Game*	$2.75
	54367-X		Canada $3.25
☐	48525-5	*Planet Run*	$2.50
☐	54371-8	*Once There Was a Giant*	$2.50
	54372-6		Canada $2.95

Buy them at your local bookstore or use this handy coupon:
Clip and mail this page with your order

TOR BOOKS—Reader Service Dept
P.O. Box 690, Rockville Centre, N.Y. 11571

Please send me the book(s) I have checked above. I am enclosing
$_____ (please add $1.00 to cover postage and handling).
Send check or money order only—no cash or C.O.D.'s.

Mr./Mrs./Miss _____

Address _____

City _____ State/Zip _____

Please allow six weeks for delivery. Prices subject to change without notice.

GORDON R. DICKSON